WASTE OF HANDSOME

Carolina Waves Series Book Two

TINA GALLAGHER

Galsalla Press

Waste of Handsome

Carolina Waves Series Book Two

By: Tina Gallagher

Published by Galsalla Press

Copyright © 2019

Cover Design: Qamber Designs

Editor: Jeannine Luby

Here's just a small list of people I'd like to thank:

My partner in crime, Pattie Giordani . All the retreats, writing days, and road trips have been amazing. I couldn't stay sane without you or them.

Cecelia Mecca for offering inspiration and support on this crazy journey.

And finally…to Mindy Kaling. I was searching for a title for this book and found it while binge watching The Mindy Project. Thanks to your awesome dialogue, I think this one is a winner.

And as always…my family

Chapter One

JACK

I WALKED through the office doors and nodded at the receptionist before continuing toward the stairs to Mr. Hanover's office. Normally I'd stop and talk with the staff, but I'm not in the mood today. I've punched up my workouts getting ready for spring training and I'm sore as hell, plus I haven't been sleeping so I'm tired. The former is something that gets worse as the years go on and the latter is because of that damn book.

In my fourteen years with the Waves, I've done my best to avoid being singled out by the team owner. Aside from a warning about partying too much my rookie year, I've been successful. And now this. It's bullshit.

I worked to keep my temper in check as I made my way through the hallway toward Mr. Hanover's office. I'm sure whatever happens at this meeting is only gonna piss me off so I can't start it with a hot head.

Stepping in front of the double doors, I took a deep

breath and knocked three times. The door opened immediately. Ken Hanover Jr., heir apparent to the Waves stood in the doorway, blocking my view of the office.

"Kenny," I said.

"Come on in, Jack."

He moved aside and I stepped into the office. Mr. Hanover sat in an oversized chair behind his gigantic mahogany desk.

"Come have a seat," he said.

The thick, blue carpet cushioned my steps as I crossed the room. I settled into one of the visitor's chairs directly across from him and Kenny sat in the chair on my right.

"How've you been doin'?" Mr. Hanover asked. "You're lookin' good. Must be workin' hard." His good ol' boy accent and small talk weren't fooling me. The man didn't call me in to tell me how good I look or ask about my workout routine. But I'll play the game.

"I'm good," I said. "Just ramped up my workouts getting ready for the season."

"Well it shows."

"Thank you, sir."

My words still hung in the air when Hannah Adams, from the public relations department, stepped into the office.

"Sorry I'm late," she said.

She gave me a small smile and sat in the chair to the left of me. Dressed in her usual bland attire, bright red glasses added the only color to her face.

"Jack, we asked you to come in today so we can discuss this book of yours," Mr. Hanover said.

I wanted to point out the fact that it's not my book, but figured he wouldn't appreciate that. Instead I focused on keeping a neutral face.

"Now I'm a live and let live kind of guy. Who you

spend your time with off the field is your business. But once it affects this team, we have a problem." He leaned back in his chair and steepled his fingers in front of his chest. "When the book first came out, we decided to ignore it. But that's not working anymore. Now it's a best seller and that woman's been all over the local circuit. Word on the street is she'll be on *Good Morning America* next week. And if she's heading to New York, that's probably not the only show she'll be hitting."

Shit.

When Cindy released that book, I thought it was a joke. Turns out, the joke is on me.

"Sir, I—" He held up his hand, halting my words.

"The problem is that this book is taking focus off baseball," he said. "We're gearing up for spring training and it's all the reporters are asking about. The phones are ringing off the hook with requests for interviews and comments. Not to mention the fact that the staff is tittering about it instead of working."

Mr. Hanover's face reddened with each word. He sat forward and took a deep breath, dragging his fingers through his hair. Resting his elbows on the desk, he looked at me again.

"Son, I understand you didn't ask for this, but you got it anyway," he said. "There's nothing we can do about the book. It's out and doesn't look like it's going away anytime soon. So, we'll just have to give them something else to focus on."

"Like what?"

"That's where Hannah comes in," he said. "She has some ideas for a, whaddyacallit?" Looking over at her, he raised his brow.

"A PR blitz," she said, shifting slightly in my direction. Clearing her throat, she continued. "We want to get you out there having a positive impact. If we show all the great things you're doing in the community, the media will look petty if they keep focusing solely on the book."

"There are tons of pictures of me visiting the children's hospital, and once the season starts, I'll be engaging with the fans like usual. What else did you have in mind?"

"You've been great with the children's hospital and we'll be able to use that. And you're always a fan favorite so that's something we can definitely highlight. But I know there are other causes you support that you've never wanted us to capitalize on. Now's the time to do that."

How the hell does she know what I support?

"I've kept them off the radar for a reason," I said. "They're not things I want to discuss."

"You wouldn't have to discuss them necessarily, just let it be known you're doing them."

"I don't want to do that, either."

She opened her mouth to speak, but it was Mr. Hanover's voice that filled the room.

"You don't have much of a choice here," he said. The fact that he didn't raise his voice didn't lessen the impact of his words. "We're trying to focus on baseball and the reporters are asking about what kind of underwear you wear instead of how the team is shaping up for God's sake."

I doubted that was true, but thought it best not to state it out loud.

Instead I said, "I apologize for that sir, but don't you think this will die down with time?"

"From what we've heard, she's making the most of the fifteen minutes of fame she's getting with this book. And once the season starts, the press will link every little thing you do to that book, stoking the fire. I'm not willing to have my **PR** department stomping out brush fires all year. Hannah here thinks we should hit this head on."

"She does, huh?" I asked, not quite keeping the sarcasm out of my tone. It's not Hannah whose ass will be on the spot answering probing questions. And no matter what she says, I know the questions will be asked.

"If you have some time before you leave, I can explain the ideas I've come up with so far and maybe we can think of a few more," she said.

I opened my mouth to answer, but once again, Mr. Hanover pulled his ventriloquist act.

"Son, I can see you're not quite on board with this, but understand, it's not an option. You know Hannah is good at her job, so let her do it. You've been a valuable asset to this team for a lot of years. I'd hate for this unfortunate incident to put a bad color on our future negotiations."

Did he just threaten my contract renewal?

His steely eyes told me he did just that.

Well damn.

Mr. Hanover prides himself on keeping the team's reputation flawless and in his opinion, this book is threatening that. I've played my whole major league career with the Waves, and plan on retiring from the team. Until now, that was never in question. I guess I'll have to play nice.

"I understand," I said to Mr. Hanover, then turned to Hannah. "I don't have any plans, so I'm yours for the rest of the day."

⚾

HANNAH

. . .

"GREAT," I said. "We can head to my office now if that works for you."

"I'm all yours," he said with a slight bow.

After wrapping things up with the Hanovers, Jack and I exited the owner's office and stepped onto the elevator. As we stood side-by-side in silence, his sweet, spicy scent found its way to my nostrils making me want to bury my face in his neck and deeply inhale.

And maybe lick.

Oh, who am I kidding? Definitely lick.

How am I going to survive this?

Despite the fact that Jack Reagan is everything I don't want in a man, my heart goes pitty-pat every time he's near. And it pisses me off because at this point in my life, you think I'd be immune to men like him.

I mean, I've been working for the Waves for nearly ten years. I shouldn't be susceptible to the charms of any of them. Not to mention where and how I spent some of my teen years. Beautiful people shouldn't even cause a blip on my radar because I know the reality behind all the glitz and glamour.

We exited the elevator on the third floor and walked down the hall to my office, fourth door on the right. I stepped behind my desk, hoping it would provide a barrier to Jack's magnetism. No such luck.

Maybe it's because he's a professional athlete and a dead ringer for Ryan Reynolds that tips my scales. It's like a double-punch to my sound judgement.

Jack slouched into the visitor's chair across from me and crossed his ankle over his knee. I assume he's trying to look relaxed, but the man is practically vibrating.

"I have a few ideas to start with and we can add on as the season progresses," I said. He didn't answer or react, so I forged on. "I know you've been a silent supporter of a variety of anti-drunk driving organizations as well as the anxiety and depression associations here and in your home state."

He sat forward. "How?"

"Excuse me?"

"How do you know that?" he asked. "No one knows that."

"It's my job to know," I said, leaving it at that.

He doesn't need to know that I stumbled on both of those facts while obsessively creeping on him a few years back. Most people don't look past the first few pages of an internet search, but the last few are where you can find some of the best stuff.

Sure, Jack is obsessive about keeping his private life private now, but back in the beginning of his career, he didn't cover his tracks as well. Which led me to the little tidbits I just shared. A few follow-ups and voila, I've got something to work with. Thankfully he didn't question me further and slouched back in the chair.

"Can't you just find me something else for me to do?"

"I can and I will, but if that's all we have, it looks like we're doing it just to up your image."

"But that's exactly what we're doing."

I chuckled, both at his words and the incredulous look on his face.

"Yeah, but we don't want the public to know that."

He sat forward, resting his elbows on my desk.

"Hannah, the reason I support those groups is personal and I really don't want to discuss it," he said, then added. "With anyone."

His New Hampshire accent appeared when he stated my name, a definite tell of how upset he is about this. But I have to say, *Hanner* never sounded so sexy.

Mentally shaking myself, I accepted his point and told

him so. "I'm sure there will be some questions about why you're supporting those specific groups, but you don't have to tell the whole story. They're both very worthy causes. Why wouldn't you support them?"

"I guess."

"Considering the time of year, I think we should focus on the drunk driving groups first. With proms coming up in the next few months, their campaigns will be in full swing. I've contacted a few schools and groups around St. Pete to work with during spring training. There's also a local event prior to that you can attend."

"What kind of event?"

"A dinner at Lucca. It had sold out but I managed to convince them to squeeze another table in for us to purchase. I was thinking maybe you and some of the other players could attend. Do you think Cal and Dan would go? They're really good with the public."

"What about you?"

"What about me?"

"You're not just going to set me up for all these things and not come along to babysit, are you?"

The twinkle in his eye mingled with that wicked grin nearly gave me an orgasm. I cleared my throat and struggled to sound professional.

"You're great with the fans. I have no doubt you'll be able to handle it without a babysitter."

"Oh no, if I'm stuck doing all this stuff, you're going to be there every step of the way."

In all my years with the Waves, I've managed to minimize my alone time with Jack Reagan. His mere presence is enough to scramble my thoughts, and his scent...well, I think I've already mentioned that. Being in close proximity to him on a regular basis will not be good for my peace of mind.

"I figured I'd set up everything, give you the details, and you could take it from there. I'm just a phone call away if you need me."

"Oh I'll need you," he said. "In fact, I'm going to tell Mr. Hanover that you'll have to be available for every little thing I do."

God help me.

Chapter Two

JACK

I KNOCKED TWICE on the kitchen door before going inside. That's something I wouldn't have done a few months ago, but with Sabrina in residence I figure I should give some notice before barging in.

The lady of the house is sitting at the island, a cup of coffee and half-eaten bowl of cereal in front of her. She turned and smiled as I stepped inside.

"Hey."

I sat, keeping a seat between us.

"Hey to you." I looked around. "Where's the rest of the family?" "Lexi is getting dressed and Dan went for a run. He shouldn't be too much longer." She glanced at her phone. "At least he better not be. He did a new workout earlier and I told him not to push it too much today."

Sabrina is not only Dan's wife, she's also his physical therapist. Last year, Dan busted his knee when he crashed into the center-field wall chasing a home run ball.

They'd been pretty hot and heavy in college until he screwed it up and she broke up with him. A decade later, he used his injury to pull her back into his life. It took some serious groveling, but he finally won her back.

Thank God.

I'd listened to him whine about her for years and now I understand why. Sabrina really is great and they're perfect together. Plus, she and Lexi love each other, which gives her my seal of approval.

"Coffee?" she asked.

"No thanks, I'm good." I looked at her forgotten cereal and remembered Dan telling me his housekeeper took off for a family emergency. "Mrs. Evans still off?"

She nodded. "She'll be helping her sister out for another month or so."

"How are you guys holding up without her?"

"We're good. Dan wanted to find someone to fill in temporarily, but I don't think it's necessary. Honestly, I'm still getting used to having a housekeeper. I can't imagine having to deal with someone new. I'm not exactly Martha Stewart, but I can cook a few decent meals and keep things semi-clean."

I looked around. Dan's house has always been more homey than mine, but since Sabrina moved in, you can tell there's a woman in residence full-time. I can't put my finger on specifically why that is, but it's definitely there.

"So what's up with you?" she asked. "Getting ready for spring training?"

"Yep. And thanks to you, Dan will be there too. You're a miracle worker."

"He did all the work."

"And you're smart enough to know when to push and when to hold him back," I said. "You're good at what you do, Sabrina. Own it."

"Thank you, Jack. That means a lot to me."

I nodded, acknowledging her words, then changed things up before they got too mushy.

"Are you and Lexi going to St. Pete?"

"We'll be heading down for a couple long weekends and during Lexi's spring break, which is the last week you're down there. So we'll all be able to travel home together." She chuckled. "I mean, Dan, Lexi, and I will."

"I'm hurt," I said around my own laugh.

"I'm sure you have your own plans," she said.

"Not this year."

Her eyes rounded, but before I could clarify or she could ask a question, I heard Lexi coming down the stairs behind us.

"Mom, can you braid my hair?" she yelled. Her feet pounded on the hardwood floors then she skidded to a stop as she entered the kitchen. "Uncle Jack!"

I slid off the stool as she closed the gap between us and bent my knees so she could throw her arms around my neck. She screeched as I stood and twirled her around. Kissing her on the top of the head, I set her back down, making sure she was steady before totally letting her go.

She climbed into the chair between Sabrina and me. "I brought a brush," she said to Sabrina.

"Did you bring an elastic, too?" Sabrina asked as she stood and pushed her stool out of the way. Lexi nodded and held up a purple hair tie.

"So what are you up to today?" I asked Lexi as Sabrina brushed the knots out of her hair.

"We're having a girls' day," she said, wiggling in her seat. Sabrina reminded her to sit still as she started braiding. "First, we're going shopping and out to lunch."

"Sounds like fun," I said.

She nodded and Sabrina stopped what she was doing until Lexi sat still again.

It's amazing that just a year ago, these two didn't even know each other and now they're so natural together. Lexi even asked to call Sabrina "mom" and Dan said they've filed paperwork for formal adoption. Since Lexi's mother gave up custody when she was born, that should be a pretty simple process.

"Lexi has turned me into a shopper," Sabrina said. As she braided the final few strands of hair, Lexi held up the hair tie. Sabrina wrapped it around then smoothed the end. "How about some cereal?" she asked.

"I'll have some Cheerios, please."

"Jack, can I get you anything now?"

"Just a bottle of water," I said.

I'm not really thirsty, but I remember how my mother wouldn't relax until she was able to serve a guest something.

"I got it." Lexi jumped off her chair, ran over to the refrigerator, grabbed a bottle of water, and handed it to me.

"Thank you," I said and gave her a wink.

Lexi stole my heart the moment we met. She was a little over a year old the first time she came to spring training. At the time, Dan and I were just starting out and stayed at the team hotel. A bunch of the players and their families were hanging near the pool as they wound down before bed. A few of the single guys and I stopped to sit for a bit before heading out for the night.

So there we all were, just hanging out, and Lexi slipped off Dan's lap toddled over to me, smiled, and held out her arms. I awkwardly picked her up and set her on my lap. She settled in, rested her head on my chest, and proceeded to fall asleep. I sat like that for two hours with her cradled in my arms, falling more in love with each second that passed.

Sabrina set Lexi's cereal in front of her and she dug in. "So you'll be going to spring training alone?" Sabrina asked as she slipped back onto the stool next to Lexi.

"Yes, I'll be both going and coming home alone."

Considering what my pattern has been, I knew it would come as a shock. I'm just hoping most people don't ask me about it. I really don't feel like explaining. Hell, I don't even know if I can.

Before she could pry further, Dan walked through the back door. Truth be told, he kind of semi-limped through, which wasn't going to bode well for him.

He kissed Sabrina and Lexi, then said, "Hey Jack, what's up?"

"Just popped in. Figured I'd see my favorite girl and find out how you're doing."

"I'm good. Real good."

"And he'd be even better if he didn't push his run," Sabrina said. Dan glanced in her direction and she shook her head. "Did you seriously think I wouldn't notice that limp?"

"Busted," I said then took a long drink of water.

"Sit with your leg elevated and put the ice wrap on," she said. "Lexi and I are going shopping. You better be on the couch when we get back. Are you sticking around for a while, Jack?"

"I can hang for a bit."

"Good. Make sure he doesn't move."

I'm not going to argue with that tone.

"Will do."

"Ready Lex?"

"Uh huh. I just have to grab my boots." She ran out of the room and was back in the blink of an eye wearing a pair of pink Uggs. "I love you, Uncle Jack," she said as she hugged me.

"Love you too, Lex." I kissed her forehead. "Have fun with your mom."

The beaming smile she directed at Sabrina could have lit the room. "I will."

Once all the goodbyes were said and Dan and Sabrina shared a semi-indecent kiss, the girls left.

"Come on, let's go to the family room. My damn knee is killing me."

He grabbed an ice wrap from the freezer and I followed him to the other room and dropped into an over-sized chair. Once he was settled with his knee propped on two pillows and the ice wrapped firmly in place, he said. "So what's up? I thought I would have heard from you yesterday after your meeting."

"I was too pissed to talk to anyone yesterday, so I just worked out until I was too exhausted to move."

"That bad?"

I shook my head. "It could definitely be worse, but I'm not happy."

"What did they say?"

"I'm sure you won't be surprised about the fact that Mr. Hanover isn't happy about the book."

"That's not surprising at all."

"Hannah came up with a bunch of PR crap I have to do, which will hopefully divert attention from the book."

"What kind of stuff?"

I took in a deep breath and let it out slowly.

"For years, I've been giving pretty heavy donations to both anti-drunk driving and anxiety and depression groups."

"Okay." He raised his voice at the end turning the word into a question.

"I never said anything about it because I didn't want anyone asking why I support those organizations specifically," I said. "So no one knew, but somehow Hannah found out and now she wants me to do a bunch of promotions and appearances for them."

"If you're not comfortable doing that, why can't she just find other groups for you to support?"

"I asked that and she said it would seem like I was just doing it to make myself look good. But since I've been giving to those two groups for years, no one could say that."

He raised his brow. "Makes sense."

"It does. I'm still not comfortable with it, though."

"Would it be awful if the reasons you support the groups got out?"

"No, my reasons are just personal and not something I want to share with the whole country." I sat forward, propping my elbows on my knees and stared at my shoes. "You know my mom died when I was in junior high. I just never told you she was hit by a drunk driver."

"Oh man, I had no idea."

I looked over at him. Might as well put it all out there.

"After my mom died, my dad crumbled. He's been battling depression for years." My sarcastic chuckle echoed through the room. "Actually, he's not even battling it, he just kind of settled into it. For years I worried he was going to kill himself. They were high school sweethearts and he said more than once that he didn't know how to live without her."

"Did he ever try to commit suicide?"

"No, he actually told me he wouldn't because of me. But he's not really living, and it's not like he was ever there for me. He used to go to work, come home, and veg in front of the TV." I cleared my throat. "Anyway, I don't want to talk about all this in a press conference any more than I want to discuss my favorite sex position, which seems to be the other option."

"I can understand that. And so far, the Waves have been keeping personal questions about the book off limits. I'm sure Hannah will come up with some PR speak about your support of those groups."

"Yeah, I guess."

"And you know all you need to do is call her if you have any issues."

"Actually, I won't need to call her because she'll be with me every step of the way."

My mouth curled into a smile remembering the look on Hannah's face when I told her that.

"Really?"

"I told Mr. Hanover that I'd feel much more comfortable with her by my side."

"She's probably not happy about that. You know she likes to stick to the office and stay out of the spotlight."

"Oh I know. But it was her idea, so if I'm going to suffer through this, so will she."

HANNAH

"MR. HANOVER, do you really think this is necessary?"

"Jack specifically asked for you, Hannah. You know that questions

will be asked and comments will be made, and he doesn't want to say or do anything that could harm the team's image."

What a jerk!

He actually played the team image card, knowing full well Mr. Hanover would agree to anything he wants.

"But what about all my work here? There's still a lot of planning to do for the season and opening day is—"

"Hannah, knowing you, I'm sure the plans for closing day are finalized, nevermind opening day."

He's not wrong, but I still don't want to be away from my desk so long. Especially with Jack. Nothing good can come from that.

But I know better than to argue with Mr. Hanover. He's generally a fair man, but he is my boss and once he has his mind set, you're not likely to change it.

"Didn't you have something set up for him to attend prior to spring training?"

"A local anti-drunk driving group is holding a fundraiser at Lucca the week before spring training. It was sold out, but I convinced them to squeeze in a table for us."

"You're amazing, Hannah. I don't ever want you to wonder if you're appreciated here. You definitely are."

"Thank you for the compliment, but having the Waves at my disposal to dangle as bait when I need it helps."

He chuckled. "Who's filling the table?"

"I was thinking Dan and Cal would help ease Jack's nerves a bit. And I'm sure Dan will bring Sabrina."

"With you that makes five. How many does the table fit?" "Six."

"Maybe Kenny will be around. Unless there's someone you'd like to bring?"

"No." I wanted to mention that I don't even want to be there, but refrained. "I can ask Kenny and if he's not available, I'll call some of the local players."

"Good plan," he said. "Thanks Hannah. I know with this in your hands, everything will be fine."

"Thank you, Mr. Hanover."

If only I could share his confidence.

This is going to happen, so I may as well accept it and make a plan to keep it organized and professional. *Definitely professional.* No ogling his abs. No listening intently to his voice to detect slips of his New England accent. And definitely no sniffing for his unique scent.

After booting up my computer, I opened Excel and created a new spreadsheet. I spent fifteen minutes filling it with the dates and events I had saved in my calendar and noted where there was room for more.

First on the list is the fundraiser coming up in a couple weeks. As much as I don't want to, I have to call Jack and see if he's spoken to Dan or Cal. I'm sure he hasn't, so my call will also serve as a reminder.

Using my desk phone so the caller ID would show as the Waves, I dialed Jack's number. Don't ask why I know it by heart.

He answered on the second ring, surprising me.

"Hi, uh Jack?"

"Hey Hannah." He didn't sound happy to hear from me, but he didn't sound totally not happy either. "What's up?"

"I uh…" I cleared my throat. "I wanted to touch base with you on the dinner at Lucca in a couple weeks. Did you happen to speak with Dan or Cal about attending?"

"No, I was kind of hoping it would go away," he said around a short laugh. "I'm actually with Dan right now. Hold on."

He must have removed the phone from his ear because his voice was a little muffled when he said, "Hey, you and Sabrina want to come to a fundraiser dinner in a couple weeks?"

I heard muttering in the back ground, but couldn't

make out the words. Then he was back. "Dan and Sabrina are in. I'll text Cal in a little bit. Can you send me your number so I can just text you back?"

"Sure."

Oh God, Jack Reagan is going to text me.

My heart is pounding like a 7th grader with a crush.

"Do we need anyone else?" he asked.

"If Cal goes, there's one extra seat. Mr. Hanover suggested Kenny attend."

"Ugh," he said. "Nothing against Kenny, but it will be more fun if Bossman Jr. isn't there."

"Any other suggestions?"

"Will there be kids at this shindig?"

"Yes."

"What about Lexi?" he asked. "She can be my date."

As if the man isn't attractive enough, he goes and says something like that.

"Sounds like a plan. I'll let Mr. Hanover know we don't need Kenny."

"And I'll text you about Cal."

"Thank you," I said. When he didn't respond, I felt compelled to fill the silence zinging across the line. "And Jack, don't worry about all this. I'll do everything I can to protect your privacy and keep focus off the book."

There was a pause between when my words ended and his began and I swear I heard him swallow.

"I appreciate that, Hannah."

Hanner.

I already broke one of my rules when I noticed that. Hopefully I'll be able to follow the others.

Chapter Three

LOOKING AROUND MY CLOSET, I'm at a loss. What to wear? What to wear?

Yes, I've had two weeks to prepare for this dinner, but have pushed it off, hoping it would go away.

No such luck.

I'm torn between donning my normal business attire and mixing it up a bit. There are enough dresses in every style hanging in front of me, so it's not that I don't have anything to wear, it's more that I'm second-guessing why I'm tempted to play dress up. I mean, I know *why* I am, I just don't want to be.

This ridiculous crush I've been harboring for years needs to go away, especially now that I'll be spending so much time with Jack. At least before, I could avoid being alone with him. Plus I feel more secure when I'm working. On my own turf I can hide behind the professional persona I've created for myself.

Grabbing a dark gray suit and pale blue blouse, I left the closet, and threw them on my bed before heading to take a quick shower. I reversed direction as my phone chimed its old-fashioned ringtone and vibrated across the nightstand.

It may not be a trendy song or fancy tune, but it reminds me of my grandmother's old rotary phone and makes me smile every time it rings. My smile faded as my father's face flashed on the screen. Declining the call, I made my way to the bathroom, closing the door to shut out the callback that would inevitably follow.

As if I'm not stressed enough about tonight, he had to call. I swear the man has a sixth sense that makes him contact me at the worst times.

Turning on the water as hot as I could stand it, I stepped into the shower and concentrated on relaxing. I took in deep, calming breaths and let them out slowly as the hot water streamed down my back. By the time I got myself together, the water lost some of its steaminess. Knowing I only had a few minutes before it was barely lukewarm, I grabbed my body wash, lathered up, and rinsed off in record time.

I went about getting ready, careful to avoid my cell. Every once in a while, it beeped letting me know I had a message, but I stayed strong while I curled my hair and applied makeup. But as I approached my bed to get dressed, I caved. Picking up my phone, I swiped and tapped the voicemail app. My father's Irish brogue filled the room.

Hannah, how ya been, ma girl? I know you're not happy with me right now, after what happened at Christmas, but I was hopin' you'd a settled down and called by now. I'm gonna be headin' to Key West for a shoot and thought we could get together. I can fly up to meet ya when yer not workin'. Or if yer wantin' a holiday, I can fly ya down. Just let me know.

There was a pause and I heard him inhale deeply, then let it out.

I love ya, baby girl. Call me.

Blinking rapidly, I reached for a tissue and dabbed at my eyes to avoid damaging the makeup I'd just meticulously applied. Thankfully I didn't ruin my face too much. I did a quick touch up then stared at myself in the mirror.

"You need to concentrate on business tonight. Get Christmas out of your head. Get your father out of your head. You can do this," I said to my reflection. It didn't look convinced, but I decided to pretend it did.

Before getting dressed, I double-checked the three boxes of swag I threw together to take to the event. This isn't an official meet-and-greet, but it's always nice to have something for the guys to sign, especially when children are attending. Although, truth be told, sometimes the adults are more star struck by the players than their offspring.

I looked down at the gray suit I'd pulled from the closet earlier and can't imagine putting it on. It's funny how just hearing my father's voice reverts me back to that girl I used to be. But I left her and that life and it's taken me a long time to figure out a balance between my two personas.

At first, I was so afraid that I lived like a monk. It took me a few years to realize I could loosen up and enjoy my life without totally falling back into dangerous patterns.

I'm still pretty buttoned up around the team, but that just helps keep things professional, which is a definite necessity with those guys. Don't get me wrong, they're all great for the most part, but personal boundaries are pretty scarce with people who routinely walk around naked regardless of who's in the locker room.

I glanced at the clock.

Crap.

I better step it up if I'm going to get there before the guys.

Grabbing the suit and blouse off the bed, I walked into my closet and placed them back on the rack. After shifting a few items out of the way, I found the dress that had called to me since I found out I had to attend this event. While it's not something I'd wear to the office, it's more professional than sexy and I think it will be perfect for tonight.

I shimmied into it, careful to not ruin my hair or makeup.

The black eyelash lace skimmed down my hips and settled a hair below mid-thigh, the silhouette hinting at my curves without putting them on full display. The high neckline and three-quarter length sleeves ensure nothing else is on display. After sliding my feet into red platform heels, I eyed myself in the mirror.

Not bad.

I turned and lifted the lid of the fitted wardrobe I'd had installed last year. The custom space keeps all my eyeglasses safe and sound. A wise investment, as far as I'm concerned.

Looking through its contents, I selected a pair of glasses with red, gray, and black plaid frames. Slipping them on, I took one last glance in the mirror, fluffed my hair, and called it good.

JACK

. . .

PULLING INTO THE PARKING LOT, I backed into the first spot on the left. Hopefully it will allow me to make a quick exit later.

I got out of the car and checked my reflection in the window, then adjusted my tie, making sure the Waves logo is perfectly centered in the Windsor knot. I figured sporting the team tie Mr. Hanover gave out at Christmas might earn me some brownie points with him. Even though he won't be here, I'm sure he'll get a full briefing, including pictures.

I searched the lot looking for Dan or Cal's cars and didn't see them. But I did spot a hot ass sticking out of a white Volkswagen SUV. Its owner pulled a box out of the car and placed it on a cart before diving back in, putting her ass on display again.

My eyes skidded down and took in her perfect calves and ankles before moving back up to her spectacular backside. She struggled with another box and I finally remembered my manners. I reached her side just before she lifted the box.

"Need a hand?"

She startled and stood to full height. In her heels, this girl is almost as tall as me, with a good portion of that being long, lean leg.

"Oh no, thank you," she said. "I'm good."

In the back of my mind, it registered that her voice sounded familiar, but before I could figure out from where, she looked over her shoulder at me.

"Hey Jack." Hannah looked me up and down. "You look great. Love the tie."

She turned back to retrieve the box. I stood frozen in place. *Hannah?*

If there'd been any question it was her, those glasses would have been a dead giveaway.

In what alternative universe is this goddess in come-fuck-me heels Hannah Adams?

Finally coming to my senses, I stepped around her and grabbed the box out of her hands.

"Give me that."

I placed it on the cart, then reached into her car to grab the third box. Once that was settled next to the other two, I closed the hatch.

"Anything else to unload?"

She shook her head. "No, that's it. Thanks Jack."

Before she could, I wrapped my hand around the handle of the cart and tugged, pulling it behind me. Hannah's heels clicked on the blacktop as she followed. A group of attendees walked ahead of us and a young boy held the door open for all of us.

"Thanks sport," I said as we entered the restaurant.

He smiled, and I heard him say, "Holy crap, that's Jack Reagan" as I passed by. I'd have to sign something for the kid.

Which reminded me.

"What's in the boxes?" I asked Hannah.

"Just some swag. There's a box for each of you."

She always thinks of everything. I've played with the Waves long enough to remember life before Hannah. Events were planned well, but nothing like they've been since she took over. The woman is a dynamo. Turns out, she's a sexy dynamo, something I never noticed before. Now that I have, I'm hoping I can go back to living in ignorance.

Hannah found the group's chairperson, Jill Sember, and introduced me to her.

"Thank you so much for coming here tonight," she said. "And for supporting the organization for so long."

"My pleasure," I said.

"We brought some items along for the guys to sign," Hannah said. "I don't want to upset your schedule, so we'll keep them under wraps until you let me know it's okay. I also have some ticket and T-shirt bundles for your raffle."

"You're wonderful," Jill said, stopping at a table near a huge picture window. "This is your table. If you need anything, just let me know. You can also talk to any of the coordinators. We're all wearing one of these," she said, pointing to the red ribbon attached to her blouse.

While the other woman was speaking, Hannah had rummaged through the boxes and now held four Waves gift bags.

"Here are the bundles." She held them out to Jill.

"Again, thank you."

That said, she was off, leaving me alone with this new version of Hannah. In the ten years I've known her, I never thought of the woman in front of me as anything more than the kickass PR person who planned every Waves event to the last detail.

Never once did I notice her shiny hair, amazing ass, or shapely calves. Or that fresh citrus scent that fills the air every time she moves.

I felt movement beside me and realized that Hannah was struggling to maneuver the cart to put it against the wall.

"Let me," I said, maybe a little too harshly.

I don't want to see Hannah as anything but the efficient executive she is. And I also don't want to think I'm so shallow that a little black dress could totally change the way I look at a person.

After pushing the cart out of the way, I stepped back.

"That good?"

"Perfect. Thank you." She looked around. "It's starting

to fill up. I'm going to head to the ladies room before it gets started."

She breezed by me, leaving the smell of citrus in her wake. I turned my back to the room and looked out the window. The pitch black outside didn't allow me to see much more than my reflection in the glass. Thankfully I'd learned how to mask my feelings years ago, so my face doesn't show the turmoil I feel. The turmoil I've felt since that damn book hit the shelves.

Since I was a teenager, I've done my best to stay in control. Keeping my relationships simple seemed the best way to do that. I pretty much stuck to one-nighters when I was in the Minors and when I was first called up, but eventually that got complicated.

By the time I settled into the Majors, I'd perfected the seasonal girl method...one girl during the season and another for the off season. I was always honest about my intentions and the girls I spent time with didn't want much more than a good time for as long as it lasted.

Until Cindy Parker, that is.

About halfway through last season, she got really clingy and eventually started making demands I had no intention of conceding to. And the book came out too fast for it to have been just a revenge thing for her. She must have been working on it right from the start, if not before.

I admit I'm a little gun shy now. My usual vetting system didn't work with Cindy, how can I trust it to be reliable with anyone else?

It's best I'm on my own until I figure it out. I can't handle any more upheaval in my life right now, I have to focus on baseball.

"Look who I found," Hannah said.

I turned and saw Dan, Sabrina, and Lexi walking beside her.

"Uncle Jack!" Lexi threw herself into my arms.

"Hey sweetheart," I said, setting her down. "Don't you look pretty?"

She twirled in a circle, making her dress swirl around her legs.

"Mom took me shopping and we got matching dresses."

I looked up and noticed that Sabrina was indeed wearing a dress similar to Lexi's. The little girl was obviously thrilled with that fact.

"Hey Sabrina." I leaned forward and kissed her cheek.

"Nice tie," she said. "Looks like great minds think alike."

Thank God men don't freak out being dressed the same because Dan and I look like twins in our gray suits, white shirts, and Waves ties.

Just then, Cal appeared turning us into triplets. I couldn't help but chuckle as he approached.

"Oh wow, we're going to have to get a picture of this," Hannah said. "You three look perfect."

That's not the word I'd use, but I didn't correct her.

I noticed the bar in the corner and figured it was time to hit it. Since I'm driving, I'm limited to one drink, but I'll enjoy the hell out of it for sure.

Stooping down next to Lexi, I said, "Would you like a drink?"

"Sweet tea."

"One sweet tea coming up." I touched the tip of her nose with my index finger, making her giggle.

"Would you like a drink, Hannah?" I asked.

"Oh, um, yes. I'll have a seltzer with lemon, please. Thank you," she said.

Cal and Dan accompanied me to the bar. We shook

hands and made small talk with the people in line. It was finally our turn and we placed our orders.

"Thanks for coming tonight guys. I really appreciate it," I said.

"No problem. Thanks for inviting Lexi. She's thrilled," Dan said.

"How are you doing?" I asked Cal.

After last season, he and his wife had decided to divorce and he'd moved into Dan's pool house. We just helped him move into a new place last month. Even though he only lives a few miles from me now, I haven't seen him since.

"I'm hanging in," he said. "I'll be happy when the season starts so I have something to focus on besides my divorce."

"How's that going?" Dan asked.

"As well as can be expected," Cal said. "You know how it is when lawyers smell money."

That's just one more reason I never plan on getting married.

The bartender set our drinks on the bar. I grabbed my beer and Hannah's seltzer, then almost knocked Lexi's tea over when Dan and I both reached for it.

"Lexi is my date tonight, remember?" I said, grabbing the glass.

He snorted. "As if I'd ever let someone like you date my daughter."

That should have smarted, but I'd never let anyone like me near Lexi either. Sad, but true.

I figure I can at least help teach her how she should be treated so she doesn't end up with some walking hormone who's only after one thing. Thankfully it'll be a few years before we have to worry about that.

Changing the subject, Dan said, "Am I the only one who barely recognized Hannah?"

Cal and I both shook our heads.

"I don't think I've ever seen her in anything besides those suits she always wears," Cal said.

Dan and I agreed.

As we approached the table, I couldn't take my eyes off the woman in question. Her dress isn't overly sexy or slightly indecent. It's just...different.

"Here you go," I said, handing Hannah her drink.

Her cheeks turned pink. "Thank you, Jack."

I placed the sweet tea down then took the empty seat next to Lexi. "Thanks Uncle Jack."

"You're welcome, sweetie," I said.

I'd felt Hannah watching me since I handed her the seltzer, and finally looked in her direction. Her eyes widened but she didn't turn away. The air crackled between us and I figured I'd better get things back to business.

"So what's the plan tonight?" I asked. "Are we supposed to just mingle?"

She took a deep breath in and slowly let it out, then smiled.

"Nothing formal has been planned, but like I said, I brought some swag for each of you. I'm sure people will be less shy as the night goes on and will approach you more. I saw you three talking to people in the bar line, which is great. You're all good with the public and have experience with different venues. So all I can say is play it by ear. If anyone gets out of line, let me know and I'll deal with it."

"Sounds good," I said.

Just then, the background music stopped as Jill Sember approached the microphone, officially starting the festivities. Waiters scurried about, doling out salads. Once our whole table was served, I picked up my fork and dug in.

"So what'd you do this week, Lex?" I asked.

"I had birthday parties on Monday and Tuesday, then me and mom went shopping for dresses on Wednesday." She shoved a forkful of salad into her mouth then scrunched her nose while she chewed. "I didn't do anything Thursday, then we had a pizza party Friday. We made our own pizzas and then watched *Frozen*."

"Sounds like a great night," I said. "You know that's one of my favorite movies."

She nodded. "And you know all the words to Let it Go."

Hannah made a choking sound and I glanced across Lexi and asked if she was okay.

"Fine thanks." She smiled, but looked like she was holding back a laugh.

I know what Hannah was laughing at and I could have pressed, but figured it'd be best if I didn't. No use engaging on anything more than a professional level. So, like the song says, I'm just going to let it go.

Chapter Four

HANNAH

MY STOMACH FLUTTERED as I watched Jack twirl Lexi around the dance floor. I've seen the two interact at various Waves events, but not like this.

It's obvious they spend a lot of time together and are pretty close. He's somehow managed to lavish her with attention without ignoring the other children when they approach.

The man is smart, sexy, and good with kids. My heart can't take much more.

I took a sip of water and glanced at my watch. This night is dragging. I'm not used to just sitting around at events. I'm usually the one in charge, taking care of the details, making sure things run smoothly.

Besides giving the guys things to sign, I've pretty much been sitting here. And once the dancing started, I've been sitting alone. Thank God for cell phones. At least I have something to look at besides the object of my obsession.

I felt someone sit next to me and prayed it wasn't Jack. Glancing over, I saw Sabrina take a drink of wine. She smiled.

"It's time for a break," she said. "My feet are killing me. I'm not used to wearing heels."

"I hear you. My toes keep falling asleep." Once upon a time, I wore heels on a daily basis, but not anymore. Glancing over at Lexi, who was now bouncing to a fast tune with Jack keeping up with her, I asked, "Does she ever get tired?"

"She'll eventually crash, but not until much later. I wish I could bottle that energy for sure."

"You three look like you've settled in well."

"We have. It's been wonderful. I can't tell you how happy I am."

"Well, Dan is just glowing, so I'd say the feeling is mutual." She blushed and looked across the room to where Dan and Cal were talking with some fans. I have to say, the people here have been very respectful of the players, and thankfully I haven't had to pry any women off them.

"Are you and Lexi going to spring training this year?" I asked.

"Not the whole time. Lexi has school and I have work, so we'll go down for a couple weekends and during her spring break," she said. "Dan said we'll be seeing you there."

While her last sentence was a statement, she raised her voice at the end turning it into a question. I nodded.

"I don't normally go, but I am this year. There are some events I need to oversee."

Since Dan told her I'd be there, I'm sure she knows why, but there's no reason to get into detail. Besides, I didn't get where I am with the Waves by blabbing the players' personal information.

Sabrina opened her mouth to speak, but then smiled and said, "Hey sweetie, did you finally give Uncle Jack a break?"

Lexi sat next to Sabrina. As if she'd been doing it for years, Sabrina poured a glass of water and handed it to the little girl, then smoothed her hair. Lexi took a long drink, put the glass down, and nodded.

"He wanted to go talk to the people with Daddy and Cal," she said. "Hey Hannah."

"Hi Lexi. You having a good time?"

"This is so much fun. I wish we could do more things like this," she said.

I'll tuck that away for later. A dance party might be fun at the end of the season. Maybe after the meet and greet. If Lexi likes it, I'm sure the other kids will, too.

Jack approached with the little boy who held the door open for us earlier.

"I wanted to give my friend Kevin here some swag for helping us out with the door before."

"Oh sure." I stood and walked over to Jack's box and pulled out a few things. He quickly signed and handed them to the boy. "And don't forget that there will be tickets for your family at the window on opening day," he said.

The boy's smile could have lit the room. "Like I'd forget. Thank you so much."

They shook hands and he took off across the room, his arms filled with loot.

"That was nice," I said.

Jack shrugged. "He's a good kid."

He walked back to the table and held out my chair. Taking his cue, I sat. Once I was settled, he took a seat on the other side of Lexi.

Sabrina's eyes shifted to Dan as he walked on the other side of the room. Besides being totally besotted by the man, I know she's also watching him for any signs of a limp. Thankfully there isn't one.

"He looks great," I said. "You're a miracle worker."

She opened her mouth to say something, then Jack cleared his throat.

Smiling, she said, "Thank you."

"When are you two leaving on your trip?" Jack asked her. "Wednesday."

"Going anywhere good?" I asked.

"We're going to Jamaica for a few days," she said.

"It's their honeymoon," Lexi chimed in. "Grandma and grandpa are staying with me and my cousins are coming over for the weekend."

"The house may not be standing when we get back," Sabrina said.

"That would be a small price to pay to spend time alone with my bride." Dan had snuck up behind us. He leaned down and kissed Sabrina's head, then straightened and held out his hand. "Another dance?" he asked.

She nodded then stood, and the two practically floated to the dance floor while Rod Stewart's voice crooned through the room.

"Tonight was pretty fun," Jack said. "If we can do things like this, my probation might not be so bad."

"You're not exactly on probation," I said.

"I'm not exactly not," he countered.

"Either way, I'll try to make it as painless as possible." "I'm sure you will since I'm dragging you along with me. There's a method to my madness."

I couldn't respond. His crooked smirk shot my heart into over drive and my mouth went totally dry. Meanwhile, other parts of me are not so dry.

If the man has that effect on me with one small smile,

what would happen if he actually touched me? I squirmed at the thought.

Thankfully Lexi asked Jack questions about his "probation" and I had some time to pull myself back together. From what I heard of the conversation, Jack answered her without getting into the dirty details. Then he somehow managed to get her off the subject of him and onto her plans for the next day.

I lost track of the conversation as I cast an admiring glance around the room, appreciating the event the committee had managed to put together. As someone who plans things for a living, I know how much work goes into making them look effortless.

Dan and Sabrina left the dance floor as the music changed tempo, and joined Cal near the bar. Just like I'd predicted, people felt more comfortable to approach the players as the night wore on and soon the three were surrounded. Lexi's voice pulled me from my observations.

"Hannah, you didn't dance at all."

"I'm not much of a dancer."

"Everybody can dance." she said, then jumped down from her chair and held out her hand. "Come on. It's fun."

I can't resist that face. Taking her hand, we made our way to the dance floor. An old rock song had ended and the radio version of a popular pop tune thrummed from the speakers. My slight detour into the fast lane as a teen came rushing back and my body easily remembered the dance moves that had graced some of the most popular clubs in Los Angeles.

"You're really good," Lexi said as she danced with a child's inhibition.

Jack slipped around me and grabbed Lexi's hand then twirled her around and back. Her giggle filled the air along with his sweet, spicy scent. I'm not sure what kind of cologne the man wears, but it makes my mouth water.

The beat kicked up as a new song started. Sabrina and Dan joined in, followed by Cal. I gotta say, these three guys have moves.

I allowed myself to relax and enjoy the moment, and I stayed on the floor for two more songs. Unfortunately, the DJ decided to slow things down and soon *The Way You Look Tonight* by Frank Sinatra floated through the speakers.

Sabrina nodded at Dan and smiled. He held out his hand to Lexi and said to Jack, "Do you mind if I have one dance with my daughter? You've been hogging her all night."

"Hey, you have your own girl," Jack said. "But sure, go ahead."

Dan pulled Lexi closer and they rocked from side to side, her smile beaming up at him. I blinked back tears and memories of dancing with my own father. We'd been so close once, but now it's just complicated.

Cal took Sabrina's hand and pulled her into a perfect dance form.

"You better keep space between you," Dan said. "I'm watching."

"Pay attention to your own dance partner." Cal chuckled and spun Sabrina so his back was to Dan.

I turned to leave the floor and stopped when a hand touched my arm. Looking back, I saw Jack.

"We can't be the only two not joining the party," he said. "Would you like to dance?"

JACK

. . .

IGNORING how perfect Hannah feels in my arms, I concentrated on dancing like my mother taught me. You know, the right way.

The times I've danced properly since high school have been few and far between. Mostly women just plaster themselves against me, throw their arms around my neck, and we sway in a slow rhythm.

Not that I'm complaining, but I have to admit this is nice.

With her in heels, we're practically eye to eye. At least we would be if she didn't have her head slightly turned, focusing on a spot over my shoulder.

Her breath hitched as I tightened my grip on her waist and she snapped her head in my direction.

"You like Frank?" I asked since I finally had her attention. She smiled. "Who doesn't? He's classic."

"What kind of music do you normally listen to?"

"A little bit of everything. My Pandora is on shuffle and it can go from Dean Martin to Metallica from one song to the next."

"I listen to a mix, too. But my go-to is classic rock. It's just easy to listen to."

It's interesting. I've known Hannah for a decade but don't know much about her beyond what she does for the Waves, which seems to be a mix of public relations, event planning, and marketing. And it's not just me, I don't think any of the players know her story.

"So are you all ready to head to St. Pete?"

She scrunched her nose. "Not yet."

That surprises me. Hannah is the most organized person I know. I figured she'd already have her bags packed and waiting by the door. Unless...

"Are you really dreading the trip?" I asked.

Telling Mr. Hanover I wanted her attending all the events with me was a knee-jerk reaction. I can tell him I'm okay on my own and I told her so.

"No, it's fine. After all these years, I should experience spring training, right?"

A small dimple peeked out on her right cheek. Another thing I never noticed.

"Are you renting a place or staying at the team hotel?"

"Team hotel," she said. "Most of the rentals close to the park were already taken. I got one of the suites, so I should be good. I'll probably only be there to sleep anyway."

"Why's that?"

"I'll have an office at the stadium. Besides, I can't hang around the hotel too much and be a buzzkill for the players staying there. That'd be like having your teacher around during spring break."

"I don't know if it would be that bad." I chuckled, letting her know I'm joking. "Seriously, the guys all think you're great."

"They still think of me as an authority figure, even if I'm not in charge of them."

"You may not be in charge of them, but you do a great job keeping them in line," I said. "And I know that's not easy."

"It used to be much easier, that's for sure. It seems like the players coming up the last few years just don't want to cooperate. They're always late to events, if they bother to show up at all. And even though they have a phone permanently glued to their hands, they don't answer my calls or text messages. I constantly have to hunt them down." She froze, then rushed to catch up to our dance and stepped on my foot in the process. "Oh God, I'm so sorry."

I pulled her tighter and righted our steps.

"No problem," I said. "What upset you?"

"I just realized what I said. I shouldn't be venting to you, or anyone for that matter."

"You can vent to me anytime and be assured I won't tell a soul." Something flashed in her eyes, but it was gone before I could decipher it. "But I know what you mean about the newer players. Most of them need to be constantly reminded where they need to be and what they should be doing. During games they're usually fine, but otherwise it's like herding cats."

Frank Sinatra ended and I was happy when another slow song started. I didn't give Hannah a chance to end the dance, I just kept twirling her around the floor.

"When I first came up, I was so in awe of the senior players," I said. "I'd follow them around, trying to soak up any morsel of their greatness I could. Some of these kids act like they could teach me how to play and can't wait for me to retire."

"Hopefully that won't happen any time soon."

"From your mouth to God's ears," I said, not wanting to talk about retirement…ever. "So besides working, what are your plans while you're in St. Pete?"

"I haven't really thought about it. Any suggestions?"

"There are a lot of great clubs down there, if you're into that," I said.

"That's not really my thing."

"It's not mine anymore, either. For the most part, I take it easy down there. I only play in about half the games, and I use the time to work on whatever needs fixing. And when I'm not doing that, I relax. Spring training is literally the calm before the baseball storm so I use the time to prepare for the season, both mentally and physically."

How did the conversation swing back to me?

"I'll probably rent a boat and get out on the water a few times while I'm down there."

"By yourself?"

I chuckled at the look of horror on her face.

"No, I usually drag at least one of the guys with me. Last year, Dan and Cal came along and we sailed down to Key West. It was a lot of fun. I think it's on the agenda this year while Sabrina and Lexi are in St. Pete. Maybe you can join us."

She froze again, but recovered quickly enough that we didn't miss a step.

"You okay?"

"I, uh, yeah I'm good."

The song ended, and she pulled away. Something had upset her...that was obvious enough, even to a shallow prick like me.

I followed her off the dance floor and had to practically run to keep up.

How the hell does she move so fast in those heels?

Once we reached the table, she sat and grabbed her water glass like it was a lifeline. After emptying the glass in one long gulp, she set it down and held onto it with both hands.

Not wanting to startle her, I slowly pulled out the chair next to her and sat. Resting my elbow on the table, I shifted in my seat to fully face her.

I'm used to seeing her poised and professional, but now she seems foggy and distant. I want to give her time to collect herself, but I obviously upset her and need to say something

"Hannah," I started, then took a breath and let it out. "I'm sorry if I overstepped out there. I wasn't...I mean, I know you and Sabrina get along and I just thought it'd be nice for her to have another woman on the boat. I didn't mean to upset you."

"You didn't," she said. "I'm fine, Jack. Really."

I studied her face. The smile that didn't quite reach her eyes and the look in those brown depths told me otherwise. But I wouldn't push. Not here. Not now.

<h1 style="text-align:center">Chapter Five</h1>

HANNAH

THE DOORBELL RANG JUST as I finished zipping my suitcase closed. Expecting pizza, I grabbed money off my dresser and ran to the front door. Instead of the delivery boy, my neighbor stood on the other side.

"Mrs. Button. Hi. Come on in." I stepped back, giving her room to enter.

"I got your message," she said as she cleared the threshold.

She'd just stepped inside when the delivery boy appeared. I handed him the cash, took the pizza, said thank you, and closed the door.

"Have a seat," I said. "I'm having pizza and wine. Join me."

"That sounds wonderful. Thank you."

She sat at the dining room table while I ran to the kitchen to get the wine.

"Lambrusco okay?" I asked.

"Ooh, my favorite. It's like grape juice for adults."

I grabbed the wine, two glasses, as well as plates and napkins and made my way back to the dining room. After I poured the wine, we each grabbed a slice and settled in to eat.

"I'm so glad you came over instead of just calling back," I said. "This is nice. We should do it more often."

"When I saw your car in the driveway, I wondered if you were sick and wanted to come check on you. You never get home this early." she said. "So I'm happy to see you're in good health." She took a big bite of pizza.

Mrs. Button lives next door and she truly is one of my favorite people. She's smart, funny, and as spunky as Betty White. After retiring from her career as a librarian, she and Mr. Button traveled extensively. Unfortunately, he passed away two years ago, and while she has tons of friends and keeps herself busy, I know she still misses him. I spend as much time with her as I can, but with my crazy schedule and her early bedtime, that's less than I'd like.

"I'm fine, but thanks for worrying."

"So why are you home?"

"I'm packing. My boss actually told me to take the whole day off, but I had some stuff to get done, so I went in for a few hours."

"In your message you said you're going to spring training. You've never done that before. Why this year? Did you get a promotion?"

"No, there are some events down there I need to oversee."

I pushed the last bite of crust into my mouth and chewed, feeling Mrs. Button's attention on me the whole time. Her eyes narrowed when I finally looked in her direction. Then she smiled.

"Events for anyone in particular?"

I'm not sure how a seventy-five-year-old woman's chuckle could make me blush, but it did.

"There are some for the whole team and a few for individual players." Not exactly a lie. There are always things happening with the team.

"Any hot individual players?" She sat back in her chair and fanned her face with her hand.

Like me, Mrs. Button has a soft spot for a certain short-stop. The only difference is that she'll tell anyone within hearing about hers. I don't even want to admit mine to myself.

"Yes, I'll be doing some things with your favorite player."

"If I was forty years younger, I'd teach him a few things. You know I loved my Manny..." She wiggled in her seat. "...but that Jack Reagan is so yummy."

After I moved here about eight years ago, I invited Mr. and Mrs. Button to a Waves game. She met a few of the players beforehand, including Jack, which started this obsession.

"Although from what I read in that book, he already knows quite a bit." Again with the dirty chuckle.

"I wouldn't know. I haven't read it."

"Why not?" she asked. "Don't you have to know what's being said about him so you can use your public relations magic to make it go away?"

Not that I'll admit it to her, but I have been tempted to buy the book. But not only do I not want to give that bitch an extra penny in profit, I also don't need any additional sexy Jack tidbits in my head.

"No I don't need to read the book."

"When are you going to admit that you have a thing for him?"

I stood and collected our plates and napkins.

"I don't know what you're talking about," I said, before heading for the kitchen. I placed the plates in the sink and threw the napkins in the garbage. Walking back into the dining room, I continued the conversation. "Jack is just another guy on the team. What makes you think I have a thing for him?"

"The way you try to not talk about him. The way you look when you do."

I'm hoping my face isn't showing everything I feel right now.

"I'm, um, I'm not sure what you mean."

"Oh honey, it's all right there on your face, in your eyes."

I hope that's not true.

I didn't realize I'd spoken the words out loud until she continued.

"Don't get me wrong, you hide it well. But I'm old. I know the signs." She winked. "And yours are practically neon where Jack Reagan is concerned."

Resting my elbows on the table, I rubbed my temples. Mrs. Button rested her hand on my arm and squeezed.

"It's okay, Hannah. Really."

"If Jack knows about my little crush, it won't be."

I dropped my hands to the table with a thud.

"I'm sure he doesn't."

"You picked up on it."

She fluffed her blonde hair. "But I'm incredibly astute."

"It is really obvious?"

"I've seen you at work and you're a closed book," she said.

"Besides, men rarely notice things like that unless you're being totally blatant. And you're definitely not."

I've hidden my obsession with Jack for ten years so I'm not comfortable talking about it. But I trust Mrs. Button with my life, and I need to unload.

"I don't understand it. I know it's ridiculous but I can't stop feeling this way."

"Well, I can't say I blame you. He is one hot dish."

"That's what I don't understand. I spent a lot of time around men too handsome for their own good. I've worked for the Waves for ten years now and most of the players can double as models. I'm immune. So what is it about this guy?"

"Remember, I've met Jack. And I believe he's more than a pretty face."

I snorted. "Jack Reagan is nothing more than a waste of handsome."

"Are you sure about that?"

"You know about the seasonal girls. He's shallow and self-absorbed and doesn't get involved. I can't be attracted to someone like him."

Pictures of him dancing with Lexi and talking to that boy at the MADD event flashed through my head. I shook the guilt away. Sure, he's good with kids, but women don't seem to stand a chance.

"And yet you are," she pointed out.

After a beat, I nodded.

"But just because I am doesn't mean I have to do anything about it. Hell, I've felt this way for ten years and this is the first time I'm even speaking about it."

"Ten years is a long time. It's obviously not going away. Maybe you should do something about it."

"No." I shook my head. "No, I definitely shouldn't. A fling with a player wouldn't be good for my career, and God knows any relationship with Jack has a short shelf life."

"Don't be too sure. If you give him a chance, he just might surprise you. The best ones always do."

JACK

"YOU'RE TALKING out of your ass," I told Dan and directed my attention back to the hockey game.

"All I'm saying is that you two looked awfully cozy on that dance floor," he said.

"I have no idea what you're talking about."

Sabrina walked into the family room carrying a plate of taco dip and a bowl of chips.

"Thanks baby," he said, patting her behind as she leaned forward to place her bounty on the coffee table. "Bri and Cal noticed it too."

"Noticed what?" she asked, her eyes shifting between the two of us.

"That Jack and Hannah looked pretty cozy on the dance floor last week."

"Oh." Her eyes settled on me and she nodded. "Yeah, I did notice that."

I leaned forward and grabbed a chip then dragged it through the dip before shoving it in my mouth. "This is delicious."

"Don't try to change the subject," she said.

I sat back and gestured between them before resting my left hand on my thigh.

"So what? You two get married and now you're finding love everywhere?"

"Just stating the obvious," Dan said.

"The obvious is that we were all out on the dance floor

and the music slowed down. You danced with Lexi and Cal danced with Sabrina. It would have been pretty shitty of me to not ask Hannah to dance."

"If you say so."

"Sabrina, help me out here before I deck him."

She chuckled. "I'm sure what you're saying is true, but you have to admit there were sparks flying between you two."

"Sparks?" I snorted. "I don't think so."

"And you have to admit that she looked beautiful," she said.

I don't want to admit any such thing, but it would be pretty shitty not to. Especially since it's true.

"Sure she did," I admitted. "But I've known Hannah for ten years. Don't you think if there were going to be sparks, they would have appeared before now?"

"Maybe, maybe not." Sabrina shifted her head from side to side as she said the words. "Sometimes all it takes is a shift in perception to make everything click into place."

I chuckled and grabbed another chip. "What is your wife talking about, Dan?"

"You know exactly what I'm talking about," she said.

"This conversation is way too heavy to have while the Bruins are on. Maybe we can pick it up another time."

Like never.

"You can count on it," she said to me. Turning to Dan, she said, "I'm going to pick Lexi up from the birthday party, then we're stopping at the store to pick up supplies for the surprise she's making for you later. Should I just grab dinner on the way home?"

"Sounds great," Dan said, with a lovesick smile on his face. "Any preferences?" she asked.

"Whatever you guys want is fine with me."

"Jack? Do you want to stay for dinner?"

"Thank you, but no. I still have to pack and I want to get a work out in tonight."

"Okay then. I'll see you in a couple weeks."

She leaned down and gave Dan what I assume she meant to be a quick peck. He had other ideas and pulled her into his lap for a full-blown Frenchfest.

I shoveled chips and dip into my mouth and glued my eyes to the TV. PDAs don't make me uncomfortable, but their obvious domestic bliss does for some reason.

Dan said, "Be careful."

I figured it was safe to look in their direction again.

"Give Lex a kiss for me," I said.

"Will do."

Then she was gone, leaving Dan and me sitting in awkward silence. And to make matters worse, a commercial was on so I couldn't even pretend to be engrossed in the game. So, I continued to shovel chips into my mouth.

"I didn't mean to piss you off bringing up the Hannah fv tthing."

"There is no Hannah thing."

I felt him watching me and looked in his direction. I wanted to punch the I-know-something-you-don't look off his face, but I know I'll have to answer to Sabrina if I do that. So instead, I tried logic.

"I don't know what you saw the other night, but regardless, you know me. You know how I am and how I live my life. Hannah just doesn't fit into that no matter how amazing she looks in a little black dress and fuck me heels."

"So you did notice."

"Of course I did. I'm not blind," I said. "But it doesn't change the fact that I spend time with a certain type of woman. Hannah is not that type."

"You have to admit that she seemed different the other night. It wasn't just the dress or the heels. She didn't seem like the same Hannah we've been dealing with all these years. I think there's more to her than what we've allowed ourselves to see for the past decade."

"It doesn't matter, Dan. She's not my type and even if she was, she works for the Waves. You don't shit where you eat," I said. "Besides, even if something was there and I pursued it, what happens when the season ends?"

Chapter Six

JACK

THE CLOCK READ 2:00 as I cracked open a Sam Adams. I shrugged. It's 5:00 somewhere, right?

I slid open the patio door, letting the fresh sea air into the condo. Stepping onto the balcony, I leaned against the railing and looked out at the ocean. After taking a long draw on my beer, I took a deep breath and slowly let it out.

This. This is just what I needed.

Back in my minor league and rookie days, spring training was a time to hustle, to prove myself, to give it my all and then some. Now it's time to relax before the season, enjoy the slower pace, and work on new skills or sharpen old ones. I still give it my all, but it's different.

For the past few years, I've looked forward to coming to St. Pete to decompress, and this year I need it more than ever. That damn book has been haunting me. I don't know how celebrities deal with having their personal lives strewn across papers and social media all the time.

What I have going on is nothing compared to that, but it's still messing with my well-ordered life. And I just don't understand why people give a shit about all that stuff.

My phone beeped and I pulled it out of my pocket and glanced at the text.

Dan: Want to shoot some hoops? Cal and Kaspryzk are in.

Me: Sounds good. I'll be down in five.

I chugged the rest of my beer, slipped into my gym shoes and was out the door.

Since it's a weekday afternoon, the gym in our complex is mostly deserted. I heard the guys before I entered the court.

"Yo! Settle down in here."

Without warning, Dan tossed the ball my way and I caught it.

"Come on, you know nothing gets past these hands," I said. They all groaned.

I turned and launched the ball in a perfect arc that swished through the net.

"Show off," John Kaspryzk said.

We settled into a circle and worked through some basic stretches. None of us are rookies anymore and we're always careful to limber up. We wouldn't hear the end of it if one of us ended up on the DL because we didn't stretch properly.

I teamed up with Cal and Dan with John, and we settled into an easy two-on-two game. Back in our crazy youth, we'd go full balls-to-the-wall, but not anymore.

After showing off his ball handling skills as he took the ball down court, John cut a move toward the basket. Cal slid sideways and plucked the ball from him in mid-dribble, took it down court and executed a perfect layup. Dan answered with a corner shot, and back and forth it went until we needed a break.

I ran to the machine and grabbed Gatorade for each of us and we stretched out on the bleachers.

"Is it me, or does the off season keep getting shorter?" John asked.

"It's definitely not you," Dan said.

"I agree, but I'm okay with it this year," Cal said. "I need something to keep my mind off the divorce."

"And I need a distraction from all the book shit going on," I said.

"There's nothing you can do about that?" John asked.

I shook my head, thinking about my conversation with my agent when the book first came out.

"Craig tried talking Cindy and then her publisher out of releasing the book, but didn't get anywhere." I took a long drink then slowly screwed the cap back on the bottle. "He said I should have had her sign an NDA because then he'd have some kind of recourse. But, I didn't, so here we are."

"Is this what the world is coming to? Anyone you get involved with needs to sign a piece of paper that states they won't try to fuck you over?"

John must be really upset because, like Dan, he rarely curses so he doesn't get into the habit and slip around his kids.

"Pretty much."

"Sad to say, even with a signed piece of paper, the lawyers find a way to get what they want," Cal added. "So an NDA may not have changed things much."

He and his soon-to-be ex-wife had a basic prenuptial agreement that somehow isn't protecting him like it should be. He's been in negotiations for months with no end in sight it seems.

"Mr. Hanover can't be happy about the book," John said.

Since it was published during the off season, the gossip mill hasn't done much churning yet, which is why John isn't up to speed.

"He's not," I said. "But the club still isn't commenting on it and they don't expect me to, either."

"I'm sure he'll try to protect you every way he can. This organization is the best I've played for."

"Yeah, he has Hannah on it. I'm going to be doing some events to add good press to the negative stuff so it hopefully cancels out." I gestured toward Dan and Cal with my empty bottle and said, "I actually dragged these two to a fundraiser a couple weeks ago."

"It was actually fun," Dan said. "Lexi had a great time."

Cal agreed. "I thought it would be another thing to get through, but I had a lot of fun."

"Thankfully Hannah thought to bring SWAG," Dan said. "Hannah was there?" John asked.

I nodded. "I told Mr. Hanover that I'd feel better if she came along. So, she's stuck going to all these things with me. At least I know she won't book anything horrible."

"Wait a minute...Hannah is coming here?" John asked. "Yep."

"But she never comes to spring training. She barely leaves the stadium."

"Well, there's a first time for everything. From what I understand, she's arriving today."

HANNAH

SETTLING ON THE COUCH, I pulled my computer onto my lap and set my planner by my side. My whole calendar is set up electronically, complete with reminders that pop up on my computer, tablet, and phone, but there's something about writing things down that helps commit them to memory. And between the usual Waves events and Jack's individual appearances, there's a lot to remember.

I looked through all my notes, ensuring everything is in order. So far, so good. I'd just flipped the calendar to look ahead to the season when my phone rang. I grabbed it off the coffee table and saw my father smiling back at me. Declining the call, I set the phone back down and sank further into the couch.

After a few seconds, my phone chirped alerting me that there's voicemail. I ignored it for a good fifteen minutes before reaching for my phone and listening.

Hannah, ma girl, I hoped I'd a heard from ya by now. We need ta talk. I'm sorry I kept things from ya, but I knew you'd be upset. I'm leavin' for the Keys tomorrow. I can fly ya down if yer lookin' for a holiday or I'll arrange ma schedule so I can come see ya. Call me. I love ya.

The words on my computer screen blurred. I blinked several times to clear the tears from my eyes and bring them back into focus.

I have no idea what to do about my father. He dropped a bomb on me at Christmas and I'm still feeling the aftershocks. Patience is not one of his virtues, but he's going to have to wait this time because I'm not ready to talk to him yet, and I'm definitely not ready to see him.

I'd almost talked to Mrs. Button about the whole situation just to get someone else's perspective, but admitting my crush on Jack had been enough emotional purging that day.

Besides, no matter what anyone else says or thinks, I have to decide how to handle things. My father is all I have and even if he wasn't, he *is* my father. I know I'll talk to him eventually, I just need to figure out what I'm going to say. And I'll put that off as long as possible.

Chapter Seven

JACK

I WATCHED as the ball left the pitcher's hand heading toward the inner half of the plate. Pulling my elbows in, I shifted my hips and whipped the bat around, sending the ball flying into the right field corner. The next five pitches followed suit. Just when I was getting into a rhythm, a pitch curved toward the outside corner. I stepped forward and extended my arms, sending it sailing into the alley between right and center.

Rocco Richmond, assistant hitting coach for the Waves and today's batting practice pitcher, chuckled. "Gotta keep you on your toes."

My spring training goal this year is to perfect my inside-out swing. It's a skill Jeter made look easy, but it's not. And it seems like more and more pitches are coming inside, probably because opposing teams noticed that I usually miss them. If I want to keep my average up, I need to up my game, too.

Raising my hand, I let Rocco know I wanted five more pitches. He threw a mix and I managed to sprinkle them around the field.

Waving, I left the batter's box and walked toward the dugout to get a drink.

"You're looking good," Wayne Brooks, the Waves' hitting coach, said. "It seems like you're seeing the ball well."

I nodded and chugged a cup of water. "I know Rocco was taking it easy, but I didn't have a problem following the ball from his hand."

"That inside-out swing has come a long way since last year. Did you spend the whole off season at the cages?"

He's kidding, but I answered anyway. "Mostly just hit off the tee. It helped me sort out the mechanics."

"It shows," he said. "And the more you practice, the easier it'll be to get the bat around on a ball so far in."

Wayne is the one who suggested I work on this and I'm happy he did. For the most part, I was missing the inside corner third strike that was coming at me more frequently. This will help turn them into hits. Which will be great, especially if there's a runner on second.

Obviously this is baseball, so nothing is guaranteed, but every little thing helps. If there's something you can do to improve skills, why the hell wouldn't you do it? I don't understand guys who hit into the shift every single time. For years, even. Fix that shit. There are enough factors in this game that you can't change...work on the ones you can.

Second basemen Oskar Marquez had stepped up to the plate after me and was peppering hits through the outfield. Dan looked good out in centerfield as he chased a good majority of them down.

"Glad to have him back," Wayne said.

"Yeah, and I know he's glad to be back."

"Is Sabrina coming down?"

I nodded. "She and Lexi are coming next weekend. Then they'll be down the last week during spring break."

"I'll have to thank her personally for getting him back on his feet." Without missing a beat, he yelled, "Marquez, quit dropping your elbow." Turning back to me he said, "I gotta go fix him."

I walked past first base and settled down on the grass to stretch. At this point in my career, I'm not looking to bulk up, I just want to maintain what I have and stay limber. That seems to be the secret to avoiding strains and sprains. That and a lot of luck.

Cal walked up next to me and slowly reached down to touch his toes. He hung there for a few seconds before standing up in small increments.

"Damn, my back is tight today," he said, then plopped onto the ground next to me. "I fell asleep on the couch last night and am paying for it."

He stretched out on his stomach, put his arms out to the side, then lifted his left leg up and over his body until his foot touched his right hand.

"Need some help?" I asked.

"I'm good," he said, although you would never know that from the tone of his voice

After a few seconds, he repeated the same motion on the other side. His foot didn't quite meet his hand this time, but it still looked like a pretty good stretch.

I spread my legs wide and moved from side to side, before walking my hands forward as far as I could go in a straddle pancake. My hamstrings and hip flexors protested, but I took a deep breath in and slowly let it out settling into the stretch. After a minute, I walked my hands back, pulled my legs together, and took a short break.

"Anything going on later?" Cal asked.

"Nothing major. Just dinner, I guess."

"When do your Hannah events start?"

"Based on the tentative calendar she gave me, there's something Saturday night," I said. "She said she'd confirm, but I haven't heard from her yet."

I stood with my legs shoulder width apart, then folded at the waist, being sure to keep my back flat. When my hands touched the ground, I bent my elbows and let gravity do its job. Once the hurt stopped, I walked my hands back further, deepening the stretch.

"Do you think it's gonna help?" he asked.

"Hannah seems to think it will, and she's the expert," I said.

"If nothing else, maybe she'll dress like she did for the last event and you'll get to enjoy the view."

I stood and grunted. That's the last thing I need. Between the book shit and the lack of someone to blow off steam with, this season is going to be hard enough. I don't need an unwanted attraction to a Waves staff member muddying the waters even more.

After twisting from side to side and arching my back in a counter stretch, I folded forward and repeated the back stretch.

"I had fun at the last event. If they're all like that, it won't be bad."

"If you need an extra for anything, count me in. It's not like I have anything else to do," he said. "I'm laying low for a while. This divorce is knocking me on my ass."

"Things getting any better?"

I don't ask Cal about his divorce unless he brings it up. For one, we're guys. Second, if he's having a good day, why bring it up and ruin his mood?

"Everything is going through the lawyers now." He

chuckled. "It's pathetic. Marsha and I were married for six years and now we can't even talk."

I sat back on the ground and stretched my legs out in front of me, crossing them at the ankle.

"The thing is, I don't know what she's so pissed about. We met when I was already playing for the Waves, so she can't say the schedule was a surprise. I never cheated on her and she's the one who surprised the hell out of me by asking for a divorce. Even though I wanted to work on it and she didn't, I offered a pretty generous settlement, which apparently isn't good enough." He stretched his right leg out and bent the left over it, then twisted at the waist, bracing his left elbow against his knee to deepen the stretch. "And it's not that I can't afford to give her more, but why the hell should I?"

He doesn't have to convince me of anything, but I nodded anyway. Right now, I'm sure he just needs someone to listen.

"I'm just trying to get through it and move on. You know I'm not a casual guy when it comes to relationships and anyone I get involved with right now wouldn't be more than a distraction from my misery."

Even though we have two totally different approaches to women, Cal's never judged me and he's been nothing but supportive through the whole book thing.

And I appreciate that. It's nice to have friends who have your back no matter what.

Cal stretched his other side, then we just both sat there, taking in the scenery.

I love my job. There are definitely worse ways to make a living than playing baseball. It's February, and instead of wasting away in an office under fluorescent lights, I'm soaking up Vitamin D on a field in St. Pete.

"Someone's coming your way," he said, nudging his chin toward the stands.

Sure enough, Hannah walked in my direction, switching her gaze between me and the steps she navigated. Dressed in her usual work attire of pants and a blouse, she should look like her usual business self, but for some reason that's not the case. She looks softer, sexier. Maybe it's just my imagination filling in the blanks since I've seen the curves that lurk beneath the boxy clothes.

She opened the low gate and stepped onto the field, pushing her glasses back into place with her index finger. As she got closer, I saw that what had looked like plain brown frames shimmered when the sun hit them.

Cal and I both stood and faced her.

"Cal, I want to thank you again for attending the event the other night. The coordinator emailed and said you guys were the hit of the evening."

"It was fun," he said. "I just told Jack I'm available if he ever needs me."

"We just might take you up on that," she said then turned to face me. "Jack, I wanted to confirm the event this Saturday night. It's only about fifteen minutes up the beach."

"It's a beach party, right?"

"Yes, from what I understand, they're having an inflatable slide and games right on the beach, so it's super casual."

"What are you wearing?" I asked.

"I, uh, I'm not sure yet," she said. A breeze floated through the stadium, blowing her hair across her face. She reached up and tucked it behind her ear. "Probably capris and a T-shirt."

I nodded. "Do I need to bring anything?"

"No, just yourself."

"It starts at seven, right?" She nodded. "I'll swing by the hotel to get you around six thirty."

"Oh, that's not necessary. I can drive myself."

"Your hotel is on my way. There's no reason to take two cars." I smiled and added, "Help avoid global warming and all that."

She bit her bottom lip and looked everywhere but at me for several seconds. I glanced over at Cal and he shrugged. Finally she nodded and looked in my direction.

"Okay, I'll wait in the lobby, so just pull in that side of the lot."

That said, she turned and walked back toward the stands. I watched her ascend the stairs with quick efficiency and disappear into the shadows of the concourse.

Cal's chuckle reminded me he was still standing there. He raised an eyebrow when I looked at him.

"What?" I asked.

"Nothing." He shook his head and laughed again. "Not one damn thing."

But I know it's something, no matter how much I don't want it to be.

HANNAH

WHAT THE HELL *did I just agree to?*

It's bad enough being in an open space with Jack, but to sit in a car next to him? Where his scent and all those pheromones he exudes will be trapped in one small area? I may not survive.

And Lord knows what he'll wear to a casual beach event. Board shorts? Faded cutoffs? A speedo?

I took that last one off the list. Jack Reagan is definitely not the speedo type.

Not that it matters. The man looks amazing in anything, especially baseball pants. I almost fell down the stadium steps when I spotted him stretching. Bent over with his amazing ass on display for my viewing pleasure like that. Rest assured, I had viewed and taken pleasure.

"Hey Hannah." I looked up and saw Ken Jr. walking toward me. "Everything okay?"

"Yeah, just mentally checking my to-do list."

"All settled in?" he asked.

"For the most part," I said. "I was just confirming Saturday night's event with Jack."

"How's he doing with all this? Is he playing nice?"

"He's actually been great. We've only done the one event so far, but he was amazing." I didn't want to sound too gushy about Jack, so I added, "Dan and Cal were, too. It was definitely a positive experience and hopefully set the tone for all the others."

"Thanks for setting this stuff up. I know you're not thrilled being down here, but for some reason, my father thought it was necessary."

"It's fine."

"I can probably talk him into letting you go home and come back down just for events."

"That's not necessary. Like I said, I'm mostly settled in. Plus, it's gorgeous here while we're having a cold, rainy spell back home. So I'm good."

"There are definitely worse places to be."

"I'll keep you updated on what we're doing and let you know if we hit any snags along the way."

"I appreciate it, but I'm sure you have it all under control."

With those words said, he continued on to wherever

he'd been headed and I walked to my office. I have some vendors to call, events to confirm, and copy to write.

Three hours later I'd managed to put a good dent in my never-ending to-do list. Not that I'm complaining about that list. I love my job. It's not what I imagined I'd end up doing with my life, but it truly is perfect for me and it's never boring.

Take these events I have planned for Jack. Getting something like this together in such a short time is a challenge. Add in his crazy schedule during the season, and it's even more difficult. But I did it. I managed to put together a calendar of events that's comprehensive but not obnoxious. Now I just have to mentally prepare myself to be in constant contact with him.

I honestly don't understand what my problem is. For whatever reason, I've always had a thing for Jack, but I've been able to keep it under wraps. Lately, it's been out of control and I'm afraid that in a moment of weakness I'm going to do something embarrassing like sniff his neck or run my fingers through his hair.

Before when the words "what are you wearing" came out of his mouth, I'd imagined the question in a whole different context. Thankfully I pulled myself together and gave a response that answered the one he'd actually asked.

I don't know if it's because I need to get laid or if I'm having some kind of early mid-life crisis, but lately my fascination with Jack Reagan has reached epic proportions. His mere presence makes me feel like a tween girl with her first crush. And I need to get over it right now.

Maybe it's time I made the effort to start dating again. Just the thought of it is exhausting, but maybe it will help me get over this ridiculous obsession.

Chapter Eight

JACK

PER HANNAH'S INSTRUCTIONS, I pulled into the hotel parking lot near the lobby door. I didn't even have a chance to put the Range Rover in park before she was opening the passenger door. Dressed in white capri pants and a yellow shirt, she looks shiny and bright.

She settled into the passenger seat and turned to buckle her seatbelt.

"Hi," she said, then did a double take and chuckled. "Nice shirt."

I looked down at my Waves-themed Hawaiian shirt, then back at her.

"Are you making fun of my shirt?"

"Not at all."

"Are you sure? Because if you are, I'll have to let Mr. Hanover know you don't approve of the gear he buys for his players."

"I seriously doubt Mr. Hanover bought that for you."

"I'm sure he didn't pick it out, but it was given to me at spring training my rookie year. I found it in the back of my closet and figured I'd dust it off for tonight. It is a beach bash, after all."

"That it is," she said as she used her knuckle to push her glasses back into place. Today's pair have white frames with tiny yellow polka dots. Adorable.

I cringed.

When the hell did I start thinking of Hannah Adams as anything but cool and efficient?

"Are you okay?" she asked.

"Yeah, why?"

"You looked like you were in pain."

"I'm good, just moved my leg a weird way," I lied. "Ready to go?"

"Lead the way, Jimmy Buffett."

A bunch of comments popped into my head, each sounding more flirty than the next, and I don't want to go there. I kept my mouth shut, shifted the car into drive, and pulled into traffic.

HANNAH

I FOCUSED on letting shallow breaths in and out through slightly parted lips. Jack's spicy sweet scent combined with the earthy smell of the leather seats is more than I can handle. Add that to his sexy dad look of Hawaiian shirt and khaki shorts and I'm in danger of losing it.

Needing something else to focus on, I pulled the tote I'd brought onto my lap. Digging through the items inside, I did another quick count to make sure I have enough.

Again, this isn't a formal meet-and-greet, but it's good PR for Jack to have something to sign if the occasion arises.

"What did you bring this time?" he asked.

"A lot of cards, a few balls, some shirts, and a stack of hats. And I found these cups abandoned in the closet of the office I'm using so I grabbed them."

I held up a sleeve of white plastic cups with the Waves logo across the front, and he took his eyes off the road just long enough to check them out. I'm actually surprised at what a conscientious driver he is.

Other than checking his rear view and side mirrors, his eyes have remained glued to the road since we left the hotel parking lot. I guess I'd expected him to be a casual, possibly reckless driver. The fact that he isn't makes him even more attractive. Ugh!

"I'm gonna take a wild guess and say that's the place," he said.

I glanced up and spotted an event banner hanging across the road just ahead. A large arrow at the bottom pointed to the parking lot up on the left. Jack turned into the lot and backed into a spot near the entrance. He shifted the car into park and turned off the engine. After looking over at the makeshift entrance to the event at the other end of the lot, he glanced over at me.

"Sorry, it's a force of habit to park as close to the exit as possible. Makes for an easy getaway," he said. "I can move closer to the entrance or drop you off."

"I'm fine walking," I said. "But thank you."

"You sure?" he asked. "It's no problem."

His sweet smile had my stomach turning somersaults.

"I'm sure."

"Then let's go. Hold on, I'll come over and help you with that bag."

Before I could protest, I heard his door slam and

watched him round the hood then open my door. He pulled the tote from my lap and extended his hand to help me out. I hesitated for a second, then realized it would be rude to ignore it.

As soon as my hand touched his, the zing that traveled from my fingertips to every erogenous zone in my body kept me frozen in place.

"Are you okay?" he asked. His hazel eyes looked down then back up my body, searching for a reason for my mannequin act. When he found none, his brow wrinkled, making him look even more adorable. Before I could get lost counting the gold flecks in his eyes, I got hold of myself and smiled.

"Sorry, I felt myself slipping and froze before I fell and looked like a total idiot."

"Don't worry," he said as he led me off the running board. "I won't let you fall."

If only that were true.

Chapter Nine

HANNAH

"WHAT A GREAT SETUP," he said.

His eyes lit up as they scanned the beach. From the parking lot, I saw a huge inflatable slide, a bouncy house, and a dunk tank. A real Shangri-La for children, and apparently thirty-four-year-old baseball players as well.

We approached the check-in table and immediately the women manning it fussed all over us. Well, over Jack. They pulled him to the side and a crowd quickly circled around. I watched as he handled the situation with ease.

"You must be Hannah Adams." I tore my gaze from Jack and his adoring fans and looked at the woman who now stood in front of me. "I'm Rose Garrett."

When I'd spoken to her on the phone, her youthful voice and energy had me picturing someone closer to my age. I was definitely wrong about that. Rose is most likely in Mrs. Button's generation.

"Looks like you have great weather for this," I said.

She held up her right hand with the index and middle finger crossed.

"So far, so good. Weather usually isn't an issue here, but last year it poured and we had to move everything inside. One of our board members has an empty warehouse we were able to use, but it wasn't nearly as successful as the previous years we've held it on the beach."

"The beach is definitely a draw."

She nodded, then nudged her chin in Jack's direction. "Although we could have held it outside in a monsoon this year and we'd probably still have a full crowd with our celebrity guest in attendance," she said. "Thank you for reaching out. Once word got around that Jack Reagan would be here, tickets sales went crazy. I've been involved with the organization for twenty years and this is the first time we've sold out prior to the event."

She just gave me some very good information. I'd hate to make any promises, but the PR person in me can't help thinking how great it would be to make some of these events annual things.

"You're welcome, I know Jack is very happy to be here."

"You said you were attending an event near you prior to this. How did that work? Is it going to be like that all night?"

She pointed toward Jack holding court with his ever-growing crowd. They'd moved further onto the beach, clearing up the entrance.

"Eventually we'll have to save him," she said.

I watched Jack sign a card and hand it to a boy wearing a Waves T-shirt.

"He's handing out goodies. Once everyone has something, they'll move on."

"I'm not so sure."

"Jack is great with fans. He'll be fine." And while I absolutely believe those words, I'm still keeping a close eye on things to make sure nothing gets out of hand. "Besides, he was eyeing that slide. I'm sure he's going to want to try it out at some point."

"Just please tell him to be careful," she said. "I'd hate for my slide to be responsible for his injury."

"I will."

"It looks like a line has formed at check-in. I'd better get back to the table," she said. "I'll talk to you later."

I stepped further onto the beach, closer to Jack. The majority of the crowd surrounding him now consisted of adults. One woman in particular seemed to be getting a little too close, and a feeling I didn't want to name raced through my body. I took a step closer then stopped myself. I stood in place and took in a deep breath then slowly let it out. After repeating that several times, I had the unnamed emotion under control.

I can't go rushing over there just because a pretty girl is getting a little handsy. He's a big boy and knows how to handle himself. If he needs help I'm sure he'll let me know.

As if he heard my thoughts, Jack looked in my direction. He widened his eyes then inclined his head the barest hint toward the woman clinging to his right bicep. I took that as my cue and walked toward his little gang, hearing more of the conversation as I approached.

"We start every season planning on going to the Series. We have the talent to get there and we'll give it our all," Jack said. "If the team doesn't suffer any major injuries, all the stars align, and the baseball gods smile down on us, we'll win it all."

I strategically worked myself into the inch of space he'd created between himself and the woman who had suction cupped herself to him.

"Speaking of injuries," one man said. "How's McMullen looking? Is he going to be back this year?"

"Dan looks great," Jack said. "All healed up and ready to play."

Before anyone could ask another question, I said, "I think they're looking for people to take their seats."

The lie seemed logical as the official start time had passed fifteen minutes ago. Jack's admirers slowly left the circle, most of them making sure to shake his hand and say a few words before departing.

A blond boy wearing a Waves jersey approached and said, "Thanks again for the ball."

"You're welcome, Jeremy," Jack said, as he shook the boy's hand. "I'll find you after dinner so we can race on the slide."

The boy's face lit up with his smile. "Great. Thanks!"

He turned and ran off, his gangly pre-teen limbs looking like they'd tangle together.

"Race on the slide?" I asked.

He shrugged. "Just trying to make the fans happy."

"Right."

"Hey Jack." The sultry voice came from behind him. His broad shoulders had hid her from my view, but when he shifted, there she stood, looking like she wanted to take a bite out of him.

"There's room at my table if you're looking for some-where to sit," she said.

"I appreciate that," he said. "But I think we're set."

Is it my imagination or did he put extra emphasis on *we're*? It must be. I can't imagine he'd do anything to alienate a potential conquest.

He looked toward me for confirmation, and I nodded. "Thanks anyway," he said.

Her eyes narrowed in my direction, then looked adoringly back at him. "I'll see you later then."

Alrighty then. I guess they already have plans. Hopefully he'll have her sign an NDA before they do anything.

JACK

WHEN DID bold women start to piss me off?

It's not that I want someone who's totally submissive, but it would be nice if they at least let me decide if I want them touching me before they're practically attached. I'm pretty sure I'd be arrested if I walked up to a woman at an event, plastered myself against her, and started stroking her chest.

"Jack?" Hannah's voice broke through my thoughts. "You okay?"

"Yeah, just taking it all in."

She didn't look convinced, but let it drop.

"We're sitting right over there with Rose Garrett," she said. "But I was going to grab a drink first," she said. "There's a non-alcoholic daiquiri over there with my name on it. Did you want one?"

"Daiquiris aren't really my thing, but homemade lemonade is and it looks like they have that, too," I said. "Let's go."

We'd just gotten our drinks when someone stepped onto the makeshift stage and asked everyone to take their seats. Hannah led the way to our table and we took the last two seats. After quietly introducing ourselves to the other six people at the table, we sat back and listened to the woman at the microphone. Once she was done, she came to our table and told us to head over to the buffet. I won't argue with that. I'm starving.

I grabbed two plates and handed one to Hannah, then waited for her to go ahead of me. Her eyes widened, but she eventually took my cue and moved forward. She proceeded to take a tiny scoop of every item as she progressed. My scoops were a bit larger.

"Everything looks amazing," she said.

"Then why are you taking portions that would only satisfy a bird?" She glanced back at me, her brow furrowed. "Please don't tell me you're one of those women that doesn't eat."

The edges of her mouth curled into a small smile and she looked down her body, then back at me.

"Does it look like I don't eat."

My eyes took the same path hers had, over every sweet dip and curve, before meeting her gaze again.

"It's hard to tell."

I need a closer inspection was on the tip of my tongue, but thankfully I didn't say it out loud. I can't go there.

We continued down the buffet line and by the time we reached the huge salad at the end, my plate was heaping. Thankfully they had smaller plates for that purpose. Hannah actually took a full sized portion of salad, adding all the amazing toppers they had available.

"All done?" I asked after she poured a small amount of dressing on her salad. She nodded and we made our way back to the table. I set my plates down then said, "I'm going to grab another lemonade. Do you want another daiquiri or would you like something different?"

She glanced at her nearly-empty drink. "Another daiquiri sounds great. Thank you."

Thankfully the line is short and I had our drinks in no time, opting to add whipped cream to Hannah's daiquiri.

She didn't get it on her last one, but when I was given the option, I couldn't resist.

I turned to walk back to the table and almost crashed into the annoying woman from earlier. She did tell me her name, but I don't remember what it is. And even if I did, I wouldn't use it. I don't want to encourage anything and experience has taught me that something as small as that would.

"Hey Jack. Thirsty?"

"Only one is for me," I said and held up my lemonade. She leaned closer and said, "Maybe we can sneak away so you can buy me a real drink."

Why the actual fuck does this woman think I'd want to buy her a drink? Or anything else? I've done nothing to encourage her.

"Sorry, but I'm booked. Enjoy the rest of your night," I said, trying to be as polite as possible. After all, I'm here for positive PR. I don't need to cause a scene.

Her mouth turned down and her lip popped out into a pout. She leaned toward me, squeezing my bicep between her fake boobs. "I'll check with you later," she said. "Maybe your schedule will open up."

She wiggled off in the other direction before I could tell her not to hold her breath.

I made my way back to my table, and placed Hannah's drink in front of her before settling into my seat. Her head was bent toward Rose Garrett, and they appeared to be deep in conversation. The older woman's silver hair gives her a matronly look, but the twinkle in her eyes hints at a youthful mischievousness. I imagine my mother would look that way if she'd lived long enough. She'd had such a joy for life and tried to make every day an adventure. Ironic since she didn't make it to her fortieth birthday.

Not wanting to go too far down the rabbit hole of

despair, I picked up my fork, speared a shrimp and popped it into my mouth. Hannah glanced over at me and frowned.

"Are you okay?" she asked.

"Mmm hmm." I finished chewing. "Why?"

"I don't know. You look upset."

"I'm good."

She looked directly into my eyes so long it made me uncomfortable. I worked at keeping my expression neutral and hoped my eyes didn't give anything away.

Even after twenty-two years, thoughts of my mother make me emotional. Obviously I miss her, but it also brings the resentment I feel toward my father to the surface. Yes, he lost his wife, but I lost my mother. He was the adult. He should have at least given the appearance that he was holding his shit together.

Fuck!

I blinked and turned toward my plate.

"The food is amazing, Mrs. Garrett," I said, changing the conversation. Thankfully the whole table picked up on the topic of food, taking my mind off my depressing thoughts for the moment.

The people at this event are definitely more in-your-face than the ones at the last had been. They're not rude or anything, just quicker to approach. Maybe it's because this event is so casual. Or maybe this dorky shirt makes me seem like someone they want to talk to. I don't know the reason, but I've had to be on all night. I'd just signed the last item from Hannah's bag and its recipient walked off happy.

"Wow," Hannah said as she folded her empty bag. "I can't believe it's all gone. Tonight has been pretty intense."

I nodded and inclined my head. "Come on. Let's walk before someone else approaches." She followed my lead.

"Keep your head down and don't make eye contact," I said, only semi-joking. I spotted Jeremy and groaned.

"What's wrong?"

"I promised that kid I'd race on the slide with him."

She looked in Jeremy's direction. "Maybe he forgot?"

"When I was his age, if I'd met Nomar Garciaparra at an event like this and he told me he'd race me on the slide, I wouldn't have forgotten."

"Probably not now, either," she said with a small smirk.

"True," I admitted. "Come on. Hopefully I won't end up racing everyone here."

Chapter Ten

HANNAH

SPENDING SO much time with Jack is going to kill me. I'm finding that he isn't a waste of handsome. I'll have to admit to Mrs. Button that she's right.

He's definitely too handsome for his own good, but he's not the self-absorbed jerk I thought him to be. Instead I'm finding that he's funny, well-mannered, and surprisingly considerate. This can only stand to make my irrational crush even more ridiculous.

Jack toed off his Sperrys and left them next to me in the sand. "Do you still have the Sharpie?" he asked.

I dug into the tote and pulled out a blue and a black marker. "Color preference?" I asked.

He took both and held them up to an approaching Jeremy. "Blue or black?" he asked.

The boy scrunched his face then said, "Black."

Jack popped the cap off the black Sharpie and asked, "Where do you want it signed?"

"On my back, right by your number." Jeremy turned and pointed to his shoulder blade.

Jack paused for a second before scrawling his name across the jersey, then added #5 just under it. He placed the cap back on the black marker and handed both back to me.

"Thanks," Jeremy said, twisting his neck to check it out. His beaming smile saying more than any words could.

"Now, are you ready for me to kick your butt on that slide?" Jack asked and was answered with an enthusiastic nod. "I'll be back," he said to me then he and the boy ran toward the slide.

Grabbing Jack's shoes, I stuffed them into the tote and made my way closer to the slide to get a better look. I have no idea how tall it is, but in order to enjoy the ride down, you have to climb up a net to get to the top.

The line had thinned significantly since the event began, but there were still people in front of them. Jack and Jeremy talked non-stop while they waited, occasionally looking up to watch whoever was on the net climbing to the top. Before long, it was their turn. Jack turned and said something, prompting a smile and a nod from the boy.

I noticed a woman off to the side with her phone held up, I assume recording the whole thing. Deciding to investigate, I moved closer until we stood only a person-width apart.

Jack and Jeremy each had one foot on the net and when the man in charge of the slide blew his whistle, they were off. Jack took a quick lead, the muscles in his forearms and calves bulging as he progressed. He looked back at Jeremy and I held my breath when his foot slipped off the net and he hung by his arms before finding his footing again. That allowed Jeremy to take the lead, and I realized Jack had done it on purpose.

They quickly scurried to the top and before I knew it, were sliding to the bottom. Jack bent his knees, allowing Jeremy to stand a split second ahead of him. The woman next to me put her phone down and I watched as she wiped a tear from her cheek.

"Excuse me," I said. "Are you Jeremy's mother?" She nodded and sniffed. I moved closer and held out my hand. "I'm Hannah Adams. I work for the Waves. I'm here with Jack."

"Karen Walsh." She looked at me with watery eyes. "I'm sorry." She dabbed at them again. "I'm not usually so blubbery, but watching my son interact with one of his heroes like that has me a mess. Thank Jack for this. He's been amazing with everyone, but in my opinion, has gone above and beyond with Jeremy."

While we were talking, Jack and Jeremy had taken advantage of the lack of a line at the speed throw. Despite the fact that the boy had put his whole body into his throw, I imagine Jack still pulled a faster speed.

"You can tell him yourself. It looks like they're done over there and are coming this way."

"Oh God. I'm a mess and Jack Reagan is coming this way." She wiped her eyes again and tucked a loose strand of hair behind her ear.

"Mom, did you see? I won!" Jeremy yelled, then added, "On the slide anyway. Jack beat me on the speed throw."

I have to give Karen credit, she kept her attention on her son while he spoke instead of gawking at Jack.

"Don't beat yourself up too much about that," Jack said. "I'm a little bigger and a lotta years older. You've got a helluva arm." But once he spoke, Karen had the usual fangirl reaction. Her face flushed and she looked like she might faint.

"Hi, I'm Jack Reagan," he said to Karen. He said it so

casually, as if he needed to introduce himself. "Jeremy's a great kid. Thanks for letting me hang with him."

Yes, the Waves does PR training with the players, but you can't teach that.

Karen shook his hand and seemed a bit dazed, but got her bearings after a few seconds.

"Thank you for being here tonight. You're Jeremy's favorite player."

Jack looked at me. "Can you hook Jeremy up with some tickets to a spring training game? And maybe for when we're playing the Rays?"

"Seriously?" Jeremy said. "Thanks Jack!"

"It's the least I can do for you representing me down here in Tampa territory."

I reached into my back pocket, pulled out a business card, and handed it to Karen.

"Take a look at the schedule and email or text me when you're available," I said. "And we'll work out the details."

We said our goodbyes and Jack gave Jeremy a high five. "See you at the park," he said as we walked away.

Thankfully no one else approached as we walked toward the exit. Jack has been surrounded all night and I imagine he's ready to get out of here. I know I am.

"Hannah."

I cringed when I heard my name, then realized it was Mrs. Garrett. She's so sweet, I can't be annoyed.

"Do you have a minute to explain the group event you mentioned to me at dinner to a couple other people?" she asked and gestured toward two women standing near the registration table. "I don't want to mess up any of the details."

"Sure." I looked over at Jack and said. "This shouldn't take too long."

"I'll go get the truck and pull it around."

He turned to walk away and I realized I still had his shoes in my tote.

"Wait, you need your shoes."

With a wave of his hand, he said. "I'm good. They're my favorites, I don't want to get sand in them." And he continued walking barefoot across the parking lot.

I spent the next five minutes talking to the women. Mrs. Garrett had mentioned they wanted to put something together for the volunteers and sponsors as a thank you for helping with this event. I suggested a day at the stadium. She said they have a small budget set aside and I can be sure they get a lot of bang for their buck. Instead of giving them the number for group sales, I handed them each a card and told them to contact me with dates.

Did I mention that I love my job? The hours are often long and the pace can be stressful, but for the most part the players are easy to deal with and I have all the team's resources at my fingertips. Mr. Hanover is dedicated to giving back to the community, so I have a pretty big budget to work with.

I expected to see Jack's truck near the parking lot entrance, but it wasn't there. I looked down the nearly-empty lot and saw the Range Rover sitting exactly where we'd parked earlier. He said he was going to pull around, but it's not a big deal for me to walk.

My phone buzzed and I stopped and pulled it out of my back pocket, groaning as my father's face flashed on the screen. I know I'll have to deal with him soon, but today is not that day.

Declining the call, I slipped the phone back into my pocket and continued toward the truck. I was focused on breathing and chasing the turmoil from my thoughts when I spotted a person slipping around the driver's side of

Jack's truck. She walked past me with a satisfied smirk on her face and I recognized her as the woman who'd been after him all night.

Guess she finally caught him.

The dome light went on as Jack slipped into the driver's seat and slammed the door behind him. The light faded as his head fell against the headrest. She must have exhausted him.

I stopped a few feet from the truck to blink back tears, trying to convince myself they'd formed because of my father's call.

JACK

STARING at the headliner of my truck, I struggled to keep my temper in check.

I can't believe that woman ambushed me in the parking lot. Did she actually think I was going to sit her in the passenger seat and take her home with me? Or maybe she just wanted a fast fuck against the truck.

It doesn't matter...she wasn't getting either. Not that I encouraged her during the event, but I think I made myself pretty clear just now that I won't be going there and she needs to back off. Hopefully that will stop her from showing up at a game.

A noise against the passenger door had me on full alert. If it's her, I swear I won't be responsible for my actions. I looked over and was relieved to see Hannah.

Shit. Hannah.

She opened the door and climbed into the seat.

"I'm sorry, Hannah." I paused to figure out what to

say. She's been around the game so long, the truth wouldn't surprise her. But I really don't want to discuss it with her, so I settled on, "I got held up."

"Not a problem," she said, clicking her belt into place.

Once she was settled, I pushed the ignition button, shifted into drive, and pulled out of the lot. Tension echoed through the truck and about a mile into the ride, I realized it wasn't all coming from me.

"You okay?" I asked.

"Fine. Why?"

"You seem upset."

"Nope. I'm good." From the corner of my eye, I saw her glance in my direction. "You?"

"Honestly, I've been better."

She faced the windshield again and mumbled something.

"I didn't catch that."

"It wasn't important," she said.

Her icy tone slapped me in the face.

"Are you sure you're okay?"

After a few seconds, she said, "I'm just tired."

We drove in silence for a few more minutes during which she seemed to be fighting an inner battle. Eventually her body language changed slightly, and she shifted into what I now recognize as PR mode.

"So, I think the event went well. Mrs. Garrett was thrilled with the outcome and plans on singing your praises to anyone who will listen."

Up until three months ago, I had no clue there was a difference between the real Hannah and the professional persona she projects most of the time. But now that I've seen the real woman, I don't want to deal with an imitation. Instead of commenting on the bullshit PR garble she just spewed, I said, "I'm in the mood for ice cream. I know a place not far from here that makes an amazing banana split. Whaddya say?"

"I really don't want ice cream."

"Are you lactose intolerant or something?"

She looked at me and frowned. "No. Why?"

"You said you don't normally order whipped cream and now you don't want ice cream. What other explanation could there be?"

"Not all of us are world-class athletes that burn millions of calories a day, you know."

I smiled. Real Hannah is back.

"Come on. You have to splurge once in a while," I said. "Besides, I'm driving so you don't have a choice."

She opened her mouth to say something then closed it and crossed her arms across her chest. "Fine."

I pulled into the lot next to its sole occupant, an orange Subaru hatchback.

"Is it open?" she asked, looking around the nearly empty lot.

I've learned that while this place has a never-ending line during the day, it's usually deserted at night. I have no idea why that is, but it works well for me.

"Yep, for another hour or so."

She didn't seem convinced, but unbuckled her seatbelt anyway. I got out of the truck and rounded the hood just as she opened her door. The fact that she didn't hesitate this time when I held out my hand to help her step down pleased me way more than it should.

We walked through the gravel lot to the window. The glass slid open and a gust of cold air floated out.

A teenage girl smiled and asked, "What can I get for you?"

Looking at Hannah, I asked, "What's your pleasure?"

"Oh, uh, I'm not sure." She glanced at the menu and

bit her lip, seeming to consider each item. "I'll have a hot fudge sundae."

The girl wrote that down, then turned her attention to me.

"Banana split."

"That'll be nine dollars and twenty-three cents."

Hannah reached into her back pocket.

"Don't even," I said, then handed the girl a twenty. "Keep the change."

The girl's eyes widened and she smiled. "Thank you. Your order will be right up."

She closed the window and walked away. I was happy to see another girl in the back. I'd hate to think she'd be closing up alone.

Putting her money back in her pocket, Hannah said, "Thank you."

"You're welcome."

She looked around and then back at me. "How did you find this place? It's a bit out of the way."

"A few years ago, Dan and I were talking about taking Lexi for ice cream after practice. One of the stadium groundskeepers heard us and recommended this place. We figured if the locals come here, it must be good, so we decided to give it a try."

"Is it always this dead?"

"At night it is, which in my mind, makes it perfect."

"I don't know how you guys handle it. I'd go crazy if I couldn't just go about my business without people staring at me or worse."

"Depending on where I am, I can usually get away without attracting too much attention."

She snorted. Actually snorted.

"I doubt that."

Before I could comment, the window slid open.

"Thank you," I said, taking the sundaes. "Come on, let's sit on the patio."

I walked around the side of the building and placed our ice cream on a table. Strands of lights woven through the beams of the patio roof added a soft glow to the space. Hannah sat and looked at her sundae.

"There's got to be a half gallon of ice cream in that," she said. "I'll never eat it all."

"Just give it your best shot." I handed her a spoon and a couple napkins. "Lexi usually gets about three-quarters of the way through, so I'm expecting at least that much," I said.

"Lexi eats this?"

"Hot fudge is her favorite."

She looked at the sundae and frowned, then tentatively dipped her spoon in and took a small taste. Then a bigger one.

"Mmm, this is amazing."

"Told you."

I shoved a heaping spoonful of banana split into my mouth and enjoyed watching her dig in with gusto. Her sexy moans and constant spoon licking made my dick twitch.

I recited stats in my head and focused on my own ice cream and anything else that would stop me from sporting full wood while eating sundaes with Hannah Adams.

I really can't go there. Hell, I've known her for ten years and until recently, never even thought about going there. What the fuck is wrong with me?

Hannah is an attractive woman, but she's definitely not my type. And if I did pursue her, what would happen at the end of the season? I'd have to deal with her, see her on a regular basis until I retire.

Something tells me she's not into casual relationships

and that's all I'm looking for. A sense of sadness rolled through me at that last thought.

I'll admit that watching Dan and Sabrina settle into wedded bliss has messed with my equilibrium. It's made me wonder what it would be like to have someone to come home to after a long away stretch.

A woman who actually cares about me and isn't just there to add another professional ballplayer to her collection. Someone who won't pay attention to every little thing I do and write a tell-all book.

I took a huge spoonful of ice cream and shoved it into my mouth, working to settle my rioting emotions. Maybe not getting it on the regular is messing up my brain.

"So earlier you said you've been better," Hannah said, breaking me out of my thoughts. "Did something happen at the event?"

I shook my head. "Just an overzealous fan trying to get a little too close."

The lights reflected off the lenses of her glasses and I couldn't see her eyes clearly, yet somehow they compelled me to continue.

"The woman that offered me a seat at her table followed me to my truck and made it pretty clear she was mine for the taking."

Hannah nodded, then looked down at her half-eaten sundae.

"So what did you do?"

"After the polite route didn't work, I made it pretty clear I didn't want her."

"Oh." So much was packed into those two letters.

What did she think I'd do? I didn't realize I'd spoken that last question out loud until she spoke.

"I saw her leaving your truck and I thought..." Her

voice trailed off and she dragged her spoon through the melting ice cream.

"You thought what?"

She squared her shoulders, looked directly at me, and said, "It doesn't matter what I thought. It's really none of my business."

"Don't do that," I said.

"Do what?"

"Hide behind that bullshit professionalism. Tell me what you thought."

"When she passed me in the parking lot, it didn't look like she'd been turned down. I figured you'd either taken care of business at the truck or made plans for later."

She'd seemed upset when she climbed into the truck earlier. Is that why? And if so, why would it bother her?

Then it hit me. Her usual reluctance to take my hand or touch me in any way. The wall she puts up when things get too casual. She feels this thing between us too. Holy hell.

"Hannah."

She looked up and I shifted forward until the glare disappeared from her glasses so I could see her eyes clearly.

"I know I'm not a saint, but I don't hook up with random groupies in parking lots. Or anywhere else for that matter."

Her eyes softened and professional Hannah was nowhere in sight. I took full advantage to plead my case.

"I know you've busted your ass putting these events together and I'd never do anything to fu—to screw them up. Please understand that. And please promise me that if I ever do something to upset you, you'll tell me. We're going to be spending a lot of time together and I don't want any misunderstandings between us."

She blinked several times.

"Okay."

"Good." I looked at the remains of her melted sundae. "Are you done?"

Looking down, she nodded. "I can't believe I almost ate that whole thing."

"It's good stuff." I grabbed her dish and stacked it on top of mine. "Come on, let's get going."

The ride back to her hotel passed in a comfortable silence. Beyond my teammates' wives, I haven't had many women friends in my life, if any, but I can easily see Hannah fitting into that category. The more time I spend with her, the more I appreciate her sense of humor and how easy she is to talk to. I appreciate a lot of other things about her too, but that's not important.

I've been controlling my emotions for a long time, I can manage to control this attraction I suddenly feel for her. I pulled into the parking lot of her hotel and circled around to the front door.

"Thanks for another great event," she said. "I know you weren't thrilled about doing this, but you've really been a great sport. And you're amazing with the fans."

She looked at me and her smile shot all my confidence that I could control anything right to hell.

Chapter Eleven

JACK

MY KNUCKLES TURNED white as my hands gripped the steering wheel.

"Jack?"

I released my fingers one at a time and turned toward her, resting my elbow on the armrest between us. Her eyes widened and she licked her lips. And just like that every ounce of restraint seeped from my body and I couldn't think of a single reason why I shouldn't kiss this woman. Right here. Right now.

Moving my hand slowly, I raised it and caressed her jaw, giving her time to back away if she didn't want this. Not only did she not back away, she let out a short breath, leaned into my touch, and shifted her gaze to my mouth.

"Hannah."

The whispered word brought her eyes back to mine. It's been a long time since the thought of a kiss made my heart pound, but mine was racing so fast, she could probably hear it.

I moved my head forward a fraction, then stopped and searched her gaze, giving her one last chance to back away. When she didn't, I tunneled my fingers through her hair and exerted a hint of pressure, tipping her head back. Her lips parted slightly and I couldn't resist anymore.

Touching my mouth to hers, I moved slowly, taking in the feel of her soft lips against mine. The kiss is relatively chaste, but I feel its impact everywhere. Needing her closer, I wrapped my arm around her waist and settled my hand against the small of her back, pulling her forward.

I forget that we're sitting in my truck in a parking lot where

anyone can see us. I forget that we shouldn't be doing this. And I

forget all about control and dive right in.

Opening my mouth over hers, I licked the seam of her lips, asking for entry. It's been a long time since I've done that and it's kind of nice. My usual women have their tongue down my throat before I even decide if I want it there.

She didn't move at first, but then with a soft moan, she opened up and I touched my tongue to hers, enjoying the lingering taste of hot fudge and ice cream. Pressing against her full lips, I added a soft suction, bringing the kiss to another level.

It went on and on, and I enjoyed every second, every taste, every touch. I shifted my other arm around and up to the middle of her back, pulling her closer. Firm, round, and full, her breasts flattened against my chest and I flexed my fingers into her back, fighting the urge to reach around and cup them.

I pulled my mouth from hers for a second, moving my

head to go at the kiss from a different angle. Her hands shifted from my shoulders to my head and she dug her fingers into my scalp, pulling me closer. Our teeth touched as our mouths clashed together and I sank into the kiss, thrusting and tangling my tongue against hers repeatedly, pulling her forward until she was halfway across the armrest.

Before my last thread of sanity snapped and things got totally out of hand, I slowed the kiss and released my grip allowing the lower half of her body to fall back into her seat. Reluctantly pulling my mouth from hers, I rested my head against her forehead, and fought to slow my breathing.

Pulling back slightly, I looked down at her swollen lips, taking in her dazed expression. Her eyes opened slowly and I had to fight the urge to take her mouth again. Instead, I leaned forward and kissed her temple, then her forehead, and her nose before meeting her eyes.

"I had a great time tonight, Hannah." My voice sounded like I'd eaten gravel. I cleared my throat. "But I should go." When she didn't answer, I added, "Will I see you at the park tomorrow?"

She blinked twice, then nodded.

"Great." I kissed her chastely and pulled back fast, fighting the urge to park the truck, drag her up to her room, and fuck her senseless. "Good night."

Reaching down to grab her bag, she looked back and said, "Good night."

The gentlemanly thing would be to go open her door and help her out of the truck, but I'll totally embarrass myself if I stand up right now.

She opened the door and glanced back, looking adorably mussed.

"Bye Jack."

That said, she stepped down, closed the door behind her, and disappeared into the lobby.

HANNAH

I STARTED AT THE CEILING, my head still spinning.

Jack Reagan kissed me.

He didn't just kiss me. He *KISSED* me. And it was amazing. Better than I'd ever imagined. And Lord knows I'd imagined.

My crush had been out of control before, but now that I've gotten to know Jack...really know him...it's turning into something much bigger. There's something sweet and real behind that amazing face and sexy body. For ten years, I was attracted to his exterior and am now finding out that what's on the inside makes him even more irresistible.

And that kiss.

I've had sex with men before and not felt as much as I did when Jack put his mouth on mine. It's been hours, and my lips are still tingling...not to mention other parts. If I was home, I'd take the edge off with my battery operated boyfriend, but I was so afraid they'd go through my bags at TSA, I left him at home. I could take things into hand, so to speak, but that takes so much longer, and I really just want to get some sleep.

I rolled over and pulled the covers up to my chin, squeezing my legs tight in an attempt to ease the ache. But something tells me that since Jack put it there, he's the only one who will be able to ease it.

And I know I can't let that happen. Ever.

Yes, he may be sweet, charming, and sexy as hell, but

he's also heartbreak waiting to happen. Years ago, I vowed to never date athletes or actors and I have no reason to change that now.

I chuckled and scooted further into the covers. I'm getting way ahead of myself here. Yes Jack kissed me, but it's probably no big deal to him. How many women have I seen him with in the past decade?

Lots, that's how many. And I'm sure there are just as many I don't know about.

One kiss, no matter how hot it had been for me, probably didn't even register on his radar. With that disheartening thought floating through my head, I drifted into a troubled sleep.

My cell phone alarm blared and I swiped to shut it off. After tossing and turning most of the night, all I want to do is roll over and go back to sleep. Maybe I should call off sick.

Groaning, I sat up and rubbed my eyes. If I call off, I'll just spend the day obsessing about Jack. At least at work, I'll have things to keep my mind occupied besides the sexy shortstop. I'll just have to hide in my office while I'm there.

Rolling out of bed, I dragged myself into the bathroom and

turned on the shower as hot as I could stand it. I'd forgotten to turn

on the exhaust fan and by the time I washed my hair and stretched

my tight muscles in the hot water, the bathroom was full of steam.

Fighting the urge to linger in my self-made steam room, I grabbed the fluffy towel from the rack outside the shower, and patted myself dry.

After wrapping the towel around my dripping hair, I

grabbed my robe off the hook and slipped into it then opened the door allowing the steam to billow out.

The rest of the room felt cold after being in my cozy confines, and I tightened my robe, then went through the motions of brushing my teeth and towel drying my hair. I picked up my brush and worked my way through the knots I'd created. Once my hair was smooth, I set the brush down and looked in the mirror.

The flush cheeks are most likely from the shower, but my swollen lips and the hint of razor burn on my jaw are definitely Jack's doing. How potent is the man that my lips still look like I sucked on chili peppers hours later?

I don't normally wear foundation, but I'll need it today to mask both my lack of sleep and the razor burn. That and mascara should do the trick. I don't need lip gloss highlighting my lips any more than they are already.

As I dry my hair, scenes from last night flashed through my head. His hands on my face, his lips on mine, his arms pulling me closer. I clicked off the hair dryer and slammed it on the vanity.

This has to stop. I'm sure it wouldn't take much encouragement from me to get Jack to scratch my itch, but that would only end in disaster. I've seen how he lives and it's not for me. I'm not a prude, but I'm also not into casual sex and that's all it could ever be with him.

And where would I be after that?

I need to exorcise Jack Reagan from my thoughts once and for all. It's time to break my dating hiatus. I've been thinking about it for a while now, and it's time to just do it.

A guy who works at the park has been overly friendly lately. He's just what I need. We can get to know each other a little bit, go out a few times, and I won't have to see him every day back home. Perfect.

Chapter Twelve

HANNAH

DESPITE BEING PHYSICALLY EXHAUSTED, I've had a productive day so far. I finalized plans for Mrs. Garrett's group to visit the stadium in two weeks and sent off an email to Doug Lane to see if he has any goodies tucked away I can give them.

I also spoke to Karen Walsh and have tickets set aside for her and Jeremy to come when we play Boston next week. Those things added to finalizing events at the stadium and coordinating Jack's PR activities made the morning fly by.

My cell buzzed and I picked it up to check the text.

Jack: I had a great time last night. Looking forward to next time.

The phone banged against the desk as it dropped from my shaking fingers. It's amazing how twelve words can throw off your equilibrium.

I picked up the phone and read the words again. Jack had a great time last night and looks forward to next time? How am I supposed to respond to that? I can't. I can't possibly respond.

I powered down my phone so I won't be tempted to answer.

A knock at my door had me jumping out of my seat.

"Come in," I said, folding my hands together and setting them on the desk.

Doug Lane opened the door and walked through carrying a box.

"Hey," he said. "I had some free time so I figured I'd just stop by instead of answering your email." He set the box on my desk and pulled out a cotton replica of the Waves' uniform jersey. "Will these work?"

"They're perfect. Thank you."

"There are twenty in this box. Is that enough?"

"More than enough."

Twin dimples popped out with his smile. I'm not sure where he's from, but with his blond hair and blue eyes, Doug looks like he just stepped off a California beach.

"Great." He closed the box and rested his elbow on the lid, seeming to study me. "I have a surprisingly quiet day. Would you be interested in getting out of here and grabbing some lunch?"

"Oh, I'm sorry I can't today. I have a lunch meeting."

His smile faltered. "Okay well, maybe some other time."

This is it. My chance to venture back into the world of dating. I thought I'd have to work harder to make this happen, but it fell right in my lap. I can't let Doug leave this office without solid plans in place.

"But I'm free tomorrow if you're available."

He looked surprised, but pleased. "Sure. That works for me."

"Great." The word sounded more enthusiastic than I felt, but I'll have to apply the fake it 'til you make it strategy here.

"Noon?"

"Perfect."

That said, he and his dimples walked out the door. Doug seems like a nice guy and he's definitely attractive. Maybe spending more time with him will help me react to those things and get my mind off Jack.

JACK

CAL SLAMMED a ball toward my side of second base. I turned and caught it on the hop on my glove side, then fired it to Monte. He caught it and dramatically shook his hand.

"Yo, take it easy. This is just practice you know."

Dale Montgomery is one of the best first basemen in the game and can handle anything thrown his way so I know he's just busting my ass. I want to tell him to stop acting like a pussy, but Lexi has made my vocabulary strictly G-rated.

Cleaning up my language was hard, I don't want to slip into bad habits again. So instead, I tipped my hat in his direction, settled it back on my head, and got back into position.

Truth is, Dale probably isn't being dramatic. I'm sure my throws to first are harder than usual today. Everything I've done today has been extra. That kiss last night has me so twisted inside, I have to release all that somehow.

I stayed on the field for a few more batters, then walked to the dugout and grabbed a cup of water. After chugging down half its contents in one gulp, I poured the rest over my sweaty head. I shivered and sat on the bench, swiping the hair off my forehead and wiping the water from my face.

How is it that a woman I barely noticed for years now has me so tied in knots? Since my mother died and my home life fell apart, I've busted my ass to be in control of all things. I worked hard to have the career I love and have worked just as hard at keeping my personal life drama free. I'm not sure which planets aligned in the past few months, but they have everything out of whack.

Thankfully my game is as good as ever, but other than that, I feel like things are spiraling out of control. First that damn book and now Hannah. The book hype will eventually go away, but I'm not so sure about Hannah. I've never felt like this. I enjoy being with her, talking to her, and I sure as hell enjoyed kissing her.

Not to sound like a total prick, but I've always found women to be pretty much interchangeable. Some I've enjoyed more than others, but at the end of the day, it didn't matter which one I ended up with.

And when was the last time I thought about any woman when I should be concentrating on baseball?

Never, that's when.

Dan jumped down into the dugout, pulling my attention to him.

"Everything okay?" he asked, grabbing some Gatorade.

"Great, why?"

He shrugged and emptied his cup in one long chug.

After crushing the cup and tossing it in the direction of the recycling bin, he sat next to me.

"You looked pissed off or something."

"Just tired. I couldn't fall asleep last night."

"You sure that's all it is?"

Sometimes it sucks to have people around who really know you. I placed my cap back on my head and shifted forward on the bench, working hard to fix my facial expression.

"I'm sure," I said and stood grabbing my glove. "I'm gonna go hit the showers. See you at the meeting."

I shifted in my seat and checked my phone for the tenth time in the past five minutes. I can't believe Hannah never texted back. Hell, I can't believe I texted her in the first place. What was I thinking?

A rumble of laughter through the locker room pulled my attention back to the meeting. Things seem to be wrapping up and I'll admit, I have no idea what was said. I'm sure it's nothing I haven't heard before...plans for spring training, welcome the new guys who just showed up, let's do it this year, yadda, yadda, yadda. Then we were dismissed.

I'm sure most of the younger guys will stick around and lift or hit the cages. Normally I'd do something like that too, but I'm too exhausted today.

"Are you hitting the weight room?" Cal asked.

I shook my head and cringed at the twinge in my neck. "I'm beat."

"Everything okay?"

"My neck and shoulders are really tight."

I moved my neck from side to side, trying to loosen it up a little.

"Max is in the training room. I'm sure he can work his magic."

"Why, what'd you do?" Dan asked from behind me.

"Nothing. Just tight."

I must look really rough. They're both looking at me like I might break. The way everyone looks at my father.

"Maybe I will go see if Max can work some of the kinks out," I said, then looked at Dan and smiled. "Unless Sabrina is around?"

Throwing that down, I walked toward my locker. My two best friends followed.

Dan snorted. "Like I'd let my wife touch you."

"I think that hurt my feelings."

"Yeah right."

I grabbed my cell from the top shelf. Still no reply from Hannah.

"They're coming in a couple weeks, right?"

"Yeah, they'll be here around dinner time Thursday. Lexi is off school Friday and Monday."

"I didn't even look that far in the schedule. Do we have games every day?"

"Day off Sunday. Maybe we can rent a boat again and head to the Keys for the day. I know Sabrina would love it and Lexi's been bugging since she missed it last time."

"I'll call Tom and see what he has available," I said. "You in?" I asked Cal.

"Definitely."

"And probably Monte, too," I said. "Anyone else?"

"I'll ask the usual suspects and let you know," Cal said.

By "usual suspects" he means guys we trust and know won't get totally wasted, act like assholes, or do anything else that will ruin the day.

"You guys headed to the weight room?" They both nodded. "I'm going to see if Max can do something to loosen me up. See you later for dinner?"

"Sure thing," Cal said. "Meet at your place at six?"

"I'm FaceTiming Sabrina and Lexi at six. I'll come down when I'm done," Dan said.

Living in the same complex definitely makes planning things a lot easier.

"Sounds good."

I checked my phone one last time before heading down the hall to the trainer's room. At this point, I don't expect Hannah to text back, but can't keep myself from checking anyway. I think the lack of sex is making me pathetic.

Surprisingly, I found Max Rigsbee alone. This room is usually buzzing with activity of some kind. Maybe the fact that it isn't is a good sign that we'll have an injury-free season.

"Hey Jack," Max said. "What's up?"

"Not much," I said. "But my shoulders and neck are a little tight. Do you have time to work your magic?"

"Sure." He patted the table he'd been cleaning when I walked in. "Hop up and let me check it out."

I settled onto the table and scooted back. Max walked behind me.

"Did you pull anything or strain it?"

"No, I just woke up tight," I said. "I stretched before hitting the field earlier and felt okay while I was out there, but once I stopped, it tightened up again."

"You're not kidding. It's like touching concrete." Max rested his hands on my shoulders and rotated his thumbs into my shoulder blades, moving them up to my neck then back down again. "Do you have some time?" he asked. "I can really dig in and loosen things up."

I nodded. "I'm done for the day."

His hands left my shoulder and he walked around the table to face me. "Take your shirt off and lie face down." He walked over to the shelf of lotions and potions and grabbed a blue tube and held it up. "This is okay for you, right?"

"Yeah, no issues last time I used it."

As a kid, my skin was really sensitive and I had severe eczema. Unfortunately both of those things followed me into adulthood. It's not as bad as it used to be and I do whatever I can to keep things under control, but it doesn't take much to throw things out of whack.

I settled onto my stomach and tried to relax so Max could do his thing.

Chapter Thirteen

HANNAH

JACK: *You can't ignore me forever.*

Jack's text speaks the truth, but I can ignore him for now and that works for me. We don't have another event until next week and I've put avoiding him on my to-do list. So far, so good.

Unfortunately the out of sight, out of mind principle doesn't apply in this case. It's especially difficult to keep him out of my mind when I'm planning events that revolve around him.

A knock on my door pulled me from my thoughts.

"Come in."

The door opened and Doug stepped inside.

"Are you ready for lunch?"

I looked at the clock on my computer, surprised to find it's a little past noon. The morning has flown by.

"Yeah definitely," I said. "I'm sorry, I didn't realize the

time." After locking my computer, I grabbed my purse from under the desk and stood.

"Have you been to the Black Whale yet?" he asked as we exited my office.

"No."

"It's a local place right on the water. Seafood dishes are their specialty, but they have a good selection of burgers, sandwiches, and salads on the menu, too," he said. "Does that work for you?"

"That sounds perfect. I love seafood."

"You're definitely in the right place for that."

Those adorable dimples made their appearance around his smile.

"I was at a fundraiser on the beach the other day and the buffet was amazing. So much fresh seafood, and the vegetables were so good," I said. "Not that we're lacking seafood back home, but it seems like there's a different variety here."

"I'm parked out front today," he said and instead of taking the right to exit toward the lot at the back of the stadium, we turned left to go out the main doors.

I avoided looking at the field as we walked through the concourse. I don't want to lay eyes on Jack right now. Hell, it's bad enough I'm thinking about him.

As I dug around in my purse searching for my sunglasses, my phone buzzed. Without thinking, I glanced at the screen and spotted another text from Jack.

> Jack: You have my favorite shoes. I'm walking around barefoot. 👟 ☹️

Emojis? It's bad enough my heart skips a beat every time he texts me, but now he's including emojis? If he keeps being so adorable, I may need a pacemaker.

Dropping the phone back to the bottom of my bag, I

found my sunglasses and slipped them on just as we stepped into the bright sunshine.

"This weather is amazing," I said as I tipped my head up to savor the feel of the warmth on my face.

"I'm right over there." He said pointed to a black BMW down a few rows on the right. "After growing up in the Midwest and attending college in the Northeast, I'm loving the weather here. Every once in a while we get a cold spell and the temperature dips into the fifties, but for the most part, it's at least seventy."

We approached the running car and cold air floated out at me as I opened the door.

"I've never lived in a cold climate," I said as I settled into the lush leather seat. "I don't think I'd like it. We had a couple cold spells this year and the temperatures dropped into the thirties and I couldn't get warm. The flurries were pretty, but I can't imagine having to deal with snow on a regular basis."

"Where'd you grow up?" he asked.

I hesitated out of habit. For years, I've avoided sharing that information, but I realize how silly that is. No one has put two and two together in over a decade. The silence was just getting awkward when I said, "California."

"How'd you end up in South Carolina?"

"The Waves offered me a job I couldn't refuse."

"Do you go back to California often?"

"No."

We pulled into the parking lot of the Black Whale before I had to expand on that. Truth is, I have no reason to go back. My grandmother died during my sophomore year in college and my father and I always caught up at whatever vacation spot he booked.

A hostess opened the door for us as we climbed the stairs leading to the restaurant. Doug requested a table outside and she led us through the dining room and out double doors to a deck overlooking the ocean. After we took our seats, she handed us menus and said that our waitress would be right over.

"Everything looks so good," I said, as I perused the menu. I don't normally eat a big lunch but may have to make an exception today.

Our waitress, Kelly, approached and recited the specials then took our drink orders. I opted for water with lemon. I have things to do this afternoon so alcohol is out of the question and I definitely don't need any more caffeine.

"What are you leaning toward?" Doug asked when she left.

"The crab cake special sounds amazing. So does the garlic shrimp pasta," I said. "How about you?"

"I'm going with the crab burger."

I flipped the menu over to check out the burgers.

"A half-pound burger seasoned with old bay, jack cheese, topped with lump crabmeat?" He smiled and nodded. "Wow."

"Once I tried it, I was hooked. I haven't ordered anything else since."

"Do you come here a lot?"

Before he could answer, Kelly appeared and set our drinks down, then took our orders. When she left, Doug took a long drink of sweet tea, set the glass down, and shifted in his seat.

"Yeah, this is one of my favorite places."

It's been a long time since I've been on a date so I'm short on getting-to-know-you conversation. Hopefully Doug will pick up the reins. After removing a couple seeds, I squeezed the lemon into my water, stirred with the straw, and took a sip.

"So what brings you to spring training this year?" he asked.

"I have some events to attend and Mr. Hanover wanted me in-house while the team is down here."

That's as good an explanation as I can give. Thankfully he didn't ask for more.

We made more small talk and soon Kelly brought our food. After topping off our drinks and being assured we didn't need anything, she walked back into the dining room.

"This looks amazing," I said then looked over to check out Doug's plate. "That is the biggest burger I've ever seen."

"They do a nice job here," he said around a chuckle.

I dug my fork into a crab cake and came away with a huge piece of lump crabmeat. The amazing flavors burst on my tongue and I slowly chewed to savor the taste.

"Good?" Doug asked.

"Mmm, delicious."

We ate in silence for a short while, then I said, "We've only talked about me. Tell me about you. How'd a boy from the Midwest end up in St. Petersburg working at Victory Park?"

"I played ball in college and had hoped to make a career of it. But that wasn't in the cards. I tore my rotator cuff the summer between junior and senior year. The surgery was successful and the recovery seemed to go well, but my arm never got back to full strength, and my throws were weak. Plus, my shoulder hurt all the time." He chuckled. "I swear, as many guys stole off me senior year as the other three years combined."

"I'm sorry about that." What else could I say?

He shrugged. "Wasn't meant to be, I guess." After taking a bite of burger and swallowing, he continued.

"After graduation, I continued on to get my master's degree as a grad assistant working with the team. After that, I made a living giving catching lessons and coaching travel ball. I probably would have done that indefinitely, but a recruiter contacted me about my current position and something made me apply. I'm glad I did because I love my job and I'm happy down here." His sweet smile should have stirred something in me, but it didn't. "And I'm especially glad now that I've met you."

That last sentence made me slightly uncomfortable and I concentrated on finishing my crab cakes and broccoli so I didn't have to comment. Thankfully he let it go and we finished our meals in silence.

He picked up the check and we made our way back to the car, which he'd once again started so it was cool inside.

"I really liked that place. Thank you for taking me," I said.

"You're welcome." He turned out of the parking lot and merged into traffic. "Maybe we can do it again when we have more time." He raised his voice slightly on the last word turning the sentence into a question.

I should be jumping at the chance to dabble in what can only be a short fling. It's been a long time between men and I could really use the distraction, but my initial reaction is to say no. Thankfully I didn't blurt it out. Instead, I said, "Sounds good."

JACK

"YOUR INSIDE OUT swing is really coming along," Monte

said as we walked into the locker room. Dan, Cal, and a few other teammates followed.

"It's getting there," I said. "Sorry to give you such a workout. It's hot as balls out there today."

Most of what I hit in batting practice went right between first and second, which is my goal. It just sucked for Monte and second baseman, Oskar Marquez, because they didn't get a break while I was at the plate.

Grabbing a bottle of water from the table in the middle of the locker room, I walked to my locker, and plopped into my chair.

Removing the cap, I chugged the whole bottle in one long gulp.

"No worries," Monte said. "What's up tonight? You want to grab something to eat?"

I peeled my sweat-soaked jersey over my head and wiped my face, neck, and chest before dropping it on the floor.

Before I could answer, Cal said, "If you're going somewhere, count me in."

"Me too," Dan said. "What are you guys thinking?"

Bending over, I removed my cleats and socks.

"Anything is good for me." I stood and stripped off my pants and sliding shorts, then tied a towel around my waist and grabbed my soap and shampoo. "I'm gonna hit the showers and see if Max can work on my shoulders again. Let me know what you decide."

Slipping my feet into slides, I walked toward the shower room, which was surprisingly empty. But I know it won't be that way for long so I'll enjoy the quiet while I can. I twisted the knob to full blast and after letting the cold water wash away the heat of the day, I adjusted the temperature as hot as I could stand it and turned my back toward the spray letting the water pound my tight muscles. I stretched my arms over my head then out to the side before folding over and touching my toes. Straightening, I twisted from side to side loosening things a little at a time.

"Did we miss the memo about a shower yoga class?" Monte asked as he and John Kasprzyk walked in.

"Just trying to stay loose," I said, then reached down to grab my soap and turned to face the spray. I made a mental note to throw more soap in my duffle bag. This bar will barely make it through this shower.

"We decided to go to Sal's for dinner," Monte said. "We're going to walk there. Since we're off tomorrow, maybe we'll hang out and have a few beers and play some pool."

"Sounds like a plan. You coming?" I asked John.

"Yeah, I'm crashing with Monte so I don't have to worry about driving."

More guys came in to shower room and before long, the room was filled with steam and a lot of hot air from all the razzing.

"What time?" I turned off the water and grabbed my towel dry off.

"We're meeting at my place at seven," Monte said.

I nodded and wrapped the towel around my waist.

"See you later."

SAL'S IS PRETTY FULL, but we managed to snag a table in the corner of the back room. Since it's close to our complex, the guys and I come here often so the patrons are used to us.

Gina, our usual waitress, stopped by the table for our drink order. We got a couple pitchers of beer, an order of nachos, and some wings to get us started. I don't plan on getting too crazy tonight, but I'm hoping a few drinks will help me sleep. I've only been getting a couple hours a night, which I think is part of the reason for the tightness in my neck and shoulders. I rolled my neck to savor the full range of motion Max managed to give me after kneading my muscles into submission for nearly an hour.

"Did Max work his magic?" Dan asked.

I nodded. "It's good right now. I just have to stay loose."

Gina placed our pitchers and five mugs on the table.

"I'll be right back with the nachos," she said, knowing full well we have no problem pouring our own drinks.

Monte did the honors and handed each of us a beer. He held up his mug and said, "To a winning season."

We all raised our glasses and took a drink before digging into the nachos.

"I talked to Tom and he has a boat we can take out next week," I said to Dan.

"Lexi will be thrilled," he said. "You guys are in, right?"

Cal and Monte nodded. John said, "I'm meeting Natalie, the kids, and her parents in Orlando. We're doing Disney before they come here for spring break."

Gina brought a platter of wings and set it down in the middle of the table. "Do you need anything else?"

"We'll finish these, and let you know," Monte said. "We plan on being here a while so we want to space it out."

She smiled and said, "Just wave me down if you need me."

Wings aren't a staple in my diet. For the most part, I eat healthy and only indulge when it's really worth it. Sal's wings are amazing with good flavor and enough kick to put them in the "worth it" category.

We dug in and soon the pile was reduced by half. I took a break and downed the remainder of my beer, then grabbed the pitcher and filled it again before topping everyone else's.

"What do you guys think of the rookies this year?" John asked.

"Lots of talent there," Monte said. "But some of them just need to get their heads out of their asses."

"Seriously," Cal said. "Were we that bad?"

"Of course not." Dan chuckled.

I started to share my conversation with Hannah on this topic, then caught myself. I trust these guys, but I'd hate to have them repeat something that would embarrass her.

"The older guys didn't let us get away with acting like that," I said.

"And I took every opportunity to soak up any morsel of knowledge they were willing to share so I didn't want to piss them off."

"That Cherry kid has an arm, but he needs to figure out how to place the ball and work his pitches. Throwing a fastball down the middle isn't gonna cut it, no matter how hard he throws," Cal said.

"But in college, I threw two shutouts in the playoffs," Monte said, mimicking Sam Cherry making everyone laugh.

"Yeah, when I signed on, I learned real fast that none of the veterans were impressed with what I did in college," Dan said.

"They cared even less about what I did in high school," I said.

"Oh I forgot we're in the presence of a prodigy who was drafted out of high school," Monte said, then ducked when I threw a dirty napkin at his head.

I caught Gina's attention and held up the two empty

pitchers. She breezed by and grabbed them then quickly returned with two full ones. I asked her to bring a pitcher of water when she had a chance.

I've learned to hydrate when I drink to avoid massive hangovers. For the most part it works, unless I go totally crazy, which I haven't done in years.

The room thinned out a little since we arrived and Cal and Monte took advantage of the empty pool table, which didn't go unnoticed by three women sitting at a table in the bar area. They didn't look like groupies but that doesn't mean they won't approach. One of them caught me looking in their direction and smiled. I kept my expression neutral and turned my back, hoping she doesn't think I'm playing hard to get. I'm really not in the mood.

When I decided to stay single this season, initially it took a lot of willpower, but now I just don't want to be bothered. Well, there's one woman I'd love to be bothered by, but she seems to be ignoring me...and honestly, both of those things piss me off.

I don't want to be attracted to Hannah for a lot of reasons, but the more time I spend with her, the more I am. And I can't stop thinking about that kiss. I don't remember obsessing over a kiss like this ever, not even back in high school. It's pathetic.

"That girl over there is doing everything short of a striptease to get your attention," Dan said around a chuckle.

Knowing better than to look toward the bar, I picked up my mug and emptied it in a single gulp. I'm getting a little buzzy so I decided to take a break and switch to water for this round.

"I'm good, thanks," I said.

"I can't believe Jack Reagan is going to be woman-free for a season," John said. "Do you think you'll survive?"

"Sure, it'll be easy. I'll just hang out with you old, married guys."

"Touché," Dan said.

Part of me wants to ask if I'm so much of a man-whore that it seems out of the realm of possibility I'd stay unattached for a while, but the other part knows why they're all busting my ass. I've lived a certain way for years and made it known I had no intention of changing.

"Is the book buzz dying down at all?" John asked.

I shrugged. "I'm trying to ignore it, but I turned on the TV the other night and Cindy was on some talk show talking about it so there must still be interest out there."

"Did you read it?" he asked.

"No. It'll just piss me off even more if I do. I got the gist from snippets and comments I saw on the internet when it first came out. It's just bullshit."

The guys just nodded at that and we watched Cal and Monte finish their game.

"Do you think the PR stuff is working?"

"I don't know. I'm not even sure how you can tell." I said, then took a long drink of water. "Doing the events isn't bad, though. So far it's been kind of fun."

"What else does Hannah have booked?" Dan asked.

"There's a fundraiser for an anxiety and depression group next week. The week after, I'm visiting a local school. It's Dr. Seuss day and I'm reading a book."

"What grade are you reading to?" Dan asked.

"I'm not sure. Why?"

"I just want to make sure they're not beyond your reading level."

"Smart ass."

They both had a good laugh at my expense, most likely fueled by the empty pitchers in the middle of the table. Cal and Monte finished their game and joined us again, signaling for two more pitchers.

When Gina brought them over, we each ordered a burger and fries.

"So who won?" John asked.

"I did." Monte's big smile looked a little wobbly.

Gina better hurry with those burgers. If we drink much more without something substantial in our stomachs to soak up the alcohol, it can get ugly. Another lesson I learned the hard way.

"Only because I scratched," Cal said.

"Still counts," Monte said.

"I gotta take a leak." Cal sat back and drained his mug then plunked it on the table and stood.

"You just don't want to talk about how you lost," Monte said.

Cal flipped him off as he walked away toward the bathrooms.

"I'm still up for attending events with you if you need backup," Dan said.

"I appreciate that," I said. "Hannah has a Little League team coming to the stadium on one of my off days. The more the merrier for that one. I'm not sure what's going on with anything else."

"Speaking of Hannah," Monte said. "I saw her going to lunch with Doug Luna today."

That sentence sobered me up real fast. "Seriously?"

He nodded and finished his beer. "I didn't think anything of it when I saw them walking to the parking lot together, but some of the office people were hanging in the stands and I heard them talking."

"Maybe it was a business thing," I said, trying not to sound too interested.

"Not according to them. And one of the women has a thing for Doug and was being a bitch about the whole thing."

Gina brought our burgers and set a bunch of extra napkins in the middle of the table.

"Do you want another one or are you slowing down?" she asked, pointing to the empty pitcher sitting next to its mate that was half-full.

"I'm good for another drink or two," John said.

She took the empty pitcher and walked to the bar and was back with a full one in no time. We thanked her and dug into our burgers.

To be honest, I didn't taste a thing. I couldn't stop thinking about Hannah. I'm here obsessing over our kiss like a teenage girl and she's dating Doug Luna. What the fuck is up with that?

"What do you think is gonna happen with that?" Dan asked, pointing toward the back of the room with a French fry.

We all looked over to where one of the girls that had been staring at Cal earlier now had him practically pinned to the wall near the restrooms. For now they were just talking, but it was obvious she wanted to do more than that. Cal's a little drunk and she doesn't look like she's taking no for an answer.

"With the shitty time he's had with his ex, he deserves to have a little fun," Monte said.

I'm not gonna deny that, but bar pickups and one-night stands have never been his thing. My first thought is that I should probably go save him before he does something he'll regret. I took a big bite of my burger and slowly chewed, reconsidering. Why the fuck do I care what Cal does? He's a grown-ass man and she's obviously of age.

Maybe Monte is right.

Cal turned to walk away and she grabbed his arm and leaned in. She rose up on her tiptoes and said something. He shook his head and her bottom lip came out as she tilted her head to the side. I'm no lip reader, but it was obvious she said please. Cal leaned against the wall and scratched his head.

If it's taking him so long to decide if he wants to get with this girl, he obviously doesn't want to. I threw the fry I'd been about to eat back on my plate.

"I'm gonna hit the bathroom," I said.

The path I took to the men's room put me right in front of Cal and the girl. I could have walked around them, but I stood there until she backed away so there was enough space for me to go through. Hopefully it will be just what Cal needs to make his getaway.

After I got rid of a couple beers and washed my hands, I went back out to find them still standing there, but at least she wasn't plastered against him anymore.

"Hey man," I said. "Your burger is getting cold."

The girl looked me up and down and said, "Hi, I'm Wendy."

I nodded acknowledging her words but my focus was still on Cal.

"My friend Molly is a big fan," she continued. "She'd really like to meet you."

This is where things get complicated. It's pretty obvious these girls want to do more than just meet us. If we spend time with them, they'll expect more but if we totally ignore them, we're dicks.

"Maybe some other time," I said. "We're just looking to relax and hang out tonight."

She looked over at our table then back to hers.

"I can get a couple more friends to come by so everyone has a partner," she said.

"Thanks for the offer, but I don't think my friends' wives would appreciate that." I smiled. "Enjoy the rest of your night."

Thankfully Cal followed as I walked away.

"Thanks for that," he said. "I'm usually better at avoiding those situations, but my head's a little muddy."

"Anytime."

We sat back down and finished our burgers. The girls made a big production out of leaving the bar, I'm assuming to get our attention.

We all noticed, but didn't react when, with three exaggerated hair flips, they walked out the door.

"Another pitcher?" Gina asked.

"One more?" Dan looked at each of us. The others nodded.

"Sure," I said. I'd lost my buzz and wanted to be that side of drunk so I fall asleep as soon as I hit the bed.

After another beer, I'd obtained that perfect state. We settled our tab and left Gina a hefty tip. She deserves it. Besides the fact we tied up her table the whole night, she always takes good care of us.

The fresh air on the walk home should have sobered me, but it had the opposite effect. Cal and I said our goodbyes as we got off on our floor, leaving the other three in the elevator. I have a shit ton to do tomorrow, so I probably won't see them and told them so.

After making sure Cal got in his door safely, I made my way down the hall to my condo. I locked the door behind me and walked to my bedroom, stripping along the way. Collapsing into bed naked, I plugged my phone in to charge and set it on the nightstand.

I'd just gotten comfortable and started to drift when a

nagging thought made its way into my brain and wouldn't go away. Rolling over, I grabbed the phone, wondering when I turned into such a pansyass.

I'm off tomorrow. Bring my shoes to my place or I'll be at your doorstep at dinnertime.

Chapter Fourteen

HANNAH

I TURNED into the parking lot of Jack's complex and
pulled into a spot in the visitors' section. I really don't want
to be here, but I want him showing up at the team hotel
even less.

Damn shoes. I should have brought them to the park,
then I could have dropped them off at his locker while he
was on the field.

And why does he need them anyway? The man has a
multi- million dollar contract. It's not like he can't afford to
buy another pair. Grabbing the shoes off my passenger
seat, I opened the car door, stepped out, and slammed it
behind me.

He really has a lot of nerve. Just because he has a day
off doesn't mean I do. Thankfully I don't have any meetings or conference calls this afternoon. Not that I plan on
being here too long, but at least I don't have to worry
about being back to the park at a certain time.

Sweat had just started to trickle between my shoulder blades when I reached the front door of the building. I still haven't adjusted to the unseasonably warm temperatures down here. Anytime I step out of my air conditioned office, my normal business attire makes me feel like I'm melting.

As I stepped onto the elevator, my ringing cell flashed my father's face. I swiped the screen to reject the call. Just as the doors opened on Jack's floor, the phone chirped, letting me know he'd left a message.

Stepping into the hallway, I stared at the phone, waging a mental war. I shouldn't listen to the message...I know I shouldn't...but the blinking notification light refuses to be ignored. I touched the voicemail app and held the phone to my ear.

Hey darlin'. I guess you're still not ready ta talk. I'm leaving the Keys Thursday. If ya want ta get together before then, let me know. I have meetings in Manhattan Friday and Monday and I'll be back home next Tuesday. I'll call ya then. Love ya, baby girl.

Leaning against the wall, I took in a deep breath and let it out slowly, then two more, until my breathing returned to normal. I wiped under my eyes to clear away tears that had escaped and turned my phone camera on selfie mode to check my face. My eyes look a little funky, but I'm sure Jack won't look at me that closely to notice.

Taking one last deep breath, I walked to the end of the hallway and found Jack's door. Squaring my shoulders, I raised my hand and knocked.

"It's open." I heard him yell. "Come on in."

I cautiously turned the knob, opened the door, and peeked inside. The most amazing smell greeted me and I pushed the door open wider to take in more. My inhale ended on a gasp when I recognized the scent. It's *him*. I'm surrounded by the scent of Jack Reagan multiplied by a thousand.

"Hannah?" Jack said, making me realize I'm standing just inside his apartment with the door wide open just breathing in the goodness.

I looked up and spotted him in the kitchen, stirring something on the stove. Closing the door behind me, I walked across the living room toward the breakfast bar that separates the space from the kitchen.

"I can't believe you just yelled for me to come in. What if I was a crazy stalker?"

"You're not, are you?" He glanced at me out of the corner of his eye then returned his attention to whatever he's cooking.

I shook my head and swiveled one of the four stools tucked against the counter toward me and leaned my hip against it. Between the contact high I'm getting from the scent of Jack in the air and the sight of him wearing loose athletic shorts and a T-shirt, I'm feeling a little buzzy.

"Did you bring the goods?" he asked in an exaggerated New England accent.

I held up the shoes and very deliberately set them on the seat next to me.

"I think your text messages were a little dramatic, don't you?"

"Not at all," he said, looking down at his bare feet, which of course are as perfectly formed as the rest of him.

"If you can't afford another pair of shoes, you need a new agent."

"I told you those are my favorite." He turned a knob on the stove and the flame disappeared. Picking up the pot, he poured whatever he'd been stirring into a clear glass bowl, then placed it in the refrigerator. "I was afraid you sold them on eBay."

"That's actually a great idea," I said. "I wonder if I'd make more if I cut them up and sold the pieces."

He placed his hand over his heart. "Don't even joke about cutting them up."

"What are you going to do when they wear out?"

"I'll figure that out when it happens."

"Couldn't you just buy another pair?"

"First of all, that pair is perfectly formed to my feet." He picked up three bottles from the counter and put them on a rack next to the stove. "And second, they don't make that style anymore."

I picked up one of the shoes and looked inside, noting the style and size.

Moving a large mixer forward from the corner of the counter, he set the beater in place then retrieved its bowl from the refrigerator. After setting everything in place, he switched the machine on high.

I had to ask. "What are you making?"

"Lotion."

"Lotion?"

He opened a drawer and retrieved a spatula, then lowered the speed on the mixer and scraped at the contents of the bowl before turning it to high again.

"Why are you making lotion?"

Placing the spatula on a spoon rest, he turned to face me. "Because I have eczema and this keeps it from getting out of control."

"Really?"

He nodded. "The batch I just threw in the fridge is more of a salve that I use at night, but this is less greasy so I can use it during the day."

So this is where his amazing scent comes from. No wonder it's not like anything else I've ever smelled.

"Comments? Questions?" His cheeky tone broke into my thoughts.

"I'm not even sure where to start," I said and let out a nervous chuckle.

"What are you thinking?" He leaned his arms against the counter, giving me his full attention.

"I've never met anyone who made lotion for themselves, nevermind a guy like you."

"Guy like me?" His right brow raised.

"You know, a guy. A jock. A professional baseball player who could probably pay someone to make it for him."

Pushing away from the counter, he turned off the mixer and checked its contents. He must have liked what he saw because he twisted off the beater, then tilted back the head and removed the bowl from its stand.

I watched as he used an ice cream scooper to distribute the lotion into six glass jars he'd lined in front of him. When they were full, he used the spatula to scrape the beater and the sides of the bowl, then topped them off.

"Want to try it?" He held the spatula up to me.

I reached out and dragged my index finger through the remaining lotion and rubbed it into my palm.

"Here," he said and reached for my hand and dragged the spatula across the back of my hand, leaving a trail of lotion in its wake. Rubbing my hands together, I enjoyed the silky feel.

"This is really nice," I said.

"Don't sound so surprised."

"What's in it?" I asked.

"Cocoa butter, almond oil, vitamin E oil, and beeswax," he said. "Then I add German chamomile, tea tree, lavender, and Bergamot essential oils."

He put lids on the jars and sealed them tight.

"How did you learn to do this?"

Looking down at the counter, he said, "My mom used to make it for me." His hazel eyes shifted up and looked at me through ridiculously long lashes. "After she died, my eczema went haywire again. The prescription creams would tone it down a little, but it never totally went away." Straightening, he crossed his arms across his chest. "I found her recipes and started making this again and for the most part, have been good since."

"That's amazing."

He shrugged. "It's pretty common, actually. Especially now. It seems everyone has jumped on the essential oil wagon."

"Like I said, this is all new to me," I said. "Do you make anything else?"

"Just soap."

"Just soap, he says like it's something everyone does."

"It's not that big a deal," he said, then turned toward the refrigerator and grabbed a pitcher of what looked like iced tea.

When he reached up to retrieve glasses from the top cupboard, his shirt raised, revealing a perfect six pack and a happy trail that disappeared into the waistband of his shorts. I resisted the urge to fan my face.

Filling the two glasses, he picked them up off the counter, walked around the breakfast bar, and nodded toward the couch.

"Come sit and have a drink." He settled onto the couch and placed the glasses on the coffee table in front of him. When I hesitated, he added, "We can discuss our upcoming events."

I slipped off the stool and walked toward him. "I don't have my calendar or computer."

His low chuckle did things to me. Sexy, clenchy things.

"Like you don't have the schedule memorized *and* backed up on your phone." When I still hesitated, he added, "And I know you like sweet tea because you ordered it at the events we've attended."

It will seem strange to decline since he's already poured, so I walked toward the couch and sat on the opposite end. He leaned forward and grabbed the two glasses then handed one to me. I took a tentative sip then a longer one.

"I'm surprised you didn't know about the lotion thing. From what I understand, there's a whole chapter dedicated to it in that book."

"Really?" He nodded. "I didn't read it."

"I find that surprising," he said.

Oh God. He knows about my obsession and is going to call me on it.

"Why?" I asked, then took a drink hoping to hide my embarrassment.

"You never do anything half-assed. I figured when Mr. Hanover stuck you with this mess, you would have read the book to make sure to cover all your bases."

Keeping a death grip on my glass, I sagged against the back of the couch.

"Mr. Hanover wanted me to set up some events and highlight your positive image. I can do that without reading a book that may or may not contain facts about you." I chuckled then added, "This is actually one of my easier assignments. You know what some of the guys get into."

He stared at me for several seconds, those hazel eyes seeming to look right into my soul. Just as it was getting awkward, he tilted his glass and finished the tea in one big gulp, then leaned forward and placed the glass on the coffee table. With his elbows resting on his thighs, he looked at me again and said, "So what had you so upset when you first got here?"

"What do you mean?"

He shrugged. "You seemed upset and your eyes looked a little glossy, like you'd been crying."

Having no idea how to respond, I remained quiet and concentrated on the couch in front of me. This man is definitely not what I expected. I've known him for a decade and didn't think he paid attention to much beyond baseball and himself, but he's proven me wrong over the last few weeks.

"Look, I'm sorry if I came on strong in those texts, but I really just wanted to speak to you." he said. "I didn't mean to upset you."

I don't want to give him details, but don't want him thinking he's upset me either.

"You didn't." I sat up straight and placed my glass next to his. "A few months ago, my dad dropped a bit of a bomb on me and instead of giving me time to deal with it like I asked him to, he keeps calling wanting to get together. He called just as I got here and left a message. I made the mistake of listening to it before I knocked on your door."

"I'm sorry. Do you want to talk about it?"

"I'd rather not," I said. "But thank you."

"If you change your mind, just let me know." I nodded, happy to let that subject drop. "So if I didn't upset you, why did you ghost me all week?"

Leave it to him to bring up an even worse subject.

How do I answer that? Do I tell him that spending so much time with him is challenging my sanity? That the crush I've harbored for years is in danger of turning into something else entirely, if it hasn't already? That the kiss we shared is the most amazing thing I've experienced in my life?

Definitely no to all three.

"I was really busy and figured I'd give you a call when I had more details about the events I'm working on."

His sexy smirk told me he wasn't buying it.

"Busy having lunch with a certain events coordinator?" he asked.

How the hell does he know about that?

I didn't realize I'd spoken the question out loud until he answered it.

"It's a small park, Hannah. You know how it is, everyone knows everybody else's business," he said. "Besides, Monte saw you leaving with him and heard comments from some of the staff."

"Great," I said, half under my breath.

"Something you want to tell me?"

"No." The word came out as a small squeak and I cleared my throat.

"Good," he said. "Because I was hoping we could talk about that kiss the other night."

My eyes widened. "Why?"

"Because it was pretty incredible and I thought maybe we could do it again."

JACK

I'M USUALLY PRETTY good at reading people, but Hannah is a total mystery. Maybe that's why I'm so attracted to her. And I'm finally admitting to myself...and now to her...that I am. Despite what people may think, I don't just jump from one woman to the next without thinking. I realize that if she's not interested or things don't work out, this could be a disaster. But if they do work...well, I won't get too far ahead of myself just yet.

She still hasn't said a word, but I can see her wheels spinning.

"Hannah?" Wide brown eyes focus on mine. "Say something."

"I'm not sure what to say."

"Just tell me what you're thinking."

"I'm wondering if I'm dreaming or maybe having some sort of psychotic episode."

"Why?"

"Why else would Jack Reagan be sitting here saying he wants to kiss me?"

"Are you saying you've dreamed of me asking to kiss you?"

An adorable blush worked its way up her neck and then spread across her entire face.

"I just don't think something like that would happen in this universe."

I shifted toward her and she backed into the armrest.

"Why not?"

"Because."

"That's not really an answer." I rested my hand next to her shoulder, moving a little closer.

"It's the only one I have at the moment."

"Why?"

"I can't think," she said, then added. "I don't want to think right now."

Now *that* I can read. I tucked my other hand onto the couch next to her hip and leaned forward, invading her personal space.

"Hannah?"

She blinked slowly before looking directly into my eyes.

"Do you want me to kiss you?"

After taking a deep breath and letting it out slowly, she nodded.

I rested my forehead against hers and whispered, "Tell me."

"Yes."

The word hit my ears just as I saw the same answer in her eyes. Thank God she wants this too, because my legendary control is nowhere in sight at the moment.

I reached out and slowly removed her glasses then carefully rested them on the coffee table. Tilting my head, I pressed my lips against hers, moving slowly, savoring their plump softness. I pressed closer and deepened the kiss. Shifting my hand from the armrest, I slid it across her jaw to wrap around the back of her head.

Wanting to taste her...*needing* to taste her...I licked the seam of her lips, begging for entry. Opening her mouth, she let me inside, touching her tongue tentatively to mine before fully kissing me back. She tastes just as good as I remember.

Pulling her flush against my body, I kissed her long and hard, creating a tight suction as our tongues tangled, exploring and enjoying her every taste and texture. I pulled back, sliding my open mouth down her neck and licked at the pulse hammering at its base, then made my way up the other side.

"Mmm, you're so sweet," I murmured against her lips.

Wrapping my arm around her waist, I shifted her down and settled between her thighs. She pushed up, and a groan escaped when she rubbed against the raging erection my loose shorts are doing nothing to contain.

"*Christ Hannah.*"

I took her mouth again, with much less finesse. She opened further for my tongue to explore, taste, and torment. Hannah moved her hands to my hair, digging her fingers into my scalp, holding me close as the kiss went on and on. I moved my hand under her now-untucked blouse and touched soft, warm skin.

Following my lead, she slid her hands down my back and brought them back up under my shirt, dragging her nails against my skin.

Needing more contact, I cupped her through her bra. Her nipple poked through the lace, demanding attention, which I was more than happy to give. It scratched at my palm, begging to be released from its confines. Slipping my index finger into her bra cup, I drew it down. Her breast popped free, filling my hand and then some.

Slowing the tempo of the kiss, I took deep breaths in through my nose and let them out the same way, not wanting to release of her delicious mouth just yet. I toyed with her nipple, rubbing my thumb against it again and again before pinching and twisting it with the help of my forefinger.

I swallowed her groan and answered with one of my own as she thrust her hips up and rubbed against me. Pressing my weight down, I held her in place before I totally embarrass myself. She moved her hands to cup my ass, trying to nudge me forward and I swallowed her groan of protest when I didn't budge. I'm glad I'm not the only one losing control here.

Moving back to shift my dick out of range, I slowly release her mouth. She's breathing hard. So am I. It's been a long time since I've gotten this worked up by kissing. I think I like it.

Spying the nipple I'd teased to a stiff peak pushing against the silk of her blouse, I lowered my head and licked, drawing a long moan from Hannah.

I make quick work of her buttons and slowly peeled

her blouse away. Her nipple hardened even more when the air touched it and my mouth watered in anticipation of tasting the perfectly pink peak in front of me. Instead of latching on like I'm dying to, I blew gently, watching in delight as it extended even further.

I looked up to her brown eyes, glossy with desire.

"You're perfect, Hannah." I kissed the curve of her breast. "So perfect."

She closed her eyes and arched her back.

Wanting more, I opened my mouth and sucked, drawing her nipple against my tongue again and again. Freeing her other breast, I gave it the same attention, then moved back and forth until they're both standing tall, glistening from my mouth. I looked down, admiring my handiwork.

"Mmm, beautiful."

This woman. I can't get enough of her and I dipped my head, laving one peak then the other.

"Jack." My name came out as a breathy sigh as her fingers dug into my shoulder blades.

Pulling back, I watched her neck muscles work as she swallowed and dragged in deep breaths. Her taste lingered on my tongue and I wanted more. Needed more. But I have to slow down and make sure she wants this too.

"Hannah." A small smile is her only response, but I need more than that. "Hannah," I said more firmly. She opened her eyes and blinked twice before seeming to focus. I smiled and rested my forehead against hers then kissed the corner of her mouth. "Hi."

She blinked again, then frowned.

"Hi." The word sounded like a question.

If this was any other woman, we'd already be naked and fucking. But this isn't any other woman. This is

Hannah, and she's different. Special. I find that thought both intriguing and scary as hell.

I don't know where this can go, but for the first time in a long time, I want to find out. If she's willing to give me a chance, I want to offer something more than I've ever given anyone. Saying all that will probably freak her out, so I decide to start with the issue at hand.

"We're getting to the point here where we need to either move to a more comfortable spot or slow things down." I placed gentle kisses on her cheek and jaw before pulling back to meet her gaze again. Her eyes look clear, the dazed expression completely gone. "I want to make sure you really want this and aren't just getting caught up in the moment, because once we do this, we can't go back."

She looked at me, seeming to see into my soul. I resisted the urge to look away because I want her to see me, really see me, so she knows I'm not just messing around here. If we do this, it's going to mean something. *We're* going to mean something. She needs to understand that.

After licking her swollen lips, she swallowed then said, "I think we should go to a more comfortable spot."

Thank God.

Chapter Fifteen

HANNAH

I THOUGHT he would have rushed me to the bedroom as soon as I said those words, but I was wrong. Instead Jack kissed me again, more slowly this time, as if it's the only thing on his mind.

The erection pushing into my hip tells me that it's probably not. Instead of thinking about that, or anything else, I kissed him back, enjoying his taste and feel.

Ending the kiss, Jack pushed back, looked down then back up my body, and smiled. The dimple that appeared in his left cheek makes him look even more adorable than usual.

"Oh, this is gonna be fun," he said, before standing next to the couch. I was about to follow when he reached down and pulled off my shoes, then slipped one arm beneath my knees and the other behind my back and stood.

"Jack," I screeched. "Put me down."

Shifting me into place, he asked, "Why?"

"I'm too heavy. You'll hurt yourself."

His sexy chuckle vibrated through every erogenous zone in my body.

"Not hardly," he said, then carried me through the living room and carefully navigated the bedroom door before putting me down on the edge of his bed.

Reaching his right hand over his head, he grabbed the neck of his shirt and pulled it off then dropped it to the floor. The sight of his bare chest had me salivating. It truly is a masterpiece.

Yes, I've seen him shirtless before, but never allowed myself to really take it all in. But now I can not only look my fill, I can actually touch. So I did just that.

I started at his waist, skimming my fingers over the sexy indents in his hips before moving them up his six pack abs, tracing every dip and ridge until I reached firm pecs.

Jack hissed, then grabbed my hands, removing them from his chest. Pushing them over my head, he arched me backward until I rested flat on the bed with my legs dangling over the edge. Standing, he unbuttoned my pants and dragged the zipper down. His hands slipped into my waistband then around and down my ass to my thighs, dragging my pants with them until he pulled them all the way off.

"You are just full of surprises." He squeezed my bare ass. "Never, in a million years, would I have pegged you for a thong girl." Dragging his hands up my stomach, he toyed with the edge of my bra. "The matching set isn't surprising though. You're always so put together."

He slid the blouse off my shoulders then down one arm and off the other, before reaching around and unhooking my bra with one hand. Tossing it on the floor, he rested his knee on the bed next to my thigh and leaned forward, taking my mouth in a searing kiss.

His hands slid against mine until our fingers intertwined.

Squeezing tight, he pulled my arms over my head, dragging his chest against my nipples. I moaned into the kiss and Jack moved against me again, seeming to understand its source.

The kiss went on and on as he tortured me, rubbing his body against mine without touching what was begging to be touched. I have to admit, being tortured by Jack Reagan is better than being pleasured by anybody else.

His hands circled my waist and he shifted me up the bed, until my legs no longer dangled. I started to move my arms to wrap around his back, but he grabbed my wrists and put them back over my head.

"No, keep them up there," he said and kissed the curve of my breast. "It keeps these right where I want them, front and center."

By slow degrees, he taunted me. He palmed and plucked first one breast, then the other, his warm mouth licking and sucking. Every touch, every stroke of tongue zinged right to my core and I moved my hips, seeking relief. His hand skimmed down my stomach, followed by a trail of goosebumps.

I held my breath as his fingers slipped into the waistband of my panties and slowly moved down. Just before he got to the good parts, he ended our kiss and pulled back just enough to look me in the eye.

"Breathe Hannah, I don't want you passing out on me," he said, then chuckled. "Not for that reason anyway."

My deep inhale made my tight nipples brush against his chest and I let it out on a long moan.

"Take a couple more," he said, watching me intently.

I took in two more deep breaths and the buzzing in my ears subsided.

Resting his chin on my chest, he said, "Okay now?" I nodded. "Good because we're not nearly done here."

His fingers slipped the rest of the way down and slid right over my clit. I grabbed the blanket behind me and squeezed until my hands hurt. My needy whimpers echoed through the room as I moved my hips, trying to ease the unbearable ache.

"Relax," Jack whispered. "I've got you." He placed a gentle kiss at the corner of my mouth, then met my gaze, his eyes looking more brown than green. "I'll take care of you, Hannah. I promise."

I don't doubt his words. We've barely gotten past second base and I'm ready to go off.

He watched me for several heartbeats then smiled. I thought I'd seen the spectrum of Jack's smiles...from the sexy to the sarcastic...but this one is different. It's sweet and intimate, but still hot as hell. Just like the man.

Before I could get too lost in that thought, Jack moved his finger back and forth, just a fraction, but it was enough to put me on the edge again. It wouldn't take more than a few small strokes to tip me right over. Seeming to sense that, he slid his hand down and dipped a finger inside me.

"Mmm, you feel so good," he said. "So wet."

Adding a second finger, he curled them slightly and pulsed his hand up and down. He shifted his leg over my thigh and moved closer. His thumb brushed my clit once, then again, before settling into place and moving in slow circles.

"Come for me, Hannah," he said, keeping up his ministrations. "Please, I want to watch you come."

As if his magic fingers weren't enough to push me over the edge, he says that. My body bowed against his as the waves pulsed through my body and my nipples tightened into painful peaks. Jack stayed with me, his hands moving in a slow rhythm, drawing out my pleasure. I dropped back onto the bed with an exhausted groan, feeling every muscle in my body relax.

Jack kissed my shoulder then my collarbone, without taking his eyes off my face. My inner walls clenched with tiny aftershocks as he removed his fingers.

"You're so beautiful, Hannah," he said. "That was amazing." His hot mouth skimmed down my stomach and nibbled at my navel, dipping his tongue inside, making me squirm. "Think you can do it again?"

"I probably could," I said, through panting breaths. "It might kill me, though."

He smiled up at me, flashing that dimple, then settled between my thighs.

"You may die, but that is a sacrifice I am willing to make," he said, mimicking Lord Farquaad from *Shrek* as he removed my thong.

I was still laughing then nearly choked when he placed an open-mouthed kiss at my core, then dragged his tongue up my folds before circling it around my clit.

"Oh God." I didn't recognize my own voice. It sounded hoarse, sultry, and needy. It's been a long time since anyone's done *that* to me and it feels so amazing I could cry.

Jack placed a restraining hand on my belly as his gaze met mine over the expanse of my body.

"You doing okay?"

I nodded, panting.

He dipped his head and continued to lick and nip until I didn't think I could take anymore. I tangled my fingers in his hair and squeezed. Jack slipped his finger inside me again then placed his mouth over my clit, alternately licking and sucking until spasms rocked my body again, this orgasm stronger than the last. Once again, he stayed with me, until every last quiver stopped.

Reaching up, he removed my fingers from his scalp and placed kisses in the center of each palm before resting them down on the bed. I felt him shift away. Cool air replaced his hot skin against my body.

Opening drowsy eyes, I saw Jack back off the bed and stand. He turned and opened the top drawer of the nightstand, reached inside, then closed it and turned back toward the bed, tossing a square packet next to my hip.

I watched as he slid his thumbs into the waistbands of both his shorts and underwear, then pushed them down his thighs, leaving him naked in front of me. The man is perfect. Absolutely perfect.

He climbed onto the bed and knelt between my wide-spread thighs, his long, thick penis bobbing with the move-ment. Reaching out, I touched him, tentative at first, then with a firmer grip.

Jack closed his eyes and muttered something under his breath. His fingers wrapped around my wrist and pulled my hand away.

"You can play next time, I promise. But right now, I can't..." He shook his head and took in a deep breath then slowly let it out. "I want this to be good for you and if you keep touching me right now, I can't promise it won't be over before it starts."

Letting go of my hand, he picked up the packet and ripped it open. I watched, fascinated, as he pinched the tip, then rolled the condom down his entire length. Task complete, he looked up and met my gaze, then shifted between my thighs. Resting his weight on his forearms, his hands cupped my face as he proceeded to kiss me senseless...even more senseless than two orgasms and seeing him naked have left me.

He slowly ended the kiss, nibbling at the corner of my mouth before pulling back just enough to look into my eyes. Shifting slightly, he reached down and lined himself up at my entrance before pushing forward and sinking into me in one, long thrust. I gasped at the same time he groaned. He stood still for a minute, his breath rough against my ear.

"Damn, you're tight."

"Maybe you're just really big."

Our fit got even tighter and he chuckled.

"Compliments will get you everywhere, Ms. Adams."

I'd just adjusted to his size when he pulled back and slowly thrust forward then started to pump...in and out, in and out, in and out...keeping it slow and steady. My inner muscles clenched along with his perfect rhythm, grabbing for him at every retreat.

He picked up the pace and I pulled my legs back, bracing my feet flat against the bed, seeking leverage against his thrusts. With every forward motion, he nudged against my clit and I wrapped my left leg around his waist, wanting more. He sank further inside and hit *that* spot. Letting out a long, low groan, my inner muscles spasmed with such intensity, I could barely breathe.

His hands on my hips, Jack slammed into me three more times before letting out a growl and collapsing on my chest.

JACK

I slowly caught my breath and rested my cheek against Hannah's temple, enjoying the clean scent of her hair. Her chest rose and fell under mine, eventually slowing to a normal rhythm. I pulled back and she squeezed my shoulders, holding me in place.

Kissing her forehead, I said, "Let me take care of this and I'll be right back."

Holding the base of the condom, I moved away from her and stepped out of bed, walking to the bathroom. I quickly disposed of the condom and wiped myself clean so I could get back to Hannah. Her eyes devoured me as I walked back to the bed, then widened when my body reacted.

Pulling the covers down, I ignored both her reaction and mine.

"Here, scoot back."

Looking dazed and sleepy, she slipped between the sheets and settled against the pillows. I moved next to her, sliding my arm around her shoulders, pulling her close. There's so much I want to say, but that can wait. Right now, I just want to relax and enjoy the feel of this amazing woman in my arms. She let out a low hum and rested her arm against my stomach. I closed my eyes and listened to her breathe.

I didn't mean to fall asleep, but one minute I was enjoying the feel of Hannah in my arms and the next she was jolting me awake with an elbow in my ribs.

"Shit!"

I sat up quickly, knocking Hannah back against the pillows. "What's wrong? Are you okay?"

She shimmied to a sitting position then scurried off the bed, yanking at the sheet and wrapping it around her, toga style. I couldn't keep the smile off my face. She could cover herself in a suit of armor, but it wouldn't stop me from mentally picturing her every delicious dip and curve.

"I can't believe I fell asleep," she said.

Struggling to retrieve her clothes from the floor and keep the sheet in place, Hannah looked flustered and totally unHannahlike. It's adorable.

Sliding across the bed, I touched her arm, halting her frantic movements.

"Hannah? Slow down."

She looked at me, over at the clock, then back at me again. "It's almost two o'clock. I have to go."

Her gaze skittered away again and I squeezed her wrist to bring it back to me. Those chocolate depths held so many emotions, I struggled to name them all. In the fore-front was embarrassment, followed by regret.

"Sit." Her eyes widened. "Please," I added, rubbing my thumb against the base of her palm. She turned, flipping the tail of the sheet behind her, wrapped it tighter, and sat a foot away from me, pulling her hand out of my grasp.

That just won't do.

I shifted toward her, closing the distance between us.

She eyed me warily, her gaze shifting down my naked form then back up to my face.

"What's wrong?" I asked.

"I have to get back to the office. I didn't plan on uh, you know, on being here so long."

She must really be freaked out. I've never heard Hannah stutter or say something like "you know" in all the years I've known her. I rested my hand on hers.

"Hannah, I want you to know that when I asked you to come here today, I wasn't expecting this to happen." I smiled. "I'll admit, I was hoping I'd get to kiss you again just to see if it'd be as amazing as the first one."

She opened her mouth, then closed it again and just stared at me.

"I'll admit that when Mr. Hanover told me we'd be

working together, I was pissed. Not because of you, but because it was going to mess up my well-ordered life."

I looked at the wall and ran a hand through my hair, then rubbed my jaw, trying to find the right words. She still looks wary, and I have to convince her that I'm sincere. Looking back into her wide eyes, I continued.

"Look, you know me. You know my reputation. You know how I've lived. And I'll admit that's how I wanted it. Until now. Ever since we've been spending time together, you're all I think about. I'm actually upset that we don't have more events because I want to see you. When you ghosted me this past week, I—" I swallowed, not wanting to say the word that had popped into my head, but knowing she had to hear it. "I missed you."

Chapter Sixteen

HANNAH

HIS LAST THREE words came out as a hoarse whisper.

Something tells me Jack is showing me a side of himself he doesn't share with many people. And I'll be honest, I'm not sure how to handle it.

Aside from the fact that he's sitting next to me stunningly, beautifully naked, he's saying things I'd never dreamed would come out of his mouth. Not directed at me anyway.

And now he's looking at me with those amazing hazel eyes...which look more green than brown at the moment...waiting for me to say something and I seem to have forgotten how to use my words.

"Are you just gonna leave me hanging?"

He chuckled, but it didn't take away the intensity of his words or the insecure expression on his face. I've never seen Jack looking anything but confident, if not downright cocky, and it's kind of unsettling.

Since he's being so honest, I will too.

"I uh," I cleared my throat. "I'm not sure what to say."

"I don't want to put words in your mouth, but I'm gonna go out on a limb here and say you're at least a little interested in me," he said. "Because if you weren't, I don't think you'd be sitting here, in my bed, after some pretty amazing sex."

A little interested?

If only the man knew.

But that had been nothing more than a crush, a fantasy, and this right now, is very real.

"Please say something, Hannah. I'm dying here," he said, his New England accent was in full force.

He shifted, drawing my attention to his...every-thing...and I felt my face heat. I looked down at my lap and gathered my thoughts before meeting his gaze again.

"You're right. I wouldn't be here if I wasn't interested. I'm not very..." I trailed off, searching for a word. "Casual. I don't do one night stands and I'm *usually* past the third date before this happens." I tightened the sheet around my chest. "I didn't do this expecting anything from you, but I'd be lying if I said I wouldn't be interested in more than this one afternoon." The smile that spread across his face was sweet and sexy and full of relief. "But Jack, we have to consider the fact that we work together might be an issue."

"Is there a no fraternization policy?" he asked, then shook his head and quickly added. "There can't be. I know of at least five couples who met working for the Waves." I wasn't talking about company policy and told him so. "Then what?" he asked.

I don't want to hurt his feelings, but he has to think about this from all angles.

"I just don't want things to get awkward."

He thought about that for a moment, then frowned.

"Hannah, I wouldn't even pursue this if I thought we'd have that kind of issue. We obviously have to take this one step at a time, but you have to know I'm not going into this with an end date in mind. I know girls like you don't normally go for guys like me, but I'm hoping —" He stopped abruptly and swallowed, then cupped my jaw and rubbed his thumb across my cheek. "I'm hoping you'll give me a chance."

Before I could answer, my stomach let out a loud growl. His laugh echoed through the bedroom. At least that broke some of the tension, even though it's a bit mortifying. Not ladylike, for sure.

"I'm sorry, you must be starving. I did plan on feeding you, but we kind of got sidetracked." He leaned in for a quick kiss. "I'll admit, I'm not upset about that." Standing, he grabbed my wrinkled clothes from the floor. "I'll steam these in the dryer to get the wrinkles out."

He crossed the room and took a T-shirt out of the drawer and walked back to hand it to me. I'm not sure if the view of him coming or going was better.

He pulled me from my Jack-induced stupor when he said, "As much as I'd enjoy the view if you sat at the table in that sexy bra and panty set, I'm afraid we'd skip lunch and go right to dessert...again. Especially when you're looking at me like that. You can wear that until your clothes are done."

After slipping back into his shorts, he walked out of the bedroom, closing the door behind him.

I sat there, trying to process everything that had happened since I arrived here. Even taking the sex...which had been ridiculously amazing...out of the equation, this afternoon has been everything I've secretly dreamed of and never thought would happen. All these years, I thought I had him pegged, but I couldn't have been more wrong. He's not the shallow, self-centered jock I thought I knew.

Making my way to the bathroom, I got cleaned up and slipped back into my underwear and his T-shirt. The bra could wait until I had to put my own clothes back on. Lifting the hem of the shirt to my nose, I inhaled. The fabric holds his scent. Delicious.

I looked over at the bed, with the covers, sheet, and pillows bunched in the middle. Before I could overthink it too much, I walked over and pulled everything off, then put it all back in place. Not exactly hospital corners, but not too bad.

After obsessing over Jack for years, I know it'll be way too easy to let myself get lost in this. I did that once before and it didn't end well.

Yes, I'd been a lot younger then, but the risks are the same. My heart needs to understand that my head is in charge here.

I walked toward the door, catching a glimpse of myself in the mirror on the way. The Waves logo on the T-shirt shouldn't make me go all gooey inside, after all I have tons of team gear of my own. But this isn't mine, it's Jack's. I turned, and my heart skipped a beat at the sight of his name and number on the back.

Oh hell.

JACK

I DUMPED pasta into the boiling water and stirred, then checked on the chicken. Everything looks good. I'm not a gourmet cook, but I can make a few things well.

Pulling a knife from the block, I rolled the prosciutto and chopped, then pulled it into a pile, and chopped again. I was repeating the pile and chop thing for the third time when I spied Hannah timidly walking through the living room. At the sight of her wearing my T-shirt, all long legs and sexy curves, I lost my rhythm and the knife slipped. I dropped it before I cut myself.

"Are you okay?" She ran into the kitchen and looked at my hands.

I nodded. Seeing her move like that with no bra on had my tongue in knots. I seriously must have been brain dead for the past decade. That's the only explanation for why I never noticed how sexy this woman is before now.

"What are you making?" she asked.

"I cleverly call it prosciutto chicken. It's those two items simmered in garlic and olive oil. Then I make a cream sauce, top it with parmesan, and pour it all over pasta. I prefer cavatappi."

I picked up the spatula and stirred the chicken before it burned. Her wide eyes watched my every move.

"What?" I asked.

"When you said you were going to feed me, I didn't think you'd actually be cooking." She chuckled. "You make lotion and soap, and you cook. A man of many talents."

I bobbed my eyebrows. "You have no idea." That adorable blush appeared again. "I love that blush."

"It's so embarrassing." She groaned.

"Well, I like it," I said, and leaned over to kiss the tip of her nose. Resting my forehead against hers, I added, "And I really like the way you look in my T-shirt." Her blush intensified, but I didn't want to embarrass her anymore, so I didn't comment on it.

Turning back to the stove, I gave the chicken another stir then added the prosciutto, mixing it through.

"Can I help?"

"I got this," I said then nudged my chin toward the edge of the counter where I'd stacked plates, napkins, and forks. "But you can set the table."

She smiled and did just that. As she leaned over the table, my shirt rose showing a nice amount of upper thigh and just a hint of the curve of her amazing ass. I had to force myself to look away before I stalked over there, bent her over the table, and fucked her hard.

Taking a deep breath, I focused on the task at hand. The prosciutto looked nice and crisp, so I twisted the cap off a box of chicken broth and added it to the pan. Once it started to simmer, I poured in some heavy cream and turned up the heat to bring it to a boil.

Hannah stood across from me, her elbows resting on the counter. I wish I could see *that* view from behind.

The sauce started to bubble and I lowered the heat, then added a handful of parmesan and stirred. It thickened pretty quickly and I lifted the strainer from the pasta pot and gave it a few good shakes to remove the water, then poured the pasta into the chicken mixture.

"That looks amazing," Hannah said as she watched me mix it all together. "It smells really good, too."

"I hope you like it," I said as I poured everything into a large serving dish. "It's one of my favorite meals."

She backed away from the counter as I walked out of the kitchen and placed the bowl on the table. I mentally shrugged. It's probably for the best. As much as I'd wanted to see that view from behind, I don't know if I'd be able to keep my hands to myself if I actually did.

"I have water and sweet tea to drink," I said. "Wine and beer, too. It's five o'clock somewhere, right?"

"That sweet tea was really good. I'll have some of that."

I went back to the kitchen and grabbed the pitcher out of the refrigerator and two glasses from the cupboard. After settling in at the table, I picked up the serving spoon and placed a healthy portion of pasta on Hannah's dish.

Her eyes widened. "Jack, I can't eat all that."

"Sure you can. I can't be the only one who worked up an appetite this afternoon." I placed twice the amount on my dish. "Speaking of five o'clock. You're not going to get in trouble for not going back to the office, are you?" I didn't think she would, but I had to ask.

"No." She picked up her fork and toyed with the pasta. "I don't have to punch a time clock or anything, but I usually work a full day, even when there isn't a game or event."

"And then some," I said.

"There's always so much going on. It can get out of hand pretty quickly if I don't stay on top of things."

"You do an amazing job." I stuffed a forkful of pasta into my mouth and chewed, then realized she was staring at me. I swallowed and said, "What?"

"You said I do an amazing job."

"Why is that surprising?"

She shrugged. "I didn't think the players even noticed what the PR department does. Except when we're bugging you to sign or attend things."

"Of course we notice," I said. "I've been with the Waves longer than you so I know how it was before you started. Things run much smoother now and you're always respectful of our time, which means a lot. You know how many directions we're pulled in and you make sure you don't add to the stress. And I know the guys with families appreciate how you plan things their wives and kids can attend. Everyone loved the end-of-season event last year. It was actually a lot of fun, definitely better than sitting behind a table signing pictures all day." Hannah's face practically glowed at my words, and I realized that she probably doesn't hear much praise for her work, especially from the players. "I'm gonna stop before your head gets too big," I said around a smile then pointed at her dish with my fork. "Now eat before it gets cold."

She picked up a forkful of the chicken and pasta and put it in her mouth.

"Mmm, this is delicious." She quickly shoved another bite into her mouth and chewed.

It was my turn to glow under her praise.

"So good," she said after swallowing another bite.

We ate in silence for a few minutes until my plate was clean and hers was nearly empty. She set her fork down, sat back in her seat, and rubbed her stomach.

"I can't believe I ate all that. I'm so stuffed." She wiped her mouth with a napkin. "But it was so good. Thank you."

"Glad you enjoyed it."

Which is true. Most of the women I've been with ate like birds and it was annoying as hell. Nothing worse than taking someone to a nice restaurant and having them order a plain salad with dressing on the side.

"Did you find that recipe in a cookbook or make it up yourself?" she asked.

I pushed my plate away and rested my elbows on the table.

"My mom used to make it all the time. I'm not sure where she got it from, I just remember helping her make it."

"How old were you when she died?" she asked.

I don't usually talk about my mother with anyone. It's still too painful, even after all these years. But something about Hannah makes me want to spill my guts.

"Twelve, almost thirteen."

"I'm so sorry. That must have been horrible."

I nodded at her words and cleared my throat.

"She was one of those moms involved in everything, so it was really strange after she was gone. No matter what I did or where I went, there was a giant hole," I said. "Plus it happened so fast. There was no long illness or anything. She went to the grocery store one day and never came home."

"I can't imagine."

She blinked several times then met my gaze with glistening eyes. Might as well put it all out there.

"She was hit by a drunk driver and died immediately, which was a blessing. At least she didn't suffer," I said.

"What happened to the other driver?"

"He was taken to the hospital and died a few days later."

"What about your dad? Is he still alive?"

"Depends on what you consider living." Her brow wrinkled and I gave an explanation before she asked for one. "He pretty much fell apart after she died and still hasn't gotten himself back together."

"Do you see him often?"

"Not really." I shrugged. "A few times a year. Usually when I'm playing in Boston." Her eyes widened, then turned sad. "I know how cold-hearted that must sound, but he seems happy in his misery. I've tried to get him help, so have other people, but he just wants to sit home and wallow. I'd get pulled into it if I spent too much time there, so I make sure he has everything he needs from the fringes."

She stared down at the table and nibbled at her bottom lip, and I have no idea what's going on in her head. I don't usually give a shit what people think of me, but she's different. I fought the urge to explain how my life had been after my mom died. How my father would sit and stare into space for days, how he stopped going to my games and school functions, stopped wanting to breathe. How losing my mother had been bad enough, but then my father spaced out and everything just fell apart.

I didn't say any of that, yet somehow she knew.

"So you basically lost both your parents," she said, then reached out and squeezed my hand. "I'm so sorry Jack, that must have been awful. I don't think you're cold-hearted, it's just sad. My father drives me crazy sometimes, but I know he's always there if I need him, no matter what."

The mention of her father gives me a good reason to get off the topic of mine.

"What's the story with you and your father? You looked pretty upset when you first got here."

Shaking her head, she said, "It'll sound ridiculous after what you just told me."

"Come on. I told you mine now you have to tell me yours."

"I don't think that's the saying." She offered a small smirk with her words.

How could she make me smile during this conversation? Not to mention make me rock hard. One minute my chest hurt talking about my father and the next my dick is throbbing because she picked up my innuendo and tossed it right back at me.

"Anytime you want to explore the real saying, I'd be happy to oblige." Her eyes glittered with interest. I stacked the dishes together and set the forks on top. "Would you put these in the sink?"

She blinked, her mouth curling into an uncertain smile.

"Oh, sure."

My T-shirt grazed her upper thighs as she stood. It took all my willpower to keep my hands to myself. She picked up the plates and carried them to the kitchen. Moving quickly, I ran to the end table and grabbed a condom out of the drawer, then followed the path Hannah had taken and didn't stop until I stood directly behind her.

She turned and screeched.

"Jack!" I grabbed her arms as she bumped into my chest. "I didn't hear you behind me."

I turned her back around, trapping her between me and the counter. Rubbing my hands up to her shoulders, I squeezed then settled into a massaging rhythm. She moaned and dropped her head back against my chest.

"Did I mention that I really like the way you look in my shirt?" I kissed her temple, then worked my way down the side of her face to her neck as I spoke. "So I'm kind of torn. I don't know if I want to take it off or enjoy the view as is. What do you think?"

Sliding my hands under her arms, I cupped her breasts through the soft cotton and plucked at her tight nipples. She squirmed and rubbed her ass along my aching dick. I moved my right hand down to her hip, pushing her harder against me while I thrust forward.

"Hannah? On or off?"

"I don't care."

"Do you care if I leave these on?" I asked, slipping my hand over her panties, rubbing my finger back and forth along the wet lace.

"Jack," she said on a groan. "I—"

"What honey?"

"I—"

She panted and her hips rocked against me. Without losing rhythm, I slipped my hand inside her panties, trapping her swollen clit between my index and middle fingers, giving it a squeeze before sliding into her slick heat. That's all it took. Her muscles tightened then spasmed as I stroked her inside, drawing out her pleasure.

Hannah gulped in deep breaths of air and sagged against me. I licked my way up her neck, taking a nip right at its curve before pulling away. I've never intentionally left my mark on a woman before, but I can't help myself with her.

Once her breathing slowed, I leaned her forward and slowly withdrew my fingers. Placing her hands on the counter, I brushed against her back and spoke directly against her ear.

"This is gonna be fast."

I grabbed the front of her panties and ripped them off then dropped my shorts. After rolling on the condom with shaking hands, I gripped her hips, pulled her back, and thrust forward.

"Hannah. *Fuck.*"

I pumped in and out, moving faster and faster until my spine tingled. I gritted my teeth, using every bit of control to hold back my release. I pushed against the small of her back, thrusting her ass further in the air and bent my knees, the new position letting me thrust even deeper, making me curve against the happy spot inside her.

"Oh my God! Jack!"

Her scream barely gave me warning as her muscles contracted, squeezing me in a tight vise and releasing repeatedly until I couldn't hold back anymore.

Chapter Seventeen

HANNAH

I JUMPED at the sound of my buzzing phone, slapping at the offending item until the blaring stopped. I'm normally awake before my alarm goes off, but today I've hit snooze three times. If I don't get my ass out of bed now I'm going to be late for my meeting.

Dragging myself to the bathroom, I carefully stepped into the shower, my muscles protesting every movement. I gradually increased the temperature of the water until the bathroom filled with steam, letting the hot spray pound away the worst of my aches. I squeezed shower gel onto my mesh sponge and quickly washed, trying not to think too much about the source of the soreness between my legs.

After turning off the water, I quickly dried and wrapped my hair in the towel before stepping out of the shower and slipping into my robe. I walked to the closet and stared at its contents.

According to the forecast, temperatures and humidity are supposed to be back to normal today, so I should be fine in my usual work attire. The Waves have a game at one o'clock so I decided to go with gray crop pants and a blue blouse. A lot of my co-workers wear team polo shirts and khakis on game days, but I've never really been comfortable in that, so I at least make sure to wear a team color.

I grabbed a powder blue bra and panty set from the drawer and Jack's words echoed through my head.

The matching set isn't surprising though. You're always so put together.

Will I ever get dressed without thinking about what we were doing when he said that?

I suppose I could purposely not match, but then I'd think about why I'm not matching, so he'd be in my thoughts anyway.

Shaking my head, I slipped into my matching set and untwisted the towel from my head, scrunching my hair with it on the way to the bathroom. I brushed the knots out and studied myself in the mirror.

The past couple weeks my makeup routine has been limited to mascara and lip gloss thanks to the summer glow I've gotten during my time down here, but today my face is glowing in a whole other way. I guess I have Jack to thank for that.

I put the brush back on the counter and something caught my eye so I turned to check it out. A small bruise stood in contrast to the pale skin on the curve of my neck.

A hickey? A hickey!

When the hell did he do that?

I braced my hands on the counter and leaned forward to get a closer look and couldn't stop my mouth from curling into a small smile. I stood back and shrugged. I've never been a hickey girl. In fact, I've never had nor wanted one before, but this one is turning my insides all mushy. And at least it's in a place my clothes will cover.

After drying and straightening my hair, I got dressed, put on my glasses, and slipped into a pair of strappy sandals. Making sure everything I need is in my laptop case, I grabbed it and my purse and walked out the door.

On the ride to the stadium, I both anticipated and dreaded seeing Jack in equal measures. Yesterday had been a fantasy come to life for me, but I can't expect that he feels the same. He said all the right things and seemed sincere, but who knows? People say things in the heat of the moment and afterglow all the time.

I pulled into the nearly-empty stadium parking lot and turned into my now-usual spot. Doug pulled into the space across from mine just as I grabbed my bags from the car and closed the door.

"Hey," he said, emerging from his car.

"Hi." I shifted my purse and laptop case over my shoulder and walked in his direction. "Why are you here so early?"

"I have a long to-do list today and I'm hoping to run through most of it in time to catch some of the game," he said.

"How about you?"

"This is actually late for me."

He swiped his card, opening the door then stepped aside for me to enter.

"A morning person, huh?"

"Not really. It's just easier to get things done before everyone shows up."

He pushed the elevator button and turned to face me.

"I had a great time at lunch the other day and was hoping we could do it again. Or maybe dinner?"

Thankfully the elevator doors opened at that moment, giving me a few seconds to formulate a response. We stepped inside and I pushed the button for the third floor and stared straight ahead as the doors closed. I don't have much time here and definitely don't want this conversation to carry on past this ride.

I turned to face Doug, straightening my shoulders. My purse slipped down my arm and I looped my thumb around the strap, setting it back into place.

"I had fun at lunch, too," I said, looking him in the eye. "And I appreciate the invite, but I'm going to have to say no."

There was more on the tip of my tongue, but I decided to leave it at that. No reason to do the whole *I'm not looking for anything right now* spiel unless he pushes for more.

His eyes widened, then he stuffed his hands in his pockets and rocked back on his heels.

"Okay," he said. The elevator came to a stop and the doors opened. Doug placed one hand against the door and gestured for me to go ahead of him with the other. "Maybe I'll see you at the game later?"

I nodded and walked beside him down the hall toward my office.

"I'll definitely be out there today. It's supposed to be perfect baseball weather."

"It's always perfect weather for baseball, you just need the right gear," he said as we reached my door.

I chuckled and tucked a stray piece of hair behind my ear. "I guess so," I said, turning the knob.

"I'll see you later."

He nodded and walked off toward his own office.

"Well that went well," I said to the empty room as I set my computer in the dock and booted it up.

See, this is why I don't get involved with people at

work. The potential for things to get awkward is way too high for me to handle. And I'd only gone out to lunch with Doug once.

I rested my head against the chair and groaned. How bad will it be when I have to face Jack?

My meeting notification dinged before I could get too caught up in that thought. Crap, I didn't realize the time.

I took a few minutes to scroll through my inbox to take care of the high priority emails. The others could wait until later. I should have a couple hours between my meetings and the game, and I can always bring my laptop down to the field and multi-task if necessary.

At eight-twenty, I left my office with my computer and calendar in hand and took the stairs to the fourth floor conference room. I settled into one of the plush leather chairs, booted my computer again, and connected it to the projector. Grabbing the remote control from the center of the table, I pushed the power button and my desktop gradually appeared on the far wall. I'll wait until Mr. Hanover arrives to connect to the meeting.

I leaned forward and glanced over at the picture window overlooking the field. It's too early for the players to be out there, but I scanned the entire area just in case, but only saw the ground crew doing their thing.

"Hannah."

At the sound of Mr. Hanover's voice, I pulled my attention away from the field. He sat at the end of the table and Kenny settled into the seat across from me.

"Good morning, Mr. Hanover. Kenny."

"Do you have the call-in number?" Mr. Hanover asked.

He's all business this morning. Good to know.

"It's actually a Skype meeting today. No phone needed."

He shook his head and mumbled, "How do you keep up with all this technology?"

Assuming that was a rhetorical question, I didn't answer. Instead, I signed into the meeting, being sure to join audio.

"Good morning," I said. "Mr. Hanover, Ken, and Hannah just joined."

The rest of the PR team was on the other end along with Mr. Hanover's assistant, Maria, who shared her screen. The meeting agenda replaced my desktop on the wall. She started on the first item and we were off.

An hour and a half later, we'd discussed everything from opening day to All-Star break. My to-do list had been completed before I came to St. Pete, but as usual, something got added. Since my laptop is presenting, I took meeting minutes on a blank page in my calendar. Maria will email a recap to all attendees, but I always take my own notes. It helps me remember things and stay organized.

Mr. Hanover asked a few questions and soon the meeting was over. Maria disconnected and my desktop background reappeared on the far wall.

"I'll never understand how that stuff works, but it does make life easier," Mr. Hanover said, referring to the Skype meeting.

"I think of technology like a car," I said. "I can use it but have no clue how it works."

"I'm too old to worry about knowing either," he grumbled.

He really isn't in a good mood today. I wonder what's up. I glanced over at Kenny and raised my brow. Kenny gave me a slight shrug and shook his head. Interesting. He doesn't know either.

Mr. Hanover sat forward and rested his elbows on the table, his hands clasped together.

I guess we're going to find out.

"I just got word that woman is making the rounds again," Mr. Hanover said. "That damn book was almost out of the spotlight, but it'll be right back in again with her hitting the talk shows she missed last go round."

His red face stood in stark contrast to the white Waves polo he wore. While I understand Cindy Parker is doing whatever she can to extend her fifteen minutes of fame and keep her book on the charts, I don't know why it bothers Mr. Hanover so much.

It's true that I haven't read *Jacked*, but from what I understand, it's pretty tame compared to some other tell-all books. She never saw Jack taking steroids and he never snorted cocaine off her ass or abused her. In the grand scheme of things, this really isn't a big deal. But I can't tell him that.

"You're going to have to up your game with Jack's PR," he said.

"I just updated the event spreadsheet," I said. "Give me a minute and I'll pull it up."

Pulling my laptop closer, I brushed my finger over the touchpad, moved the cursor to the file, and double clicked. The spreadsheet appeared on the far wall.

I summarized the events he'd already known about then explained the others I'd just set up in greater detail.

"I also have some people we met at the local event coming to games here in the next couple weeks. He'll meet with them either before or after the game, depending on if he's playing. We can have some of the other guys join in too so it doesn't look like we're just focusing on Jack."

"Good thinking," he said. "Do you plan on adding anything else?"

"I don't think so. Between these and the usual meet-and-greets at the stadium, the schedule is pretty full."

"Are you sure it's enough?"

"Dad, you know how crazy the season is for those guys,"

Kenny said before I could answer. "You can't expect Jack to be running all over the place just to make the media happy."

"That's not what I expect," Mr. Hanover said.

"It seems like it is," Kenny said. "I don't even know why you're so hopped up about this book. It's not even that bad," he added, echoing my earlier thoughts.

"And exactly where does it cross over into *that bad*?" Mr. Hanover practically shouted the last two words and stood, pushing his chair back. It bumped against the wall with a dull thud as he crossed the room, opened the door, and slammed it behind him.

Kenny and I looked at each other in stunned silence.

He dragged a hand through his hair and rubbed the back of his neck.

"I have no idea why he's making such a big deal about this book," he said.

I closed my laptop and unplugged it from the projector.

"You know how he is about team image."

"I know, but *Jacked* is probably the tamest tell-all book out

there. And it's not like Jack is some screw up we just recruited." He rubbed his brow. "Don't plan anything else just yet. I'll talk to him."

I took the stairs down one floor and walked into my office. Setting my computer and calendar down, I looked around. My chair is tucked neatly into the desk instead of backed away like I'd left it. I opened the bottom drawer and found my purse and cell phone still there, and it didn't look like anything else was missing or moved. The garbage can is still full, so it wasn't the cleaning crew.

I mentally shrugged. Whoever it was didn't take anything, so I guess it's not a big deal. Just strange.

I docked my computer and pushed the power button. My monitors came to life, and I pulled out my chair, ready to get back to work. Just before I sat, I spotted something on the seat. I reached down and picked up a gray shirt, it's familiar softness leaving no doubt in my mind to its origin, but I unfolded it anyway. Jack's name and number appeared and I hugged the material to my chest and closed my eyes, remembering it sliding over my still-tingling nipples the day before. Raising the shirt to my nose, I inhaled the scent of laundry detergent and *him*.

I dropped into my chair, my face still buried in the shirt. My head got buzzy and I had to stop. Is it possible to get intoxicated from a man's scent? I chuckled out loud, the sound echoing in the empty room. I'm probably just making myself hyperventilate.

The notification light on my cell caught my attention and I picked up the phone and swiped, bringing it to life. My heart pounded when I spotted the text from Jack.

> Jack: That shirt looked better on you than it ever did on me. See you after the game.

I have no idea how we got here or where here is exactly. One thing I do know is that if this continues, Jack will own me heart, body, and soul.

JACK

. . .

"LOOKING FOR SOMEONE?"

I tore my attention from the stands and looked over at Dan's smug face.

"Nope, just doing some final stretches."

He nodded and stood next to me and grabbed his right elbow with his left hand then pulled to stretch his shoulder. He repeated the process on the other side while I raised one knee into my chest, then the other.

Setting my feet shoulder-width apart, I lunged from side to side, going deeper at every pass, stopping when I felt a twinge in my right hip. No idea what's going on there.

Maybe I'll talk to Sabrina about it when she gets here next week. If I mention it to Max, he'll have to document it and then it'll be a whole thing, and that's the last thing I need.

Dan twisted from side to side, looking at me like he was trying to figure something out.

"What?" The word came out louder than I'd expected, drawing attention from some of our teammates. I glared at them until they went back to playing catch.

"Something you want to tell me?"

"Nothing I can think of."

He glanced at the stands then looked back at me.

"There's not a certain PR person you want to talk about?"

How the fuck does he know?

Dan chuckled and leaned his arm on my shoulder. "I saw her leaving the apartment complex last night looking a little disheveled."

I rubbed my hand down my face and groaned.

"Does she know you saw her?" He looked surprised by my question and shook his head. "Don't tell her, okay?"

His surprise turned into a big smile.

"I won't say a thing."

"Don't be a smug fucker," I mumbled and walked away. His laugh followed me all the way to the dugout.

I stepped into the on-deck circle. Thanks to two walks and a line drive double to the right field corner by Oskar Marquez, we took a one-run lead over Philadelphia here in the fifth inning. I slipped the doughnut onto my bat and, holding it in my right hand, swung my arm in big circles loosening my shoulder then repeated the process with the left.

I'd managed to make contact my last two at bats, but the hits didn't go anywhere...a line drive right at second base and a long fly ball caught by the center fielder on the warning track. That last one had the distance, but not the location. If it had been a little to the right or left, it would have been at least a double.

Moving through the rest of my routine, I watched Monte take two strikes followed by two balls. He fouled a couple off, giving some happy fans souvenirs, then took two more balls and jogged down to first base.

I banged the handle of the bat on the dirt and dislodged the doughnut. With the bases loaded and one out, I walked toward the plate and stepped into the box. A loopy curveball came in wide for ball one. The pitching coach called time and ran out to talk to the pitcher. It was only his second inning and he seemed to be losing his shit. A fact I planned to take full advantage of.

I stepped out of the box, leaned the bat against my hip, and tightened my batting gloves. Looking around the stadium, I zeroed in on Hannah sitting in the owner's section right next to Kenny and Mr. Hanover. She had her head turned, listening to Kenny speak, but suddenly looked in my direction, as if I'd pulled her attention to me. I smiled and felt all warm inside when she smiled back. I have no idea what it is about this woman, but she makes me feel things I've never felt before.

Like the raging jealousy that tore through me the next second as Doug Luna plopped down in the seat on the other side of her. He leaned closer to her and said something. She looked over at him and replied, making him chuckle, but he didn't move away. Instead, he rested his elbow on the arm rest.

Didn't the mother fucker ever hear of personal space?

The umpire stepped into position before I could see her reaction. I got into the box and took my stance. The pitcher looked over his shoulder at Monte then stepped his foot off the rubber.

Seriously?

The bases are loaded. It's not like he's going anywhere until I hit the ball.

As everyone got back into position, I fought the urge to glance over at Hannah to see what's going on. While my reaction to her is new, I can't have it interfere with baseball. As I've been doing since I was thirteen, I channeled all my emotions into the game.

I stepped back into the box and glared at the pitcher. He glared back. Throwing from the stretch, he released the ball and I knew from the minute it left his grip, the pitch was my idea of perfect. A fast ball, waist high, right between the center of the plate and the outside corner.

The feel of the ball hitting the bat vibrated through my hands a millisecond before the satisfying crack sounded in my ears. I took off toward first base and looked up just in time to watch the ball sail over center stadium wall. Slowing into my home run trot, I circled the bases and stepped on home plate.

My teammates congratulated me with fist bumps, chest bumps, and pats on the back that could dislodge a lung.

The crowd continued to cheer so I tipped my helmet then looked over at Hannah and smiled. Her smile widened and she continued to clap and jump in place.

I have no idea how she normally reacts to home runs, but based on the look Kenny was giving her, I'm thinking this isn't it. I stepped into the dugout and tossed my helmet to the batboy.

Dan came up behind me and squeezed my shoulders.

"You know you're fucked, right?"

He tossed the words I'd said to him right before coming up with the plan to get Sabrina back into his life. I should have wanted to punch the knowing smile off his face, but instead I returned it and shrugged.

Chapter Eighteen

HANNAH

THE WAVES WON, thanks in part to Jack's grand slam. He'd also made some amazing plays, letting nothing get past him. One time he dove deep into the pocket, grabbed the ball, and fired a one-hopper from his knees that Monte picked to end the inning.

He ran onto the field with gauze on his forearm the next inning, so he must have torn it up on that play.

After the game, I watched Jack talk to one reporter after the other. I'm sure his grand slam would top the baseball news for the night. When the ball is hit out of the entire stadium, it usually garners some attention, even if it happens in spring training.

Mr. Hanover left as soon as the game ended and Kenny and I chatted for a while, trying to figure out the source of his bad mood. The book may have him a little upset, but it can't be the only thing bothering him. In all the years I've worked for the Waves, I've never seen him so short-tempered and miserable.

I mentally shrugged as I made my way back to my office. Kenny can figure it out. I like Mr. Hanover, but we really only have a professional relationship. A friendly one, but professional nonetheless.

I'm not someone he'd confide in. Give orders to? Definitely. And as long as I follow those orders, I'm doing all I can to keep him happy.

After booting up my computer, I made some phone calls, sent a few emails, and updated my calendar. I sat back and glanced at the clock and was surprised to find two hours had passed.

I'll admit, I was worried being here would mess with my normal work routine, but so far, so good. I have my own office and the rhythm here is the same as at First Allegiant Bank Park so I have plenty of quiet time to get things done before everyone else shows up and after they leave.

I tilted my head from side to side, working some of the kinks out of my neck. My whole body is achy today. A few amazing orgasms apparently take a toll on unused muscles.

Not that I'm complaining.

Last night was worth every ache and pain I'm feeling. I made a mental note to pick up Epsom salts on the way home. Maybe a long soak will fix me. Or maybe I just need to work those muscles more.

Jack had lived up to my every fantasy, and Lord knows there've been many through the years. I swear he could make me orgasm with his voice. Hell, with this scent. Speaking of his scent...I sniffed, catching a hint of that spicy sweet smell I love. Looking up, I found the subject of my thoughts lounging against the doorway.

Am I that tuned into him that I can pick up his scent from across the room?

"Jack."

He pushed off the doorframe and slowly walked toward my desk, dropping the duffle bag that had been slung over his shoulder to the floor just as he reached me. His gaze didn't leave mine as he placed his hands on the arms of the chair, leaned down, and softly kissed me. He tilted his head to the other side and kissed me again, lingering just a bit longer. Pulling back, he nipped at my bottom lip and the corners of his eyes crinkled with his sexy smile.

"Hannah," he said and his warm, minty breath brushed against my face.

The man is a walking, talking wet dream. I took in a deep breath, filling my lungs with the scent of fresh-from-the-shower Jack.

Mm, so good.

I didn't realize I'd said that out loud until he chuckled. "Thank you." He straightened and took a step back. "You wouldn't have said that about a half hour ago. Be thankful I hit the showers before coming up here."

I've been around Jack post-game and he smelled amazing despite the dirt and sweat. But I won't share that with him. It might sound creepy.

Instead I said, "Thank you for the shirt."

His eyes took a lazy tour of my body, slowly down then back up again, lingering on my breasts, making my nipples tighten and tingle. My face heated as he raised his gaze, pausing at my neck, where his mark lingered beneath the silky blouse, before looking into my eyes again.

A small smirk had played at the corners of his mouth during his perusal, but he was full-on grinning now, a naughty sort of smile that made my thighs quiver.

"You're welcome," he said. "Do you have plans tonight?"

It took me a couple seconds to catch up with the change of subject.

"No."

"Dan and I are grilling some steaks at my place. Want to join us?"

"I don't know if that's a good idea," I said.

I sat forward and shut down my computer. Grabbing my laptop case from under the desk, I put my calendar and a few files in, then undocked my computer and secured it in the padded section of the bag. Jack's hand covered mine just as I zipped it closed.

"Hannah." He didn't speak again until I looked at him. "It's just Dan, and he won't make a big deal out of this."

Whatever this is.

"*This* is you and me, getting to know each other better, enjoying ourselves, figuring it out along the way," he said.

What is it about this man that makes me lose control of my inner dialogue?

I closed my eyes and shook my head.

"I don't know if I'm ready to announce this to the world. It's too new."

My entire body broke out in goosebumps as Jack's fingers skimmed my cheek then stroked my jaw, his thumb resting under my chin, tipping it up slightly until I opened my eyes.

"No matter what he thinks, Dan is not the world," he said around a soft chuckle. "But seriously, we'll grill some steaks, drink a few beers, and relax." His eyes shifted away and he took in a deep breath then slowly let it out before meeting my gaze again. "I wasn't going to mention this because it's really not a big deal, but Dan saw you leaving my place last night."

I groaned. "What did he say?"

"He dished out some payback on the ball busting I gave him about Sabrina."

"I thought you liked Sabrina."

"I do, and I really liked watching him get whipped by her. Still do," he said. "So I guess I deserve the payback now that the tables are turned."

Is he implying that he thinks we can be like Dan and Sabrina?

Thankfully I didn't utter that thought out loud.

He took my hand in his, raised it to his mouth, and placed a kiss right in the middle of my palm, then curled my fingers closed as if to hold it in place.

"Hannah, I'd like to spend time with you, see where this goes. But we can't live in a bubble. If we don't sneak around and make a big deal of this, maybe no one else will either." Those soft hazel eyes broke down every last bit of my resistance. "So what do you say?"

"What can I bring?"

JACK

"Promise me you won't be a dick tonight," I said to Dan.

"Why would I be a dick?"

"Because for some reason you think this is hysterical."

I handed him six potatoes and pointed to the sink. Taking

the hint, he turned on the water and rinsed them off.

"For some reason? Seriously Jack?"

If he wasn't my best friend, I'd punch the smartass smirk right off his face. Hell, if he pushes me or makes Hannah feel uncomfortable tonight, I might anyway.

After finishing his job, Dan placed the wet potatoes on

a plate then proceeded to poke the hell out of them with a knife.

"You don't need to kill them," I said. "Just make a few holes to allow the steam to escape."

He stopped murdering the potatoes and leaned his hip against the counter. Crossing his arms over his chest, he watched me unwrap the cowboy ribeyes from the butcher paper and place them on a cutting board.

"Do you really not know why I find this thing with you and Hannah so amusing?"

He crossed his arms over his chest and stared me down as I sprinkled a generous amount of seasoning on the steaks. When I finished, I mimicked his pose and waited for him to answer the question my raised brow was asking.

"I've seen you with a lot of women over the years, some I think you've liked more than others, but not one of them even put a dent in that brick wall you have around yourself," he said. "But since that event at Lucca, I've watched you knock it down piece by piece and let Hannah in."

I'm not a big drinker, but this is way too heavy of a conversation to have without at least a beer in my hand. I walked over to the refrigerator and grabbed two Blue Moons, twisted off the caps, and handed one to Dan. I downed half of mine in one long chug.

"When I told you I saw Hannah leaving last night, your first reaction was to worry about how she'd react if she found out I knew. Not to mention the fact that you look at her all sappy-eyed."

What can I say? I know he's right. Well, maybe about everything but the sappy eyes. I hate to think I'm following her around looking like a pathetic puppy.

I put the potatoes on a plate and popped them into the

microwave to partially cook before I throw them on the grill. I picked my bottle up from the counter and raised it to my mouth.

"I like her," I said, then finished my beer and tossed the bottle into the recycling bin. "And I have no idea why it took me a decade to notice that, but it doesn't change the fact that it's true."

"Have you told her that?" I nodded. "And?"

I shrugged. "She was here last night and she's coming back tonight so I guess she's interested."

"And are you open to giving this a chance to last beyond September?"

The doorbell rang before I could answer. I've told Hannah that I'm not starting this with an end date in mind, but I'd be lying if I said that doesn't scare the shit out of me. And even though I didn't say that out loud, Dan seemed to know anyway. Sometimes it sucks to have people know you so well.

I walked across the living room and just before I opened the door, looked back when Dan called my name.

"Just don't fuck this up," he said. "I got lucky when Sabrina gave me a second chance. You might not be as fortunate."

Even though I told her she didn't have to bring anything, Hannah held a plate of cupcakes as she stepped through the door. The smell of rich chocolate tickled my nose as I leaned down to give her a small kiss. I closed the door and she walked past me to place them on the counter.

Dan had moved from his perch in the kitchen to greet her.

"Mm, those smell amazing. German chocolate?"

She set her purse on a stool and shook her head. "Guinness cupcakes with Bailey's cream cheese icing."

"Can we eat dessert first?" he asked.

"You can wait. It builds character," I said, then cringed. It still freaks me out when I open my mouth and my mother's words come out. Hannah's eyes widened and I smiled. "I'm going to go light the grill."

From out on the balcony, I heard them making small talk. I turned the gas to high and pushed the red igniter button. Once the flames got going, I shut the lid to let the grill get hot.

"So far, I'm having fun down here," Hannah said as I walked through the sliding glass door. "I see why you guys like it so much. It's definitely more laid back."

"Not for you," I said. "You've been working as many hours here as you do at home."

"No rest for the wicked," she said around a chuckle.

"Want a beer?" I asked.

"Sure."

I grabbed three beers from the refrigerator, twisted the top off one and handed it to Hannah, then gave the other to Dan.

"I have to open my own?"

"Don't be a pussy," I muttered.

"What was that?" he asked, then settled into the living room chair. "I didn't catch what you said."

I flipped him off and set my beer on the coffee table.

"Have a seat," I said to Hannah. "I'm going to go throw the steaks on the grill."

"Do you need me to do anything?"

"Just relax. I've got everything covered," I said. "Thank you for the cupcakes. You really didn't need to bring anything, but they look amazing." I leaned in for a small kiss then said against her lips, "And I can think of a few things we can do with that icing later."

I'd love to explore that last thought right now, but Dan is sitting in the living room and I have steaks to grill. I smiled and nudged her toward the couch.

She pushed her glasses into place with her index finger. The frames are a soft pink now and match her shirt. She'd had blue on earlier. I've met women with a shoe fetish, but have never known anyone who owned more than a couple a pair of glasses. She seems to have a pair for every occasion. I'll have to find out more about that later.

I grabbed the steaks from the counter as she sat on the side of the couch closest to Dan.

"When are Lexi and Sabrina coming down?" she asked him then took a sip of her beer.

"Next weekend," he said. "Then they'll be back again for the last week while Lexi is on spring break and we'll head home together."

"Do you have any special plans while they're down here?"

They continued their conversation as I walked out to the balcony. I threw the steaks on the grill and glanced at my watch. In four minutes, I'll flip them, turn down the heat, and let them cook for fifteen minutes before flipping again.

Leaning against the banister, I looked out at the water and realized that one nice thing about hanging out with Hannah is that she knows my friends and their families and they like her. I won't have to make sure I'm with them every second to run interference.

Some of the women I've spent time with didn't always mesh well with my friends or their wives...especially their wives. Things got real awkward when I didn't stick by their side.

I checked my watch, pushed back from the banister, and opened the grill, the aroma of the steaks making my mouth water. After flipping them, I closed the lid, and stepped back inside.

Taking a seat next to Hannah, I grabbed my beer, twisted the top off, and took a drink.

"We're all set, right?"

Both Dan and Hannah looked in my direction and I realized the question was directed toward me.

I swallowed my beer and said, "With what?"

"The boat to go to the Keys."

"Yeah, we're set."

"Are you coming along?" he asked Hannah.

She choked on a sip of beer then composed herself.

"I uh, I don't think so."

I glared at Dan. I'd mentioned a possible trip to Hannah before we got involved, but not since. I'd like to think her answer will be different now.

"I hadn't gotten a chance to ask her yet." I directed my attention to the embarrassed woman at my side. "It's going to be a lot of fun and I'd love it if you'd come."

She didn't look convinced, but I decided to let it go. I'll talk to her about it when we're alone.

"So how about this guy today," Dan said, saving me from the silence that had been turning awkward. "Damn, you crushed that ball. Your bat loaded or what?"

"He threw a pitch in my sweet spot and I went with it."

"And those plays you were making," Dan went on. "Don't give it all away here. Make sure you save some of that stuff for the season."

"Don't worry," I said around a chuckle. "There's enough to last."

"How's your arm?" Hannah asked.

She wrinkled her nose when I twisted my hand and looked at the brush burn and open wounds on my forearm.

"It's okay."

"It doesn't look okay," she said. "Does it hurt?"

"Right now it just burns. The fun stuff comes in a few days when it starts to heal and gets all scabby."

That led to a conversation about the worst injuries Dan and I had seen through our careers. Hannah had a few to add that were pretty impressive. I honestly can't remember having this much fun spending time with a woman. Well, a woman I'm involved with.

I glanced at the time. "I'm gonna grab the potatoes and check on the steaks. You need another drink?"

Hannah shook her head. "I'm not finished with this one."

"I'll have a water," Dan said, then added. "I'm Face-Timing with Sabrina and Lexi later. Don't want to be shit-faced for that."

I pulled the potatoes out of the microwave, quickly wrapped them in foil, and set them back on the plate. After pouring a glass of water, I walked through the living room and handed it to Dan.

"I'll be right back."

Opening the grill, I flipped steaks, then lined the potatoes in a row on the top rack to finish cooking.

"They'll be done in about ten minutes," I said, then realized I never asked Hannah how she likes her steak. "I always cook them medium rare. Does that work for you or do you want them cooked more?"

"Medium rare is perfect."

I walked to the kitchen, took the salad out of the refrigerator, and grabbed a couple bottles of dressing, butter, and sour cream. After placing them on the table, I went back into the kitchen and took a platter out of the cupboard large enough to hold the steaks and potatoes.

Hannah laughed at something Dan said and the sound gave me a warm feeling right in the center of my chest. I rubbed at the unfamiliar sensation...no idea if I want to hold it there or make it go away.

My relationships have always been controlled and uncomplicated. Some people might say superficial. Even though this thing with Hannah just started, I know it can't be described with any of those words.

Chapter Nineteen

HANNAH

I LOOKED around the table at Jack and Dan's empty plates then down at my own nearly full one. "How did you eat all that?" They both looked at me like they didn't have a clue what I was talking about. And I suppose they don't.

Jack frowned. "You barely touched your steak. Was it cooked okay?"

"It was perfect."

"Then why didn't you eat it?"

"Seriously Jack? I ate a lot," I said. "This steak could feed a family of four. There's no way I could eat the whole thing."

"We did."

"Yeah, but you're professional athletes. You burn a zillion calories a day."

Dan chuckled at that and said, "Speaking of calories. I cleaned my plate. Time for a cupcake."

He stood and grabbed the plate and placed it in the

middle of the table. Opening the plastic wrap, he stole a cupcake, peeled back the liner, and ate half in one bite.

"Mmmm," he said around a mouthful. "These are so good."

Jack took one and agreed. "This is seriously the best cupcake I've ever had." He looked at me. "Aren't you having one?"

I shook my head. "I'm stuffed. Maybe later."

They'd each just finished a second when Dan's phone beeped.

"Time to call my girls," he said, then licked his fingers.

He stood and put his knife, fork, napkin, and crumbled cupcake liners on his plate then brought it to the kitchen.

"Just leave it," Jack yelled to him. "I'll clean up."

Dan stood at the sink and the water turned on then off. He walked back around the counter and said, "Great steaks, man. You are the master." Then he looked to me. "It was fun, Hannah."

I agreed, it had been fun. Through the years, I've spent a lot of time with these guys, but not like this. It's always been at the stadium or a team event. This is different. The last few weeks, I feel like I've gotten to know the real Jack and tonight's given me some insight into the real Dan.

Dan left, leaving Jack and me alone.

"You cooked, so I'll clean up," I said.

He shook his head and picked up both of our plates.

"I got it."

"Jack, you know how I hate sitting around doing nothing."

I felt his sexy chuckle in every erogenous zone in my body.

"Do you want me to wrap this steak so you can eat it tomorrow?" he asked.

"That'd be great."

I picked up the cupcake plate and secured the plastic wrap then walked over and placed it on the counter. Leaning against the stool, I watched Jack bend down and retrieve a container from the bottom cabinet. I'll admit I ogled his ass and enjoyed every second of it.

He glanced back and caught me looking. With the wicked glint in his eyes, I'd expected a sexy comment, but the words that came out of his mouth shocked me.

"Do you want some salad, too?"

It took me a second to process the question.

"Yeah, sure," I said.

He stood with two containers in his hand and placed them on the counter. He cut the remainder of my steak off the bone and placed it in one and secured the lid. Then he picked up the tongs and filled the other with salad. *How does he make even domestic chores look sexy?*

"Dinner was amazing, Jack. Thank you for inviting me."

*This man has cooked for me two nights in a row. If whatever *this* is continues past spring training, I'm going to have to reciprocate once we're back home.*

"It was my pleasure," he said as he put the containers in the refrigerator. "And thank you again for bringing the cupcakes."

He glanced down at the items in question and the corner of his mouth kicked up. Reaching out, he carefully pulled up the plastic wrap and removed one from the plate before closing them back up. His gaze met mine again and I forgot what I was about to say. *How does he make me wet with just a look?*

I closed my eyes and swallowed. When I opened them again, Jack stood directly in front of me.

"No closing your eyes," he said, his soft gravely tone

putting my nipples on full alert. His soft groan told me he'd noticed. "Lick."

I opened my mouth and did as he said, the flavor of the icing bursting on my tongue. Jack moved in and licked my upper lip then the corner of my mouth.

"Mmm, it tastes even better off you."

Before I could respond, he kissed me as though he was starving for the taste of my lips. I shifted and spread my legs so he could move closer. He wrapped his arm around my waist and pulled me forward until even air couldn't fit between our bodies, his erection pressing against me. At first I fought the urge to rub against him, but when he brushed his chest against my painfully tight nipples, I couldn't hold back. I rocked forward, shifting to the left until he hit just the right spot. A groan vibrated between us, but I couldn't say if it came from him or me.

Next thing I knew, I was floating through the air, my legs wrapped around Jack's waist, his hand cupping my ass. If I wouldn't have had to end the kiss, I may have been asked how he was carrying me using just one arm.

He ended the kiss and I opened my eyes, blinking to bring him into focus. As he loosened his hold on my butt, I unwrapped my legs from his waist and slowly slid them down until I stood between him and the bed. Bending to the side, he placed the cupcake on the nightstand, seeming to make a point of grazing my nipples on the way out and back.

"Your nipples are so responsive." He cupped me with both hands and leaned down to nibble behind my ear and whispered. "I love it." Standing tall, he looked down at me and said, "I love how real you are, how honest. Your reactions to me, your words. I never have to wonder why you're here, what you're thinking or feeling."

I smiled, acknowledging his words, my heart nearly

pounding out of my chest. Jack Reagan just used the word love in reference to me twice. And looking into his eyes, I know he's not just throwing me a line.

Sometimes when he looks at me, something shifts in his gaze, like a shade is being lifted and I feel like he's letting me see a part of him he doesn't share often.

"Now I think this needs to come off." He tugged at the hem of my shirt. Slowly sliding my glasses off my face, he asked, "How much can you see without these?" Closing the arms, he turned and carefully placed them next to the cupcake on the nightstand before facing me again.

"I'm nearsighted, so I can't see far," I said. "Things get blurry about a foot out."

He placed his hands on my waist, flashed a wicked smile, and shimmied my shirt up and over my head.

"I'll have to make sure to stay within range then so you know it's me."

As if I could forget.

He reached behind my back and unclasped my bra, caressing my shoulders and arms as he slowly slid it away from my body. My nipples tightened even more when the cool air hit them.

"Jesus, Hannah." He backed me up until the back of my knees hit the bed. "Lie down."

I sat then scooted back against the pillows. Jack rested his knee next to my hip and whipped off his shirt then tossed it to the floor. He moved forward and nudged my left nipple with his nose, then flicked it with this tongue.

Resting his chin on the curve of my breast, he smiled and said, "As sweet as you are, I've been thinking about licking that icing off these babies since you showed up at my door."

He pushed back and grabbed the cupcake. Holding it upside down, he smeared icing over one, then the other nipple. After taking a second to appreciate his handiwork, he leaned down and licked just the tip of one nipple before opening his mouth and laving it with the flat of his tongue, pulling me into his mouth and sucking, drawing me in further.

My hips shot off the bed and streaks of fire raced between my nipple and my clit. Jack shifted over me and settled between my wide-spread thighs, holding me in place. Releasing my nipple with an audible pop, he said, "Just relax and enjoy." And moved to the other side.

Easy for him to say. He's not the one having every erogenous zone stimulated through a single point of contact. I moaned and thrust up, shamelessly rubbing myself against his rock hard erection. He sucked harder and his hand moved up to slowly roll and twist the other nipple between his thumb and forefinger.

I let out a long groan and pressed my head into the pillows.

Jack pulled back and I felt the cupcake against my nipples again. I opened my eyes and watched him slowly smear icing over the twin peaks.

"You're so beautiful, so responsive," he said, making them tighten even further. Glancing up at me, he smiled. "It's fucking sexy as hell."

I watched his tongue come out and lick some of the icing off, leaving my elongated nipple peeking out between stripes of white on either side. It wasn't nearly enough and I wiggled beneath him. He blew gently and I shivered as sweet sensation zinged throughout my body.

"Think you can come this way?" he asked, the wicked gleam in his eyes making my insides melt even further.

At this point, it wouldn't take much to put me over the edge. Again, I lost control of my inner dialogue and said that out loud. His low, sexy chuckle vibrated against my nipple.

"That's good, honey. Real good."

Moving back and forth between each breast, he licked and lapped, removing all traces of icing. His lips closed around one nipple and I watched his cheeks hollow as he sucked, drawing it further into his mouth.

"Please," I begged, grabbing onto his shoulders.

Back and forth he went, his mouth and fingers continuing their slow, sensual assault. My nipples felt raw, the sweet agony spreading throughout every single nerve ending in my body.

"Jack."

His name came out as a hoarse whisper. I arched my back, thrusting myself further into his mouth. I can't take much more and he didn't seem in any hurry to stop.

"Jack," I said again, and continued to chant his name with each panted breath. Thank God it's only one syllable because I don't think I could handle much more than that.

My legs stiffened and I pressed up against his hips, searching for relief. He dropped more of his weight on me, his erection resting against the exact spot begging for attention.

I couldn't move. Couldn't think. Couldn't do anything except lose myself in the pleasure coursing through my entire body.

Jack pulled back and his teeth closed around one nipple as his thumb and finger pulled hard on the other. That's all it took. I tumbled over the edge as my body convulsed, shattering into a thousand pieces, the amazing orgasm leaving me limp and tingling.

He braced himself on his elbows, his hands cupping my face. I barely had enough breath to return his sweet kiss.

JACK

I PULLED BACK and looked down at Hannah as she came back to reality. Her normally pink nipples stood rock hard and cherry red as her chest heaved with every breath.

Hannah coming apart like that is probably the sexiest thing I've seen in my life, and God knows I've seen a lot. I shook my head to dislodge that last thought. I don't want anything or anyone to intrude on my time with this amazing woman.

She looked up at me and blinked a few times, as though she was trying to bring me into focus. Maybe she is. I moved closer.

"That was so amazing," I said, placing a kiss at the base of her throat. "And hot as hell." She took a deep breath and let it out slowly, dropping her gaze to the side. "Oh no." I kissed her jaw, forcing her head back, then looked into her eyes. "Why do you look embarrassed?"

Shaking her head, Hannah chuckled. "How do you see right through me?"

"Because I pay attention," I said. "And don't try to get out of answering the question."

"You barely touched me and I went off like that," she said. "You have to admit, it's a little embarrassing."

"Barely touched you?" I asked. "I'll have you know, I did some of my best work just now." I tried to look indignant, but couldn't stop the corners of my mouth from curling up. "And regardless, the fact that I can affect you like that is hot as fuck."

She smiled and kissed me, lingering long enough to nip at my bottom lip.

"You're very sweet," she said when she pulled back and rested her head on the pillow.

"I'm really not, just stating the facts," I said. "And besides, you haven't touched me at all and I'm hard as steel and ready to come in my shorts."

I pushed against her, feeling her heat even through the layers of our clothes. Her eyes widened and her pupils dilated just before I felt her fingers move between us to fiddle with the button of my shorts until it popped free. She reached inside my boxer briefs and wrapped her hand around my dick, slowly stroking.

Without letting go, she pushed at my shoulder with her other hand, urging me onto my back. Settling back against the pillows, I watched her shift to her knees.

She grabbed the waistband of my shorts and pulled them and my underwear off in one swipe. My dick bobbed toward my stomach and she leaned forward and flicked her tongue against the tip before opening her mouth wide and sliding her lips down my shaft.

Wrapping her hand around the base, her nostrils flared as she slowly moved down until her mouth met her fist. She squeezed and lifted her head. Just when I thought she'd release me, she swirled her tongue around the head and sucked before lowering all the way down again, repeating the process again and again.

I recited baseball stats to keep from coming as I watched her head bob up and down in a hypnotic rhythm. My balls tightened and the tingle at my spine had me grabbing at her shoulder.

"Hannah." She didn't stop so I said her name louder. With her lips still wrapped around my dick, she looked up at me with those big brown eyes and I nearly lost it right then and there. For a second I forgot what I was about to say, but when my balls squeezed even tighter, I said, "Stop. You have to stop."

She slowly slid her lips up my shaft and let go.

"Give me a minute," I said, taking deep breaths in through my nose and letting them out slowly through my mouth.

Once I gained control, I looked at her watching me. The flush on her cheeks had nothing to do with embarrassment and everything to do with the fact that she'd been really into what she was doing. This woman truly is perfect.

Raising up on my elbows, I said, "You might be more comfortable if you take those shorts off."

I sat up and repeated the process she'd done to me minutes before. After tossing her shorts and panties onto the floor next to mine, I followed the expanse of her long legs all the way up to heaven. She's not totally bare, and her neatly trimmed hair glistened. I reached out to touch her, sliding my finger along the seam.

"You're so wet." I couldn't stop myself from taking a taste. Rolling onto my belly, I let my tongue follow the path my finger had just traced. "Mmm, so sweet," I said before fully opening her so I could lick at the treasure I'd revealed.

I added some suction, but didn't quite give her what she needed. Her fingers curled into my scalp and I continued to nip, suck, and lick her until she was writhing beneath me. My dick throbbed against the mattress, wanting to get in on the action, but I didn't want that yet. I wanted at least one more good orgasm from her before letting him loose.

Thrusting two fingers inside her, I curled them then stroked and sucked on her at the same time. She let out a garbled sound that was either my name or a prayer just before she clamped down on my fingers, her clit throbbing against my tongue. I stayed with her until her muscles slowly relaxed. Kissing her inner thigh, I looked up and smiled at the sated look on her face.

I moved back to pull a condom from the drawer. Hannah watched me roll it down my length and licked her lips. This woman is seriously going to kill me. I chuckled, thinking about my *Shrek* quote when she told me I was going to kill her last time we did this.

"I'm glad you find this funny because I can barely breathe," she said, resting on her elbows, putting those amazing breasts front and center.

I grabbed her hand and pulled her forward, kissing her cheek then tip of her nose. She took a deep breath and let it out on a long sigh.

"Okay?" I asked, resting my forehead against hers. She nodded.

"I feel like I just ran a marathon."

"Want to take a break?"

She glanced down at my dick and it got even harder. He's really not happy with me right now.

"No, I'm good."

"Are you sure?" I asked. She looked down again.

"Don't worry about me. If you need some time, we can stop, maybe watch a movie or something." She raised her brow. "Seriously."

"I'm fine, Jack. You just make me forget how to breathe."

I sat back against the pillows and pulled her toward me. She shifted her leg across mine and straddled my lap.

"Just take it slow, and please don't forget to breathe," I said. "I don't want you passing out on me."

She raised up on her knees until my dick rested against her entrance, then she slowly lowered down until I was buried deep inside her. Leaning back, she rested her hands on my thighs and moved back and forth, slowly at first before settling into a good rhythm.

With every thrust and pull, she tightened and pulled me in deeper, and I clenched my jaw and started on those baseball stats again. I may make her forget how to breathe, but she erodes every bit of my control.

Widening her thighs, she slipped down further and closed her eyes, letting out a low moan. She shifted forward and pressed her hands against my chest, rocking back and forth, moving faster and faster until we were both breathing hard.

"Hannah, I'm gonna come."

She was gasping now, right on the edge. I reached between us and circled her clit. On the first pass, she quivered against me. I got in one more stroke before my release began. Her muscles clamped down on me again and again, milking every last drop.

Chapter Twenty

JACK

I STROKED my fingertips along Hannah's spine, slowly up and down, enjoying the feel of her soft skin. She snuggled her cheek against my shoulder and sighed.

"As much as I'd love to stay here like this, I need to take care of the condom."

She lifted herself up on her elbow then rolled to the side and dragged the sheet up, ruining my view. I leaned forward and kissed her.

"Don't move. I'll be right back."

I went to the bathroom and took care of business as quickly as possible so I could get back to Hannah. After washing my hands, I walked back toward the bed, happy to find her in exactly the same position. With her tousled hair, rosy cheeks, and the sated look on her face, she looked like a goddess.

My goddess.

My eyes devoured her, wanting to commit this moment

to memory. I'd love to take a picture, but I don't think she'd be comfortable with that.

"What?" she asked, tightening her grip on the sheet and pulling it higher.

Climbing back into bed, I settled on my side next to her.

"Just taking a mental picture," I said, tucking a stray strand of hair behind her ear, before resting my hand on hers. "I want to be able to see you like this in my mind anytime I want."

The corner of her mouth curled and her eyes took a lazy tour of my body before meeting my gaze again.

"Same," she said and licked her lips.

Thoughts of that sweet mouth wrapped around me made my dick twitch. I can usually recover pretty quickly, but this is definitely a record. Normally I'd look for a second round, but I want things to be different with Hannah. I want more with her.

"Feel like watching a movie?" I asked.

Her eyes widened. "Sure."

I grabbed the remote and clicked on the TV hanging across

from the bed. Pulling up the menu, I asked, "What's your preference? Drama, mystery, those sappy chick flicks?"

"Nothing scary and nothing sad," she said. "Other than that, I'll watch pretty much anything."

I scrolled through the listings until one caught my eye.

"Looks like there's a Mac Flynn movie coming on." I switched to that channel and set the remote back on my nightstand.

Every woman I've ever known has loved Mac Flynn movies as much as I do, if for a different reason. Similar to James Bond, Mac Flynn is an agent for a fictionalized secret service and the movies are filled with action, drama, and sex. Which is what I like. Women usually watch because they find the man himself attractive.

The title sequence filled the screen and I settled back against the pillows and opened my arm, inviting Hannah to rest against my chest. She moved closer and held herself stiff against me.

"You okay?" I asked. She nodded and her cheek rubbed against my left pec. "We can watch something else."

"No, this is fine," she said.

She didn't seem fine, but I didn't want to push and make her uncomfortable. Maybe she's just not used to this kind of intimacy. I'll admit it's new for me, too. Not to say I've never snuggled in bed with a woman, but it's usually just to rest between rounds of sex. But Hannah is different. Right now, I just want to hold her and watch the movie with no other agenda in mind.

"Do you need your glasses?" I asked.

"No, I don't usually wear glasses when I watch TV in bed. If I don't lie on my back, the frames bend," she said. "It's a little blurry, but unless I have to read something, I'm good."

The movie started with a car chase, and I pulled Hannah closer and watched the action unfold. Eventually she relaxed against me and by the time the end credits rolled, she seemed to be enjoying it as much as me.

I ran my finger along her jaw, then nudged her chin until she looked up at me.

"Thank you," I said, then placed a gentle kiss on her lips. "I enjoyed that."

"I did too." She looked surprised by that fact, but at least she was more relaxed than before the movie started. "But I should probably get going. It's getting late."

"You could always stay here." I stroked her cheek and she turned her head into my palm and took a deep breath. After taking in another breath and letting it out, she looked up at me.

"I love the way you smell. It's intoxicating."

Intoxicating?

A woman once told me I smelled like an old hippy, so Hannah's words surprised me.

"I always wondered what kind of cologne you wear, and now I know," she added.

"Now you know," I agreed. "No cologne, just eczema cream."

"That you make with your own two hands."

For some reason, she finds that fact fascinating and I don't feel any need to discourage anything she likes about me. I leaned forward and nibbled at her plump lower lip before sealing our mouths together and dipping my tongue inside for a taste. Talk about intoxicating.

I could kiss her forever, and settled in to do just that.

Later I watched Hannah slip back into her clothes.

"Are you sure you don't want to stay?" I asked.

She nodded and picked her glasses off the nightstand and slid them into place, then smoothed her hair.

"I'm sure, but thank you for offering," she said. "And thank you for a great night. Dinner was amazing."

I stood and stepped into my boxer briefs then closed the distance between us.

"So was dessert," I said, and watched the blush spread across her face before kissing her forehead.

We walked into the living room and I continued to the kitchen to retrieve Hannah's leftovers from the refrigerator. She moved to the other side of the counter to retrieve the keys from her purse.

"Do you want to take a couple cupcakes home?"

"No, I'm good."

"Are you sure?" I asked. "You didn't get to eat one."

"I had to taste test, so I had one before I got here."

"No wonder you couldn't finish your dinner."

"I couldn't finish my dinner because you could feed an army with what was on my plate."

I walked around the counter and placed my hands on her hips. "Before it was a family of four and now it's an army? I think you're just making excuses."

She rolled her eyes and laughed. "How about, big enough to feed a baseball player?"

"That works."

I echoed her laughter and gave her a quick peck, enjoying how easy this feels. I've always liked Hannah and even though we were more friendly co-workers than friends, I respected her. She's smart, no-nonsense, and keeps the team whipped into shape.

Now that I've noticed her in a whole new way, those old feelings are still there, but the new ones mix in, adding layers to this relationship that I've never experienced before. I don't want to just keep her around so we can fuck and go out occasionally, I want to *make love* to her, get to know her, spend time with her. That last thought reminds me.

"Dan opened his big mouth before I could ask, but we're renting a boat next week and taking a slow ride down to the Keys. Would you like to come along?" I saw the hesitation in her eyes so I kept talking to both stop her from saying no and convince her to say yes. "We did it last year and it was a lot of fun. Sabrina and Lexi are coming this year so you won't be the only female on the boat."

"Who else is going?"

"Cal and Monte."

Her brow furrowed. "I don't know if it's a good idea, Jack."

That's not a no. I shifted closer and squeezed her waist.

"I know you want to keep this quiet, but these guys are my

best friends. They won't say anything if we don't want them to." I kissed her forehead, then the tip of her nose. "It'll be fun. I promise."

She let out a long sigh then looked up at me through her eyelashes. "Does anyone ever say no to you?"

"Surprisingly, yes," I said. "But I'm hoping you don't."

"Okay, I'll go."

HANNAH

I SHUT down my computer and slipped my cell phone into my pocket. Will Call just texted to let me know Rose Garrett and her crew picked up their tickets and were on their way into the stadium. Picking up the box of T-shirts from the edge of my desk, I made my way out of my office and through the corridors that will lead me to the field.

The sounds of the stadium got louder with every step...the crack of the bat, the ball hitting the glove, and the arriving crowd. I wasn't raised around sports, but in the past decade, baseball has seeped into my system and the sights, sounds, and smells that surround me during the season feel like home.

I turned right on the concourse and continued toward the third base side. Two girls walked in my direction, giggling and glancing back over their shoulders. A little further down, I spotted the source of their interest. He leaned against a table, looking at his cell phone. Wearing uniform pants and a form-fitting Under Armour shirt, Jack Reagan is a sight to behold.

I was still studying his profile when he turned and looked in my direction. My stomach fluttered at his slow smile that promised all sorts of things. Dirty things. Hot things. Things I know he's more than capable of delivering.

As if my hardened nipples were a homing device, his gaze shifted down and lingered for a heartbeat before meeting mine again.

"Let me help you with that," he said.

I handed him the box I'd been holding against my hip and he set it on the table behind him.

"How'd you know I'd come down this way?" I asked, hoping to calm my raging hormones.

He shrugged. "This seems like the most logical way to this section, so I took a chance. I saw Mrs. Garrett's group arrive, so I knew you'd come down."

"I'm surprised you didn't cause a riot standing up here."

Obviously the players can go wherever they want, but they usually stick to the spots not open to the general public.

"I just kept my head down and didn't make eye contact. A couple of twittering girls just passed, but they didn't approach me." Resting his hand on the small of my back, he moved me in front of him and picked up the box. "What's the plan?"

"I was going to say hello to the group and hand out the shirts. I planned on bringing them down to the field after the game to meet you and whoever else is available, and the kids can run the bases."

I preceded Jack down the stairs toward Mrs. Garrett's

group. Thankfully she was seated on the end so I didn't have to climb over people to get to her. She stood and hugged me.

"Thank you so much for setting this up," she said.

I looked over my shoulder at Jack.

"You remember Jack Reagan." Her eyes opened wide. "Shouldn't you be out there?" she asked.

"I'm not starting today. So I figured I'd come up and say hi," he said and placed the box he was holding onto the step. "And give you guys these shirts Hannah brought."

Jack treated the group like old friends, talking and answering questions like he's known them forever. He passed out the shirts and when one of the kids asked for an autograph on his, I handed him the Sharpie I had stashed in my pocket. Soon a crowd surrounded Jack and he signed whatever they handed him. He really is a PR dream.

"So, it looks like there have been some developments since I last saw you two," Mrs. Garrett said from just behind me.

"What do you mean?" I asked and took a step to the side to face her.

"You and Jack."

I fought the urge to stutter, but couldn't control the blush I felt creep across my face.

Shaking my head, I said, "I still don't know what you mean."

"Oh honey, at the beach bash it was obvious you two were attracted to each other. I'm just happy to see you've finally acted on it."

I shook my head again, not sure of what to say. If it's obvious to a woman we've met once, everyone else will eventually notice, too.

"Don't worry, it's probably only obvious to meddling old ladies like me." She patted my hand. "Plus I'm a retired psychologist. Body language is something I'm tuned in to."

I nodded to acknowledge her words, then decided to change the subject. I'm not ready to acknowledge my relationship with Jack with people I know, nevermind a woman I've just met, no matter how sweet she may be.

"The kids can come onto the field and run the bases after the game if they'd like. Some of the other players will be around to meet the group as well."

"They'll be thrilled."

I looked around at the stadium, which was starting to fill up. Jack was still signing things, posing for pictures, and talking to the group, which had grown since we got here. I figured I'd better wrap things up before every fan in the stadium decided to join in.

"Jack." He finished signing a baseball card and looked up. "You need to get back to the field," I said. The crowd surrounding him glared at me, but better they're angry with me than him.

"Okay guys, last call. Who hasn't had something signed yet?" Two kids held up their hands and he signed a glove and a picture, then thanked them all for supporting the Waves.

Thankfully his little crowd dispersed, clearing the stairs. Jack walked down the two steps that put him next to Mrs. Garrett and me.

"Thank you for being such a good sport again," Mrs. Garrett said.

"It's my pleasure," he said.

"There was a significant donation made to our group shortly after the beach bash," she said. "Would you happen to know anything about that?"

Jack looked around the stadium and shook his head. "No ma'am."

"For some reason I don't believe you," she said. "But I won't push."

We said our goodbyes to Mrs. Garrett and Jack waved to the group and we walked down the few remaining steps to the field gate. He walked through then closed it and faced me from the other side.

"You'll be down here after the game, right?"

"I'll be here."

"And afterwards? What are you doing then?"

"Nothing," I said. "I mean, I don't have any plans."

"Come over to my place? I haven't been alone with you in

forever."

That last statement isn't quite true. It may seem like forever, but it's only been four days. The Waves played away all week so we didn't see each other at the stadium and I had my period and didn't feel up to going anywhere after work.

"Okay," I said.

"I'm sure I'll get there before you because you work way too much, but just in case, the code is 0921623."

I noted that in the memo app on my phone. "Got it."

I'll have to make sure I leave the stadium before he does just so I can prove him wrong.

"And Hannah," he said, leaning closer. "When I get you alone, I'm gonna kiss the ever-loving fuck out of you."

Chapter Twenty-One

JACK

I KNOW I should keep things professional when we're working, but I couldn't help myself. She looks so put together and professional in her capri pants and blouse, I wanted to shake her up a bit. Unfortunately, I shook myself up in the process because the heated look she flashed at my words made me instantly hard.

Thankfully my sliding shorts kept the big guy compressed. Baseball pants aren't very forgiving, and I wouldn't hear the end of it from my teammates if they caught me sporting wood.

The game was about to start and I grabbed a bag of dill pickle seeds and an orange Gatorade preparing to spend it on the bench. Dan walked over and handed me his cell.

"Sabrina and Lexi are stuck in Atlanta and their flight was just delayed again. Hold onto this and let me know if she sends any updates."

Dan's always been a little on edge whenever Lexi wasn't around but with this being his first season married to Sabrina, he's worse than usual. It's going to be a long season for both of us.

This will be the first time I'll be leaving someone I want to spend time with when I go on the road. In fact, it's the first time I have someone I actually *want* to spend time with outside the bedroom. Before I could get too bogged down with thoughts of how shallow my adult relationships have been, Cal took a seat next to me.

He nudged his chin and said, "Give me a handful of those."

I opened the seeds and poured a pile into his palm and took some for myself before zipping the bag closed.

"Your protege is glowing today."

"He's not my protege." I spit some empty shells onto the floor. "He thinks he's my replacement."

Which might be the case, but if I have my way, that won't be for a long time. My agent has started the lengthy process of negotiations and I'm looking for at least a five-year contract renewal. That should give me enough time to figure out what the hell to do once I retire.

We stood for the national anthem and the game started. The rookie pitcher, Sam Cherry lived up to his Cherry Bomb nickname throwing heat and striking out the side.

Dan ran down the steps and straight over to me.

"Nothing yet," I said.

"They were supposed to be here two hours ago," he said then walked across the dugout to grab his bat and helmet. "Let me know as soon as you know something. Call time out and run onto the field if you have to."

Thankfully Sabrina called just before the middle of the third inning and said they were getting on a plane and would be here in a couple hours. I met Dan at the top of the dugout stairs and filled him in.

"She said they're going to Uber to the stadium from the airport so don't leave before they get here," I added.

"Thanks man." He smiled and slapped me on the back. We walked down the stairs and he grabbed a drink. "I was getting ready to hop in the car and go get them."

"Sabrina said to tell you to relax. They're fine and will be here before you know it."

The Waves won the game 6-2, despite three errors by the shortstop. The kid has talent, but he needs to get his head out of his ass and pay attention. Play is different at this level and if he doesn't adjust, he won't make it. But that's not my problem. He views me as a rival instead of a mentor so I'm the last person he'd look to for advice.

I walked out of the dugout looked up into the stands. Hannah stood at the top of the stairs next to Doug Luna. She laughed at something he said then walked down the stairs toward Mrs. Garrett's group.

Thankfully he disappeared into the concourse because I couldn't be responsible for my actions if he followed her. I have no reason to believe Hannah is interested in the man, but my blood still boils every time I see them together. Apparently jealousy is another first I'm feeling with Hannah.

She led the group onto the field and I walked to her side.

"You guys ready to run?" I asked.

I spent the next half hour standing at home plate, telling each kid when to go. Dan, Cal, and Monte stood at each of the bases, acting as coaches, waving their arms in a dramatic circle advancing the kids to the next base.

We wrapped things up and Hannah led the group off

the field and up the stairs. I'm sure she'll go back to her office to do some work before leaving.

"I'm gonna hit the showers," Dan said. "My girls will be here soon and I gotta smell good for them."

I don't need to shower, but I followed him to the locker room to change. After sliding on jeans and a T-shirt, I slipped my feet into my favorite Sperrys and said my good-byes. I walked out of the stadium toward to the player's parking lot. The door had just closed behind me when a red Ford Focus pulled up. The back passenger door opened and Lexi came bounding out.

"Uncle Jack!" she yelled and jumped into my arms.

"You made it," I said and kissed her forehead before putting her back down.

"I didn't think we would. We were in the airport so long," she said, dramatically drawing out the last two words.

Sabrina walked over, and dropped two suitcases and a backpack next to her.

"How are you holding up?" I asked, kissing her on the cheek.

"Not quite as energetic as our girl here, but I'm good," she said.

Lexi filled me in on their airport adventure, which is par for the course for her. After all, she's been traveling to games her whole life. Before she started school, she was usually with us on road trips.

Dan burst through the stadium doors and ran toward us. Pulling them into his arms, he kissed them both.

"I'm so happy to see you guys," he said. "I missed you both so much."

"Daddy, you're squeezing too tight." Lexi wriggled until he loosened his hold.

Sabrina stayed right where she was and rested her head on his shoulder.

"I wasn't sure if you'd be hungry, but ordered take out just in case," Dan said. "We can pick it up on our way to the condo."

"Are you coming over, Uncle Jack?"

"No, I have plans," I said. "I'll see you tomorrow at the game though and then Sunday on the boat."

"Plans?" Based on Sabrina's smirk and raised brow, I'd say Dan told her about Hannah and me.

"Plans," I confirmed with a wink. "I'll see you guys tomorrow."

Chapter Twenty-Two

HANNAH

I KNOCKED on the door of Jack's condo and waited, listening for signs of life inside. I hadn't noticed his car in the parking lot, but didn't want to just go barging in.

When he didn't answer, I carefully pushed the code he'd given me earlier into the touchpad and smiled when the light turned green and I heard the lock disengage. I turned the knob, opened the door, and slowly stepped inside. The door sounded extraordinarily loud as it closed behind me.

Standing in the foyer, I took a deep breath, inhaling the faint remnants of his scent. He can't be that far behind me and it would be really strange if he walked in and found me standing just inside the door sniffing the air.

I moved forward and placed my purse on its now-usual stool then settled onto the couch and grabbed the remote from the coffee table in front of me.

I scrolled through the menu a couple times then clicked

on an old episode of *The Office*. My sophomore year of college, I interned at a marketing firm and can totally relate to some of the antics that go on in the show. Yes, they're exaggerated, but apparently craziness is the norm when you get people together in a cube farm.

The Waves' offices are a bit more segmented, but still manage to get a little nuts at times. I can't imagine what would happen if we were all in the same room all the time.

After slipping off my shoes, I placed my glasses on the coffee table and curled my legs onto the couch, resting against the decorative pillow. Turning up the volume, I relaxed and watched one episode of *The Office* end and another begin. The opening sequence had just ended when I heard the front door open. I shifted up and looked over my shoulder.

"Don't move," Jack said.

I froze in place and watched him walk toward me. When he reached the couch, he dropped to his knees and leaned toward me, forcing me to lie back against the pillow. Placing his hands on either side of my face, he devoured me with his gaze and my heart pounded at its intensity. When he lowered his mouth to mine, I'd expected a full-blown, tongue-tangling kiss, but instead, he nibbled at my bottom lip before placing his mouth over mine and applying a wonderful suction that I felt right down to my core.

My mind whirled as Jack's mouth opened and closed in a steady rhythm. Long and hard, soft and gentle, our tongues tangled in a hot, sexual assault. He literally made love to my mouth and I didn't want him to stop. I twisted my fingers into his hair and held on tight.

"You drive me crazy," Jack whispered as he pulled back just far enough to tilt his head and come at me from a different angle.

With our mouths still melded together, he shifted on top of me and I opened my legs to make room. Taking the invitation, he settled into place, and I shamelessly rubbed against his erection. He moved so suddenly, I barely had time to let go of his hair.

"Come here."

I took his offered hand and he pulled, hauling me over his shoulder in a fireman's hold.

"Jack," I screeched. "What are you doing?"

He spanked my ass then rubbed his hand against the spot in a soothing caress.

"Getting you into my bed the fastest way possible."

My stomach bounced against his shoulder but before I could protest again, he lowered me to the bed. He ripped his shirt off and threw it to the floor then stepped out of his jeans. I caught sight of his erection peeking over the waistband of his boxer briefs a second before he rested his knee next to my thigh and urged me to lie back.

"I think we can get rid of these for a while, don't you?" The words were barely out of his mouth when he pulled my capris off with one tug and tossed them on the floor.

Jack settled his hands against my waist and pushed me farther onto the bed. Leaning forward, he opened my blouse, one button at a time then slowly peeled it apart, leaving goosebumps where the material had been.

"I don't want to embarrass you," he said. "But I can see right through this material."

His looked at my breasts, encased in a sheer white demi bra. The matching panty shows just as much. I've always liked wearing sexy underwear and Jack's appreciation makes me happy for that fact. After taking a lazy tour of my nearly-naked body, his gaze met mine again.

"I'll have to see if I can get a refund since they're defective," I said.

He lowered his mouth and nibbled at the mound peeking over the material of my bra.

"I didn't say anything about them being defective. They're actually kind of perfect, like you."

Before I could think about that last statement too much, he brushed his lips against mine and picked up where he'd left off in the living room. He settled between my widespread thighs and I wrapped my arms around his neck, putting my breasts in contact with his brick wall of a chest.

He slid his hand up my back and flicked my bra open then shoved it out of the way. I groaned when my nipples made contact with his skin. They've always been sensitive, but with Jack, they're at a whole other level.

He pulled back. "Christ, Hannah." His gaze roamed over my body as he dragged in deep breaths. "I wanted to go slow this time, but you erode my control until I act like a horny teenager with his first girl."

He stood and removed his boxer briefs then leaned over and grabbed a condom out of the nightstand drawer. I watched, fascinated, as he covered his hard length with latex.

That done, he leaned down and slipped his index fingers into the waistband of my panties and slowly dragged them down my legs. He settled my calf onto his shoulder and leaned forward, shifting my other leg to the side, opening me to his gaze.

His finger traced my folds then dipped inside.

"Mmm, perfect."

He leaned down and brushed his mouth against mine then

filled me in one long stroke. Our breath mingled between kisses as he thrust into me, slowly at first then with more force.

I tightened my leg against his shoulder and grabbed onto his arms. His muscles flexed as he pushed his upper body up and away from me, shoving his pelvis deeper into mine. The new position had him brushing against my clit with every thrust.

"That's it," he said, picking up the pace. Every time he pulled out, my inner muscles clenched and tightened, then fluttered when he pushed back in. "You feel so good."

He slipped his hand around my ankle and raised my other leg onto his shoulder and thrust forward, pushing deeper than before, the tip of his penis hitting *that* spot while his pelvis brushed against my clit. Talk about sensation overload.

"Oh my God, Jack! Don't stop. Please, don't stop."

He picked up the pace and said my name on a low groan. "Come for me, baby."

My nipples tingled and a wave of sensation crashed through my body as I clamped down on him over and over again. Jack stiffened and throbbed inside me.

After the storm passed, he turned his head to the side and kissed my knee before sliding first one leg then the other down to rest on the bed. He lowered himself against my chest and my inner muscles clenched with aftershocks.

He kissed my collarbone and looked up at me, his eyes sleepy and sated. I imagine mine look the same. Then something felt strange.

"Jack?"

"Hmm?" He kissed the curve of my breast.

"Jack, something doesn't feel right," I said, trying not to sound too panicked.

Shifting onto his elbow, he looked down to where we were still joined and back into my eyes.

"Are you okay? Did I hurt you?"

"I'm fine, but something doesn't feel right. Down

there," I added, as if there was any question to what I was talking about.

He backed away slowly, and pulled out of me, then cursed. "Fuck!" he said, not quite under his breath. "The condom broke."

JACK

I GRABBED a tissue and dragged the busted condom off, cleaning myself in the process. I pulled a washcloth off the shelf and ran it under warm water for Hannah so she could do the same.

Looking at myself in the mirror, I cringed at the freaked out expression on my face. But I guess I have every right to be freaked out. I've been having sex since I was sixteen and have never had a condom break. Ever.

I guess I've just been lucky.

After squeezing the excess water from the washcloth, I left the bathroom and handed it to Hannah.

"Thank you," she said.

I walked around the bed and kept my back to her as I pulled my underwear back into place and grabbed a pair of shorts from the dresser giving her a little privacy.

"Can you hand me my clothes?"

She sat in the middle of the bed with the sheet clutched against her chest. Instead of doing what she asked, I pulled a T-shirt from the drawer and brought it over to her. I don't want her to leave right away and I have a feeling if she gets into her own clothes, she will.

I'd expected a protest, but instead, she slipped the shirt

over her head without saying a word. She smoothed her hair into place and looked over at me.

"You okay?" I sat next to her on the bed.

She nodded. "I'm sorry I reacted like that. It just freaked me out for a minute."

I chuckled and laced my fingers through hers and squeezed. "Understandable," I said. "It freaked me out, too."

"Just to ease your mind, I'm on the pill," she said.

"That's good to know." I stroked my thumb against hers. "But pregnancy isn't the only issue with a broken condom and I want to put your mind at ease. I'm clean. You know I get regular physicals that include blood work." I said.

"I'm clean, too," she said.

Not that I had any doubt, but it was nice to hear.

I shifted further onto the bed and pulled her against my chest. We stayed that way for a long time and I just enjoyed the feel of her in my arms. Her breathing deepened and as carefully as possible, I reached down and pulled the sheet up to her shoulders. I settled further into the pillows and closed my eyes.

I woke slowly with Hannah still in my arms and looked over at the clock. It was just past six so my alarm won't go off for another couple hours. The game is at one o'clock today, and I don't have to be at the field until ten, but I'm not sure about her.

"Hannah," I whispered, then kissed the top of her head. She snuggled further into my chest and sighed. Rubbing my hand up and down her back, I repeated her name.

"Hmmm?"

"What time do you have to get up?"

"Not yet," she muttered.

I'll give her another half hour. I can't imagine she has to be at the stadium super early, and Hannah doesn't strike me as the kind of woman who takes hours getting ready for work.

I slid my hand under the sheet and rested it on her waist. She still wore my T-shirt but it had ridden up during the night so I touched warm, soft skin. Then I remembered she'd never put her panties on last night, so I let my hand drift lower until it reached the firm globe of her ass. I squeezed and slowly caressed, just enjoying the feel of her.

Hannah moaned and pushed against my thigh, then shifted her leg over mine. Instead of dragging her on top of me to impale her with my growing erection, I closed my eyes. But instead of dozing back off, I started thinking about what happened last night.

I guess I've just been really lucky, because I've never had a condom issue. I know Lexi exists because of a broken condom, and while Dan fought hard to keep her and loves her more than life, he was less than thrilled the moment it happened.

When Hannah told me the condom broke, I definitely panicked, but it wasn't as bad as it could have been. I suppose it was bound to happen eventually and I'm glad it was with Hannah. At least she's honest and I trust that when she says she's on the pill, she really is. I've had women swear they were protected and we could skip the condoms, but I never felt comfortable enough to do that.

My first Minor League coach warned about girls who'd get pregnant on purpose hoping to hitch themselves to a future Major League star. At the time, I thought he was exaggerating, but I've seen it happen since then. I've also personally witnessed girls poking holes into condoms, which is why I always make sure to always use my own.

You'd think all that would put a damper on sex, but the

MLB is just as active as ever. Until Cindy wrote that book, I never thought twice about it.

I was careful and avoided the usual groupie scene and thought that was enough. While I didn't trust the women enough to go bareback, there was a degree of familiarity there that made me feel like things were under control. The guys always busted me about being a serial monogamist, but it worked for me.

Until it didn't.

And now there's Hannah. For some reason with her, I'm not preparing for the end. In fact, I'm thinking about all sorts of things that never entered my mind before. Things I've avoided my whole life.

I don't need a psychiatrist to tell me why I've lived the way I have. It has more to do with my father than baseball. He loved my mother so much that more than twenty years later he still can't move past her death. I never wanted to feel that way about anyone. Didn't want to give someone that much control over my life. And until now, I didn't.

I had women that lasted for a season then went away. I always made it clear up front what they'd be getting...a few months of travel, good meals, and some great sex. Over the years, a few got clingy, but most just enjoyed the relationship for what it was, took the perks as they came, and left when it was time. I never had any real issues until Cindy. She took clingy to a whole other level and when the end came, she refused to go away

After the whole book debacle, I planned on spending this season alone, but finally got my head out of my ass and noticed Hannah...really saw her...and I'm so happy I did. She's different and I feel different with her. Feel more with her. She makes me jealous. She makes me horny. She makes me want things I've never wanted before.

Before I could dig into that last thought too much, the

subject of my musing suddenly pushed herself off my chest and sat, grazing my balls with her knee in the process. Not enough to cause any real damage, but I definitely felt it.

"Ugh!" I grabbed my junk and bent my knees, trapping her leg between mine and my abs.

"Oh my God! Jack! Are you okay?"

She shouted those things as she extracted her leg from my hold and shifted onto her knees next to me. I took a few deep breaths and nodded.

"I'm fine." I let go of the boys and settled back against the pillows. "You didn't get me too bad. It was just a shock." Her glistening eyes met mine and my stomach flipped. "Hannah, I'm fine." I reached out and pulled her against my chest again. "Please don't cry. It's all good. No damage done."

"I can't believe I did that. I'm so sorry."

"It's okay." I kissed the top of her head. "Really."

"I had a dream that I overslept then woke up and was afraid

I actually did."

"I was gonna wake you in fifteen minutes or so. I wasn't sure what time you want to be at the stadium."

"Eight thirty," she said. "I really should go so I'm not late."

"Let me cook you breakfast."

"Thank you, but I don't normally eat breakfast."

I shifted onto my side so I could look at her.

"Didn't anyone ever tell you it's the most important meal of the day?"

"I've heard, but I'm not usually hungry in the morning."

"Maybe I'm not giving you enough of a workout." I kissed the tip of her nose. "Maybe I need to step up my game."

"Your game is fine. If it was any better, I wouldn't be able to handle it."

Her giggle echoed through the room when I tickled her ear with the tip of my tongue.

"You need to have more faith in yourself. I'm sure you'd manage to keep up."

"Think so?" she asked.

I licked my way down her neck to her collarbone and nibbled, then nodded.

"I believe in you."

Her pebbled nipple pushed against the fabric of my T-shirt and I couldn't help myself. I opened my mouth wide and sucked her through the soft fabric. She dug her fingers into my hair and moaned. I moved my head to give her other nipple the same treatment. Don't want to play favorites.

I was about to lift the shirt so I could taste her sweet skin, but she had other plans. Hannah pushed against my shoulders, urging me to roll onto my back.

"I want to make sure I didn't do any real damage," she said.

My dick was practically busting out of my shorts and when she pulled the waistband down, it sprang free and she caught it in a tight grip. The sight of her watching her hand move up my full length then back down again nearly did me in.

"Everything looks like it's in working order, but I want to be really sure."

She wrapped her hand around the base and her lips around the head then slowly slid down until they met in the middle. Moving up and down, she licked and sucked, going deeper at every pass, pulling me into her mouth further and further until her hand was gone and I nudged the back of her throat.

"Hannah. *Fuck.*"

Moving her head back, she wrapped her fist around me again and held me in place as her tongue swirled around the tip and sucked before taking me all the way in again. I dug my fingers into her hair and held on for the ride.

Her free hand stroked up my thigh and cupped my balls, squeezing and gently tugging, dragging me closer to the edge.

"Hannah." I squeezed her scalp. "Baby, I'm gonna come."

Instead of pulling back, she sucked harder and squeezed. That did it.

"*Hannah.*"

Her name came out as a garbled grunt as I felt my dick pulse over and over again inside her warm, wet mouth. She stayed with me the whole time, drawing out my release.

When it was over, I loosened my hold on her hair and fell back against the pillow, pulling in deep breaths. She released me and placed a soft kiss on my hip bone, her mouth curled into a small smile as she looked up at me.

"Well, it seems like everything is in working order."

Chapter Twenty-Three

JACK

I CIRCLED around the stadium and spotted Hannah's car before continuing to the players' lot. After blowing my mind earlier, she'd refused to let me reciprocate, saying she needed to get home to get ready for work.

While she got dressed, I made a couple ham, egg, and cheese sandwiches and we ate them at the kitchen table. It was all very domestic. I think I'd like to start every day that way, with or without the world-class blow job beforehand.

Pulling into my usual spot, I grabbed my duffle and plastic bag from the passenger seat and got out of the truck. Hannah had reminded me that Jeremy Walsh would be at the game today so I brought along a new practice shirt and glove to give him. I'm sure Hannah put together a goodie bag, too. She has a never-ending supply of team swag that she's not afraid to hand out.

I walked through the parking lot to the players' entrance, chatting with the security guards for a few minutes before going inside. Country music echoed down the hallway and blasted out at me when I opened the locker room doors. That means Kasprzyk controlled the music this morning. At least it's the newer rock-style country and not that old-fashioned twangy crap he listens to sometimes. This stuff is pretty decent and doesn't give me a migraine.

Besides the music, it was pretty quiet in the locker room. No bickering or busting. I settled in at my locker and started my usual pre-game ritual. Some guys are really superstitious and do things the same way because they think it's bad luck not to. I do things the same way because the ritual helps me get into the right frame of mind.

"Hey," Dan settled into the chair at his locker next to me.

I glanced at the clock. "I'm surprised you're here so early."

"My wife slash physical therapist gave me some extra stretches to do today. She said my leg needs to be a little looser."

"I'm not even gonna comment on that."

He shook his head and chuckled.

"She was speaking as my physical therapist, not my wife when she said that."

"I'm sure she was." I held my hands out in front of me, palms up. "No judgment here."

"I'm just happy they're here. The three of us lived in a bubble last year. I got used to being with them all the time," he said. "We've been working on a schedule for the season so we're not apart too long. Thankfully Sabrina has a lot of vacation time and can set her own schedule now that she's a partner."

"What's Jeff doing now that Sabrina is around?"

"He still hangs with Lexi when Sabrina works and the

rest of the time, he deals with my accounting and investments. Now that he has more free time, he's thinking about taking on some other clients. He definitely doesn't want to go back to working on Wall Street."

"If he is taking on new people, I'm definitely interested."

"I'll let him know."

I stood and grabbed my duffle and the bag for Jeremy.

"What'd you bring a snack?" Dan asked.

"That kid I met at the beach bash is here today. I have a couple things for him."

We both walked out of the locker room toward the tunnel leading to the field.

"Are Sabrina and Lexi coming today?" I asked.

"They'll be here. Which reminds me. Did you tell Monte and Cal that Hannah is coming with us tomorrow?"

"Not yet. I'll tell them before the game."

I looked around the stands, disappointed there was no sign of Hannah. But it's still early. After dropping our things in the dugout, Dan and I walked onto the field to stretch.

Cal and Monte were limbering up in right field so we joined them. Talk about a break. I thought I'd have to do some serious maneuvering to get them alone.

"I wanted to tell you guys something about the trip tomorrow," I said as I started my stretching routine. They continued to stretch but gave me their attention. "Hannah and I have been seeing each other the past few weeks and she's coming along."

As if it was rehearsed, their eyes rounded and they looked to Dan then back to me.

"Hannah *Adams*?" Monte asked.

I nodded and looked back and forth from him to Cal who said, "Wow."

"I just wanted to give you fair warning so you don't do what you're doing right now."

"I appreciate that," Monte said. "I'll have it under control for tomorrow."

"Yeah," Cal agreed. "I like Hannah, but it would definitely be a shock if she showed up and I wasn't expecting her."

"So we're good?" I asked.

They nodded and I breathed a sigh of relief. Thankfully my friends have some respect for Hannah because if she was anyone else, I know they'd be busting my ass. Then again, if she was anyone else, I probably wouldn't be bringing her along.

I'd just finished batting practice when I spotted Jeremy and his mom walking down the stairs toward the field. They settled into their seats three rows back, just to the right of home plate. I reached down and grabbed a ball then walked toward the wall.

"Jeremy," I yelled.

He looked down at me and I held up the ball then tossed it his way once I knew he was ready for it. I gestured for him to come down and he ran down the steps.

"Glad to see you here," I said. "How's it going?"

"Great," he said. "I made that travel team I told you about. I'm the starting shortstop."

"That's awesome." I gave him a high five. "Hold on a second, I have something for you."

I ran to the dugout and grabbed the bag. Jeremy watched Derek Moss scoop up a ball at shortstop then twirl around in a circle, leap, and sidearm it to first base. Fucking hot dog.

Leaning my elbow against the wall, I said, "See that

right here?" He nodded. "That's exactly what you don't want to do. Yes, it looks impressive, but there are too many things that can go wrong when you ham it up like that. The ball could take a wicked hop, you could trip, throw the ball away." I shrugged. "And there's no reason for it. My high school coach used to say that a mediocre player makes the easy plays look hard and a great one makes the hard plays look easy."

"I'll remember that."

I held up the bag. "This is for you."

He grabbed the glove out of the bag and looked back and forth between it and me.

"This is so cool. It has your name on it and everything." He ran his fingers along each letter of my name stitched in pale blue thread along the back of the little finger. "Thank you so much. This is so awesome."

"You're welcome," I said. "I have to limber up some more before the game starts but I'll catch you later."

"Good luck today," he said then turned and ran back up to show his mother every detail of the glove.

I walked toward the first base line and placed my feet shoulder-length apart and leaned forward to stretch my hips out some more. After bending down to one leg then the other, I stood straight and spotted Hannah at the top of the stairs watching me. I met her gaze and the corner of my mouth kicked up. She answered with a shy smile that twisted my guts. I have no idea how this woman can affect me with a single look, but I definitely like it.

HANNAH

. . .

"HI HANNAH."

Lexi's voice pulled me from the Jack-induced daze I'd fallen into. I dragged my gaze from his and turned toward her and Sabrina.

"Hi guys," I said.

Lexi waved to Jack, her whole body getting into the motion. Jack waved back, though his was a bit more subdued. His smile glowed with love for the little girl, though.

"Do you know if Ava is here yet?" Lexi asked, as she looked toward the family seats for Ava Kasprzyk, John's daughter.

"I haven't seen her, but I just got down here," I replied.

"And you were busy looking at someone else," Sabrina muttered. I've only met her a few times, but I really like Sabrina.

"That obvious, huh?"

She shrugged. "Probably only to someone who knows who you're looking at and why."

"There's Daddy. I'm gonna go say hi," Lexi said and ran down the steps toward the home plate wall.

"I seriously wish I had half of her energy," Sabrina said.

"To see you two together, you'd never know you met less than a year ago," I said.

"She's very easy to love, and thankfully she's willing to share her father with me."

"You make a great family, and I know Dan is thrilled you're here."

"It's nice to be back together and I can't complain about being in this perfect weather, especially since it's been cold back home," she said. "What about you? Dan said you don't normally come to spring training."

"I don't, but Mr. Hanover insisted so here I am.

Honestly, I could have just traveled down for events but he wanted me on site every day. I thought I'd be totally off my routine, but I've managed to get things done without any issues."

"And your events with Jack?"

"They're going well. He's so great with fans, especially the kids, my job is easy. Speaking of," I said and held up the bag in my left hand. "These are for a boy Jack met at an event we did a couple weeks ago. He and his mother are down in the family section."

"I'm heading that way."

We walked down the steps and I said hello to Karen and Jeremy and introduced them to Sabrina.

"It looks like Jack already gave you a couple things, but here's some more." I handed the bag to Jeremy.

"Thank you!" Jeremy took the bag and dug through it with his right hand, never taking Jack's glove off his left. "This is so awesome."

With the game about to start, Lexi left her perch at the wall to sit next to Sabrina in the row behind Karen and Jeremy. Just after the national anthem, Natalie Kasprzyk arrived with Ava, her parents, and in-laws in tow.

After introductions were made, I decided to sit next to Karen to watch the game.

There was no real action until the fourth inning when Oskar Marquez hit a line drive double to left field to start off. After that, the Waves' bats came alive and by the seventh inning stretch, they were ahead six to nothing.

I left the group and headed back to my office to finish up a few things. I clicked on the TV hanging on the wall across from my desk so I could listen to the end of the game. Jack and some of the other starters were taken out in the eighth inning, giving the rookies and Minor League players extra playing time.

After making a few phone calls and answering some emails, I decided to officially call it a day. I have a few errands to run after work and still have to decide what to wear on the trip to the Keys.

I still can't believe I have plans to hang out on a boat with Jack and his friends. Hell, I can't believe I'm *with* Jack. I never thought I'd act on the ridiculous crush I've been harboring for years. Besides the fact he never seemed interested, I always said I'd never get involved with an athlete or an actor. At this point, I've done both.

Hopefully things with Jack will end better than they did with the actor. I'm older and wiser now so I'm pretty confident they will. Besides, Jack is already established in his profession, he definitely doesn't need me for my connections.

Before my thoughts could go too far down memory lane, I heard a knock on my door.

"Come in," I yelled.

Doug Luna popped his head in and looked around. "I wasn't sure if you were in a meeting."

"Nope, it's just me," I said. "What's up?"

"A bunch of us are going out to happy hour and I was wondering if you wanted to come along."

"Thank you, but I have a bunch of errands to run after work."

"Maybe next time," he said. "Are you in tomorrow?"

"No, I'm taking the day off."

"Doing anything special?"

"Just relaxing." That's not a total lie. I'm sure I'll be relaxing on the boat and in our final destination.

"Well enjoy. I'll be here all day moderating a baseball camp."

"Have fun."

I shut down my computer and sat back to wait for

updates to complete before undocking. A knock sounded on my open door and I looked up to find a fresh-from-the-shower Jack standing just inside my office, looking good enough to eat.

"Hi," I said, the word coming out in a husky whisper.

He walked across the room, his delicious scent filling the small space with every step. Leaning his hip against the desk, he struck a casual pose, even though he looked anything but. He looked like the old Jack, the one the whole world sees. Not the one I've gotten to know the past few weeks.

"Was Doug Luna just in here?"

"Yes."

"What for?"

"He invited me to happy hour with the rest of the gang."

When he didn't say anything, I added, "Is something wrong?"

He looked down at his clasped hands and took a deep breath before meeting my gaze again.

"Every time I turn around, he's with you," he said. "And it's obvious he's interested."

While he stopped speaking, the question hung in the air anyway. I answered it before he felt the need to ask.

"Jack, there's nothing going on with Doug and me," I said, then decided to be completely honest. "We went on one lunch date when I first got here, but that was it."

"Why?"

"Why what?"

"Why was that it?"

"Because we got involved and I told him I wasn't interested."

"Were you interested before we got involved?"

A hundred answers ran through my head, but I

decided to go with the truth. At least a good portion of the truth. He doesn't need to know about my decade-long obsession with him.

"He's nice enough and I like him as a person, but honestly, I only went out with him to distract me from my growing attraction to you."

The corner of Jack's mouth kicked up into a small smile and he leaned forward, placing his hands on either armrest, trapping me in the chair.

"Growing attraction?" I nodded and his mouth curled into a sexy smile. "Is it still growing?"

"Every second of every day."

"That's real good." He leaned down and kissed the corner of my mouth. "Because I don't share."

His mouth took mine in a searing kiss that had my head spinning. He pulled back and resumed his perch on the edge of the desk.

"Now, the reason I came here in the first place was to ask what you're doing tonight."

"I have a few errands to run then I have to figure out what I'm wearing tomorrow."

"Why don't you stay at my place tonight? We can order some dinner, maybe watch a movie."

I chuckled. "Did you just ask me to Netflix and chill?"

His laugh echoed through my office. "I hope I have a little more game than that," he said. "I thought it would be easier if you stayed at my place tonight since we're heading out early."

"Sounds good," I said. "Can I bring anything?"

Jack bobbed his eyebrows. "Have any more cupcakes?"

My nipples tightened at the thought of what he'd done with the last batch I'd made. There's no way he could see that through the bra I have on today, but his gaze dropped anyway, as if he knew.

"I can make some," I said.

He shook his head and dragged his gaze back up to meet mine.

"Just come over as soon as you can."

"What about for tomorrow?"

"We have it all covered." He leaned forward and gave me a quick kiss. "I'm gonna head out now so you can finish up here and run those errands." He stood and took a step back. "Don't be too long. I'll be waiting."

This man does know how to make my heart go pitty-pat. He walked toward the door and looked back over his shoulder, his cocky smile promising all sorts of wicked things. I need to say something to knock him down a peg or two.

"Jack." He stopped before stepping out into the hall-way. "I don't share either."

His smile grew larger, and a look that I could only call relief crossed his face.

Rapping his knuckles against the door jamb, he said, "Understood."

Chapter Twenty-Four

JACK

TOM PHILLIPS expertly docked the *Lucky Catch* in the slip and killed the engine. Monte jumped off and dropped the rope over the piling, securing her in place. We decided to change things up a little this year, starting with having a captain on board.

We usually ride by ourselves, but with the addition of Sabrina and Lexi, and then Hannah, decided it would be nice for someone else to be in charge of navigation. And it worked out great.

Tom anchored us off a barrier island and we spent the day there, snorkeling, exploring, and relaxing. There was a lot of eating and drinking too, but not enough that I'm not craving cold beer and conch fritters at Arnie's Place.

With my duffle and Hannah's bag slung over my shoulder, I stepped onto the dock then turned and held out my hand to help her off the boat. As she stepped forward, I pulled her toward me so she fell into my chest. I lowered my lips to give her a small kiss, then held her close.

"Thank you for coming today."

"Thank you for inviting me."

Throughout the day, enough comments have been made so she knows it's not normal for me to bring the women I'm seeing on outings with the guys. Not these guys anyway.

It wouldn't have been fair to have them get to know all the women through the revolving door of my love life on a personal level. They may have crossed paths a time or two, but for the most part, contact was limited.

"Trust me when I say the pleasure has been all mine." I kissed her then pulled back and looked down her body, now covered in a long sundress, then back up. "Especially getting to watch you frolic in a bikini all day."

She opened her mouth to comment, but Lexi's laugh grabbed her attention. Dan had picked her up out of the boat and swung her in the air before placing her on the deck. She ran toward Hannah and me as her father grabbed their gear and helped Sabrina out of the boat.

"Uncle Jack, that was so much fun," she said.

I bent down and asked, "What was your favorite part?" "Snorkeling. I did it in the pool before but not in the ocean.

It was so cool," she said, then looked over my shoulder. "Daddy, we're going to eat now, right? I'm starving."

Cal, Monte, and Tom finished their conversation and walked our way.

"Are you guys dropping your stuff at the hotel before you head to Arnie's?" Cal asked.

Our game isn't until tomorrow night, so we're staying in Key West for the night and chartering a plane to fly us back to St. Pete early in the afternoon. Tom plans on staying down here for a few days before sailing back.

Everyone looked around our little circle, waiting for someone else to answer. When no one did, I decided to pawn the decision off on the rookies.

"Let's let the ladies decide."

The guys liked that idea and we turned our attention to Sabrina and Hannah...and Lexi of course.

"Honestly, I thought I'd want to shower and change before dinner, but now I'm afraid that once I'm in the room, you won't get me out again," Sabrina said.

"How far is this Arnie's Place from the hotel?" Hannah asked.

"It's on the way to the hotel, about four blocks from here," I said. "Then if everyone is okay with going as they are, it makes more sense to go to dinner first then continue on to the hotel," she said.

Leave it to my Hannah to take the logical approach. Everyone agreed that it made sense, especially Lexi, who reminded her parents that she's starving.

"Tom, you want to join us?" I asked our captain.

He stepped toward me and slapped me on the back.

"Thanks for the invite, but I have plans of my own."

Walking past me, he joined his "plans" waiting a few feet away.

"Alrighty then," Monte said. "Old man has more game than us," he said to Cal.

"The only game I want right now is on the field, but you feel free to find some," Cal answered. "Ready to go?"

Our little mob walked the short distance to Arnie's and I was happy to see that aside from two old men sitting at the bar, the place was empty. Then again, it's never been crazy busy anytime we've been here...which is why we like it.

It's a local hangout more than a tourist trap, and any people here usually just leave us alone. Plus, the food is amazing. Arnie's husband, Ted, had been a chef at a Michelin-rated restaurant decades ago before they decided to get out of the rat race and move to Key West.

Arnie greeted us and I introduced him to the girls. He made a fuss over Lexi, then took our drink orders and brought her over to the bar to pour her own drink from the soda gun. I pulled out a chair for Hannah then sat next to her. Everyone else settled in around the table and Dan left a seat between us for Lexi.

The two returned from the bar, Lexi holding her glass carefully in two hands and Arnie had two pitchers of beer in one hand and a stack of glasses in the other. He expertly set everything down on the table, then took Lexi's glass from her and helped her climb into her chair.

"I had Ted drop some fritters for you," he said. "Anything else you'd like to start with?"

"Garlic parmesan wings," Monte said.

"Shark bites," I added.

"Do you think Ted would whip up some of those crab nachos he made last time we were here?" Cal asked.

"I'm sure he will as long as you promise to kick Boston's ass this year," Arnie said.

Both he and Ted were born and raised in New York and are rabid baseball fans. The flip side of that is that they hate Boston baseball.

"You know we'll do our best," Cal said, and the rest of us agreed. Arnie turned his attention to me. "Want to add anything?"

"I think that's good." I said. "I want to save room for a burger and dessert."

He went to place our orders and take refill drinks for the guys at the bar.

"You want to save room for a burger and dessert?" Hannah's lips curled into a small smirk as she repeated my last sentence back to me. I nodded. "The burgers here are amazing, and both the strawberry shortcake and brownie a la mode are delicious. Ted makes everything from scratch, including the ice cream."

"I may not make it through all the appetizers, so I'll have to live vicariously through you," she said.

"Oh no, you better step up your game tonight. I don't want to choose between those two desserts I mentioned and I'm counting on you to order one so we can share," I said, then nodded my head toward Lexi. "I know better than to ask this one to share a dessert because I won't get any."

Lexi laughed. "I can't help it. I love ice cream," she said. "And chocolate."

"I understand that," Hannah said. "And I'll do my best to keep up with all the food tonight."

Cal poured beer for everyone and held his up for a toast.

"This was a great day. Thank you for distracting me from my current situation."

His ex-wife was really putting him through the wringer, and we've done our best to be supportive without acting like total pussies or hovering like helicopter moms. We all raised our glasses and took a drink.

Arnie walked over with a platter of conch fritters and a stack of small plates. After placing both in the center of the table, he went back to the kitchen and returned holding a tray of small bowls.

"Here's your dipping sauce," he said, I assume speaking to Hannah, Sabrina, and Lexi because the rest of us know the drill. He always gives people individual bowls of sauce so there's no issue with double dipping. Apparently, it's one of his pet peeves.

"Enjoy."

"These are delicious. I expected them to be greasy, but they're so light," Sabrina said. "And I've never tasted anything like this sauce."

"Wait until you taste Ted's blue cheese sauce that comes with the wings," Monte said. "I don't even like blue cheese and I could eat that stuff like soup."

We'd just about finished off the platter of fritters when Arnie and Ted walked out of the kitchen, each carrying a tray heaping with food. After they set platters on every available inch of the table, introductions were made. Sabrina and Hannah complimented the food and Ted started a serious discussion with Lexi. Apparently there's a debate on whether or not Tinkerbell...whose likeness covered the front of Lexi's shirt...is a princess.

After spending so much time with Lexi, I'm aware of the fact that she was considered one a few years ago but now isn't, and Ted knows this because he has two daughters and four granddaughters.

From what I understand, he married young and had three children, then divorced years later when he realized, or should I say admitted, he's gay. I met his son, one of his daughters, his ex-wife, and her husband when they all came "up north" when we played New York and they all seem to get along well.

I didn't hold the fact that he rooted for the other team against him. Hell, in my mind I'm still a Boston fan, though I don't share that with the world.

Ted excused himself to get back to the kitchen and Arnie checked to see if we needed anything else.

"Just let me know when you're ready to order entrees," he said, then took his place back behind the bar.

We dug into the feast in front of us, and did very little talking. It's been a long day on the boat and even though we kind of grazed all day, everyone was hungry. It didn't take long for the seven of us to put a good dent in the food and finish both pitchers of beer.

Hannah consolidated the remaining food onto a few plates to make room. She is seriously the queen of organization. A very attractive trait to a man who likes everything in order.

I stood and said, "I'll take these over to the bar and get some more drinks. More beer?"

Lexi jumped off her chair. "I want another soda. Do you think Arnie will let me pour again?"

"We can ask," I said and handed her one of the empty pitchers to carry.

I managed to balance the empty plates in one hand and carry the other pitcher in the other. Lexi handed Arnie the empty pitcher and he ushered her behind the bar to fill her glass. I set my load on the edge of the bar closest to the kitchen.

"Two more pitchers of beer and one of water," I said.

Lexi and I managed to get everything over to the table unscathed and on the way, she noticed the vintage jukebox tucked into the corner.

"Can we play some music?" she asked before we sat back down.

"Sure, let's go see if it takes bills," I said.

Thankfully it had been modified to accept bills, so I pulled a five from my wallet and handed it to Lexi. She put it in the slot and surprisingly it went in on the first try.

"Now remember, we have to play songs everyone will like," I said.

For a kid, she has decent taste in music, but every once

in a while, she wants to listen to the new crap being put out nowadays.

I showed her how to punch in the codes and she'd entered three before she screeched.

"Uncle Jack! They have our song," she said. "Will you dance with me?"

"Sure," I said. "Punch it in."

We were still picking songs when the first chords of *Stone in Love* by Journey started to play. Lexi loves Journey. but only with Steve Perry singing. Her father is raising her right.

We selected a few more songs and with all our money spent, returned to our seats and waited for *our* song to play.

"I'm going to the ladies' room," Sabrina told Dan. "Lexi?" She nodded and hopped off her chair.

"I'll join you." Hannah stood and the two left the table.

"So Jack, who was that kid you were talking to at the game yesterday?" Monte asked.

"Jeremy Walsh," I said. "That's the kid I met at the beach bash fundraiser."

"That was his mom with him?" I nodded and popped a nacho in my mouth. "Was the dad at the game, too?"

"The dad was killed by a drunk driver," I said.

"That's awful," he said. "They live here?"

"Somewhere close by, I guess."

He was about to say something else when Cal interrupted.

Leaning his elbows on the table, he gestured for us to move closer.

"I don't want to sound like a fangirl here, but I'm pretty sure Mac Flynn just walked through the door," he said.

I glanced over my shoulder and watched the man in question walk toward a table in the corner of the bar area.

The woman with him looked around the room then sat in the chair he'd pulled out for her. I'd have to agree with Cal. He looks exactly like the star of all the Mac Flynn movies.

The girls came back and before we could say more on the subject, *Down Under* by Men at Work ended, and the beginning of *Cotton Eye Joe* echoed through the restaurant.

"Come on, Uncle Jack!" Lexi held out her hand.

"*Cotton Eye Joe* is your song?" Hannah asked, one brow raised.

"You know it." I leaned down and kissed her then allowed Lexi to pull me toward a clearing near the jukebox.

We stood next to each other, with enough space between so we could dance. I looked at Lexi and she nodded and we went through the steps, repeating them over and over as the song went on and on.

Instead of doing the basic line dance, I usually add things in that I know will make Lexi laugh. At one point, I leaned down and hooked my elbow with hers and we spun around in one direction three times, then turned and repeated the action on the other side. That had the desired effect.

My table clapped in time with the music, and between spins, I saw Hannah smiling as she watched. At least there's not a crowd in the restaurant. I really don't want a video of this showing up on the internet because it's personal. I'm okay with having my public persona out there for everyone to see, but I'd feel exposed if something like this was out there.

Toward the end of the song, I got down on one knee and reached my hand out for Lexi. She held on as she continued doing the dance moves while circling around me. The final notes played as she completed her second rotation and I pulled her in to sit on my knee and into a dramatic backward dip. She laughed, then sat up and threw her arms around my neck and kissed my cheek.

"That was awesome, Uncle Jack!"

"Sure was."

I held on to her and stood, picking her up with me.

"You guys get better and better," Sabrina said.

I set Lexi in her chair and watched Mac Flynn walk toward our table and stop directly behind Hannah. I know he's just a person, but it's freaking Mac Flynn, and I'm at a loss for words. Obviously everyone besides Hannah is too, because they're all just staring at him. Hannah is oblivious to the fact that one of the biggest stars on the planet is right behind her.

Which means her beaming smile is just for me.

"That was so great," she said. "You must practice a lot to be that good."

She directed the question at Lexi, whose attention was focused on Mac with the rest of us. Instead of answering Hannah's question, she said, "Who are you?"

Hannah realized Lexi spoke to a point above her head, and she glanced over her shoulder. Her entire body stiffened and every ounce of color drained from her face.

"Hello darlin'," Mac said.

Chapter Twenty-Five

HANNAH

I SAT against the arm of the couch, my knees bent, a pillow clutched against my stomach. Jack handed me a glass of water then settled into the other end, seeming to strike a casual pose, but with every muscle in his body tense, didn't quite pull it off.

He looked so worried, I wanted to put him at ease but couldn't find the words. In fact, I couldn't seem to find any words. I knew my father had been down here shooting his latest movie, but he was supposed to have gone home a couple weeks ago. What kind of divine intervention not only put us in the same city but would have him walking into Arnie's?

I took a few sips of water and cradled the glass in my hands. Looking at Jack, I opened my mouth to speak, but nothing came out. How do I explain the fact that one of the biggest celebrities on the planet is my father?

Obviously if our relationship continued, I would have

told Jack eventually, but I'd hoped things would be settled with my father by then. My feelings where he's concerned are still a mess and running into him like that, without warning, was definitely a shock to the system.

"Are you okay?" I looked into his worried eyes and nodded. He pulled my legs onto his lap and rubbed his hand up and down my shin. "What can I do to help?"

This man is so not what I ever expected. I'm seriously falling here. Besides being gorgeous and sexy as hell, he's sweet and kind and has a knack for knowing exactly what I need at any given time.

I'd managed to greet my father and not be a total bitch, but Jack noticed my distress and got me out of Arnie's before Melanie came over to the table.

Thank God.

Facing them both for the first time in months is not something I want to do in a public place in front of my new friends.

Tears blurred my vision and I blinked them away. He deserves an explanation, and it will be nice to get another perspective on the situation.

"First I want to thank you for getting me out of there before we caused a scene."

"The few people in Arnie's were probably still trying to get the vision of me dancing to *Cotton Eye Joe* out of their minds. I'm sure they didn't even notice you and your father."

A fresh wave of tears blurred my vision at the thought of him dancing with Lexi. It's obvious he loves her very much and would do anything for her. If he's like that with his friend's child, what would he be like with his own?

I shook my head to dislodge that last thought. If I'm going to survive in this relationship, I can't start imagining white picket fences and babies.

"I mentioned to you before that my father and I were having some issues." He nodded and I continued. "He told me something at Christmas and I haven't spoken to him since. I'm not sure what to say, what to do about the situation. I've asked him to give me time to think, but patience isn't one of his virtues and he keeps calling. Thankfully he's been busy or he would have shown up at my door."

"I know all about having father issues," he said, then smiled. "Of course, my father isn't Mac Flynn."

"Aaran Diskin." His raised brow prompted me to explain. "My father's name is Aaran Diskin. The character he plays is Mac Flynn."

Jack nodded and his hand continued to slowly stroke up and down my shin. I shifted my butt to get more comfortable.

"How is it possible that your father is one of the biggest movie stars of his generation and no one knows?" he asked.

I took a drink, then leaned forward and placed the glass on the coffee table before settling back into position.

"My father didn't hit it big until I was entering high school. Until then, he made his living doing bit parts and construction jobs. His big break came with a movie called *Shooting Holes in the Sky*. The movie wasn't a huge hit, but one of the big network executives noticed my dad and thought he'd be perfect for the Mac Flynn character."

Jack cupped my foot in his hands and started a slow massage and, despite the fact that I'm talking about a history I'd rather not discuss, I relaxed. The only other person who knows all this is Melanie and I haven't spoken to her in months either. I've never shared my whole story with anyone I've dated, but I find myself wanting to tell Jack everything.

"Things kind of went crazy after that. You know how

nuts celebrity can be and trust me when I tell you that Hollywood takes it to a whole other level." He moved onto the other foot and I shifted even further into the couch. The man truly has amazing hands. "And they have no limits. Absolutely none. My father had always been popular with the ladies, but it got ridiculous. Everyone either wanted a piece of him or a connection he could make for them and he was invited to every event, every party. Some of that extended to me, of course. What better way to kiss up to the star than by doting on his geeky, backwards daughter?"

"That description of you doesn't register," he said.

"I was a naive book nerd and definitely no match for kids who'd grown up in that world. But my dad's publicist gave me a makeover and I tried to fit in. It's amazing what's available to kids at those parties. Alcohol, drugs, sex...anything they want. I wasn't stupid enough to get caught up in all the excess, thank God, but what teenage girl isn't flattered when good-looking guys are hitting on them left and right? Especially after being invisible for years."

Jack continued to hypnotically knead the pad of my foot as I collected my thoughts. We sat quiet for a while, then I took a deep breath and continued.

"My father trusted that when his publicist or agent extended an invite to me, the events were safe for me to attend. He had no idea adolescent Hollywood parties are just as bad as the adult ones. And even though we were close, I wasn't going to tell him. I liked going to those places and figured that as long as I wasn't doing anything wrong, it was okay for me to be there. And for a while, it was.

"I had fun wearing the popular name brands, the sky-high heels, and hanging out with the pretty people. We moved to a nicer house in a new zip code and I changed school districts my Freshman year. I wasn't very popular at my old school, but at least the friends I had were real. I was too naive to know the people who flocked to me at my new school weren't. Most of them had parents in the business and we traveled in packs from party to party."

I looked at Jack and shook my head. "It still amazes me how much is available to these kids. They're still in high school and they have access to anything and everything. Nothing is off limits, and no one seems to care or even think it's strange. The rules just don't apply to them."

Jack continued to massage my feet, but tension radiated off him in waves. The man has a knack for reading me and he obviously knows something happened.

"So I spent the first couple years of high school attending upscale parties and dancing in the hottest clubs. My Junior year, there was a big party the day school let out for Christmas break. Looking back, I could see something different was happening, but that night I had no clue. I was drinking soda but halfway through the second, I felt sick. That's the last thing I remember until I woke up in the hospital the next day."

"Someone drugged you?"

"Nothing showed up in the blood tests, but that's the only explanation for my blackout. There are pictures of me at the party, but I don't remember any of it. Apparently I had sex too, but I don't remember that either."

"You were raped?" Those words came out as a growled whisper, the lack of volume not dulling their intensity.

"There was no sign of force, so it was never called that," I said. "And even if it was, it wouldn't matter. No one at that party would talk so it's not like whoever did it would ever be caught."

With a final squeeze, he let go of my foot and reached

for my hand then pulled me toward him. I shifted on the couch until my hip rested next to his. He removed my glasses and carefully set them on the end table then put his arm around my shoulders and tucked me against him until my cheek rested on his chest. His heart pounded against my ear as he squeezed me tight.

"I'm so sorry, honey." He kissed the top of my head and rubbed my back. "Were you okay?"

"Physically I was fine. I had bruises on my hip and shoulder from being dumped on my front lawn and I was sore from the sex, but there were no lingering issues. Mentally, I was a mess. I had no idea who'd drugged me and when I talked to my so-called friends, none of them had even thought to question my behavior that night. They thought it was funny and took plenty of pictures of me acting like a fool. Looking back, I'm pretty sure one of them did it because they'd been acting strange, like they were waiting for something to happen."

Jack's heartbeat had settled into a normal rhythm and I snuggled closer and buried my nose into his shirt, enjoying his amazing scent. Even after a day on the boat and at the beach, it's still there.

"I'm not even sure my father initially believed my story. I feel like he just thought I made some bad decisions and was afraid to tell him. But as the days went on, he realized something was seriously wrong because I barely got out of bed. When he talked to me about the party again, I repeated my story and told him I didn't want to go back to school. I wanted out of the whole Hollywood scene.

"By that time, the first couple Mac Flynn movies had been huge hits and my dad's star continued to rise. He'd been contracted to do two more movies, so obviously he wasn't leaving, and I'd never ask him to give up the dream he'd worked so hard to achieve. But that party really opened my eyes. Most of the people in my school were somehow connected to the entertainment industry and just used each other. One guy I dated for months stopped calling me after he got a part he wanted. Of course the only reason he got the part is because my father introduced him to some people. I didn't want to live like that. It's so shallow and isolating. My grandmother lived in Glen Lyon, a small town about an hour outside of Hollywood, not far from where I grew up. I asked if I could live with her and thankfully she was happy to let me."

"So you just disappeared?"

"Pretty much. Adams was my mom's maiden name, and my middle name, so I dropped the Diskin and became Hannah Adams. I went back to my old look, started the second half of Junior year at a new school, and no one was the wiser. My grandmother became my legal guardian so my dad never had to sign anything or be hands-on. And it was only for a year and a half. After that, I got swallowed up in the anonymous world of college where I could be whoever I wanted to be."

"Did you see your father at all?"

"He'd come visit and we'd go on vacation. We talked on the phone all the time. He even managed to attend both my graduations."

"Didn't he cause a riot?"

"No one even noticed him."

"How?"

"He grew a beard, dressed differently, kept a low profile. Most people recognize him by his voice, so as long as he

wasn't speaking, he was usually okay."

Often dubbed as the Irish Sam Elliott, people recognize my father's voice as much as they do his face. Over the years, he's perfected a variety of accents for when he wants to remain anonymous.

I pushed back to look at Jack. "Don't forget, he wasn't quite as famous then. I'm not sure he'd get away with it so easily now." I shrugged and rested my cheek back on his chest.

"So you were close?" I nodded. "What happened?"

"Growing up, I had a friend who lived next door to my grandmother named Melanie. Anytime I stayed there, we were inseparable. We even managed to stay close during the crazy Hollywood days. It was great when I moved in with my grandmother because we were together all the time, then we were roommates in college. After Granny Bea died my Sophomore year, I stayed with her family on breaks and they were really good to me. It was tough moving away after graduation, but I got offered a great job at a PR firm in South Carolina, so I took it and since that led to my current position, I'm glad I did. We kept in touch, vacationed together every year, and stayed as close as ever."

The last words came out as a hoarse whisper. I swallowed, but the lump in my throat wouldn't go away. Before I could stop them, all the emotions I've pushed down the past few months welled up like a tidal wave and I clutched Jack's waist as I sobbed against his chest. He rubbed my back in soothing motions as he kissed the top of my head and whispered sweet nothings.

When the storm passed, I took in deep breaths and let them out slowly to regulate my breathing. I moved my cheek against his T- shirt, trying to find a dry spot to rest against.

"Come here," Jack whispered. He placed his hands on my waist and pulled me across his lap, settling my butt onto his firm thighs. My head fit perfectly in the space between his neck and shoulder, as if it was made just for me. I sighed and snuggled into his embrace. His fingers stroked through my hair, the motion soothing the hurt I've bottled up for months. He kissed my forehead. "Better?"

I nodded and looked at him through teary eyelashes. "I'm sorry about that."

"Don't apologize." He massaged the back of my neck and I rested my head against him again, enjoying the comfort he offered. "You obviously needed to let all this out." He kissed the top of my head. "And I'm guessing there's more to the story."

"You haven't heard the best part," I said. "This past Christmas, my dad rented a cabin on Lake Ontario so we could spend the holidays together. He'd do that sometimes. Just rent a place somewhere out of the way so we could hang out and relax. We had a low-key holiday and a couple days after Christmas, Melanie showed up. I figured my father invited her to surprise me."

"That's the woman he was with tonight?"

"Yeah, Melanie Reade, my former best friend and soon to be step- mother," I said. "Turns out they've been involved for over a year now and she quit her job about nine months ago to travel with him as his assistant." I took in a shuddering breath and slowly let it out. "And it's not so much the fact that they're involved that has me so upset...although that's kind of messed up...it's that they lied to me for months. I regularly spoke to both of them, even saw them a few times, and neither said a thing."

"What made them decide to finally tell you?"

"She's pregnant. Due in July."

"Fuck."

Leave it to Jack to sum up this whole screwy situation with

one growled word. And with that one word, my hurt

faded away and the ridiculousness of it all bubbled up in me and erupted in a string of laughter. Not sexy little chuckles, but huge guffaws, complete with snorts. I don't know how long it lasted, but Jack held me until all the laughter faded and I rested against him, limp and exhausted with an aching belly.

"Thank you," I said.

"I'm not sure what I did, but you're welcome."

I shifted to straddle his lap and kissed his cheek. "You were here and you listened." Cupping his jaw, I stroked the soft stubble with my thumb. "I've kept all this to myself and for months it was like a hard ball of hurt wedged deep inside. I feel so much better now, and not just because I was able to talk to someone, it's because it's you."

I dropped my hand to his chest and traced the wet spot from my tears, trying to collect my thoughts. I didn't plan on sharing every emotion I'm feeling with him tonight, but that seems to be where I'm headed. I don't want to totally freak him out, but he has to know. He's said this thing between us doesn't have an expiration date, but that doesn't necessarily mean his feelings are the same as mine. And if that's the case, I have to know now.

"Hey, what's going on in that beautiful head?" He stroked the outside of my thighs. "Talk to me Hannah. Tell me what you're thinking."

His soft words urged me to meet his gaze.

"Jack, this whole thing between us is not what I expected it to be when it started. *You're* not what I expected."

"In a good way, I hope."

Even though the words were said lightheartedly, the look in his eyes told me my answer was important to him.

"I never expected this to be more than a good time.

We're both adults and I figured we were just exploring this sudden attraction the way grownups do. And despite the fact that I've always found you insanely attractive, I didn't know that was more than skin deep. I never thought you'd be so sweet and kind and considerate, or that I'd fall so hard so fast."

He cupped my ass and pulled me closer until our chests touched and we breathed the same air.

"I don't know why it took me a full decade to notice you like this, Hannah. Maybe I wasn't ready for you or maybe I just had my head up my ass." Those last words were said around a soft chuckle. "But now that I have, I want you to know that I'm all in. I'm not ready to put everything I'm feeling into words, so I'll use yours. I'm falling hard and fast for you, too." He kissed me softly, lingering for a moment before and resting his forehead against mine. "I'm here for you Hannah. I hope you know that." He kissed the tip of my nose and pulled back just enough to look into my eyes. "Just tell me what you need."

"Make me forget."

JACK

HANNAH'S WORDS made me feel like someone punched me in the gut. In all the years I've known this woman, I've never seen her any way but confident and in control. Now she's looking at me as though she may shatter at any moment and I'm the only one who can keep her together.

I'm touched. I'm humbled. And I'm gonna make her come so damn hard she'll be lucky to remember her own name.

Taking her mouth in a tongue-tangling kiss, I shifted forward on the couch, readjusted my grip on her ass, and stood. She wrapped her legs around my waist and held on while I walked the short distance to the bedroom.

Without releasing her mouth, I set Hannah on the bed and settled between her widespread thighs. Her moan vibrated against my chest as I pressed against her and deepened the kiss, giving her everything I have.

When we were both in danger of passing out from lack of oxygen, I ended the kiss, and dragged my mouth along the long column of her neck. She arched her back as I licked and nipped my way over her collarbone down to the sweet crease of her cleavage.

I shifted back just far enough to pull her shirt up and over her head then dragged her bra down until her nipples popped free. I teased first one then the other, moving back and forth between the two, teasing and sucking, until they tightened into hardened little buds.

I could do this forever, but her insistent thrusts against my rock-hard dick tells me she needs more. Without taking my mouth off her sweet skin, I kissed my way down and nipped at her navel before unbuttoning her shorts and revealing the baby blue lace beneath. I decided to leave her panties on and sat back on my knees to drag her shorts down her long legs. After tossing them on the floor, I leaned forward and kissed my way back up toward paradise. When I got to the juncture of her thighs, I rested my chin against her mound and looked up the expanse of her body.

"Hannah, look at me," I said. She slowly opened her eyes and blinked several times, most likely trying to bring me into focus. Without her glasses, she probably can't see me clearly, but I still want her eyes on me. "Watch."

I opened my mouth and sucked until I could taste her

sweetness through the lace. She arched and pushed herself closer against my mouth, but never once closed her eyes or looked away. Slipping my tongue between her folds, I licked and laved her clit, using the soft lace to increase the sensation.

"Jack." My name came out on a hoarse plea.

As much as I'd love to tease her all night, I know she needs the release. I moved her panties to the side thrust two fingers inside.

"Mmm, you're so damn wet."

With my gaze locked on hers, I licked at the skin I'd revealed, lapping up her sweetness. Curling my fingers slightly, I stroked her deep inside and sucked on her clit. That's all it took to push her over the edge.

I stayed with her, offering soothing kisses and sweet words until her body sagged against the bed, relaxed and replete. Her inner muscles grabbed at my fingers as I pulled them free and she watched as I slowly slid her panties down and off.

Holding them up, I said, "I know I've mentioned this before, but I really like your taste in underwear." After tossing the scrap of lace to the floor, I reached behind her back and released the clasp of her bra. Holding it up to emphasize my words, I said, "Every time I see you, I wonder what you're wearing under your professional clothing. It's a little distracting."

I threw it in the direction of its mate and slid up the bed until I rested next to her.

She shifted onto her knees and her eyes took a lazy tour of my body.

"How is it that you always manage to get me naked and stay fully clothed?" she asked.

"Just lucky I guess."

Placing her hands on my waist, she dragged them up my

chest, taking my T-shirt along for the ride. I lifted my shoulders and yanked it over my head before resting back against the pillows.

"Better?"

She nodded and ran her soft hands over my pecs and down my abs. Before she could get any ideas, I reached down to intertwine my fingers with hers and pulled her forward. Her tight nipples dragged against my chest as I took her mouth in a kiss that would hopefully leave no doubt in her mind that I'm not done with her. One orgasm isn't nearly enough to distract her from what's going on with her father.

Ending the kiss, I looked into her glazed eyes, happy to see they looked less troubled than before. But she still needs more. I need to give her more.

"Come here." I wrapped my hands around her elbows and lifted her until she straddled my chest. Hannah started to shift back and I grabbed her ass to hold her in place. "Not that way," I said and nudged her forward. Her eyes widened when she realized my intent and I couldn't hold back my smile.

"Jack, I can't do that." Somehow her words came out as both a whisper and a shriek.

"Sure you can."

I shifted my shoulders down until they rested flat on the bed with my head raised slightly on the pillow. I pulled her forward until her knees tipped over my shoulders and her calves straddled my biceps. The muscles in her thighs felt rock hard against my chest as she held herself back. Mere inches from my face, the sweet scent of her release made my mouth water. I wanted to taste her more than anything but I need to make sure that, despite her words, she's okay with this.

Looking up at her face, I watched her nostrils flare with her deep breath then she licked her lips as she met my gaze.

"Just relax," I said around a small smile.

She nodded and the corner of her mouth curled slightly as some of the tension left her thighs, putting heaven within reach of my tongue. I licked her from back to front, lingering on the still- distended nub at every pass. Bending my elbows, I rested my hands on her hips and tilted them forward allowing me to give her a good tongue fucking.

Hannah leaned back and rested her hands on my waist, thrusting herself into my face, opening her fully to me.

Looking up, I watched a trickle of sweat run from her neck and down the middle of her chest until it absorbed into her skin. Her tight nipples rose and fell with every panting breath she took. The look of pure bliss on her face made me want to beat my chest like a caveman, but I still have work to do here.

I licked, laved, and sucked, feasting on her until one orgasm crashed through her, then I kept it up until another followed.

"Jack!"

Hannah's screech echoed through the room as she leaned forward and smacked her palms against the wall behind my head. Her new position put her clit in the perfect position. I tickled it with the tip of my tongue then nibbled before fully drawing it into my mouth and sucking.

Hannah's legs trembled with another orgasm and I heard her hands sliding down the wall as more of her body weight settled against me. I pulled her down until her head rested against my chest and her hot heat teased my dick through my shorts. He's not happy about being left out of the action, but tonight isn't about him.

I ran my hand up and down her back, enjoying the feel of her silky skin. Her breathing slowed and I thought she'd fallen asleep so she surprised me when she sat up and shifted down my legs. Gripping me through my shorts, she slowly stroked.

"We should do something about this," she said. "It can't be very comfortable."

"I'm fine," I said. Maybe I should take up acting because that actually sounded convincing.

She unbuttoned my shorts then slid both them and my boxer briefs down my legs. I kicked them off and reached for Hannah. Shaking her head, she tucked her hair behind her ear then leaned forward and dragged her tongue along my throbbing erection, from base to tip before swirling it around and sucking at the head, pushing me dangerously close to the edge.

"Hannah." My voice came out as a strangled croak.

She looked up at me through her lashes then slowly slid down, taking me all the way to the back of her throat. I closed my eyes and focused on breathing in an attempt to get myself under control. If Hannah stopped what she was doing, I might have been successful, but she didn't. She kept moving up and down in a slow rhythm, taking me deeper with every pass.

"Come here," I growled and grabbed her shoulders to pull her away.

Tossing Hannah back onto the pillows, I settled between her thighs, and pressed my lips against hers. Our tongues thrust and tangled and I opened my mouth wider, deepening the kiss, taking and giving and losing myself in her sweetness.

Hannah shifted, dragging her hot, wet core against my now- throbbing erection. I groaned against her mouth and pulled back, taking her bottom lip between my teeth and giving it a tug before releasing it and looking down at the beautiful woman beneath me.

"You're killing me, you know that?" Her sly smile didn't look the least bit apologetic. "The condoms are in the nightstand on the other side of the bed." I gave her a quick kiss. "I'll be right back." She twisted her leg around my waist, holding me in place. "Hannah?"

Looking away, she licked her lips and swallowed before meeting my gaze again.

"You don't have to." I raised my brow, silently asking her to explain. "You don't have to get a condom. I'm on the pill and we already had that one issue and..." She trailed off and shook her head. "Nevermind, it was stupid."

This isn't the first time I've had a woman offer to skip the condom, but it's the first time I'm seriously considering accepting. I cupped her jaw and stroked her cheek, drawing her eyes back toward me.

"It's not stupid, but it is a big step." I kissed the tip of her nose. "Are you sure?"

The certainty in her big brown eyes as she nodded tugged at something deep inside me. I've *never* had sex without a condom and more than anything I want to experience it for the first time, right now, with this amazing woman.

I reached down and positioned myself at her entrance then thrust forward, filling her in one long stroke, and froze.

"Holy fuck." She's so tight and wet, even baseball stats aren't going to slow this down. "Hannah, I'm not gonna last very long here. You feel too fucking good."

She dragged her leg further up my hip, opening herself more and pulling me deeper inside.

"Mmm, you feel amazing," she said.

Once I mustered a semblance of control, I pulled out slowly then pushed in and repeated the motion, settling into a comfortable rhythm. Her inner muscles gripped and tightened around me every time I retreated, bringing me closer and closer to the edge.

Knowing I wouldn't last much longer, I shifted onto my knees, creating a tiny gap between us and reached down to stroke her clit.

"Oh God! Jack! I can't...I..."

She tightened with every pass of my finger and when I pinched the hard bud between my thumb and forefinger, her muscles clamped down on me over and over, and for the first time in my life, I came inside a woman with nothing between us. I pulsed between her legs, drawing out the sensation, enjoying the aftershocks.

Once I caught my breath, I pushed back and looked down at Hannah. Her blissful smile and glowing cheeks gave me a sense of inner peace I've never felt before. I slowly withdrew and gave her a small kiss.

"I'll be right back."

In the bathroom I wet a washcloth, then studied myself in the mirror as I cleaned myself off. I don't know what I was expecting to see, but I don't look any different. But I have to admit, I feel different. Peaceful. Content. Happy. I don't know. All three, I suppose. The antsy feeling that's been beneath the surface as long as I can remember is noticeably absent at the moment.

I shook my head and ran the washcloth under warm water before ringing it out. Grabbing a towel, I walked back into the bedroom and found Hannah sound asleep. I sat on the edge of the bed and kissed her forehead, then ran the washcloth between her folds and along her inner thighs. She thrust into my hand as I washed then dried her off, but didn't wake.

Between the long day, running into her father, and four orgasms, she's probably down for the count. I stood and threw the washcloth toward the bathroom and heard it land on the tile floor with a splat. Climbing into the other side of the bed, I pulled Hannah back against my chest, wrapped my arm around her waist, and tucked my hand between her breasts.

I relaxed and matched my breathing to hers, pushing everything I'd learned today out of my mind until only one thought existed. Before I drifted off to sleep, I muttered it out loud.

"Hannah Adams, what are you doing to me?"

Chapter Twenty-Six

HANNAH

THE SCENT of coffee and frying bacon tickled my nose and brought me fully awake. My muscles protested as I rolled over and sat on the edge of the bed. We'd gotten back to St. Pete yesterday with just enough time for me to get to work at a decent hour. The Waves lost by one run, but that didn't dim Jack's enthusiasm in the bedroom afterwards.

I'd asked Jack to make me forget, and for the past couple nights he'd done that and more. I'm not sure if I fell asleep or passed out after that last orgasm. I half woke at some point during the night and snuggled further back against Jack's chest before drifting off again as he tightened his hold on me. But other than that, I slept like the dead.

I stood and stretched, working out the kinks. Sex with Jack is definitely a full-body workout. Not that I'm complaining. Padding to the bathroom, I took care of business, then studied my blurry reflection in the mirror as I brushed my teeth. My breasts are sporting light whisker burns and Jack left a love bite on my right hip. The man does like to leave his mark on me, but as long as they're in discreet places, I don't mind. In fact, I kind of like it.

Back in the bedroom, I collected my clothing from the floor, shook out the wrinkles, and decided not to get fully dressed just yet. After slipping into my panties, I pulled Jack's discarded T-shirt over my head instead and followed the delicious smells to the kitchen. I grabbed my glasses off the end table where Jack had placed them last night and slipped them on, bringing the room into focus.

Speaking of delicious. Standing at the stove with a spatula in hand, wearing only a pair of jogging shorts riding low on his hips, Jack looks good enough to eat.

Something must have alerted him to my presence, because he quickly turned his head. The naughty smile he flashed not only upped his yumminess factor, it also told me he'd caught me shamelessly ogling him and didn't mind one bit.

"Good morning," he said, then turned his attention back to the stove. I watched him expertly flip four eggs in turn. "Have a seat, I'll bring your plate over in a minute."

I sat at the table and took a sip of orange juice he'd already placed on the table. The cool drink soothed my throat, that was a little sore from all the panting and screaming I did last night.

"How'd you sleep?"

He filled two plates with bacon and toast, then picked up the pan and tipped it, somehow managing to slip two eggs onto one plate then the remaining two on the other. His kitchen skills astound me.

"I'm not sure if I slept or died," I said.

Picking up both plates with one hand, he snagged the handles of two coffee mugs with the other and walked in my direction. His shorts slipped lower, fully revealing the cut of his hips. As he placed a plate in front of me, I resisted the urge to turn my head and run my tongue along the sexy V-line in front of me. I'm sure Jack wouldn't mind, but I have to go to my hotel and change before work, and he has a game later, so it's better to hold off on any licking until later.

"Yeah, you kind of passed out." He sat across from me and picked up a strip of bacon. "But you needed it." He shoved the entire piece into his mouth, chewed, swallowed, and said, "How do you feel today?"

"Good." I picked up my fork and dragged it through the perfectly cooked, over-easy eggs, and watched the runny yolk seep out. "Thank you for being there for me the last couple nights."

Jack didn't say a word as he chewed his toast but he didn't have to. His sweet smile and warm look said everything. We ate in silence for a while, the perfectly cooked meal quieting my rumbling stomach. I don't normally even eat breakfast, but it seems like when I'm with this man, all my appetites are bigger.

He pushed his empty plate toward the center of the table and sat back in the chair, coffee in hand.

"Any idea what you want to do now?" he asked. "About your father, I mean."

I put down my fork and shrugged. "I told him I'd call him, and I know if I don't, he'll come find me."

"If you're not ready, I'll talk to him and explain that if you want me to."

Jack's image blurred and I blinked the tears away.

"Thank you." I cleared my throat. "Thank you for offering, but I have to deal with this eventually. I'd really like it if you'd be there when I do talk to him though. If not in on the conversation, at least close by."

"If you're sure that's what you want, I'll be there," he said.

I dragged my toast through a pool of yolk. "He said he'd come up to St. Pete."

"You can meet him here if you'd like."

"Are you sure?"

He nodded. "You can't meet him in public and it's more

private here than at the team hotel."

"That'd be great. Will tomorrow after the game work for you if he's available?"

"I'll make whatever time you set up work."

"I really can't thank you enough," I said. "For just being here.

Talking about it the past couple nights really did help. I still find the fact that my father knocked up my best friend a little icky, but they're both adults." I flashed him a small smile. "Something you said the other night helped me with that." His right brow rose in that sexy way prompting me to explain. "You said that you didn't know why it took you ten years to notice me this way. Maybe it's the same thing with my dad and Melanie. Kind of like us, maybe it just happened."

"You're amazing, you know that?"

"You're kind of great yourself."

He met my gaze and smiled, the elusive dimple popping out on his right cheek. My lady parts started to tingle and I decided it was time to get out of here before I end up jumping his bones. I blinked, breaking the sizzling connection and pushed back from the table.

"I'd better get going. I have to go to my hotel to shower and change. I also want to call my dad before heading to the park."

I finished my coffee in one long gulp and placed the mug on my plate and reached for Jack's.

"I got it," he said.

"You cooked. I'll clean."

Jack stood, took my plate, and put it back on the table. Taking my hand in his, he placed a kiss in the center of my palm before resting it on his shoulder. He wrapped his hands around my waist and tugged gently, forcing me to take a small step forward, and rewarded me with a small kiss.

"Go take care of whatever you have to so you can get to work. I'll clean up here. I'm sure you're mentally freaking out because you weren't at the stadium at the crack of dawn."

"Come on, I'm not that bad."

"That's debatable." He tilted his head slightly to the side, making him look even more adorable. "But before you go, I wanted to discuss something you said the other night."

"What's that?"

"I didn't want to ask at the time because you were so upset." The teasing glint in his eyes didn't quite prepare me for his words. "But I'd like to find out a little more about how *insanely attractive* you've found me for years."

Oh God, I did say that. His low chuckle told me that once again, he could read my thoughts.

"Doesn't your ego get stroked enough by all your adoring fans? If I start chiming in, your head will get too big for your helmet."

After slowly removing my glasses, I watched his smile widen before he took my mouth in a hot kiss that was in no way tamed by its brevity.

"To answer your question, now that we've gotten to know

each other a little better, you should realize that I'm not really affected by ego stroking or what people think about me." He kissed me softly and rested his forehead against mine and closed his eyes. "Unless I really care about them." His lashes tickled mine when he reopened them and he pulled back just enough to meet my gaze with hazel-green eyes. "And you are most definitely in the people I care about category."

I've always agreed with Alice in Wonderland when she said the falling isn't bad, it's the landing you have to be concerned about. And for weeks now, I've enjoyed every second of falling for Jack, that fear of landing always in the back of my mind. But now that I've ended up snug and secure in his arms, totally, madly, and completely in love with him, I can't remember what I was so afraid of.

JACK

I TUCKED my shirt in and took one last look around the condo. It'll do, I guess. I usually keep things pretty neat, but I arranged to have someone come in to clean earlier today to make sure it passes the white glove test.

Settling onto the couch, I put my feet up on the coffee table and waited for Hannah. I'd high-tailed it here after the game to make sure everything was in order. She shouldn't be too far behind me.

I'm thirty-four years old and am about to meet the parent of someone I'm dating for the first time in my life. Back in high school, I knew most of the parents of the girls I went to school with, so I never had to do the whole formal introduction thing. After that, meeting the parents would never have been a part of the kind of relationships I was involved in.

I don't know if I would have been more or less nervous if this had happened years ago. Then again, I suppose age isn't really a factor. Until now, I've never been in a relationship with someone I cared enough about that I wanted to both meet and impress her family.

But Hannah is different. This whole thing between us is different. And of course the fact that her father is one of the biggest movie stars on the planet isn't doing anything to calm my nerves. I'm not often star struck, but I am a huge Mac Flynn fan and today may have me as tongue-tied as the day I met Nomar Garciaparra for the first time. Thankfully I hadn't made a huge fool of myself then and hopefully the same will be true today.

A beeping sound from the keypad outside pulled me from my thoughts. I looked over my shoulder and watched Hannah walk through the door and close it behind her.

"Hey," she said as she set her purse in its usual spot on the stool at the kitchen counter.

In the past, anytime any woman I was spending time with got too familiar in my space, I'd make it clear they needed to stop. But the fact that she's comfortable here has me wondering how she'll make her mark in my real home when we get home. Time will tell.

She sat next to me and gave me a small kiss.

"You look nice," she said taking in my khaki pants and blue and white-checked button-down shirt. I even put on my good Sperrys for the occasion.

"Thanks."

"Great game today, by the way. How's your hand?"

An inside fastball caught me on the back of my left hand in the sixth inning. I held it out for Hannah to inspect. Right now, it's swollen and red, but experience has taught me that it will be bruised and stiff as hell tomorrow.

She placed a gentle kiss on the injury and said, "Shouldn't you have ice on it?"

I definitely should, but I don't want to greet Aaran Diskin that way.

"I'll wrap an ice pack on it later."

Hannah opened her mouth to speak, but a knock sounded at the door before she got any words out. Her eyes widened and filled with so many emotions, I was still sorting through them when I heard a second knock.

"I better let him in before he breaks the door down," I said. "I've seen him do it."

That brought a smile to her face, erasing her panicked look.

I stood and walked to the door then took in a deep breath and let it out before pulling it open. The man on the other side of the threshold looked me up and down with his world-famous blue eyes before meeting my gaze.

"I'm lookin' fer Hannah."

Nodding, I stepped to the side and opened the door wider. "Come in, sir." I held out my right hand. "We didn't meet formally at Arnie's. I'm Jack Reagan."

"I know who ya are."

Logically, I know this man is Hannah's father, but with his icy glare and bone-crushing handshake, I had to remind myself that Mac Flynn wasn't here to kick my ass.

"Daddy."

With that one word, the man in front of me transformed from a terrifying intelligence agent ready to incapacitate me with his pinky into a nervous father, unsure of his place in his daughter's life. He stepped around me and slowly walked toward Hannah, looking equal parts nervous and excited. She took a small step toward him and that's all it took to break down the wall that's kept them apart for months.

He took two giant steps and pulled her into his embrace. She wrapped her arms around his neck and buried her face in his chest, and they stood there holding each other.

I felt like a voyeur, watching the intimate scene play out, but I couldn't look away. My dad and I see each other a couple times a year and there's never this kind of emotion when we meet. Then again, in order to show emotion, you have to actually give a shit, and my father hasn't cared about anything since my mother died. Including me.

Before I could spiral down that depressing rabbit hole, Hannah pulled back and wiped her eyes. Her father did the same.

"Ah darlin, I missed ya so much," he said. "I know why ye stayed away, but I'm hopin' we can work this out, that ye'll let me explain." He shifted his eyes to me then back to Hannah. "In private."

Hannah looked in my direction and held out her hand. That was enough of an invitation for me. I walked to her side and wrapped my fingers around hers.

Her father looked at our joined hands and met Hannah's gaze. "So it's like that, is it?"

She looked up at me and smiled. "It's like that."

"All right then," he said.

I squeezed Hannah's hand. "Why don't you two get settled and I'll go grab some drinks?" She nodded and sat down on the couch. I looked at Aaran. "Sir, would you like water, sweet tea, or beer?"

He sat on the chair and said, "I wouldn't say no to a beer."

I looked back at Hannah and raised my brow. She

nodded and I walked into the kitchen, grabbed three bottles of Sam Adams off the shelf, and opened them in turn. When I returned to the living room, they were just sitting there looking at each other, the love between them obvious.

I handed them each a bottle before sitting next to Hannah. She took a long drink before leaning forward and setting it on the coffee table.

Leaning her elbows on her knees, she said, "I'm sorry I haven't called, but it took me a long time to figure out how I feel about this whole thing." She sat back and pulled my hand into her lap, intertwining her fingers with mine. "Honestly, I avoided thinking about it."

"I know it must a been a shock when we told ya," Aaran said. "Ya know there have been women since your ma...maybe too many women. But this is different. Melanie and me love each other. That's one of the reasons we waited so long to say somethin'. We wanted to make sure it was real before upsetting ya."

Hannah slowly nodded. "And after being together over a year and having a baby on the way, you're finally sure?"

"I admit we waited too long to tell ya, but with my filmin' schedule, time just passed us by."

She tightened her fingers around mine, and I stroked the back of her hand with my thumb, soothing her the only way I could at the moment.

"I've come to terms with the fact that my father and best friend are intimately involved. I understand that things just happen sometimes. That you can know someone for a long time and then all of a sudden notice them in a different way." She looked up at me and smiled before turning her attention back to her father. "I just can't understand why you both lied to me about this for so long. For over a year, we spoke regularly, spent holidays with each other, and went on vacations together and neither of you mentioned a thing." She sniffed and wiped a tear from her cheek. "I spent time with both of you at Thanksgiving, and she was already pregnant and neither of you said a thing. Not about the baby and not even about the fact that she'd quit her job to work as your assistant."

With Hannah's every word, her father seemed to shrink into his chair, but his gaze never left his daughter. It's obvious he knows he screwed up, but he seems willing to do whatever it takes to repair their relationship.

"Darlin' I'm sorry. I should a told ya sooner, but I was a coward," he said. "Don't blame Melanie. She wanted ta tell ya long ago, but I held her off. I was afraid of what ya would think, how ye'd react. I was wrong. We've always been honest and this should a been the same. I just hope ya can forgive me. I miss ya, baby girl."

I turned my attention to Hannah, giving Aaron some privacy as he blinked tears from his eyes. Her eyes glistened as she looked at me, but she seemed to be at peace. I squeezed her hand and leaned down to whisper in her ear.

"I'm going to Dan's so you two can have some privacy." I kissed her cheek. "Text if you need me." Standing, I approached her father and held out my hand. "Sir, it was nice meeting you. I'm a big fan of both your work and your daughter."

He stood and shook my hand, less aggressively than he had upon arrival.

"Thank ya. I'm a fan of your work as well. Hopefully we'll be gettin' together again so I can ask ya some things about the game."

"Anytime."

I closed the door behind me and walked to Dan's condo. Normally I'd just barge in, but with Sabrina in residence, I knocked. The woman in question opened the door a few seconds later.

"Hey Jack."

I smiled. "Mind if I hang here for a little bit?"

She opened the door wider. "Not at all." Closing the door,

she followed me to the living room. "Lexi is with the Kasprzyks. She'll be sorry she missed you."

"If I'm interrupting something, I can find somewhere else to go."

"You're good," Dan said as he pushed up into a sitting position on the couch.

Sabrina curled up next to him, and I sank into the leather recliner. They both looked at me expectantly.

"What?" I said.

"We've been dying to find out what's going on. Hannah's father is Mac Flynn?" Sabrina practically squealed the last two words. "How is that even possible? Did you know? Are they close?"

Dan kissed her forehead. "Baby, you should probably let him answer one question before you pile on more."

"Sorry," she said. "Do you need me to repeat the questions?"

"I think I'm good," I said around a chuckle. "Hannah's father is Aaran Diskin. The character he plays is Mac Flynn," I repeated the words Hannah said to me. "She told me that after the Mac Flynn movies became popular, she didn't like the whole Hollywood lifestyle, so she went to live with her grandmother and dropped his last name, using her middle name instead, which also happens to be her mother's maiden name. It surprises me that no one seems to know about their relationship, but I guess it's not an interesting enough story for them to dig up. I found out at

Arnie's, the same time as you. And they've had some issues the past few months, but yes, they're close."

Sabrina smiled. "Well done. I think you answered everything I asked."

"They're at my place getting their relationship in order right now."

"At your place?" Dan asked at the same time Sabrina squealed, "He's in this building?"

"They can't exactly meet in public and this building is more private than the team hotel," I said. "Things were getting pretty intense so I wanted to give them some privacy. I figured I'd come here so I'm close in case Hannah needs me."

They both smiled at me. Not small, polite smiles, but huge dopey ones.

"Cut it out," I said. "You look like idiots sitting there with those goofy smiles."

"I'm sorry," Sabrina said. "It's just nice watching you finally spend time with someone who makes you happy."

I could have called Sabrina out on the fact that she hasn't been around long enough to witness enough of my relationships to judge. But I didn't because for one, she was with Dan during the end of my days with Cindy and of course, she's had a front-row seat for the aftermath of that debacle. And two, I love her like a sister, and I know she means well.

"Hannah is great and I enjoy spending time with her." Christ, I sound like I'm answering an interview question. I decided to amend my answer. "I really like her and want to see where this goes."

Chapter Twenty-Seven

HANNAH

I TOSSED my hair dryer into my suitcase and zipped it closed. Looking around the room one last time, I made sure I wasn't leaving anything behind. It's amazing how much I settled into this place in such a short time.

When Mr. Hanover said he wanted me to come down to spring training, I'll admit I was less than thrilled. Little did I know how much this whole experience would change my life. There had been a few sparks flying between Jack and me back home, but I'm not sure anything would have happened between us there.

I'd been told things are more relaxed down here, but until I experienced it, I didn't understand. I live in a laid-back beach town, but St. Pete takes chill to a whole other level.

The events I had Jack attend were so casual, I think it allowed both of us to really relax. Being down here also allowed me to have groups come to the stadium on short notice, so we didn't have to actually go out as much as I'd initially thought. Plus being in-house gave Mr. Hanover a chance to see his plan in action.

Speaking of plans. I totally changed mine when Jack asked me to drive home with him instead of flying back. We've spent a lot of time together recently, but nine hours in a car should let us know if we're truly compatible.

We're also meeting up with my dad and Melanie for lunch along the way. They're staying a couple hours up the coast from St. Pete and we're hooking up at a beach shack my dad found. He's the master of discovering out of the way places...both to stay and hang out. We've never vacationed or dined where people go to see and be seen. It's always somewhere off the beaten path, which works for me.

After that initial meeting with my father at Jack's condo, I got together with him and Melanie to talk some more. I still feel a little awkward around them...after all, having your dad knock up your best friend is definitely the stuff of soap operas...but I think we'll be okay in the long run.

Besides the fact she's my best friend, Melanie will be giving birth to the sibling I've always wanted. I would have liked to have had said sibling prior to my third decade of life, but I guess you can't always plan these things.

My cell sounded just as I plopped the last of my things in front of the door. I couldn't stop the smile that crossed my face at the sight of Jack's number on the screen.

"Hey," I said.

"Hey yourself." Mmm, just the sound of his voice makes me tingle.

"All set?"

"I just gave the room a last look. I'm all ready."

"I'll come there and load your stuff into my truck, then we'll head to the rental place to drop off your car."

We had this discussion last night. His sense of chivalry or whatever you want to call it won't allow him to let me load the car myself and meet him at the car rental place. My fear that all the rookies will see Jack and me together makes me want to keep him as far away from here as possible.

"I can load up myself and just meet you there."

Silence zinged between us for what seemed like an eternity. I'm sure the little noises I did hear were his teeth grinding. I don't want to spend nine hours in the car with a hostile driver.

"I'll be here waiting."

"See you in ten minutes."

True to his word, Jack stood outside my door ten minutes later, looking amazing in khaki shorts, a white polo shirt, and his favorite Sperrys. Yes, I can tell them apart from the rest.

He stepped inside and slipped his Ray Bans to the top of his head before wrapping his hands around my waist and pulling me forward until I stood flush against him. Spinning me around, he pushed me back against the door and proceeded to kiss me until I barely knew my own name.

His lips teased and tasted, his tongue thrust and tangled, and I followed his lead, taking what he offered and giving back what I could. He rocked against me and I wrapped my right leg around his hip to hold him tight so I could rub against his hard length.

Jack squeezed my ass, holding me still and slowly ended the kiss.

"You erase every bit of my self-control."

I'd be lying if I said that statement didn't give my self-confidence a big boost. Making a man like Jack Reagan lose control is quite a feat.

"Sorry." I raised my voice slightly at the end of the word making it sound more like a question.

He slowly dragged his fingers up my side, over my breast, and cupped the back of my neck. His thumb stroked over my jaw and caressed my cheek.

"I don't think you are," he said around a sweet smile. "I think you enjoy it."

"Well you do the same thing to me, so I guess we're even."

His intense gaze met mine, seeming to search for the truth of my words. The man has to realize the reaction I have to him is unique. As usual he read my mind. A slow, sexy smile spread across his face and that damn dimple peeked out, making my knees weak.

We just stood there, smiling at each other for I don't know how long.

"Hannah, I —"

Jack looked away for a second before meeting my gaze again. He kissed me and straightened, his fingers slowly trailing along my neck as he pulled his hand away. Stepping back, he cleared his throat and said, "I think we better head out so we're not late meeting your father."

JACK

HANNAH WATCHED the scenery pass as I navigated along the coast. I'd decided to drive to spring training this year, figuring the quiet time would help clear my head. Nothing gets my mind straight better than some windshield time and good tunes. And the ride down had done just that. I was able to mentally sort out some stuff and cool off the anger simmering beneath the surface.

The whole book thing had pissed me off more than I wanted to admit to anyone. I've always been honest with the women I've gotten involved with right from the start and treated them well during our time together. Only one relationship ended badly, and that was with Cindy.

As the end of last season neared, she started acting more clingy and erratic...two things that drive me totally insane. So even if I was inclined to continue the relationship, her behavior would have changed my mind.

And considering the timing of the book, she obviously had the deal before things ended between us. It just really sucks. No one would want a book out there spilling all kinds of private details about their life. Just because my job puts me in the public eye doesn't make me any different.

I glanced at Hannah and couldn't help but smile. Our relationship is the one good thing that came out of this whole book debacle. If we weren't forced to spend so much time together, I'm not sure I would have ever noticed her as anything more than a kickass PR person. And that would have been sad.

For the first time in my life, I'm in what people would consider a real relationship and I really like it. I really like her. The fact that I asked her to join me on the drive home shows just how much. There are very few people I'd want sitting next to me on a long car ride.

I shifted my eyes her way again and found Hannah watching me. At least I assume she's looking at me. I can't actually see her eyes through the dark lenses but her head is turned in my direction.

"You okay over there?" I asked.

She nodded. "This is a really good playlist," she said as The Outfield ended and the Eagles began.

"It's a 70's and 80's mix I think is perfect for road trips."

"It definitely is." She looked down at her lap and toyed with the hem of her shorts before turning back toward me. Shifting her glasses up higher on the bridge of her nose, she said, "So, we're almost a couple hours in now. Do you regret inviting me along yet?"

"Not at all."

"You sure?"

I took my eyes off the road long enough to look her in the eye. Well, look her in the eye as much as I can considering both of us are wearing sunglasses.

"I'm sure." I turned my attention back toward the road then chuckled with the thought that entered my head. "What if I wasn't sure? Would you just have me pull over and dump you on the side of the road?"

"Hopefully you'd at least be willing to suffer my presence a little longer so I can meet up with my dad."

"Just curious. I don't plan on dumping you anywhere," I said. "But seriously, I'm glad you agreed to come with me. This is nice. Different, but nice."

"Different?"

"I don't normally take passengers on road trips, so this is a whole experience for me. But that's par for the course where you're concerned."

I reached over and squeezed her hand, then laced my fingers with hers. She shifted in her seat, sitting up straighter, her lips curled into a small smile. I've told her she's different enough times now that she obviously believes it. What I haven't said are those three little words that almost slipped out earlier. Thankfully I'd stopped myself. I have no doubt that my feelings for Hannah are real, but I'm not sure I'm ready to put that out there just yet. Especially not before we're trapped in a car together for hours.

What I've just said has made things feel kind of intense. Time to lighten it up a bit.

"Can I ask you something?"

"Sure."

"How many pair of glasses do you own?"

She burst out laughing.

"What's so funny?"

Settling her head against the headrest, she shifted onto her hip and crossed her right leg over her left. Our joined hands rested in her lap as her body turned slightly in my direction.

"I thought you were going to ask something serious."

"I am serious. I've known you for years and don't think I've seen you wear the same pair more than once."

"That's a bit of an exaggeration, don't you think?"

"Not much of one."

"It has to be. I only have 126 pairs."

"Only?"

"I know it's a lot, but it's kind of an addiction." She shrugged. "There are worse things."

"True," I said. "How did your little addiction start?"

"Like many people before me, I fell during my Hollywood days," she said. "When my dad's agent had me made over, the stylist wanted me to switch to contacts, but I have an astigmatism and they didn't sit right and bothered my eyes. She suggested the funky frames and got me started with my first ten pairs." She tapped the arm of the transparent frames with pink polka dots with her index finger. "These are a pair of the originals. I've have the prescription updated when necessary and just recently put in transition lenses so I can use them as sunglasses."

"So those are fifteen years old?"

"Something like that." She shrugged. "Through the years I've gotten rid of a few frames that have broken or are uncomfortable, but for the most part, I just update the lenses when I need to and keep them in my collection. Insurance pays for new frames every couple years and there's a consignment shop near the stadium where people bring old glasses and sunglasses to sell, especially designer ones. It's amazing how many I've accumulated over the years."

Looking down, she stroked the back of my hand with her thumb. The GPS directed me to take the exit a mile down the road, and we drove in silence until I did just that.

"The glasses are the one thing I kept of those Hollywood days," she said. "I ditched the fake eyelashes, hair extensions, sky-high heels, and fancy clothes. But the glasses quickly became part of me and I didn't want to let them go."

"They definitely suit you," I said. "Recently, I've found myself trying to guess what color you'll have on every day."

"Really?"

I shrugged. "Sad but true."

"Have you ever been right?"

"Not once."

"Glad I can keep you guessing about something."

"Oh, you keep me guessing about a lot of things."

"Me?"

I thought about my response as I listened to the GPS and

followed the left fork of the road.

"Why do you find that so surprising?"

"I'm just plain Hannah Adams," she said. "There's nothing

surprising here."

I took the next right into the parking lot of a shack of a restaurant with a sign out front boasting ice cold beer and the best conch fritters in the state. Extracting my hand from Hannah's, I pulled into a parking space and shifted the car into park. Unfastening both my seat belt and hers, I shifted in my seat and cupped her cheek.

"Let's get one thing straight. You're not *just plain Hannah Adams*." I brushed my lips against hers. "You're amazing."

Chapter Twenty-Eight

HANNAH

I PRACTICALLY FLOATED across the parking lot and through the door of the restaurant. Jack says the sweetest things and it's amazing how he makes me feel with his words or even just a look. He keeps telling me this is all new to him and I have no reason to doubt that. It's new to me, too.

It took my eyes a few seconds to adjust to the dim interior, but I eventually spotted my father and Melanie seated across the room, his arm draped across the back of her chair, their heads tipped together as they talked. Jack bumped into me from behind as I hesitated in the doorway. His fingers trailed down my arm and he squeezed my hand.

"You okay?"

I nodded and glanced over my shoulder at him. "It's still a bit of a shock to see them together like this."

"I can imagine," he said. "Just say the word when you

want to leave." He pressed a kiss against my forehead. "I'll follow your lead."

"There ye are." My father's voice boomed from across the room. Jack stepped next to me and wrapped his arm around my waist then led me across the room. I reluctantly pulled away from him and stepped toward my father, who stood to hug me.

"I'm happy yer here, darlin'." He pulled back to look at me.

I nodded and swallowed the lump in my throat, then stepped back. Out of the corner of my eye, I saw Melanie watching us from the edge of her seat.

"Hi Mel."

I leaned down to give her an awkward hug. I'm trying to move forward so things can get back to normal between us, but it's not easy. We may not be blood related, but I always considered Melanie my sister. And now she's sitting here, pregnant with my little brother or sister. Before my thoughts could fall down that rabbit hole and ruin the mood, my father settled back into his seat.

"Sit," he said.

Jack pulled the chair on the other side of Melanie away from the table and waited for me to sit before taking the space between my father and me.

"So are ya ready fer the season?" my father asked Jack.

"Yes, sir."

"Think ye'll win it this year?"

Before Jack could answer, the waitress approached the table with two glasses of water in one hand and menus in the other. After placing the glasses in front of Jack and me and handing us each a menu, she asked if Jack and I wanted anything to drink besides water, directing our attention to the drink and draft list above the bar.

"I don't want a drink," I said. "What do you have besides soda?"

"Sweet tea and lemonade."

"The lemonade is amazing," Melanie said, holding her glass out to me. "It tastes just like my grandmother's."

Before I could overthink it, I took a sip of Melanie's lemonade. "I'll have a glass of lemonade," I said, setting her glass back on the table.

"Make that two," Jack said.

"I'll go get those and give you some time to look at the menu," the waitress said.

We sat quietly, perusing the menu. Everything looked so amazing, we decided to order a bunch of appetizers to share so we could sample it all.

"So, do ye think ye'll win it this year?" my father asked Jack again.

"We go into every season planning on winning it all," he said. "This year we look better than most. If the baseball gods smile down on us and we keep injuries to a minimum, we'll get it done."

He continued to ask Jack questions about the upcoming season and baseball in general. For a man who never even watched a baseball game before I started working for the Waves, I'm pretty impressed with my father's insight and knowledge. He's learned a lot in the last decade.

While the two men in my life talked, I figured Melanie and I should do more than just sit there listening.

"Your mom must be thrilled about the baby. She's been bugging your brother for a grandchild for years."

"She is," she said. "This was a shock to my parents too, but she's looking forward to spoiling the baby."

"When did she find out about your relationship?"

"I held off telling her as long as possible, but when I

quit my job and started traveling with A—your father, I didn't have a choice." I nodded and sipped my lemonade. "I wanted to tell you then too, but he didn't think it was a good idea. I guess I should have pushed him more."

I'm not sure what to say to that. I imagine the shock level of finding out would have been the same if they told me sooner, but the betrayal I felt from their lies may have been less. I don't know. Either way, my relationship with both of them would have been affected and we'd have to rebuild.

"It doesn't matter," I said. "We just have to move forward now."

Melanie blinked away tears. She opened her mouth to speak, but the waitress arrived with our food. After setting her tray on a stand, she placed baskets and plates of mouthwatering goodness on our table until it was completely covered then refilled our glasses and left us to our feast.

We ate and laughed and talked about how amazing the food was until our plates were empty.

"Now that yer bellies are full, we have somethin' ta discuss," my father said. He placed his hand over Melanie's and toyed with the huge diamond ring he'd given her. "Melanie and me plan on gettin' married before this babe comes along, and we'd like ya ta be there."

"Oh." I glanced between the two of them. "When's the wedding?"

"We haven't set a date," Melanie said. "We wanted to find out your schedule first. It's not going to be anything big, just a small ceremony at my parents' house so we can do it whenever you can make it."

"A *small* event at your parents' house? Really? Has that ever happened?" I asked.

Melanie laughed. "I'm sure the whole neighborhood

will be invited, but it's not going to be a big Hollywood event." She looked at my father and smiled. "Neither of us wants that."

I pulled my phone from my purse and opened the calendar. The next few months look crazy as usual, but I have to make time to attend. If I don't, it will always be between us, and don't want that. I'll put in for vacation and make a long weekend of it.

"Other than the next two weeks, I can make any date work."

Melanie's eyes widened then she grabbed my arm and squealed. I'm sure that squeal would have been a full-blown scream if we weren't in public.

"Thank you so much." She squeezed my hand. "It means a lot to both of us."

I leaned over the arm of my chair and pulled her into an awkward hug.

"Of course I'll be there," I said. "We're family."

JACK

AFTER A TEARY GOODBYE, Hannah and I hit the road again and for the past few hours, haven't said a word to each other. She seemed content to pass the miles just listening to the music and I didn't feel the need to break the silence.

That's another thing that makes Hannah different from every other woman I've been with. She doesn't need to fill the air with idle chatter like the rest of them. I never knew how nice it could be just spending time with a female in comfortable silence. And this is a comfortable silence. I'm sure she's thinking about the intense scene at the restaurant and her father's upcoming wedding to her best friend, but she doesn't seem upset or stressed.

Needing to touch her, I reached over and squeezed her hand then laced our fingers together. I watched her mouth curl into a small smile before returning my attention back to the road. We'd put quite a few more miles behind us when Hannah spoke, her voice just above a whisper.

"Thank you for today." I glanced over and found her watching me. "I know they're my people, but it was nice having you there in my corner."

"Anytime."

"You must think we're the most dysfunctional people on Earth."

I lifted her hand to my lips and brushed them against her knuckles.

"I think nothing of the sort. I'll admit the situation is a bit fucked up, but it's easy to see how much love is between you." I chuckled. "Wait until you meet my father. Then you'll see true dysfunction."

I pulled into Hannah's driveway and killed the engine. After I'd basically promised to introduce her to my father, we'd chatted for a while, then she dozed off. I looked over and couldn't stop a smile from spreading across my face at the sight of her. Hannah is such a force when awake, I love getting to see her all soft and snuggly like this.

Leaning over, I kissed her forehead.

"Hannah," I whispered. She shifted and snuggled into the seat. "Time to wake up."

She slowly opened her eyes and blinked me into focus. Looking a bit dazed, she sat forward, but the seatbelt engaged and she fell back. Unbuckling, she turned to face me, rubbing the sleep from her eyes.

"I can't believe I fell asleep. I'm so sorry."

"Nothing to be sorry about. You obviously needed the rest."

"But I wasn't very good company."

I unbuckled and leaned over the console to kiss her.

"You're always the best company."

Her cheeks reddened as a shy smile crossed her face. "Come on, let's get your stuff inside."

I stepped out of the truck and twisted from side to side, stretching my back. After touching my toes and loosening my hips, I met Hannah at the back of the truck and opened the tailgate. I stopped when she started to reach inside for her bags.

"I got it." I grabbed two suitcases and her duffle and set them on the ground then closed the hatchback and picked them up again. "Lead the way."

We walked up the sidewalk and Hannah opened the front door and stepped to the side, gesturing for me to enter. I walked inside and set the bags down and turned around, expecting Hannah to be right behind me, but she wasn't. I heard her talking to someone outside and peeked my head out.

"Well hello, Jack. Fancy meeting you here."

Hannah's neighbor, Kate Button, hopped up the last two steps and breezed right by me through the door. She and her book club are semi-regulars at the stadium and I always enjoy talking to them.

"Mrs. Button." I leaned down and kissed her cheek. "How are you?"

"I'm well, thank you," she said, looking very prim and proper for a woman whose hand was practically cupping my ass.

"And you? Are you ready for the season?"

I pulled out of her reach. "I am."

Hannah closed the door and took a few steps closer until she stood between Mrs. Button and me.

"Would you like a drink before heading out?" Hannah asked. "The refrigerator is bare, but I can manage a glass of water."

"No, I'm good," I said. "I should get going, though. I want to get in a run and go to bed early.

Thanks for riding with me. It was fun."

Hannah nodded. "It was. Thank you for having me along."

Mrs. Button looked like she was watching a tennis match as her gaze bounced between us. As much as I'd love to kiss Hannah goodbye, I'm not into PDAs and Mrs. Button would probably enjoy watching a little too much. Instead, I squeezed her hand and smiled.

"I'll talk to you tomorrow," I said to Hannah. "Mrs. Button, will I see you opening day?"

"The ladies and I will be there," she said.

"I look forward to seeing you all."

Hannah walked me to the door and opened it.

"Be careful," she said and I stepped over the threshold.

It's been a long time since anyone's said that to me. My mother is probably the last person who cared enough about me to say those simple words that basically mean *I love you*. That's what I read somewhere anyway and I'm choosing to believe it, especially now, with this woman.

"Will do."

Chapter Twenty-Nine

HANNAH

I WATCHED Jack get into his car before closing the door. Mrs. Button stood right behind me and I almost bumped into her as I turned around.

"I don't know if that man looks better coming or going," she said. "What's your opinion?"

"Hmm, that's a tough one." I walked past Mrs. Button and over to the kitchen island, where she'd stacked my mail into neat piles. Picking up a stack of envelopes, I dismissed the junk mail one by one. "All junk mail, just like you told me."

Mrs. Button had hiked herself onto a stool on the other side of the island and leaned back, her arms crossed over her chest.

"Yes, during our many phone conversations, I was very honest with you about what's been happening," she said. "It seems the same can't be said for you."

I could act like I don't know what she's talking about, but I'd never hear the end of it.

"I'm sorry I didn't tell you about Jack and me, but when it started, I wasn't sure it was going to continue. Then when it did, I kind of treated it like a perfect game. I didn't talk about it for fear I'd jinx it."

"So no one knows about you two?"

She leaned forward, resting her elbows on the granite.

"Jack's close friends know and we ran into my dad in the Keys, so now he knows."

"I'm going to tuck that dad comment away and we can talk about it later. For now, I want to hear all about you and Jack. And please don't leave out any details. Remember, I'm living vicariously through you," she said, resting her chin on her hand and waited for me to start.

I settled into bed and turned on the television. Mrs. Button had stayed for hours and while I enjoyed catching up with her, I'm exhausted. She'd seriously wanted to hear every detail about Jack and me and had managed to slip in a few *I told you so's* without actually saying those exact words.

She's always been a huge fan of Jack's and did tell me more than once that I should go after him. That seemed ridiculous at the time because Jack saw me as nothing more than a fixture at the stadium and despite my crazy crush, I thought he was an arrogant ass.

My phone rang and the arrogant ass's name popped up on the screen.

"Hey," I said.

"Are you alone or is Mrs. Button still grilling you?"

I chuckled. "She left a few minutes ago, but you're right about the grilling. How did you know?"

"The rabid look in her eyes. It was obvious she was just

waiting for me to leave so she could pounce," he said. "So what did Mrs. Button have to say about us?"

"She's thrilled. You know she's your biggest fan," I said. "Plus, I think she's hoping you'll spend time here and she'll get to ogle you."

His sexy laugh sounded in my ear, making all my lady parts tingle.

"If having Mrs. Button ogle me is the price I have to pay to spend more time with you, I'll be sure to dress sexy," he said, then added, "I miss you."

"We just spent an entire day trapped in the car together. I figured you'd be sick of me," I said.

"You figured wrong," he said. "In fact, if Mrs. Button hadn't been chomping at the bit to interrogate you, I may have tried to convince you to let me stay."

"Really?"

"Mmm Hmm." That sexy sound vibrated in my ear. "But instead of being curled up next to you, I'm lying here in my big, lonely bed. It's very sad." He sighed. "Tragic even."

Thankfully he'd added the dramatic sigh and those last two words, because when he mentioned being alone in bed, I was ready to run over to his place and remedy that issue. Instead, I decided to match his silliness with my own

"So, what are you wearing?" I said, my voice soft and sexy.

"I think you know what I wear to bed."

Yes, I do have the good fortune to know that Jack sleeps in boxer briefs. He said he used to sleep nude but he rolled over one night and pinched "the boys" between his thigh and the mattress. So now he's paranoid.

"What about you?" he asked. "I've only seen you sleep in my T- shirts. What do you normally sleep in?"

"A tank top and shorts."

"Let me see."

"What do you mean?"

"I'm switching the call to FaceTime."

"I hate the way I look on that."

"Well you'll have to get used to it because I plan on seeing you when I'm on the road."

His voice sounded farther away and a second later, my phone beeped. I pulled it from my ear and accepted his FaceTime request. Jack's image filled my screen.

"So let me see," he said.

"See what?" I asked, although I know exactly what he's talking about.

"Your jammies," he said, his sexy purr punctuated by the naughty smile I've come to know so well.

Sometimes it still seems surreal to me that we're together like this. I spent so many years harboring my stupid crush while thinking we were worlds apart. Turns out, we're a lot alike.

"These jammies?" I tipped my phone slightly, giving him just a glimpse of my cleavage.

"Oh yeah, those are the ones." He licked his lips. "Keep going."

I slowly panned down my body, giving him a good look at my baby blue tank top and black Soffe shorts. Just for good measure, I continued all the way down my legs and wiggled my toes at him before tilting the phone back toward my face.

Somewhere during my sensual tour, Jack had bitten his lower lip and now he let it slowly slide from his teeth.

"Remind me why I'm at my place instead of being there with you."

"Because you were afraid of a sweet, little old lady." I got a good view of his Adam's apple as he tossed his head back and laughed. "What's so funny?"

"That sweet, little old lady was practically cupping my ass a few hours ago."

A raised right brow punctuated his words. He obviously thought he'd scored a point with that last statement.

"Can't say I blame her. It's a mighty fine ass."

I raised my right brow to match his, but have to admit his looks more impressive.

"Ms. Adams, I'm shocked. What happened to that quiet woman I knew? She never talked about my ass."

I snort-laughed. "Maybe not to your face."

"What am I gonna do with you?" he asked around a wide

smile.

"I'm sure you'll think of something."

"I'm sure I will." He looked at me for several seconds then his smile faded. "I did call you to talk about something."

"What's that?"

"This whole Mrs. Button thing made me realize that we have to discuss coming out, for lack of a better term."

"Coming out?"

"Yeah, letting people know we're a couple."

"You really think we should do that?"

Some of the spark left his eyes.

"Are you not sure about this, Hannah?" he asked, his voice a mere whisper.

I shrugged and shifted onto my side, resting the phone against the pillow.

"It's not that I'm not sure, but it's nice having this be just between us. For the most part anyway. Once the world knows, it'll get crazy."

"Hannah, I don't plan on broadcasting it on the Jumbotron. I just want to tell the powers that be so we can actually interact out in the open."

The thought of having everyone know about Jack and me gives me palpitations. There's not a no fraternization rule at work, but I don't want to be known as one of *those* girls. You know, the ones who fool around with the players. We've had our share of them through the years and their time working for the Waves was usually short- lived.

"What's going on in that beautiful head?"

I shook my head and smiled.

"Nothing." Meeting his gaze through the screen, I asked,

"What's your plan?"

Chapter Thirty

JACK

I SLIPPED on my sunglasses and stepped onto the field. The sun hovered low in the cloudless sky and I know it will be right in my eyes until the end of the first inning. At this point I'm used to it and it's a small price to pay for such a perfect day. I'm of the opinion that any day at the ballpark is a good day, but weather like this is like icing on the cake.

Settling onto the grass just off the first base line, I leaned forward and held onto the sides of my feet, pulling forward for a good stretch.

"Great day for baseball."

I sat back and looked over at Dan, who sat next to me.

"That it is," I agreed.

"How was your meet and greet?"

"I was my charming self, Hannah handed out swag, and everyone seemed to have a good time."

The big wigs of the HVAC company responsible for the climate comfort of the stadium are partying in their private box. Hannah set up a meet and greet with them after I took batting practice. The need to get back onto the field kept it short and sweet. Thankfully I get credit by the meeting not the minute.

We continued stretching and watched the stadium fill. I've been playing ball for nearly three decades and the thrill of opening day hasn't dimmed. There's just an energy that's different from every other game.

Back when I was a kid, the parade and free nachos ranked right up there with playing, but since teener league, I've only focused on the game. Baseball has been the only constant in my life since my mother died.

"So does your relationship with Hannah give you immunity from more events or get some tacked on?" Dan asked. "How did the coming out meeting go?"

I shrugged and twisted toward him.

"It seemed to go well. He didn't freak out, just told us to keep it off the field and away from team business."

"Do you think that's possible?"

"We've done it so far." I stood and leaned down to touch my toes. Wrapping my arms around my calves, I deepened the stretch and held it. "We're not making a formal announcement or anything. The only reason we told Mr. Hanover is because of the whole book thing." I let go of my legs and slowly straightened. "He's finally not up my ass and I don't want to do anything to put him up there again."

HANNAH

. . .

I STOOD against the concourse railing and watched the teams pregame. As interviews and historical footage showed on the Jumbotron, the players worked through their various routines. It's a beautiful night for a game and the stadium is quickly filling, the fans eager for the start of another season after a long winter.

Jack and Dan stood on the first base line stretching. As Jack bent to touch his toes, I'll admit my eyes strayed to his amazing ass. And I now know for a fact that it looks even better naked. Good enough to bite...which I may have done once or twice.

The man in question stood and twisted from side to side. After watching him for years, I know he's done warming up. True to form, he walked toward the dugout, Dan at his side. He looked across the stands and right at me. I'd like to say he sensed me there, but I'm a creature of habit too. I tend to stand in this same place before every game.

His gaze didn't leave mine as he crossed the field. Dan disappeared into the dugout, but Jack paused just long enough to smile up at me before stepping inside. Like a schoolgirl with her first crush, my heart pounded and I'm sure my face is bright red.

What can I say? He just does it for me.

"Ready for another season?"

I'd been so wrapped up in Jack, I didn't notice that Kenny had leaned on the railing alongside me.

"Absolutely." I chuckled. "At least I'd better be."

"My father said Jack's meet-and-greet went well earlier."

"It did. He's so good with fans, he makes my work easy."

"That's good to hear."

As the noise from the Jumbotron ceased, Warren Tucker's voice filled the air, welcoming everyone to First Allegiant Bank Park and the start of a new season. The longtime voice of Waves celebrated his seventy-eighth birthday last season and has no plans of retiring anytime soon.

The crowd yelled out its usual taunts and boos as Warren announced the visiting team. The insults got especially harsh when the starting pitcher for Chicago, who started his career as a Wave, was introduced.

A hush fell over the stadium as Warren took a pause, building the anticipation before segueing into the Waves' starting lineup. The crowd went wild as each player was announced and took his position. I split my attention between shortstop and Jack's picture on the Jumbotron, enjoying both views. Once the field was filled, Warren asked everyone to rise for the playing of the national anthem.

Chris Russell aka Rusty took the mound and Chicago's leadoff batter stepped up to the plate. After two well-placed fastballs, it was a pitcher's count. A wasted slider set the stage for another fastball, high and tight this time, that struck the batter out looking.

"Rusty looks amazing," I said.

"For what we're paying him, he'd better."

Kenny isn't usually what you'd call jovial, but he seems especially grumpy today.

"Everything okay?"

He leaned his elbows against the railing and let out a long sigh.

"Holly decided not to move here after all. She told me this morning." Kenny's been dating a woman who lives in Manhattan for a few years now, and at the end of last season, he told me she planned on moving to Myrtle Beach after the holidays.

"I'm sorry to hear that."

He nodded. "Thanks."

"Are you going to keep doing the long distance thing?"

"We've done that for five years now. And for the last two, we've talked about taking the next step. Obviously I can't move. The team is here. Unless I tell my father I don't want it, I have to be here, too. She understands that." Shaking his head he said, "At this point, it's time to either move forward or end it." He chuckled. "I thought we were moving forward. I guess I was wrong."

During our conversation, the number two hitter had popped out to center field and the third batter just grounded out to third base. Three up, three down on six pitches. Nice way for a pitcher to start a game.

"Maybe she'll change her mind."

"Deciding not to come *was* her changing her mind," he said. "She had a great job lined up and had most of her apartment packed."

"So what happened?"

"I'm not sure. She said she doesn't want to leave the life she's built in the city, her friends..."

He trailed off and I focused my attention on the field as the Waves' second baseman, Oskar Marquez stepped up to the plate. The crowd went wild as he lined the first pitch to left-center field and ended up with a double. The stadium got even louder as John Kasprzyk slipped a ground ball between third and short, putting men on the corners.

A familiar *Jack, Jack, Jack* chant filled the stadium as my guy stepped into the batter's box. I've always loved watching him play, but there's a whole new element to it now that we're involved. He rested the bat on his shoulder and watched the pitcher shake off signs with narrowed eyes. As the pitcher and catcher finally came to an agreement, Jack settled into his stance.

After checking the runners one last time, the pitcher faced the plate and, from the stretch, sent a fastball hurling toward Jack.

Literally.

The ball sailed toward his head and he hit the ground just before it hit him. The crowd yelled and booed as Jack stared the pitcher down and slowly stood, refusing to dust himself off. I learned early on that the latter is a thing they do, or don't do as the case may be, to show they're not shaken. Not rubbing the spot after getting hit by the pitch says the same thing. Men are funny creatures, for sure.

After watching the pitcher and catcher go through the same routine as before, Jack once again settled into his batting stance. Another fastball sailed toward the plate, but this one was right in Jack's sweet spot. His whole body seemed to tense just before he stepped and swung, bringing the entire stadium to its feet at the crack of the bat as he sent the ball flying in a high arc into the upper deck behind left field.

He ran around the bases and stepped on home plate a few steps behind John. The players greeted Jack with their various high fives, chest bumps, and whatever else they use to celebrate a home run. The crowd continued to cheer and chant his name as he stepped down into the dugout. After a few seconds, he reappeared at the top of the dugout stairs and tipped his hat. Before stepping back inside, his gaze met mine over the sea of fans and his smile widened. Setting the cap on his head, he disappeared back into the dugout.

"My father said he had a meeting with you and Jack earlier."

Despite all the noise surrounding me, I jumped when

Kenny spoke. I was so focused on Jack, I'd totally forgotten he was standing next to me.

"We did."

I'm not sure what Mr. Hanover shared and I don't plan on volunteering anything.

Kenny shifted onto one elbow, turning slightly toward me.

"When I first met Holly, it was pretty clear that her career was the most important thing in her life. Over the years, it seemed like that had changed and she led me to believe I ranked at least as high, if not higher, than her work. But if that were the case, she'd be here now." He stood up straight and put his hands in his pockets. "I like you, Hannah. You're a good person and an excellent employee."

"What, exactly, are you saying, Kenny?"

"People don't change," he said. "They might mix things up for a while, maybe try something new, but eventually end up going back to their comfort zone." He glanced at the field at the crack of the bat and watched the designated hitter, Philip Riddle, get thrown out at first base. "You've known Jack for ten years. You know how he's lived. Just be careful. I'd hate to see you get hurt."

Then, after vocalizing my deepest fear, he walked away.

Chapter Thirty-One

JACK

I STRETCHED across the bed and clicked on the TV. After flipping through the usual ridiculous reality shows, I finally found a keeper. Charlie Sheen had just knocked the head off a wooden batter with a fastball when I settled on *Major League*.

At this point, I've lost count of how many times I've seen this movie, but it doesn't matter, I'll still watch it anytime it's on. It's a classic.

We're in day five of an eight-day road trip and I'll admit I miss Hannah. I figured I would, but didn't anticipate how much. The guys had a good laugh about it during dinner. Dan said I looked "mopey" and "pathetic." I don't know about that, but I do know that my days aren't the same without her. Besides, it's not like he's much better.

My phone beeped and, as if my thoughts conjured her, Hannah's beautiful face filled the screen. I swiped right and her image came to life.

"Hey you."

"Hey yourself," she said. "Great game today. How's the arm?"

"Not too bad."

I tilted the phone to show her the ball-shaped bruise on my bicep from a wild hop. I'd managed to keep it in front of me and throw the runner out, but I'll admit, it hurt like hell for the rest of the game.

"What lovely colors, and I love how you can see the imprint from the stitches. It really adds something." I moved the phone back so I could see her face. Her brow furrowed as she added, "But seriously, does it hurt?"

"Not more than any other bruise. It'll be fine," I said. "How was your day? Where'd you and Mrs. Button go to dinner?"

She rolled her eyes and laughed. "I went to Dino's with Mrs. Button *and* her friends. If you think the team gets rowdy, they have nothing on those ladies."

"The same ones that come to the games?"

"No, that's her book club. These were the ladies she quilts with." She tucked a stray strand of hair behind her ear. "A couple glasses of wine in and no topic was off limits. I know way more than I want to about their sex lives, past and present."

I don't know the ladies she's talking about, but if they're anything like Mrs. Button, I imagine the conversation was pretty interesting.

"Learn anything?" I raised my brow. "Hear anything you'd like to try?" She rolled her eyes and then her face disappeared and I found myself looking at her ceiling. "Where'd you go? I'm just curious. Those ladies are a lot older than me, have a lot more experience."

The room seemed to bounce up and down, then the phone tilted and Hannah's face filled the screen again.

She'd settled onto her side, her head resting against a pillow.

"I doubt that, but they did have a lot to share." She adjusted her glasses and scooched down further against the pillow. "And of course, they all love you and were asking all kinds of questions."

"What kind of questions?"

"First they were asking about the book. Apparently they've all read it. I shut that down pretty fast when I told them that I *haven't* read it and have no intention of doing so." Her eyes shifted to the side for a second before looking directly at me again. "Then Mrs. Button alluded to the fact that we're involved and they pounced. When I wouldn't give even a hint about our sex life or what you look like naked, they took it upon themselves to discuss the intimate details of their lives in great detail. I think they were hoping I'd feel compelled to join in." She yawned and pushed her glasses back into place. "I didn't, in case you're wondering,"

"How'd they take that?"

"After trying to convince me to at least take a picture of you in just boxer briefs to share with them, they tried to outdo each other with their own stories." After rolling onto her back, she added, "I had a lot of fun listening to them, but good Lord, there are some things I'd rather keep private." She shrugged. "Maybe I'll feel differently when I'm their age."

"So you're not one to kiss and tell?"

"Nope. Your kisses are safe with me."

I know she's being silly, but her words still settle deep in my heart and fill it with reassurance. I'm a private person. And, despite the fact that my chosen career has me in the public eye, I've managed to keep most of my private life out of it until recently. I didn't enjoy my time in that spotlight and really wouldn't want a repeat. It's good to know I'm with someone who feels the same.

"Good to know," I said, speaking part of that last thought out loud. I turned onto my side and propped the phone on the pillow next to me and just looked at her.

"Everything okay?" she asked, picking up on my mood change.

I nodded. "Nothing that being in the same room as you won't fix. I miss you." Her lips curled into a shy smile as a blush spread up her neck and across her cheeks.

"I miss you, too," she said. "But it's only three more days and then you're here for a ten-day home stretch."

"I can't wait."

Three days later, the game started after a two-hour rain delay, and quickly turned into a pitcher's duel. There'd only been three hits in nine innings...two for the Waves and the other for New York...but none produced a run. A night game on the last day of a road trip is not when you want to go into extra innings, but here we are.

All hell broke loose for both teams as both of our bullpens had trouble finding the strike zone. A few walks and a couple hits later, we found ourselves tied 2-2 in the top of the thirteenth inning.

Oskar Marquez managed to pop a little flare between second base and right field and ended up on first base. After Kasprzyk's perfectly executed sacrifice bunt, Oskar stood scoring position for me as I stepped into the box.

The pitcher narrowed his eyes at me before turning to his catcher for the sign. To someone else, he might look intimidating, but I know the mental game as well as the physical. And I also know that he only has two decent pitches...a fastball and a slider. According to his stats, he also has a changeup, but nine times out of ten, it ends up in the dirt when he throws it.

I tightened my grip on the bat and settled into my stance, blocking out the screams of the crowd. The pitcher hurled the ball toward the plate. To me it looked low and outside, but the umpire had a different opinion. Other than glancing at him out of the corner of my eye, I didn't react. I learned a long time ago that arguing balls and strikes just pisses the umpire off.

I stepped out of the box and stretched my shoulders and neck then, putting the previous pitch out of my mind, got back in to be ready for the next one. It looked identical to the last, but this time the umpire called it a ball. The next pitch was a changeup and, following the odds, it was in the dirt. A foul ball and a high pitch later, I had a full count.

The catcher ran out to the mound and while they talked, I met the third base coach, Jeff Clopton, halfway down the line.

"You know what you're looking for here?" he asked.

I looked out at the mound and tightened one batting glove then the other before turning my attention back to Jeff.

"I'm thinking fastball."

"Me too." He smiled, revealing crooked teeth. "Be ready

for it."

The crowd started cheering as everyone got back into position. Stepping back into the box, I tuned them out once again. Settling into my stance again, I waited. As soon as the ball left his hand, I knew it was perfect.

Tightening my grip on the bat, I swung and felt the vibration as it made contact with the ball. Finishing the swing, I still felt the contact humming through my body as I dropped the bat and ran toward first base as I watched the ball sail in a high arc toward left-center field. I was rounding the bag as it dropped into the crowd for a two-run homer.

A blend of cheers and boos from the crowd echoed through the stadium as I jogged around the bases. I rounded third and saw my teammates waiting for me and as I crossed home plate, they walked me toward the dugout with a series of back slaps, chest bumps, and high fives.

I chugged a cup of water and leaned against the railing to watch the rest of the inning. Riddle flew out to center for the second out, but Dan kept our half of the inning going with a line drive double over the shortstop's head.

Cal stepped into the box and after falling quickly into an 0-2 count, he fouled off four pitches before sending a ground ball between short and third, putting runners on the corners as Monte stepped up to bat. He swung at the first pitch and ended the inning with a groundout to second.

I grabbed my glove and ran out to shortstop, followed by my teammates. Monte tossed me a practice ball and I scooped it up and threw it back to him as Malik Walters warmed up. Our closer is one of the best in the league and I have confidence he'll shut this down now so we can all go home.

That last thought had just left my head as the first batter stepped up to the plate. Malik's first two pitches were a bit wide, but he finally found the strike zone with the third. The fourth pitch was well placed, but the batter still managed to get his bat squarely on it and send it sailing over the short porch in right field.

That rattled Malik just enough that he walked the next batter. New York quickly sent in a pinch runner, obviously geared to steal. After sitting out a couple games to nurse a sore knee, Xander McKay is back behind the plate tonight.

He called timeout and ran out to the mound, to give Malik a minute to settle down.

"You got this," I yelled when X ran back to position. "Let's go!"

I kept half an eye on the runner at first as Malik released the ball toward the plate. The batter swung at the pitch as the runner took off for second. X threw a perfect rope to me, but the guy's foot hit the bag a split second before I slapped him with the tag. I shook my head when Elmer looked at me to see if the play should be reviewed. There's not a doubt in my mind the guy was safe.

Every player has an occasional bad night, and unfortunately tonight is Malik's. It's not that he's horrible, his stuff just isn't as sharp as usual. The next batter hit a ground ball to third. Cal looked the runner on second back before throwing over to first, getting us the first out.

The stadium vibrated with noise and energy as the crowd screamed, cheered, and chanted. It took extra concentration to tune them out as the next batter worked his way to a full count before hitting a pop fly toward the third base line. Running at full speed toward the ball, I saw Shawn Riggs doing the same from left field.

The ball kept carrying toward the stands and I slowed to a jog, resigned to the fact this would not be the coveted second out of the inning. Riggs must have come to the same conclusion because he slowed down, too.

I watched in horror as Cal continued running at full speed then reached out his glove and caught the ball just as he approached the wall. His momentum sent him sailing into the stands head first. The crowd went silent as he landed on the concrete, the top half of his body wedged under the seats.

I jumped over the wall and pushed my way through the

fans surrounding Cal, followed by Riggs. Cal looked up at me and struggled to move.

"Sit tight," I said, but he wasn't having it. Leaning onto his right arm, he shifted and I helped him into a sitting position. As the medical crew raced over, he held his glove up high, with the ball squeezed tightly inside. Even the New York fans clapped when they saw the movement.

Blood dripped from his eye and ear, pooling into the neckline of his shirt.

"You're a crazy son of a bitch, you know that?"

Cal smiled at my words and cringed, then investigated his fat lip with the tip of his tongue.

I stepped aside to let the professionals do their thing. Cal refused to get on the board they brought and instead, with their help, stood and leaned against the back of a seat. It was pretty obvious he was in a lot of pain and just wanted to get out of sight.

Riggs and I followed as the medical crew flanked him on all sides and guided him through the seats to the gate that led onto the field. We walked toward our positions and they continued to the dugout as the entire crowd chanted Cal's name. That's an extraordinary thing to happen in another team's stadium. Cal waved as he stepped inside then disappeared into the tunnel.

Mitch O'Moore grabbed his glove and ran out to third base. I paced along the grass and looked out at the stands as Monte threw a few warm up ground balls to him. More fans had their faces in cell phones than were looking at the field. I'm sure videos of Cal's leap into the stands are already flooding social media.

Once Mitch was warmed up, everyone got back into position and the umpire stepped behind the plate and called the next batter up. Malik got ahead with two strikes then followed with two balls just outside the zone. The crowd was on its feet, screaming as the next pitch went sailing toward the left field fence. Thankfully it hooked foul.

Mixing it up, X called for a changeup and was given a perfect one. The hitter's swing was way ahead, but he managed to graze the ball, sending it into the ground just behind the plate.

Malik walked around the mound talking to himself. I know from past experience, he's giving himself a pep talk. He grabbed the rosin bag and threw it back to the ground before stepping back toward the rubber. After taking the sign, he looked the runner back, then threw a fastball toward the plate just inside the outside corner. I watched the batter swing and heard the crack of the bat a split second after I saw it sail toward the gap in right-center field.

Since there are two outs, the runner took off on contact and was rounding third while Dan and John were still tracking the ball. It looked like New York was going to tie the score when Dan dove and snagged the ball just before it hit the ground. It peeked over the edge of the webbing as he slid to a stop. Jumping to his feet, he held the glove high as he ran toward the infield.

The entire bench cleared and ran onto the field and we all met on the mound in a heap of back slaps, high fives, and chest bumps. Endorphins from the win gave us a shit-ton of energy but I know that won't last. I just want to hit the showers and get the fuck out of here and home to Hannah.

Chapter Thirty-Two

HANNAH

I KNOW I should be paying attention to the ceremony. After all, it's not every day your father and best friend get married, right? But instead, my gaze keeps sliding to the man next to me. After four months, you'd think my hormones would have settled down some, but they seem to be just as out of control as ever where Jack is concerned.

At the sound of my father's world-famous voice, I turned to face the happy couple, who are now exchanging vows. It's still bizarre that Mel is going to be my step-mother, but I have to admit, they look happy. And despite the odd situation, I know she loves truly loves him for the man he is and not his money, celebrity, or movie persona.

My father managed to choke back tears as he finished his vows, but lost the fight as Melanie recited hers. Their images blurred and I blinked away my own tears as they exchanged rings, dabbing under my eyes to keep my makeup intact.

As I lowered my hand, Jack's fingers wrapped around my wrist, then entwined with mine. I looked down at our joined hands as he rested them on his firm thigh, then up toward his face. Warm hazel eyes met my gaze and his mouth curled into a small smile. I sniffed and smiled back.

Jack tightened his hold on my hand and I rested my head against his shoulder and watched as the officiant declared the happy couple man and wife. Everyone stood and cheered as my father kissed his bride then led her down the makeshift aisle. I turned and watched them walk the short distance to the tables that were set up to create a reception area.

A backyard wedding with less than a hundred guests doesn't qualify as a Hollywood blowout, but it's exactly what I'd expect from both of them. My father steps into the spotlight when necessary, but he's made it a point to keep his personal life out of it. And the fact that they've kept their relationship secret all this time shows how Mel feels.

Jack wrapped his arm around me from behind and kissed the top of my head.

"Sorry I was so late," Jack said. "The game ran long and traffic was a bitch."

I turned in his arms and smiled up at him.

"I'm just happy you're here."

"Me too." He looked around. "This reminds me of Dan and

Sabrina's wedding. Just family and close friends in the backyard."

"I guess it's the easiest way to control the environment. There are too many unknowns and possibilities for details to leak with a venue."

He chuckled. "I forgot I'm with the master planner."

"Lucky for me, when I plan an event, I usually want

everyone to know who's going to be there so I don't have to worry about leaks."

During our little talk, the chairs had emptied out and the rest of the attendees had made their way to the party area, and more importantly, the food. Melanie's mother is full-blooded Italian and she, her sisters, and her mother have gone all out with this wedding. Hell, Sunday dinner is an event at this house. The food for a special occasion like this could feed a small country.

"So who are all these people? I don't see anyone I recognize so I'm guessing no Hollywood bigwigs are here."

"Nope, strictly family and friends. My dad's agent doesn't even know about this." I spotted two of Melanie's brothers standing by the bar. "Come on, I'll introduce you to everyone starting with Mel's brothers." I smiled up at Jack. "They're huge Anaheim fans. So if the subject of baseball happens to come up, please feel free to mention the fact that the Waves swept their team earlier this week."

"You sure you want me to go there?"

Jack's raised brow and sexy smirk made me want to drag him out of the party and get naked. Ten days apart is way too long. I took a deep breath and reminded myself that we have all night and part of tomorrow to spend together. Not to mention the flight home. Jack has chartered a private plane to bring us back east so we can really relax or...whatever. With the way I'm feeling right now, *whatever* is more likely.

"Trust me. I've taken enough abuse from them through the years. They deserve the payback."

"Can I help with anything?"

Melanie's mother, Angela, busied herself consolidating food and stacking empty trays. I've seen her do it hundreds of times at various gatherings. Past experience tells me she won't let me help, but I have to offer anyway.

"No, I'm good. You know I have a system." She turned her head and smiled. "But stay and keep me company. We can catch up." She reached out and squeezed my hand. "How are you doing? With all this?"

I wiped the powdered sugar she left on my hand when she let go and returned to her task.

"I'm okay." Looking at me out of the corner of her eye, Angela managed to call bullshit without saying a word. "I'll admit, it's strange and the whole thing freaked me out when they told me. But what can I do? Disown my father? Cut ties with my best friend? Never get to know my little brother?"

She surprised me with one of her world-famous hugs. "You're an amazing young woman, you know that?"

Pulling back, she kissed my forehead. "And I'm honored to call you my second daughter."

With three sons, and only one daughter, Angela had always said she loved having me around because it helped ward off all the testosterone. As an only child, I loved being welcomed into their crazy family dynamic.

Angela winked and nudged her head in Jack's direction. "Your young man seems to be fitting in just fine, too."

I looked over at Jack talking to Melanie's brothers and cousins. To say he's fitting in is an understatement. They love him, despite the fact he plays for the Waves and not their team. He caught me looking and smiled, then tipped his drink in my direction without missing a beat in the conversation.

"Do ya think ya could stop playing' googly eyes with yer boyfriend and dance with yer da?" My father walked up behind me and grabbed a cookie off the platter Angela had just filled and took a bite. "This is all amazing', Angela. Thank ya for putting' all this on."

"It's my pleasure, Aaran." She hugged her new son-in-law, who is only five years her junior. "Welcome to the family."

He pulled back and smiled. "Thank ya. It means a lot."

"Now go dance with your daughter." Angela patted his shoulder. "Thank you for your help," she said and kissed me on the cheek.

A slow, bluesy tune started as father led me to the makeshift dance floor and pulled me into a perfect frame. We danced in silence for several beats before he pulled his head back and looked me in the eye.

"Thank ya fer been' here."

His husky voice tore at my heart. I know our months apart affected him as much as they did me. As long as I remember, it had been the two of us against the world, and even when I went to live with my grandmother and he built himself into a megastar, he was my rock. I know that if I ever needed him, he'd drop everything and be at my side in a minute, no matter what.

"I'll always be here," I said. "No matter what."

He wrapped his arms around me and pulled me into a tight hug and we swayed from side to side as the song came to an end.

"Yer a good girl," he kissed my forehead and pulled back. "Make sure he treats ya right."

I swallowed and nodded. "I will."

We walked to the edge of the dance floor as the familiar strains of Frank Sinatra filled the air. I felt Jack behind me before his hand brushed my arm, leaving a trail of goosebumps in his wake.

"Excuse me sir, can I steal your daughter?" He asked my father then turned to me. "I believe they're playing our song."

My father kissed me on the cheek and stepped back.

Without a word, he walked across the yard toward his bride.

Jack wrapped his arms around my waist and stepped closer, leaving me no choice but to loop my arms around his neck. The last time we danced together, you could have fit a truck between us and I'd breathed through my mouth to avoid inhaling his intoxicating scent. Now our bodies touched in all the best places and I rested my cheek against his shoulder as we swayed to *The Way You Look Tonight*, much slower than the beat warranted.

"This is much nicer than the last time we danced," he said, echoing my thoughts. He kissed my temple and rested his cheek against the top of my head.

I nodded and, taking in long, slow breaths, settled in to enjoy his amazing smell and savor the moment.

JACK

I climbed into bed and set a gift bag on the pillow next to me. The shower shut off a while ago, so Hannah should be out any minute. I'd been half-tempted to join her, but decided against it. After ten days away, I want her stretched out on a big bed, not against a wall in some hotel shower. No matter how nice said hotel might be.

Melanie's mother had offered us a room at her house. Thankfully Hannah turned her down. As welcome as the Reade family made me feel, I know alone time would have been in short supply if we stayed there.

The bathroom door opened and Hannah walked across the room all shiny and clean, her legs looking impossibly long below the hem of my T-shirt. I saw a quick flash of pink lace panties as she kneeled onto the bed. Facing the headboard, she pointed to the bag.

"What's this?"

"A present."

Her eyebrows shot up. "For me?"

I looked around the room and settled onto my side.

"I don't see anyone else here."

Her eyes shifted between me and the bag. "I can't believe you got me a present."

"It's nothing big," I said. "But it's something I thought you'd like."

She settled onto the bed with her legs crossed and pulled the small bag into her lap then gingerly removed the tissue paper. Reaching inside, she slowly pulled out its contents. I watched her inspect them for several seconds and worked to tamp down my nervousness.

I've bought things for women before, but never something personal like this. Then again, none of my relationships were personal like this. And Hannah isn't the kind of woman who'd want flashy jewelry or a trendy purse. She's the type who couldn't wait to get out of her designer dress tonight so she could jump in the shower to scrub away layers of makeup and a helmet of hairspray.

Hannah looked up at me, a smile lighting her face.

"These are amazing. Where did you find them?"

She picked up one pair of glasses then the other and inspected them.

"I went to dinner with the guys the other night and there was a consignment shop next door to the restaurant. These were in the window and caught my eye so I went back the next day to check them out." I shifted onto my elbow and shrugged. "I thought you'd like them."

"I love them," she said. "I don't have any ombre frames and these other ones are so unique. They look like plain tortoise shell, but tiny flowers make up the pattern."

"I understood tortoise shell, but what the hell is ombre?"

Holding up the frames in question, she said. "When the color goes from light to dark like that."

"I had no idea there was a name for that."

"Well now you know," she said and pulled off her black-framed glasses and placed them on the discarded tissue paper. Setting the "ombre" frames into place, she asked, "What do you think?"

"Nice," I said. "Hold on." Grabbing my phone, I turned on the camera and snapped a picture. "Now the other ones." She swapped glasses and struck a pose. "Got it."

She put on the glasses she could actually see out of and carefully wrapped the other two in the tissue paper, put them back in the bag, and set it on the nightstand.

"Let me see." Crawling to the middle of the bed, she set her head next to mine on my pillow. I pulled up the pictures and watched as she flipped back and forth between them. Turning to me, she placed her hand on my cheek and looked into my eyes.

"They're perfect, Jack. Thank you."

Leaning in, she placed her lips on mine, then lingered, deepening the kiss. I rested my hand on her shoulder and pulled back, holding her in place when she would have followed.

"What's wrong?" she asked.

"I just wanted to warn you and give you a chance to back away."

"I have no idea what you're talking about."

"We've been on opposite coasts for ten long days," I said.

"FaceTime and phone calls have been like extended

foreplay. So the next time we kiss, I'm not gonna let you come up for air until dawn."

Her lips curled into a slow smirk. "Sleep is highly overrated."

After Hannah uttered those words, I hate to say I jumped her, but that's basically what happened. Pushing the T-shirt out of my way as I slid up her body, I rested my hands on her cheeks then dragged my fingers through her hair before resting them on either side of her head. Tilting her face to one side, I pressed my lips to hers and took small tastes, nibbling and licking before opening my mouth fully and devouring hers.

Hannah gave as good as she got, meeting my tongue stroke for stroke. Her fingers dug into my scalp, holding me in place as our mouths opened and closed, taking and giving. I pressed against her, creating a tight suction, exploring and enjoying her every taste and texture.

She shifted her legs wider, pulling me closer to heaven. My hips moved, thrusting slowly against the heat surrounding me, her lace panties doing very little to dull the sensation. Without even touching me below the neck, Hannah had my dick peeking out of the waistband of my boxer briefs looking for attention.

The kiss went on and on, long and hard, our mouths fused together in a hot, sexual assault. Hannah's hands slid down my back and squeezed my ass, pulling me harder against her. A muffled moan vibrated through her chest when I thrust forward, pushing the tip of my dick between her folds to press against her clit.

I swallowed her low groan then pulled back, tugging her bottom lip between my teeth until she opened her eyes and met my gaze. Releasing her, I kissed her again, slower this time, savoring her sweetness, trying to set a new pace. The woman normally erodes my control and being apart for so long hasn't helped that. Hannah slid her right leg against my thigh and wrapped it around my hip, opening her to me even more.

So much for control.

I slanted my mouth over hers in a fierce, possessive kiss as our bodies thrust against each other. Her tight nipples dragged across my chest and I couldn't wait to feel them against my tongue. Tearing my mouth from hers, I fought to slow my breathing and backed up until I knelt between her thighs.

Her gaze dragged over me from head to abs. Zeroing in on the erection playing peek-a-boo with the waistband of my briefs, she reached out and tugged them down, catching my dick in a tight grip as it bobbed forward.

"Oh no you don't," I said and peeled her fingers away. Taking both of her hands in mine, I raised her arms above her head and wrapped them around her pillow. "Keep those there."

"Jack." Her voice came out somewhere between a whine and a groan.

I leaned forward and kissed my way from the corner of her mouth to her ear.

"Trust me. It'll be better this way." I nipped at her lobe then left a trail of open-mouthed kisses along her jaw, down her neck, and against her chest. Taking one nipple between my thumb and forefinger, I licked the other, then gazed up at her and sucked it into my mouth. She arched her back, but kept her hands in place above her head.

I licked, laved, and sucked, first one nipple then the other, her soft mewls urging me on. I could do that forever, but her thrusting hips became more insistent telling me she needed more. Pulling my mouth away with a pop, I kissed my way down to nip at her navel. Hannah watched my every move, her fingers white as she gripped the pillow.

Dipping my fingers into the waistband of her panties, I tugged them down her long legs and shifted away from her just enough to slip them off. I settled back into place and took a deep breath, inhaling her sweet scent. Using my thumbs, I held her open and stared at her glistening lips and engorged clit.

"You are so beautiful," I said, my voice hoarse.

I had every intention of teasing her a bit, but that plan went out the window as soon as I heard her ragged groan. She needs this as much as I need to give it to her.

Sliding first one, then another finger into her wet heat, I curled them forward and pumped slowly, dragging against her G-spot with every pass. Her hips lifted in tiny thrusts and I rested my hand on her stomach to hold her in place, leaned in, and took a long, firm lick.

"Jack, please." She panted. "*Please.*"

I pulled that tiny bundle of nerves into my mouth and sucked. Hannah's pussy clamped down on my fingers then continued to spasm as I feasted. Her shaking thighs clamped the side of my head and I pulled back giving her time to take a breath. Aftershocks squeezed at my fingers as I slowly pulled them out of her.

Resting my chin against her mound, I looked up the length of her body and couldn't help the chuckle that escaped. With her fingers digging into the pillow, she held it tight against her forehead, just above her tightly clenched eyes.

"What are you laughing at?" she asked, but sounded too exhausted to care.

"You can let go now."

Leaning forward, I stroked her white-knuckled grip with my thumb. She peeked one eye open and, finger by finger, loosened her hold on the pillow until it flopped back into place on the bed.

I lowered her arms until her hands rested on her stomach and massaged her fingers, working my way past her wrists to her forearms and biceps, then her shoulders. Stroking my way back down to her hands, I held them loosely in mine and kissed one then the other and smiled.

"You okay?" I asked.

She took in a deep breath and slowly let it out then nodded. "You're not stopping, are you?" she asked.

My answering laugh ended on a groan when she thrust her hips up, rubbing against my cock.

"As if I could stop."

Shifting off her, I got naked and rolled onto my back, pulling her on top of me. I usually like to be the one controlling the action, but with Hannah, I love watching her, love being able to touch her while she moves over me.

My eyes rolled back as she reached down and lined me up at her entrance and slowly slid down my entire length. The feel of sinking into her bareback is still new and I grit my teeth to hold off the orgasm that's never far away when I'm inside her.

I curled my fingers into her hips as she settled into a slow, steady movement. Her inner walls tightened, squeezing me closer to the edge with every stroke. Time to get this show moving before I totally lose control.

Sliding my fingertips up her sides, I cupped her breasts and dragged my thumbs across her nipples. She lost rhythm and grabbed onto my forearms to steady herself then pulled in a deep breath and let it out on a slow moan as she resumed her previous rhythm.

She froze in place when I pinched then rolled her nipples between my thumb and forefinger. Her knuckles turned white as she squeezed my wrists.

"Jack." My name came out on a throaty sigh.

"Come here." I let go of her nipples and, with her

fingers still wrapped around my wrists, pulled my arms down, taking her with them. Her tight nipples dragged against my chest when she rested her hands just above my shoulders. "You're killing me," I moaned, just before I lifted my head to press my lips against hers.

I'd meant to just give her a quick peck, but as usual, I lost control and ended up kissing the ever-loving fuck out of her.

Hannah's hips pulsed and I cupped her ass, angling her so her clit dragged against me with every thrust. With her pussy squeezing me tight and her sexy sounds, I know I won't last much longer. I pulled my lips from hers and leaned up onto my elbows and pull her right nipple into my mouth, licking and sucking, until her movements become more frantic. I moved onto the left, giving it the same treatment.

Hannah shifted back and dug her fingers into my scalp, holding me in place. Her inner muscles quivered and I knew she was close.

Thank God.

I rested my head back onto the pillow and thumbed both of her nipples at the same time, dragging them along the underside, just how she likes it.

"Jack!" she screamed just before she clamped down on my dick and milked me dry.

I held her tight as she rested against my chest, our heartbeats settling into a matching rhythm.

Before Hannah, the only thing I ever felt after sex was a physical release. But with her it's so much more than that. Yes, it's physically satisfying, but it's also so damn emotional, sometimes I feel like my chest will burst. I've avoided putting a name to what I feel for her, even though deep down inside I know. Someday I'll nut up and tell her.

My heartbeat sped up and slowed down with my

thoughts. Under normal circumstances I'd be worried I have an arrhythmia, but these aren't normal circumstances. Nothing with Hannah is normal.

She tilted her head back and looked me in the eye. "Everything okay?"

"Yeah, why?"

Leaning up on her elbow, she rubbed the center of my chest.

"Your heart is beating funny."

"I'm fine. I—" Those three little words were on the tip of my tongue, but I pussied out and said, "I'm just trying to figure out how you make my heart beat faster and slower at the same time."

My heartrate kicked up again at her answering smile.

"You do the same thing to me," she said, her voice barely a whisper, but her eyes said so much more.

And I like that more. I like it a lot.

Chapter Thirty-Three

HANNAH

I WALKED through the concourse and settled against the railing just as Sam Cherry threw the first pitch across the outside corner of the plate for a called strike one. The batter fouled the next pitch back, putting him way behind in the count. The crowd chanted and cheered as Sam went into his wind up. My view of the field was blocked as the fans jumped to their feet when strike three was called on the batter.

The stadium is extra loud tonight. It's always a bit crazy when we play New York, but there's extra energy for this game because if we win, we'll be tied with them for first place.

Batter number two popped out to shallow right field for the second out.

"Sam looks good tonight," Kenny said as he leaned on the railing next to me. "Hopefully he finally has his head together."

The strike zone has evaded our phenom pitcher the past couple weeks, and it doesn't matter how hard you throw if you can't put the ball over the plate. Sam has been a real Wild Thing for more starts than I want to think about, but tonight he looks good.

I smiled at my mental *Major League* reference. I'd seen the movie years ago but have watched it at least three times in my months with Jack. Then again, I've introduced him to *Baby Boom* and he's willingly watched Diane Keaton acclimate to life in a small Vermont town just as often.

Sam mixed it up and tossed in a breaking ball, throwing the batter off balance. He managed to get his bat on the ball, but ended up hitting a weak line drive toward Cal, who snagged it for the third out of the inning. He and Jack bumped gloves and jogged toward the dugout.

"Cal seems to have made a full recovery." Kenny phrased it as a sentence, but it came out more like a question. I nodded in agreement. "What do you think?"

I chuckled. "You'd know better than me."

Cal's neck injury after chasing a foul ball into the stands took him out of the game for a few weeks, but he seems to have made a full recovery. He looked amazing during his rehab games and this is his first series back with the Waves.

"Not necessarily." He turned to face me, resting his right arm on the railing. "You're part of their inner circle now."

As if I'd ever share any information my status as Jack's girlfriend makes me privy to with Kenny, or anyone else for that matter. Instead of commenting, I let Kenny's words hang in the air as the Waves came up to bat. Eventually he turned back to the field and we watched the game in silence through four full innings.

Both pitchers are on tonight and neither team has

managed to reach first base, so the game is moving fast. Kenny's phone buzzed just as Sam took the mound for the fifth time. He checked it, then put it back in his pocket.

"My father wants to see both of us in his office," he said.

"Now?"

"That's what the text said."

Mr. Hanover usually watches home games from his suite so the fact that he's in his office is a bit strange. That he wants to see both of us there is even more odd.

We left the concourse and headed toward the owner's suite.

"Any idea what this is about?" I asked.

"Not a clue."

The office door stood open as we approached. Kenny stepped aside and gestured for me to enter ahead of him. Mr. Hanover sat behind his big desk flipping through papers. We settled into the chairs across from him and waited. The fact that he didn't look up when we entered didn't make me think for one minute he was unaware of our presence.

"Thank you for coming," he said. Resting his elbows on the desk, he glanced between us. "I got word of something you both need to know."

Kenny and I shared a clueless look before returning our attention back to his father, who was now totally focused on me.

"Word is out about you and Jack," he said.

I sat back in the chair and crossed my legs. Considering the fact that Mr. Hanover is missing the game to hold this meeting, I thought he'd have something worse to share. Jack and I knew that eventually people would find out about us. We haven't announced our relationship but we haven't exactly been hiding it either.

Jack might have to field some questions about us, but I'm sure he'll handle it like the pro he is. I don't imagine anyone is going to bother me.

"I appreciate the head's up," I said.

"That's not all." Mr. Hanover's grim face and wrinkled brow warned me he was about to say something big, but I never imagined what a colossal turn the conversation was about to take. "I'm not sure how to say this so I'm just gonna put it out there. The media knows you're Aaran Diskin's daughter and that he just married a woman your age."

"What?" Kenny practically shouted, then looked from me to his father and back again. "Aaran Diskin is your *father?*"

I slowly nodded. My fingers and toes turned to ice as my ears buzzed. Taking in deep breaths through my nose and letting them out through my mouth, I struggled to ward off the panic attack that was fighting to take over. I haven't had one since high school and I certainly don't want one now.

I've managed to live my life out of the limelight attached to my father for over half my life and I don't want to step into it now. Especially not when his marriage to Mel will be fresh news. The fact that she's my best friend and having his baby will only add fuel to the fire.

"How the hell have you managed to keep that quiet all these years?" Kenny asked.

I gave him an abbreviated version of the story I told Jack a few months ago.

"Still, it seems impossible to fly under the radar nowadays," Kenny added. "How does no one know about you?"

"There are obviously people who knew me as Hannah Diskin, but I left her behind a long time ago. And the people who knew me are too absorbed in themselves to worry about where I disappeared to."

Kenny opened his mouth to speak again, but Mr. Hanover interrupted.

"The details of this aren't our business." He directed that comment at Kenny, then turned to me. "I know you like to stay behind the scenes, but you're going to be up front and center with this. Security will keep the media away from you here at the stadium, but you have to be prepared. You and Jack dating is small news compared to this."

Mr. Hanover seems pretty calm about this. Then again, it really doesn't affect him or the team. It does, however, affect my entire life. And Jack's by default.

Shit, Jack.

"Does Jack know about this yet?"

"Not yet," Mr. Hanover said. "The team journalists know at this point, but have been warned not to bring it up in the post-game interviews, but it's probably gonna be on those gossip shows."

"Thank you for letting me know" I said. "Is there anything else you wanted to discuss?"

Despite the turmoil churning within me, I managed to sound professional.

Mr. Hanover shook his head. "Just hang in there. It won't take long for another story to bump yours out of the spotlight."

Those words of wisdom from the man who freaked out because of a book. But since I value my job, I didn't call him on that fact. Instead, I excused myself to retreat to my office so I could have a nervous breakdown in private.

JACK

I FOLLOWED Dan down the tunnel.

"Sucks to admit they outplayed us today," he said. "But they did."

"Can't argue with that."

After seven nearly perfect innings for both teams, New York's clean-up hitter smashed a hanging curve over the right field fence giving them a one run lead. And we never managed to get that run back.

Thankfully Cal's return is the story of the night. The reporters will all want to talk to him and I should be able to shower and sneak out without much fuss.

Echoing my thoughts, Dan said, "If we keep our heads down, we might get out of here in record time."

Neither Dan nor I had done anything newsworthy in the game so we managed to remain invisible in the crowded locker room. After showering and dressing in record time, we practically tip-toed out the door.

He checked his phone and smiled. "I'm meeting Sabrina and Lexi at the ice cream shop. Want to come along?"

"Thanks, but I'm meeting Hannah at my place."

"You sure about that?" he asked.

"Yeah, why?"

Instead of answering me, he said, "Hey Hannah."

She stood at the end of the hallway, next to the stairs leading to the players' parking garage.

"Hi Dan—"

"I thought we were meeting at my place," I said, cutting off whatever else she was going to say.

Something must be wrong. Hannah never comes down

here and behind her bright blue glasses, her eyes look red and puffy, like she might have been crying.

"Hey, what's wrong?" She looked down and shook her head. I took her hand in mine and squeezed. "Hannah?"

Out of the corner of my eye, I saw Dan smile. The guys love the fact that I'm with a woman I actually care about. I'm glad they think it's funny because sometimes it freaks me the fuck out.

"I'll see you guys tomorrow," Dan said. "Gonna go meet my girls."

Hannah used her knuckle to push her glasses into place and stood taller, like she was trying to pull herself together.

"See you tomorrow," she said.

Dan took the steps to the parking garage two at a time, obviously in a rush to meet his wife and daughter. I threaded my fingers through Hannah's and turned to face her. I have no idea what has her so upset, but I want her to know I'm here, whatever it is.

"What's wrong?" I asked.

"Mr. Hanover called me to his office earlier to let me know that word of our relationship is out."

"Jesus, Hannah, you scared the shit out of me. I thought something awful happened. We knew that was going to happen eventually," I said. "We'll handle it."

"The media also knows about my dad."

"That he got married?"

"That he's my dad."

Oh fuck.

Chapter Thirty-Four

HANNAH

THE RINGING DOORBELL gave me an excuse to put down the book I was trying to immerse myself in. Placing my Kindle on the coffee table, I stood and walked to the door. After looking through the peephole, I pulled the door open wide for Mrs. Button.

"You're back," I said, unnecessarily. "How was your trip?"

I ushered her inside and closed the door behind her.

"I had a wonderful time, but it's good to be home." She settled into the overstuffed chair and put her feet up on the ottoman. "That's how I know I'm not ready to move."

She and Mr. Button had relocated from the Boston area to Myrtle Beach after he retired and her children have been bugging her to move back since his death.

"I love my children and adore spending time with my grandchildren, but right now, my life is here. Maybe I'll go back someday, but not today," she said. "But enough about me. How are you holding up?"

"I'd be lying if I said I'm happy it all came out. But it could be much worse." I shrugged. "For the most part, I'm able to lie low and I ignore the stories as much as possible."

Most people take anonymity for granted, but not me. Having a front row seat to my father's fame made me appreciate being in the background. Thankfully I left Hollywood in time so I was allowed to live most of my life out of the spotlight. I suppose I was crazy thinking that could last forever.

"Thankfully Myrtle Beach isn't a breeding ground for paparazzi."

I nodded at her words, then stood.

"I think I'll have a glass of wine. Join me?"

"That sounds wonderful."

I walked to the kitchen and opened one of the bottles of Pinot Grigio Jack bought at a winery we visited a few weeks ago. Pouring two glasses, I grabbed them in one hand and carried the bottle in the other and returned to the living room.

After setting the bottle on the coffee table, I handed Mrs. Button her glass and settled back onto the couch, tucking my feet beneath me.

"How's Jack handling all this?"

I shrugged. "On the surface he's fine, but he's boiling underneath. He blames himself."

"Why?"

"He rented a private jet to bring us home from my dad's wedding and from what we understand, someone from that company talked about our relationship. Once someone had a reason to dig up information about me, it was only a matter of time before they found out the whole story. Obviously it wasn't his fault, but he doesn't see it that way."

She smiled and took a sip of wine, looking at me over the rim of the glass with twinkling eyes.

"When I met you however many years ago, I never would have imagined that your father is one of the biggest movie stars in the country, if not the world. And..." She drew out the world dramatically, "you'd hook one of the hottest baseball players that ever played the game."

"I'm sorry I never told you about my father," I said. "I'd thought about it many times, especially in the last few months, but keeping the secret had been second nature for so long, I talked myself out of it."

"I understand, dear." She took another drink, then added, "And don't think you can ignore the last thing I said."

I circled my finger along the rim of the glass, deciding on a response. Have I *hooked* Jack? I've been determined to not name this thing between us and take it as it comes. So far, I've been successful...or at least I convince myself I have.

"Jack and I are enjoying each other's company, but that's it for now."

"Hannah, *I* enjoy that man's company. What you two have is way beyond that," she said. "It's obvious to anyone who sees you together that you're in love."

My face grew hot and I'm sure it's bright red.

Damn Irish skin.

I took a few slow breaths in an attempt to slow my racing heart.

"I uh, I'm not sure about love. It's kind of soon for that."

"I knew I was in love with my Manny by our third date. We married six months after we met." She sat forward and patted my knee. "There's no timeline for love. It will come and tap you on the shoulder when you least expect it. Choosing to turn around and embrace it is up to you."

That said, she finished her wine and placed her glass on the coffee table before standing and walking out the front door in dramatic silence.

JACK

I TURNED the water on hot enough to melt my skin and stood under the spray, willing it to pound away the tightness in my shoulders. Despite regular massages and stretches, my muscles feel like one big knot.

Normally I'd just deal with it, but it's starting to affect my bat speed. Not enough that anyone would notice, but I know my swing is slower than usual. Chicago's pitcher was throwing heat today for sure, but I only managed to foul off a few pitches I'd normally send into a gap.

Turning off the spray, I grabbed a towel off the rack and dragged it over my head and chest before tying it around my waist and stepping out of the shower.

My phone dinged as I stepped out of the bathroom, signaling a message. I picked it up and smiled at Hannah's name on my screen. I touched the voicemail app and her voice filled the room.

Tag, you're it. Sorry I missed your call. I was discussing our itinerary with Mr. Hanover. Give me a call when you can.

Pulling up FaceTime, I touched her name and waited half a breath before her smiling face filled the screen.

"Hey you," she said. "How's Chicago?"

"Boring without you." The words were out before I could stop them.

She laughed and sat back in her desk chair. I decided not to obsess over my flowery statement and instead got comfortable and rested against the pillows.

"What are you up to tonight?" she asked.

"Going out with the guys to get some deep dish. How about you?"

"I'm picking Mrs. Button up from her hair appointment and we're going out to dinner. I'm not sure where yet. I told her it's her choice."

"Please be careful."

"I'll be fine." Her eyes softened. "But thank you for worrying."

I hated to leave Hannah in the midst of the shit show I'd created, but duty calls. At least I'd just started a home stretch when the news broke so I was with her, but today's game in Chicago starts a seven-day road trip in the Midwest.

"If anyone bothers you, let Mrs. Button loose on them."

I rubbed the center of my chest as Hannah's answering laugh caused a warmth to spread through it. The action dragged her eyes downward.

"So." She drew out the word in a low, husky voice. "What are you wearing?"

I slowly moved my arm down my side until she could see me from hip to face.

"Mmm, nice," she said and licked her lips.

My body had its usual reaction to her interest in it, tenting the towel.

"Have anything interesting to show me?" she asked.

She'd spun her chair and I can tell by the way she's

slouched down that her feet are resting against the wall behind her desk.

A smile spread across her face as I slowly untucked the towel, loosening it around my waist. Moving the flap aside, I opened it, exposing my hip. Her smile widened.

"You know, normally when I show you mine, you show me yours," I said, bringing her eyes back toward my face.

"I'm still at the office so you're just going to have to use your imagination."

I closed my eyes and pictured Hannah spread out in my bed like she'd been just a couple nights ago.

"Jack?" I heard her, but instead of answering, I smiled and let out a low groan at my thoughts. "Jack!" I slowly opened my eyes and took in her laughing face. "Stop that!"

"I was just using my imagination like you told me."

She rolled her eyes.

"What am I going to do with you?"

"I'm sure you'll come up with something."

Hannah opened her mouth to answer, but instead sat up straight and swung her chair around. I looked at the side of her face as she glanced toward her office door.

"Yes?" I heard a voice in the background, then Hannah looked back at me. "Jack, I have to go. Marianne wants to speak with me before I leave."

"Call when you get home so I know you're safe," I said.

"I will. Have fun tonight."

"You too."

Even though I had the phone focused on just my face, before she hung up, her eyes looked down as though she could see everything below my neck. That did nothing to calm my raging erection. Thankfully I have a half hour before I have to meet the guys.

Being on the road can be exhausting, but I always enjoy

the hole-in- the-wall places we've found to eat in every city we visit. Back in my early playing days, I frequented the hot spots, but now I just want to go somewhere quiet where I can be left alone and enjoy a good meal, maybe a few drinks.

Dan bumped my arm with his elbow.

"Lexi got the game ball today." He tilted his phone in my direction, showing me a picture of his smiling daughter holding a dirty softball. "She hit a homerun. Not over the fence, but the ball went over the center fielder's head and she made it all the way around."

"That's my girl," I said.

"No, that's *my* girl."

He showed the picture to Cal, Monte, and Kasprzyk then put the phone back down next to his plate.

I shrugged. "Whatever you say."

Before he could respond, the waitress showed up at the table carrying two large pies. A young guy stood behind her with a heaping platter of chicken wings in one hand and two pitchers of beer in the other. They squeezed everything onto the table and she grabbed our empty pitchers. The kid stayed just behind her, staring at us with his mouth hanging open.

"You guys need anything else right now?" she asked. We told her we were good and she said to give her a shout if we needed anything. Otherwise, she'd leave us alone. Which is how we like it. She dragged her co-worker away with her.

He must be new. We've frequented this place often enough that the regular staff and patrons don't give us that wide-eyed look anymore. When we're done eating, I'll have the waitress send him over to sit with us for a few minutes.

My mouth watered at the combined aroma of pizza goodness and spicy wings. Knowing better than to dig into the pie before it cools a bit, we focused on the wings.

They're probably just as hot, but at least they won't fall apart.

"I have some news to share," Kasprzyk said, after we'd put a good dent in the platter of wings. We all sat back in our seats, giving him our full attention. "Natalie is pregnant." He smiled. "We're expecting baby number four."

We all congratulated him, then finally felt confident the pizza had cooled down enough to stay together when taken out of the pan. Monte grabbed the spatula and served slices all around.

"So when's she due?" Dan asked.

"December 12th," John said.

I did the math in my head and said, "So she's four months pregnant?" He nodded. "Didn't I just see her? She didn't look any different."

"She has a little bump, but has been hiding it well. Now that we're telling people, I'm sure she'll be wearing things that make it a little more obvious." He shrugged. "After the miscarriage, we wanted to wait to announce it."

Natalie had been pregnant at the end of last season, but lost the baby around her third month. I can't blame them for waiting to tell everyone this time.

"You hoping for another girl?" Monte asked.

"I know Ava is for sure," John laughed. "A girl would be nice so we'd have two of each, but honestly, it doesn't matter to me. Healthy is all I care about."

After we finished all the food and settled the tab, I asked the waitress to send the guy who'd delivered our chicken wings over when he had a chance. He showed up next to the table almost immediately and I invited him to sit in the sixth chair at our table.

Unnecessarily, I introduced myself and the guys and found out his name is Tim, although he hesitated before offering it, like he may have forgotten for a second. We talked for a while, mostly about baseball, before the wait-ress walked past, making eyes at him that said it was time for him to get back to work. He stood and thanked us for calling him over.

"We'll see you next time we're in town," I said. "This is our usual hangout when we're in the city."

"I'll see you then," Tim said, having mostly lost the star-struck look he'd had earlier.

When he left, Cal said, "All your extra PR must be rubbing off on you."

"Maybe it's just Hannah rubbing off on him," Monte added.

I looked at him with a raised brow. The wives and girl-friends rule never really applied to the women I've spent time with, but Hannah is different. Sometimes the guys need to be reminded of that fact. My look did it better than any words could. Monte lifted his glass to me in apology.

To lighten things, I said, "Maybe I'll get extra credit for coming up with it on my own."

We finished our drinks and hung out for a little while longer when Cal looked toward the back room.

"Anyone up for a game of pool?" he asked.

"I'm in," Monte said.

"I'm actually gonna head back to the hotel," Dan said, then smirked. "My personal physical therapist gave me some extra exercises to do. I want to get them in before bed."

"I'll go with you," I said, surprising them. I'm usually one of the last to leave whenever we go out. "I'm beat. It's been an exhausting couple weeks," I added, stopping any ribbing they might have thrown my way.

"I'll hang out for a while longer," John said. "I'm not

tired at all and will just end up flipping through the nonsense on TV if I leave."

We all stood. Cal, Monte, and John walked toward the back room to the pool table. Dan and I walked out the front door and continued the five blocks to the hotel, mostly in silence. Before we went inside, Dan stopped.

"I'm actually kind of glad the guys decided to stay," he said, nodding toward a bench to the left of the sliding doors. "I wanted to talk to you alone."

"What's up?" I hesitated a second, then sat. "Everything okay?"

"Relax, everything is fine," he said, settling next to me. "More than fine, actually. This is totally classified information, but I got Sabrina's permission to tell you."

Between his smile and the look on his face, I knew what he was going to say.

"Holy shit! Sabrina's pregnant?" He nodded, looking like he might give himself whiplash. I reached out and patted his back in a sideways hug. "Congratulations! That's awesome."

He kept nodding at my words.

"When's she due?"

"March 10th," he said. "We didn't think it would happen so

fast, so the timing sucks with the season starting, but we're too thrilled to care."

"Does Lexi know?"

"Do you think it would be a secret if she did?" he asked around a chuckle. "No, I just convinced Sabrina to tell our parents a couple days ago. The doctor said everything looks great, but Natalie's miscarriage has her a little freaked out."

"That's understandable."

"At least now the parents know just in case she needs

them." He looked at me. "And now you know in case I need you."

Baseball has given me a makeshift family, but Dan has definitely become the brother I never had. It was my turn to nod and I had to swallow down the lump in my throat before speaking.

"I'm sure you won't, but I'll be here if you do."

He slapped my back and stood.

"Besides, how could we not share this news with *Uncle Jack*?" he asked, lightening the mood.

I stood and followed him into the hotel. We'd just gotten off the elevator on our floor when his phone rang.

"Hey Bri," he said, a huge smile on his face. "I just shared our good news with Jack."

I yelled my congratulations toward the phone.

Dan's smile faded. "No, we didn't see that," he said, eyes shifting in my direction, then toward the floor. "We'll check it out. Thanks for letting me know. I will. Love you, too."

"What's wrong?" I asked as he ended the call.

He glanced up and down the hallway before looking at me again. "Sabrina said there's a bunch of shit about Hannah on the internet. She caught the end of the story on one of those entertainment shows and checked it out."

I looked at my phone to see if Hannah had called. No missed calls or texts showed. So either she didn't see it yet or she's already dealing with the fallout.

"Let's get in your room so we can find out what's going on," Dan said.

We walked the short distance to my room and I stopped looking at my phone long enough to unlock the door and step inside. Dropping into the chair, I Googled Hannah's name and fought to keep my dinner down. My vision blurred as a helpless rage coursed through my body and I blinked furiously, bringing my screen back into view.

"Shit." Based on Dan's whispered curse, I assume he's looking at the same thing I am.

Flipping through the pictures, I cringed as the horrible night Hannah described to me a few months ago unfolded in full color. She looks so different...younger for sure, but with her designer dress, fancy updo, and full face of makeup, she looked older in some ways. The article accompanying the pictures depicts her as a typical Hollywood wild child with too much money and not enough sense.

I tossed my phone on the table next to me, afraid if I kept looking I'd either smash it or find the guy who published that shit and go smash him in the face.

Chapter Thirty-Five

HANNAH

"I JUST DON'T THINK it's a good idea for you to go with everything happening," Mr. Hanover said.

He'd summoned me to his office to drop that bomb. I'm supposed to head up to Boston in two days to meet up with Jack to attend a benefit. Then we're venturing over to New Hampshire for another fundraiser and to visit Jack's father, which I'm excited and nervous about in equal measures.

"I apologize, Mr. Hanover. I never thought my past would come back at me like this."

I've been in the same room when Mr. Hanover stared down a player, but have never been on the receiving end of his steely gaze until now. I fought the urge to hunch my shoulders and sink into the chair.

"I understand you didn't ask for this, but it's here and has to be dealt with."

He'd said a variation of that sentence to Jack a few months ago and ironically, I was the one enlisted to help clean things up. Now here I am sitting in the middle of my own mess.

"Would you like me to resign?" I asked.

It's a serious question. He's traded players who cause crests in the Waves' organization. Why would I be any different?

"Resign?" He muttered under his breath then leaned forward, resting his elbows on the desk. "No I don't want you to resign, but you have to admit that keeping yourself behind the scenes is probably a good idea at this point."

Behind the scenes is my favorite place to be, but I'm not sure that's possible for me anymore. Even after this all settles down, I'm sure that on a slow news day, some bored reporter will check out what I'm doing. But I didn't tell him that.

And as a PR person, I'll admit that there's some merit to what he's saying, but as the woman in Jack's life, I want to go see him and meet his father.

"We can send someone in your place if you think it's necessary," he said, pulling me from my thoughts.

"Since I've been accompanying him all season, don't you think that would draw more comments?"

He grunted, which I took as agreement since he didn't rebut my point.

"If we were in LA or New York, it may be more of a concern, but I can't imagine the paparazzi is going to flock to a fundraising event in Boston to snap a picture of me."

Leaning back in his chair, he rubbed his eyes, then dragged his hands down his face. Meeting my eyes, he said, "You really believe that?"

"I do." I shrugged. "Besides, me hiding away won't

minimize any curiosity people have about my past or my relationship with my father."

He folded his hands over his stomach, seeming to consider my words. As usual, Mr. Hanover's expression gave nothing away, so I was surprised when he said, "All right." At my raised brow, he added, "You can go."

That said, he leaned forward and started sorting through the paperwork on his desk. I decided to take his statement and run before he could change his mind, throwing a quick *thank you* over my shoulder as I left.

JACK

I took the fastest shower possible, packed my duffle, and was out of the locker room before some of my teammates even entered it. We'd split the series with Boston, with three of the games going into extra innings. I'm exhausted and looking forward to a day off.

Well, the day off and spending time with Hannah.

The benefit we attended last night was a stiff, formal Boston affair, but I still had a good time. Hannah looked amazing in a black dress that should have been nondescript, but it put her every curve on display. Her black heels weren't sky high, but they had the coveted red bottom, and added just enough to her height to align all our good parts.

Not that Hannah has any bad parts.

But the cherry on the sundae was the fact that she wore the glasses I had given her a few weeks ago. She had debated between the ones she calls *ombre* and the tortoise shell but in the end decided on the latter.

I'd managed to get her on the dance floor for most of the slow songs. Her body pressed against mine had the usual effect, but thankfully the jacket of my tux hid that fact.

I walked out the gate and spotted the Audi convertible I'd rented for this venture parked at the curb. I'd convinced her to drop me off earlier and go back to the hotel for some well-deserved R&R.

"Hey," I said, not wanting to scare her as I approached the car.

She looked in my direction and smiled as I opened the car door and slipped behind the steering wheel. I leaned over the console and kissed her. I'd intended on just quick peck to say hello, but it ended up being a full-blown, tongue-tangling kiss. And I would have loved for it to continue, but I heard voices in the distance and figured we should get out of here.

I ended the kiss and rested my forehead against hers, breathing in her sweet scent.

"You ready?" I asked. "Are you okay with the top down?"

She nodded. "That's why I put my hair in a ponytail."

I moved back into my seat before I forget where we're at and start kissing her again. Hannah took a deep breath and slowly smiled before moving into her own seat.

"You smell so good."

"You wouldn't have said that a half hour ago."

"I've been around you after games and you still smell amazing," she said.

A lot of women have complimented me through the years, but their flowery words never meant a thing. But when Hannah says something like that, I get a warm feeling in the center of my chest that chips away at my stone-cold heart. Maybe it's because I see how happy Dan and Sabrina are, but instead of freaking me out, it makes me want to explore where this relationship with Hannah can go.

I looked in the rearview and shifted the car into drive. Looking at her out of the corner of my eye, I smiled and said, "Here we go."

Chapter Thirty-Six

HANNAH

"HOW HAVE I gone my entire life without eating one of these?" I shoved the last bite of lobster roll in my mouth.

"I don't know, but I'm gonna go grab you another one because I really enjoyed watching you eat that.

I rolled my eyes and swallowed.

He kissed my forehead and whispered, "I'll be right back."

As he walked away, I chuckled, thinking of something Mrs.

Button always says.

It's sad to see him leave but so nice to watch him go.

That statement most definitely applies to Jack. The man's ass is seriously a work of art.

"Enjoying yourself ?" Marie Daniel, the event coordinator, appeared from somewhere behind me and sat on my side of the long bench.

I nodded. "It's a beautiful day and the food is amazing. You've put together a great event."

"Thank you, but I can't take all the credit. I had a lot of help," she said. "And honestly I've planned so many of these, I could do it in my sleep. As long as the weather cooperates, I'm good."

"Is it always adult's only?"

"This event is," she said. "Initially we had it as a family event, but when we moved it to this location, we decided to make it twenty-one and up. It's such a large area, it would be easy for children to run off. Plus it gives me an excuse to leave my kids at home." She gave me a conspiratorial wink. "We host a basketball tournament that's all ages in November, and the kids love it."

Jack stood across the clearing, a plate in each hand, talking to three men as they watched what appeared to be a riveting cornhole match. When we first got here, he'd spoken to pretty much everyone, and the attendees were either star struck or teased him for not playing for Boston. But now they seemed to have relaxed a little and it looked like everyone was enjoying themselves.

Wearing khaki shorts and a blue Waves polo, he should blend in with the rest of the similarly-dressed men, but that's not the case. Or maybe it's just me because I thought the same thing when he wore a tuxedo for the blue-blood benefit in Boston.

He caught me watching him and said something to the men surrounding him and walked in my direction, his eyes not leaving my face. When he reached the table, he set the plates down and sat across from me.

"Thank you again for being here," Marie said. "And for dealing with being surrounded by rabid Boston fans with such grace."

"It's my pleasure," he said then leaned slightly toward

Marie. "And you know I grew up a rabid Boston fan, so I get it."

"We usually have a good turnout here, but your presence really bumped it up." She stood and held out her hand and shook his. "I'll leave you two alone to finish eating."

We said good-bye and she left us to go check on the buffet table. I picked up my fork and dug into the clams he'd brought me. Elbows resting on the table, he held a buttery ear of corn with both hands.

"Please give me fair warning before you start eating that lobster roll. I don't want to choke on my corn," he said, then smiled and took a big bite.

Jack's New England accent was slipping all over the place here, which I love. I looked down at my *lobsta roll* and smiled. Might as well give the man what he wants.

"Here's your fair warning," I said as I picked up the roll. "Let me know when you're ready."

He put his nearly-eaten corn back on the plate and rested his chin on his fist.

"I'm ready. Bring it on."

JACK

WATCHING Hannah wrap her mouth around a lobster roll is better than any porno I've ever seen. And as if the visual isn't stimulating enough, she keeps making soft little moans in the back of her throat every time she takes a bite.

I kept my gaze glued to her lips, even after she was done, which is how I realized she was speaking to me, because I certainly hadn't heard her.

"Hmm?" I cleared my throat. "What did you say?"

"What time do we have to leave?"

"It'll take us about a half hour to get there." I glanced at my phone. "If we leave in an hour we should be good."

I told my dad we'd be there in time for dinner, which is at five sharp in his house. For the past couple decades, he's been very regimented about his meals. They happen at eight, noon, and five without fail, and I'm not going to mess with that.

He ended up in the hospital a few months after my mother died because he basically stopped eating. By the time I graduated high school, he'd gotten himself pulled together enough to implement the schedule, which had been recommended by his doctor.

But the not eating thing and subsequent illness freaked me out. Especially since it had been so soon after my mom died. Even years later, once I moved out to play ball, I used to call him to make sure he'd eaten something.

I stabbed the last potato on my plate, shoved it in my mouth, and chewed clearing those thoughts from my mind. I have an hour left here to enjoy Hannah's company and then we have the whole night and all day tomorrow to spend together. I refuse to let thoughts of my father or whatever happens at his house ruin that.

Pulling into the driveway of my childhood home, I rolled my shoulders, trying to relax. Hannah placed her hand on my knee, and I looked over at her. She knows how much I hate coming here and also knows how much I hate myself for hating it.

"Ready?" she asked pulling me from my thoughts.

I nodded and opened my door, then rounded the car to open hers. She got out, holding the box of goodies Marie Daniel had insisted we take when she found out we were coming here. I had planned on bringing pizza, but my dad will enjoy this more.

The house and lot both look well-kept thanks to the property manager I hired years ago to keep it maintained. I also pay for a housekeeper to visit once a week so I know the house is being cleaned and straightened.

I noticed a shadow behind the front door and it swung open just as we stepped onto the front porch. Well, that's a first. I can't remember the last time my dad had greeted me at the door.

Normally when I visit, he's in his recliner watching TV so I know his eagerness today has nothing to do with me.

I held the screen door open and motioned for Hannah to go inside, then followed her, closing the door behind me.

"Hey dad," I said giving him an awkward hug. "This is Hannah Adams."

I didn't add anything after her name. Calling her my girlfriend seems juvenile. But if you're not married or engaged, what other term do you use when you're in a relationship as an adult?

He watches the news so he knows exactly who she is and the nature of our relationship. Then again the fact that she's here says it all. I haven't brought anyone into this house since high school.

"What d'ya got there?" he asked Hannah.

"We were just at a fundraiser and they had the most amazing food. The woman in charge insisted we bring some for you," she said. "I highly recommend the lobster rolls. They're amazing."

"Hannah had her first lobster roll today," I said as I rummaged through the cupboard for some plates.

"Where'd you grow up?" he asked.

"California," she said as she removed the items from the box one by one and placed them on the kitchen table.

"Then I moved to Myrtle Beach, and they're more about hush puppies and fritters down there."

"What do you want to drink, dad?"

"Just water," he said. "But I should be waiting on you two since you're my guests."

He really is putting on a good show for Hannah.

I grabbed three bottles of water from the refrigerator, quickly taking an inventory before closing the door. The housekeeping service I hired also keeps his cupboards and refrigerator stocked.

I pulled out a chair for Hannah to sit. She'd made my father a plate and I asked if he wanted it warmed up.

"No, it's good," he said.

I settled into the seat next to Hannah and picked at the potatoes, eating them straight from the container.

"Do you want me to make you a plate, too?" she asked.

"No, they taste better this way."

She shook her head and chuckled.

"This is a pretty good lobster roll. Why don't you have another one?" he said to Hannah. "It looks like there are plenty."

"I already had two," she said.

"Yeah, but third one's the charm," he said. "It'll taste even better."

Who is this man?

Since my mother died, I've endured conversations filled with his single-word responses. But, much to my surprise, the conversation between him and Hannah flowed. The man spends his days watching TV and reading so he's well versed in everything from Harry Potter to the latest Hollywood gossip. Naturally he knew about her father but didn't ask too many questions. He seemed much more interested in the woman sitting across from him, and I can't say I blame him.

"Can I use your restroom?" Hannah asked when there was a break in the conversation.

I pointed toward the door just across from us, but my father said, "That one has been acting up. Use the one upstairs." Before I could ask, he offered, "I have a plumber coming to look at it next week."

Standing, I gestured to Hannah and said, "Follow me."

I walked through the living room and up the stairs and she followed a few steps behind. I know she's trying to get a good look at the pictures that are hanging on the wall and scattered on tables without being too obvious.

We stood outside the bathroom and she looked at the other four doors in the hall then asked, "Which room was yours?"

I pointed to the one at the end of the hall.

"Will you show me?"

Hannah followed me down the hall and I opened the door, gesturing for her to step inside. She stopped and looked around then took a few more steps into the room. I watched her, trying to see it from her point of view.

The room is like a time capsule. Nothing has changed since I left. Trophies and awards line the shelves I'd helped my father hang when I was about nine years old. Signed baseballs sit on one dresser and a scattering of baseball caps on the other. The full-size bed is decked out with Boston sheets and the windows are covered with curtains to match.

"Was this your girlfriend?" she asked, pointing to my senior prom picture stuck in the dresser mirror.

"Just a prom date," I said. "She lives a couple doors down so we grew up together. Her boyfriend broke up with her a few weeks before prom so I stepped in."

She smiled. "What a guy."

"Yeah, I'm a regular knight in shining armor."

I smiled and kissed the tip of her nose, then turned and walked out of the room, hoping she didn't ask about the framed picture of my mom and me sitting on the night-stand. Thankfully she took my cue and I closed the door behind me.

"I'll see you downstairs," I said and left her standing outside the bathroom.

"I thought you got lost," my father said when I entered the kitchen.

"Just showing Hannah my old room."

He picked up his plate and stood, then placed it in the sink. His back still to me, he said, "I like her. She's not like those floozies I've seen you with."

I took a long drink of water, hoping it would drown the sarcastic comment on the tip of my tongue. Thankfully it worked so I took another quick sip before putting the bottle down.

He joined me at the table again.

"And I can tell you like her, too."

"No denying that," I said.

"Jack, I know I haven't been a great father to you, but..."

He closed his eyes and shook his head.

I clenched my jaw, fighting the urge to unleash more than twenty years of frustration on him. Instead of letting him have it, I focused on peeling the label off my water bottle in tiny strips. My father hasn't said this much to me in years and I'm hoping he gives me a clue what this is all about.

Opening his eyes, he looked directly into mine.

"I've been seeing a counselor for the past four months."

And there it is.

I snapped my head up to look at him.

"Why didn't you say something?" I asked.

"I wanted to make some progress first," he said. "And I was hoping that maybe now that you have someone in your life that you love like I loved your mother, you'll understand a little better."

"Dad, it's not like that." My stomach twisted with my words.

His laugh sounded rusty. "I wish I could take a picture so you could see how you look at her."

I heard the sound of running water and the floor above us creaked. I want to get this conversation over before she came back.

He blinked and looked directly at me with watery eyes.

"Jack, the Reagan men love hard. You have generations of happy marriages and love stories in your history. Granted, your path has been a little different than all of ours, but the destination is the same."

He took a drink and slowly screwed the cap back on the bottle.

How the fuck is my father who's been in a deep state of depression for the better part of my life giving me relationship advice? I wanted to ask him, but I'm not that much of a prick.

"When that drunk driver took your mother away from me..." He trailed off and shook his head.

I should have gone back to peeling the damn label, but my hands were shaking too hard. Should have kept my mouth shut too, but I couldn't seem to do that either.

"Did you ever once consider the fact that that drunk driver took my *mother* away from me?" The words came out as a vicious whisper and once they started flowing, I couldn't stop them. "And my father too because you couldn't keep yourself together enough to actually be a parent."

I swallowed and took a breath, trying to slow my

pounding heart. I heard Hannah's feet on the stairs, the pauses letting me know she was taking the time to check out the photos she'd missed on the way up.

What the fuck is wrong with me?

I don't lose control like this. Ever.

Well, not since right after my mother died and I realized I was going to have to be strong because the man in front of me couldn't be. Before either of us could say anything else, Hannah entered the kitchen. It was obvious from the look on her face that she felt the tension in the room. She looked from me to my father and back again, and her lips curled up slightly, offering me a slight smile.

My heart skipped a beat at her small show of support and that familiar warmth spread through my chest.

"You ready to go?"

My voice came out more harsh than I'd intended, but she didn't react or seem surprised by my question. She simply nodded and told my father how nice it was to meet him and thanked him for his hospitality.

I swallowed, hoping my tone would be somewhat softer next time I spoke. I swore I wouldn't let my father ruin this time with Hannah and I won't. We're gonna have an amazing night and a great day tomorrow.

And after that, I have to work on getting my shit back under control.

Chapter Thirty-Seven

HANNAH

"OH MY GOSH, HE'S GORGEOUS."

My new little brother blinked sleepy blue eyes at me. You gotta love FaceTime. This live action is better than a video for sure.

"Melanie was splendid," my father said and I dragged my eyes from the baby to look in his direction.

He tilted his iPad so I could see Melanie propped up against the headboard of the bed behind him. They both looked exhausted but the happiness shined through.

"Does he have hair?" I asked.

Since my dad's hands were full, Mel leaned forward and pulled off the baby's beanie, exposing soft tufts of light blond hair.

"Blond haired and blue eyed like his daddy," she said, making my dad beam with pride.

My dad and I have similar features, but I really wish I'd

inherited his eyes. They're a cerulean blue and dip slightly at the edges, giving him a perpetual look of sincerity.

"So did you decide on a name?" Last I'd heard, they'd narrowed it down to three and were waiting to see which suited him.

"Jacob," my father said.

"Hey Jacob. I can't wait to meet you in person and hold you."

Jacob was obviously unimpressed by my words because his mouth twisted into a wide yawn. The three of us watched the little miracle as he settled back into place.

"I'm gonna take this little man to the nursery and rock him a bit," he said. "You girls can enjoy a chat." He kissed the screen and said, "Love ya baby girl."

After handing the iPad to Mel, he stood and she watched them leave, a sappy look on her face, then turned to me.

"So how was it?"

"Wonderful. Horrible. Amazing. Painful as hell." She smiled wide. "And I'd do it again in a heartbeat."

"He's perfect, Mel. Congratulations."

Her watery eyes met mine through the screen.

"Thank you."

Before things got too mushy and we both ended up blubbering, I asked, "So how was the home birth? Would you do *that* again?"

Much to my father's chagrin, Mel had wanted to have the baby at home. They've kept a low profile since the wedding and she didn't want to jeopardize that by going to the hospital. She'd made her final decision after the story about me was published.

"I would do it again. At least I was comfortable in my own home during the hours of labor. I could pace the hall without worrying someone was gonna snap a picture of me."

"How'd my dad hold up?"

"He was great. I know he wasn't sold on the home birth, but he was still supportive."

"You look so happy," I said. "I feel like I'd be a mess after giving birth, but you're camera ready."

"I don't know about that last statement, but I am happy." She settled further into the pillows and her eyes looked into mine.

"How about you? Are things still good with Jack?"

"Things are still good." I shrugged. "But there's definitely something different."

"Bad different?"

"I'm not sure." I saw my frown in the little window on the screen and relaxed my face. "On the surface, things are great. Jack is as sweet and attentive as ever, but he just seems off sometimes."

"Have you talked to him about it?"

"About what?" I asked. "There's really nothing specific to ask about."

"Well, when you were at our wedding, I thought something was going to spontaneously combust with all the heat between you two."

That had been a hot trip for sure.

"Things didn't feel off then."

"Do you think he's upset because the news came out that you're Aaran's daughter?"

"I know he blames himself since the leak came from the charter company he used," I said. "But no, things were okay after that. I didn't feel a difference until after our trip to Boston."

"Did something happen there?"

"Not really. We attended the events then visited his father."

"You didn't tell me you met his father," she screeched. "Tell me all about him. Does Jack look like him?"

Jack's story is his to tell, but I can answer her questions without giving it all away.

"They do look alike. I saw a picture of Jack and his mother and I can see some of her features in him too, but he and his dad share a strong resemblance," I said. "He's very sweet. It's obvious he still misses Jack's mother, but some people never get over the death of a loved one."

"Are he and Jack close?"

I shrugged and gave a non-answer. "As close as they can be considering Jack doesn't live near him."

She shook her head dramatically. "Okay, now that I'm semi filled in on the father situation, let's get back to Jack," she said. "Is the sex still good? I mean, we haven't discussed details, but I'm assuming it's good."

"And we will never discuss details," I said. "Besides the fact that you know I don't kiss and tell, I definitely don't want to hear any of *your* details."

Her laugh echoed through my living room.

"Understood." She wrinkled her nose. "That would definitely be icky," she admitted. "And I don't need details, just an answer."

I thought about the times we've been together since Boston.

"It's still good," I said. "If anything, it's the only time things don't feel off. And don't get me wrong, I don't have that feeling all the time. He'll be normal and then it's like something shifts. Like there's a glass divider between us." I rolled my eyes. "It sounds ridiculous. Maybe I'm being crazy. The schedule hasn't had many breaks since Boston. He could just be tired."

"Could be. It's a busy schedule for sure. Is he home now?"

"No, he's in Texas for the next three days then Detroit for another three. But then he'll be home for a ten-day stretch."

"You'll have to let me know how it goes."

I nodded. "You should get some rest while the baby is sleeping." She didn't argue, so she must be exhausted. "Call or text anytime. I'll be out to visit soon."

She yawned and turned onto her side. "Love you," she said.

"Love you, too."

JACK

AFTER STRIKING out my first at bat, I managed to sneak one between short and third. Detroit's first baseman practically leaned against me as he held me to the bag and I shifted away from him, looking for some space. He wasn't having it.

The guy is a hothead who still holds a grudge from our Minor League days. On one drunken night, I made him look like an ass in front of a girl he was trying to score with and he still messes with me anytime I play against him. After all these years, you'd think he would have either gotten over it or realized that I'm not going to rise to his bait.

After the pitcher settled onto the mound, I took a step and a half toward second.

The asshole at first made some comments questioning both my sexuality and parentage, but I focused on the pitcher instead. I don't want to get picked off because I'm focusing on some prick with a chip on his shoulder.

Phil Riddle took two high pitches, putting him ahead in the count. I took advantage of the situation and chanced an extra step in my lead, figuring the pitcher would be concentrating on putting a strike across the plate instead of me.

Turns out, I was wrong.

He stepped off the rubber and snapped the ball toward first. I dove back to the bag and the umpire called me safe a split second before I felt the first baseman's mitt smack down on my forearm with just a little too much force. I glared at him as I stood and adjusted my helmet.

"Got a problem, pussy?" he asked.

"What the fuck is wrong with you?"

"Pathetic shits like you piss me off."

I took in a deep breath and let it out slowly as I stepped back into my usual lead.

Riddle lined the ball over the third baseman's head and I ran the ninety feet and rounded second base, but stopped there. The left fielder got the ball in pretty quickly, so I played it safe.

I glanced back at first, thankful I wouldn't be there for another batter. I'm in no mood to deal with that asshole.

I ran out to my position in the bottom of the ninth, thankful this game is almost over. We just need three more outs and we can get the hell out of here with another win in the books.

My shoulders feel like concrete and I just want to sleep in my own bed. If Hannah is in my bed with me, that's even better.

Shaking away that last thought, I watched our pitcher, Chris Russell aka Rusty, warm up. He looks good, so hopefully this will be a quick inning.

The umpire stepped behind the plate and the first batter got into the box. Rusty is throwing heat tonight and the guy couldn't catch up to the first two fast balls. The next two pitches were fouled off, but Rusty finished him off with a slider.

The asshat of a first baseman stepped into the box. He's not much of a hitter, so I had visions of a quick second out. That looked like a good possibility when Rusty threw a fastball on the outside corner for strike one. Unfortunately, he followed that with a hanging curve that went flying into right field. My vision of a one, two, three inning wasn't totally lost though. Kasprzyk got to the ball quickly and came up throwing.

I got into position to receive the ball, my feet on either side of the bag. Out of the corner of my eye, I saw the guy barreling toward me while I kept my attention on the ball flying over Oskar's head toward my glove. Just as I was about to catch it, my legs were taken out from beneath me and the ball hit my cheekbone and bounced off.

My head banged against the hard clay as he landed on top of me with an elbow lodged against my throat. I pushed him away, but he shifted back with more pressure.

"Get the fuck off me!"

When he didn't move, I pushed at, then punched his shoulder. "You're nothing but a cocky pretty boy mother fucker."

He pushed off me and dug his spike into my calf as he stood. I started to get up but he pushed on my shoulder knocking me back down.

I jumped up and lunged toward him, but Oskar grabbed me from behind. Rage-fueled adrenaline coursed through my body and I struggled against his hold.

"Settle down, Jack." Oskar's voice came from directly behind me as he pulled at my arms. "He's not worth it."

Those words stopped me in my tracks.

I stopped struggling and focused on breathing.

"I'm good," I said. "You can let go."

Oskar slowly released his hold.

The whole scene had taken mere seconds. No benches were cleared, no one was ejected, and no warnings were issued. The umpire asked if I was okay and I nodded even though my head and cheekbone are both throbbing, and my calf hurts like a son of a bitch. I got back into position and forced my stormy thoughts away so I could focus on the game.

Thankfully the altercation didn't ruin Rusty's rhythm and he took the next two batters down with ease. I participated in the celebratory antics on the field then headed for the showers. A few minutes later, I stood under the ice cold spray, trying to figure out what just happened on the field. Hell what's been happening since the outburst in my father's kitchen.

I turned off the shower and wrapped a towel around my waist. As I walked by the mirrors, I spotted the cut and bruise on my swollen cheekbone. I also noticed the wild look in my eyes. I haven't seen that in years.

For the past few months, I've fooled myself into thinking I could release my hold on certain feelings while keeping control of the others. Obviously that's not the case. The question is, what am I going to do to fix it?

Chapter Thirty-Eight

HANNAH

I HEARD Mrs. Button's giggle and knew Jack must have arrived. As I opened the door, I found the man in question standing in front of my porch steps, pizza in hand. Wearing loose basketball shorts, a green T-shirt, and his favorite Sperrys, the man looks good enough to eat.

"You kids have fun," Mrs. Button said.

"Would you like to join us?" he asked.

"I'm going out with my girls tonight, but thank you for the offer."

"Uh oh, girls night. Don't get too crazy, okay?" He winked at her. "And if you do, give me a call."

"You shouldn't say things like that to old ladies." Mrs. Button dramatically fanned her face. "It's not good for the blood pressure."

"I'd never say that to an old lady," he said, putting emphasis on the last two words.

She shook her head and smiled at me. "This one is definitely a charmer," she said.

"That's for sure," I agreed.

We said good-bye to Mrs. Button and I held the door open for him. He gave me a quick kiss as he walked past and I took in a deep breath. We've been together for months and I'm as addicted to his scent as ever.

"You can set that on the coffee table," I said, then closed and locked the door.

He put the pizza down then settled onto the couch, looking exhausted. The baseball season is long and by August it takes a toll on even the sturdiest players. A day off after an afternoon game like the Waves have this weekend is a welcome relief.

"Would you like a beer?" I asked.

"Sounds good."

I went to the kitchen and pulled two beers out of the refrigerator with one hand then grabbed the cupcakes I made for dessert before I went to work this morning with the other. I looked down at the platter and smiled. Last time I made Guinness cupcakes with Irish creme frosting, I'd ended up part of Jack's dessert. Maybe that will happen again tonight.

Setting the platter next to the pizza, I handed Jack his beer then placed a couple slices onto the plates I'd put out earlier. After giving one to Jack, I settled next to him on the couch.

"Thank you for picking this up."

He took a big bite and chewed. "You're welcome." He looked at the cupcakes. "Thank you for baking. Are those what I think they are?"

"You'll just have to taste one and find out."

We ate our pizza and talked, and I watched him, trying to figure out what's different. Like I told Mel, he's as sweet and attentive...and charming, as Mrs. Button said...as always, but something is definitely off. He acts more like he did when we first got together. Not that that was awful, but it's not the Jack I've come to know in our time together.

I placed my empty dish on the coffee table and scooched sideways, resting my back against the arm of the couch debating my next words. A million things went through my mind, but I finally decided to keep it simple.

"Is everything okay?" I asked.

Jack had finished his fourth slice and he leaned forward and placed his empty plate on top of mine. Looking at me out of the corner of his eye, he said, "Yeah. Why?"

I shrugged and pushed my glasses back into place.

"I don't know, you just seem preoccupied the past few weeks," I said, then added. "Ever since we got back from Boston I feel like something is different."

He settled back against the cushion and shifted slightly to face me.

"Different?" he asked, his tone neutral, but his eyes were anything but. Then he blinked and whatever I saw there was gone.

My stomach twisted and I nodded, afraid the lump in my throat would make my voice sound hoarse. I remember the exact moment Jack really let me in. I knew then that I was seeing a side of him he doesn't share with many people. Now that's gone and in its place is a decent imitation, but nothing close to the real thing.

"Hannah?"

I cleared my throat. "You just seem different and I wanted to make sure nothing is wrong."

His brow wrinkled and he looked away, shaking his head.

Jack has kept his relationships pretty drama free so the last thing I want to do is get hysterical, but he's making me nervous. I took in slow, steady breaths as I waited for him to speak.

After what seemed like hours, but was probably less than a minute, he looked over at me.

"Hannah, you're amazing."

Oh God, nothing good ever follows those words.

"You know what my relationships have been like up to now. All surface and no substance, with a predetermined end date." He looked into my eyes and I saw *my* Jack. "But you're different. *This* is different. I love spending time with you and miss you like hell when I'm away." Leaning forward, he rested his elbows on his knees and stared at the floor. "The problem is, I'm not sure how to do this and keep everything else together."

"Jack, this is all new to me too, but I think we're supposed to help each other keep it together." My voice came out sounding strangled, ruining the light-hearted effect I'd been aiming for.

Turning his head, he met my gaze again.

"Between the book and Mr. Hanover on my back, then all the craziness when the media found out about your father..." He shook his head. "Hannah, in my entire career, I've never gotten into a fight. That asshole in Detroit has been taking cheap shots for years and I always managed to keep my cool. But if Marquez hadn't held me back a couple weeks ago, I would have pounded that guy into the ground. And that's something that I never would have even thought about last season. I was always in control before, but it's all different now. It's like when I loosened up and let my feelings for you grow, I lost control of everything else. I've been trying to figure out a way to open my heart to you *and* keep all the other bullshit out, but it's just not working."

"So what, exactly, are you saying?" I asked.

"I'm trying my best to explain what's going on. I didn't think I was acting different, but if you noticed, I guess I am." He shrugged. "Right now, I'm on sensory overload and I've been working on getting myself under control again, like I was before."

That last word is like a knife to the heart. *Before.* What he means is before *me.* These months with him have been some of the most amazing of my life. Jack is everything I've ever wanted in a man and after my initial reserve, I jumped in with both feet. Now he's telling me he wants his life to be the way it was *before* our relationship. We're definitely on different pages here.

"So you don't want us to see each other anymore?"

JACK

HANNAH'S VOICE cracked on the last word and she looked toward the floor, but not before I saw the tears in her eyes. I leaned toward her and took her hand in mine, stroking her knuckles with my thumb.

"I'm not saying that at all," I said. "I can't imagine not having you in my life, but I need to get my shit together and to do that, I have to pull back a little bit."

"Pull back?" she asked. "What does that mean?"

"I need to be in control Hannah, or things just get too chaotic."

"Control?" She narrowed her eyes then shook her head. "Like in *Fifty Shade of Grey?*"

"No, I'm not into BDSM," I said. "Don't you think I would have mentioned if I was before now?"

"Then I don't know what you mean about being in

control." She shrugged and pulled her hand out of mine. "And I also don't understand how letting yourself feel something for me messes everything else up."

She stood and stacked the empty plates on top of the pizza box then picked everything up and carried it to the kitchen. I thought about following her, but figured she probably needed a break from me.

Resting my head against the back of the couch, I rubbed my eyes until I saw stars. I'm in unfamiliar territory here. This relationship stuff isn't easy.

I sat up straight when I heard Hannah walk back into the room. She perched on the other side of the couch and watched me with cautious eyes.

"I'm sorry I ran off like that, but I needed a minute." She rubbed her forehead then met my gaze. "Jack, I don't totally understand what's going on with you, but I have a feeling that I'm right in thinking whatever it is isn't good for us."

"Nothing really has to change with us," I said. "I just need to make sure I keep all my emotions in check so nothing gets out of control."

"So you're essentially telling me that you want our relationship to be like all the others you've had through the years."

"Not exactly, no."

"What *exactly* would be different?"

"Everything with you is different."

"Everything with me may have been different so far, but from what you're saying, that won't be the case going forward."

"I don't understand why you think that's true."

"Because you can't control your emotions or pull back and still be in a real relationship."

The fact that she used air quotes for the majority of the words in that sentence can't be a good thing.

"Real relationships are messy," she said. "Look at any relationship between any two people and that's probably the one thing they all have in common."

"Why do they have to be messy? Why can't a relationship just be two people enjoying each other's company without drama?"

The look on her face had me questioning my own intelligence, like she was obviously doing.

"Jack, we're going in circles here so I'm just going to lay it on the line," she said. "If our relationship never developed beyond the surface level, I'd be okay with what you're saying. Hell, I wouldn't have known the difference."

She leaned forward and rested her elbows on her knees, hands clasped in a white-knuckled grip as she stared at the floor.

"But at some point, everything became more intimate, more *real*." Her sad chuckle made my heart ache. "I once told Mrs. Button that you were a waste of handsome, but as we spent time together, I realized that just isn't true. And at some point during all this, I fell in love with you." She looked up and met my gaze with glistening brown eyes. "I can't be in a half relationship with you, Jack. I'd hate myself if I agreed to that."

The word love echoed through my head and before the joy that flooded my system at her declaration took over, I tamped it down. So many thoughts scrambled my mind, but I know if I open my mouth, I'll say those three little words back to her. And that would only complicate this even more.

She stood and walked toward the door. With her hand on the knob, she said, "I think you should go."

Chapter Thirty-Nine

HANNAH

ITS'S DAY twelve post-Jack and I think I might actually get through it without ugly crying. I glanced at the clock for the third time in the last half hour. If I go to sleep right at sunset, I may be able to avoid regular crying, too.

I couldn't stop my groan at the sound of the doorbell. I love Mrs. Button, but I really just want to be alone right now. My head started pounding the minute Jack walked out the door and no matter how much Advil I take, it won't let up. But she knows I'm in here, so I left my sanctuary on the couch and opened the door.

Only I didn't find Mrs. Button across the threshold. It was Sabrina.

"Oh Sabrina, hi." I opened the door wider to let her in.

"I apologize for just popping in, but I was afraid you wouldn't see me and I really wanted to talk to you."

I walked to the couch and picked up the blanket I'd been snuggling and tossed it across the back.

"Why would you think that?" I asked, settling into the couch and gesturing for her to do the same.

"Because technically, I'm on Team Jack." She rolled her eyes. "But that's only because I'm married to his best friend. If I had my choice, I'd hop over to your side."

"While I appreciate the support, there's no reason to choose sides." I offered her a small smile. "But out of curiosity, what tipped the scale in my direction?"

"The fact that men are idiots."

I shrugged. "Can't argue with that."

I fought the urge to look away from her as she looked at me with eyes that seemed to see way too much. I know how awful I look. I'm not a pretty crier and after nearly two weeks of nonstop tears, I'm an absolute mess. My glasses can mask the occasional eye bag or dark circle, but what I have going on right now is more than they can fix.

"I'm not going to ask how you're doing because I have eyes," she said. "I just wanted to come by and talk, let you know I'm here if you need me."

I blinked furiously but a few tears managed to escape anyway. Wiping them away, I said, "Please don't be nice to me. I'm hoping to get through the night with dry eyes."

"He looks just as bad, you know."

"Not helping," I said around a sad chuckle.

"I'm sorry," she said. "If you don't want to talk about him, I'll respect that, but it might help."

My first instinct is to shut this conversation down, but I can't help being curious.

"Do you know what happened?" I asked.

"Jack said you broke up with him because he wanted to get his shit together."

"That's the gist of it, I guess."

She shifted on the couch, tucking her ankle under her leg.

"I haven't known Jack all that long, but we've gotten pretty close in a short time. I mean, he's Dan's best friend and Lexi thinks he hung the moon. I couldn't be the odd man out." She smiled. "And besides that, he's just a really good guy. I wasn't sure what to think when I first met him. But the way he's lived his life isn't who he is. Not really."

I leaned forward and pulled a tissue from the box I placed on the coffee table earlier. Guess it's not going to be a dry-eyed night after all.

"When we first got involved, I swore to myself I'd enjoy it for what it was and move on when it was over." I dabbed at my eyes with the soggy tissue. "But somewhere along the line, things changed. Instead of being him and me, we became *us*."

"And then he got his head stuck up his ass."

I burst out laughing at her words. Partly because she delivered the line perfectly, but mostly to ward off the tears.

"The question is...if he got it unstuck, would you give him another chance?"

JACK

"YOU LOOK SAD, UNCLE JACK."

I smiled in what I hoped was a reassuring way. "Why?"

Lexi shrugged. "You just do."

"I'm hanging with my favorite girl. What's there to be sad about?"

She'd just executed a perfect flip into the pool...a skill

her mother had taught her...and was now swimming circles around me. Her parents sat in lounge chairs in the shade deep in conversation. From the looks they keep throwing my way, I'd bet anything they're talking about me.

Instead of obsessing about that, I grabbed Lexi around the waist as she passed me and tossed her toward the deep end. Her head bobbed above the surface and she giggled and swam back toward me.

"Can I dive off your shoulders?"

"Sure."

She stepped behind me and I reached back so she could grab my hands and climb up to my shoulders. Her fingers dug into my scalp and I held her ankles as she found her balance. I felt her stand and a second later she jumped off, diving into the water a few feet in front of me.

We did that a few more times before Sabrina walked toward the edge of the pool and told Lexi it was time to get out so she could get ready for a sleepover.

"Okay, mom," she said then swam up next to me. "I can stay here if you want, Uncle Jack."

Shit, I must look really pathetic.

"You go have a good time," I said. "I'll see you next week."

She wrapped her arms around my waist and squeezed.

"I love you, Uncle Jack."

"Love you too, Lex." I kissed the top of her head. "Have fun tonight."

She climbed out of the pool and dried off, then wrapped a purple towel around her shoulders and ran into the house. I wasn't far behind her, but instead of running into the house, I wrapped a towel around my waist and settled onto the lounge chair next to Dan's.

"That girl is something else," I said.

He chuckled. "I'm aware."

"What did you tell her about Hannah?"

"Why do you think we told her anything?

"Because this is the first time in months she didn't ask about her."

"We just told her not to bring her up. Surprisingly, she didn't ask questions." He gave me a pointed look. "What do you want me to tell her if she does ask?"

I rested my head against the lounge chair and closed my eyes.

"I don't know," I said. "I'm still not sure what to tell myself."

"Want to talk about it?"

"Not really."

"You sure?" he asked. "You listened to me talk about Sabrina enough through the years. Consider it payback."

I took in a deep breath and slowly let it out then looked over at him.

"I don't know what to say," I said, then quickly added. "I shouldn't have anything to say. I should be happy it ended so smoothly considering."

Dan chuckled. "Looking at you, I'd never guess it ended smoothly."

"What's that mean?"

"Jack, you look like shit," he said. "And Hannah isn't much better. Are you sure this isn't something you two can work out?"

"You're asking the wrong person since she's technically the one who ended it." I realized how whiny that sounded as soon as the words left my mouth. "Besides, I was trying to pull back a little anyway."

"You mentioned that. I just don't understand why."

"That shit in Detroit made me realize that I need to get it together," I said. "This next contract might be my last. I have to focus on the game and keep everything else under control. There are enough variables without me adding to them because I'm caught up in some relationship drama." Dan sat forward in his lounge chair and looked at me like I'd lost my mind. "What?"

"Do you realize that you didn't have any relationship drama until you decided to change things up to avoid drama?"

"It's not that cut and dried," I said.

"Okay, then explain something to me," he said. "You wanted your life back to what you consider normal...drama free with you in total control." I nodded. "Now that you have that again, what's the problem?"

"What do you mean?"

"You're a half a step behind at short and your bat speed is down," he said. "You're drawn tighter than a guitar string, and as I already mentioned, you look like shit."

"Jesus Dan, don't worry about sugarcoating it."

"I can sugarcoat things or I can be a good friend. Right now, I think you need the truth more than you need to be stroked."

"And what do you think the truth is?"

"You love Hannah and are miserable without her. And until you face that and do something about it, you'll never be in control.

Chapter Forty

JACK

I GLANCED at the clock and groaned. The sun will be up soon and I haven't slept a wink. My brain wouldn't shut down long enough to allow me to drift off.

Dan's words kept running through my head. He really didn't say anything I haven't thought myself more times than I can count through the past few weeks. But hearing it from him made it harder to shake off.

My logic had seemed sound. I thought that opening myself up to Hannah had left me vulnerable in other areas and that if I shut those feelings down, the other gaps would close as well. Apparently that's bullshit because we've been apart for weeks now and I'm a mess.

For years I've channeled all my feelings into baseball and that worked for a long time. Getting involved with Hannah did change that, but only because the rage that fueled me since my mother died had lessened while I was with her. I felt relaxed and truly happy for the first time in years.

Visiting my father had brought all that old shit back and instead of dealing with it like a normal adult, I panicked and fell back into old habits.

What a dumbass.

I've been in love with Hannah for months, but was too much of a pussy to admit it. And now that I have, I need to figure out what to do to get her back.

For the first time in weeks, I'm happy with my performance on the field. I made a couple great plays and went three for four, with a two-run homer in the first inning to put us on the board.

The tightness in my shoulders has loosened and the headache I've been living with for weeks is mostly gone.

As much as I wanted to get showered and up to Hannah's office, duty calls. I gave a handful of interviews, discussing and dissecting both my play and that of the entire team. Every minute of delay seemed like an eternity and when I finally answered my last question, I decided I needed to see Hannah immediately.

Cal and Dan stood at their lockers as I crossed the room to get to my own. I toed off my spikes and replaced them with turf shoes. My friends sat back in their chairs watching me with interest.

"You look like you're in a hurry," Dan said.

"I need to talk to Hannah." I wedged my finger between my heel and the back of my shoe and wiggled my foot into place. "Now."

They looked at each other and smiled.

"Good luck," Cal said.

"You know what you're gonna say?" Dan asked.

"I think so." I chuckled. "Hopefully I'll remember it all when I'm in the same room as her."

"You'll be fine," Cal said. "Just be honest and tell her how you feel."

"Thanks guys." I smiled. "If you don't hear from me, consider it good news."

Dan patted me on the back and I walked out of the locker room, heading toward the staircase. I don't want to waste my time waiting for the elevator. I burst through the doors on Hannah's floor and ran to her office.

Standing outside her door, I took a few deep breaths to slow down my breathing and knocked.

Nothing.

I knocked again.

Nothing.

I opened the door and peeked inside.

Where the hell is she?

Hannah normally starts and ends the day in her office, but she's definitely not here now.

I closed the door and started back down the hall. One of

Hannah's co-workers walked toward me.

"Have you seen Hannah?" I asked.

"She left for the airport a few minutes ago."

"The airport?"

She nodded. "Yeah, she's going to visit her father."

Obviously Hannah hadn't told people about our split because this girl looked confused.

"I have no idea how I forgot that was today," I said. "Thanks."

Running down the hall, I took the stairs again and ran to my car as fast as humanly possible.

Chapter Forty-One

HANNAH

I TRIED to immerse myself in my book, but wasn't being very successful. What on earth made me think bringing a romance novel along was a good idea?

Tossing the book back into my purse, I shifted in my seat to get more comfortable. My flight doesn't leave for another hour.

I've been dying to get out to California to meet my new baby brother and managed to work a small break into my schedule. This is going to be another quick trip to the coast but it'll be worth it to see the little guy before the end of the season.

If I'm being honest with myself, I need a break. The past few weeks have really taken a toll on me. It's taken a lot of energy to avoid seeing Jack. But even though I haven't seen him in person, he still surrounds me.

The Waves are his team. Pictures of him line the hallways and walkways, and flash on the multitude of TV screens scattered throughout the stadium.

I'm hoping this time away, even though it's only a couple days, will help pull me out of my Jack-induced coma. Maybe the change of scenery will shift my world back to the way it was before I knew that kissing Jack Reagan is better than anything I'd ever imagined.

I'm not a teenager who thinks six months is an eternity. In the grand scheme of things, logically I know that my time spent with Jack should just be a blip on my radar. Once I convince my heart of that fact, I'll be able to get my life back under control.

Control.

That's what Jack said he wanted. Hopefully he's gotten it.

"Are you okay?"

I looked up and realized that those words were meant for me. Nodding at the woman sitting across from me, I said, "I'm fine."

"You're crying," she said. "Are you sure you're okay?"

I dragged my fingers along my damp cheeks. I hadn't realized.

"I'm sure," I said. "But thank you for asking."

She studied me a moment longer then went back to her knitting. I reached into my purse and dug around for a tissue. The pack I found at the bottom only had one left, but hopefully that's all I'll need. I dabbed at my eyes then blew my nose and tucked the tissue in my pocket.

Picking up my phone I turned the camera on selfie mode and lifted my glasses. My eyes look a little red and puffy, but I managed to keep the concealer I'd applied to the dark circles intact.

I was about to turn off the phone when something behind me caught my eye. Holding up the phone, I watched what appeared to be Jack jogging through the terminal. I whipped my head around so fast, my neck cracked.

I'm not hallucinating, it is Jack. And he's pretty easy to pick out because he's still wearing his uniform. In my peripheral vision, I saw no less than a dozen cell phones trained on him.

And then he turned and looked directly at me and everything else faded out of sight.

JACK

"HANNAH!"

I yelled and ran in her direction, dodging my way through all the people. I'm sure I look like a maniac and every cell phone turned in my direction is capturing it. But I can't worry about that right now.

I finally made it to the gate and ran the short distance to her. She hadn't left her seat but her eyes remained glued to my face. Kneeling down in front of her, I fought to catch my breath.

"Thank God I found you."

"What are you doing here, Jack?"

Looking at her, everything I'd planned to say disappeared from my brain. All the flowery words and explanations were gone, and only one thing remained.

"I love you, Hannah," I said. "I love you so much and being without you physically hurts."

Her eyes widened then shifted from side to side. I looked around and realized a lot of eyes...and cell phones...were watching us. But at this moment, none of that matters. All I care about is making things right with the woman in front of me.

"Jack." Her eyes shifted left and right again before looking directly into mine. "Are you sure you don't want to take this somewhere a little more private?" she whispered.

I shook my head.

"Hannah, you're the best thing that's ever happened to me. Please tell me I didn't totally fuck this up." I swallowed the lump in my throat. "Please tell me you'll give me a chance to prove that I'm not a total idiot and I know how priceless you are."

She blinked and when I saw the tears roll down her face, I couldn't keep my distance any longer. I leaned toward her and placed my hands on either side of her face, wiping her tears away with my thumbs. I continued stroking her cheeks as I spoke.

"I'm so sorry for treating you like anything other than the most important woman in the world." I looked into her eyes, willing her to see the truth in my words, looking for a sign that she still loves me. The small flicker of interest I saw there gave me hope so I continued.

"I panicked. Instead of dealing with some shit that has nothing to do with us, I freaked out and ended up pushing you away."

I lifted her glasses to the top of her head so I could see her eyes without the glare of the lights on her lenses obstructing my view. My pounding heart thrummed in my ears. I haven't been this nervous since the first game I played for the Waves. And as big as that moment had been, so much more is at stake here.

"Hannah, I love you." I offered a small smile. "Please give me another chance."

My stomach tightened as she looked away and shook her head. I moved my hands from her face and rested them on her lap. After what seemed like an eternity, she finally met my gaze again.

"Jack, the last few weeks have been torture," she said, doing nothing to calm my nerves. "I never, ever want to feel like that again."

The tears flowing freely down her cheeks caused an ache in my chest. Which is nothing less than I deserve after what I put us both through.

"Hannah, I love you and I swear if you give me a chance, I'll spend the rest of my life making this up to you." Her eyes widened at that last statement. I hadn't meant to blurt that out right now, but I don't regret the fact that I did. But first things first here.

"Please."

My voice cracked and I blinked away the tears I feel fighting to get out. Hannah's lips touched mine and I opened my eyes wide allowing them to flow free.

"I love you too, Jack," she whispered against my mouth. "And yes, I'll give you another chance." It was her turn to wipe away my tears. With her hands on my face, she pulled me in for a soft kiss then held me in place and opened her mouth over mine.

I'm not sure how long that kiss went on before I heard a voice over the loud speaker announcing our flight. I slowly ended the kiss and rested my forehead against hers before pulling back.

We still have an audience and I'm sure some, if not all, of this will end up on social media, but I don't give a fuck. The only thing I care about is that Hannah loves me and is giving me another chance.

I shifted off my knees and sat in the chair next to Hannah.

"I'm going to meet my little brother," she said.

"I heard."

"I'll be back in a couple days and we can figure all this out."

"I'm sure we'll be able to carve out a few minutes either on the flight or in California to sort out the details."

"You bought a ticket for this flight?" I nodded. "I couldn't get through security without a ticket."

"How did you know which flight I was taking?"

"I didn't know for sure," I said. "But I assumed you'd use this airline and knew where you were going, so I took a chance and bought two seats next to each other. I figured if everything worked out, you could sit next to me. If they didn't, I'd have the row to myself." I chuckled. "When I ran through here I didn't see you at first and I almost freaked out. Then I turned and there you were."

She smiled and rested her head against my shoulder.

"Why are you still in your uniform?"

"I needed to talk to you and didn't want to waste time." Around a smile, I added, "Plus, I wanted to see if you really think I smell good after a game."

She leaned in and took a deep breath.

"Oh yeah."

"It's gonna be a long flight," I groaned.

The woman at the counter announced boarding for first class passengers.

"Ready?" I stood and grabbed her suitcase.

She followed me to the counter and I scanned both of our

boarding passes. We walked down the tunnel and boarded the plane. I stowed Hannah's bag in the overhead bin and sat next to her.

"My head is still spinning over all this."

"Then settle in and we'll get you a drink, and we can figure out what I'm going to say to your father."

"About what?"

"I basically proposed out there and I should probably talk to him about that before I do it all nice and official." I winked. "Maybe even fancy."

Hannah's wide smile made that warm feeling spread through my chest. I rubbed at the spot, welcoming the feeling.

"You are so much more than I ever imagined, Jack Reagan."

"Considering you thought I was a waste of handsome, I appreciate you saying that," I said. "And I promise that for the rest of our lives, I'll prove to you that I'm worth all this handsome."

Hannah's laughter echoed through the small space.

Her smiling eyes met mine.

"What am I going to do with you?"

"I don't know, but we have the rest of our lives for you to think of something."

Are you ready for Cal's story?

Barbara

I stared out my office window, looking down at the factory below. Conveyor belts carried candy in various stages from one station to another, then moved completed confections toward the workers who would package and ship them out.

I used to be one of those workers. One of the packers responsible for boxing perfect chocolate creations and distributing them to the masses. But that was a long time ago. Before Stewart Mack came into my life and I lost myself in his world. Why I'm still in his world three years after the divorce is beyond me.

Not that he's totally to blame. When we met, I wasn't in a good place emotionally speaking, and was ripe for the picking. After breaking up with my college sweetheart, I shifted to team Stewart with minimal sweet talk from the man himself.

Even after all this time, I'm still not sure what put me on his radar. Stewart barely pays attention to the factory workers—or any of the workers, for that matter. He generally lives in his ivory tower and doesn't mingle with the masses.

Before my thoughts could get too Stewart-centric, I spun my chair around to face my desk and the task at hand. Molly Mack Chocolate's expansion and renovation depends on me acing my presentation at the bank this afternoon. If I can convince First Allegiant Bank to loan us an insane amount of money, the company will be able to expand, improve operations, and increase market share. That's the plan anyway. Stewart's plan.

And I have to say, despite the fact that he's a class-A jerk, the man has a good head for business. So far, most of his ideas have had a positive impact on the bottom line. It really pisses me off, too. Not that I want the business to tank, but it would be nice if something bad happened to the asshole. I keep waiting for the karma train to run him down, but he's managed to avoid it so far. He just strolls through life with everything going his way.

Well, maybe not everything. I'm still here. I know if he had his way, I would have been in the unemployment line before the ink dried on the divorce papers. The fact that I live in his mother's pool house doesn't sit well with him, either. I smiled at the thought.

"You look happy." I jumped, knocking my stack of handouts to the floor. "Sorry, I didn't mean to startle you."

My mother-in-law—make that ex-mother-in-law—settled into the seat in front of my desk.

"It's fine. I just didn't hear you come in."

"It's been a long time since I've seen a smile like that on your face. What put it there?"

I chuckled. "You don't want to know."

I love Molly. We bonded the first moment we met and I love her as much as I loved my own mother. But she *is* Stewart's mother so I avoid making any nasty comments about my ex-husband in her presence. It's an unspoken agreement between us that we don't discuss him.

Understanding, she refocused her attention to the handouts, which were once again stacked neatly in front of me.

"Ready for the big presentation?"

"Yep. You?"

"You have the hard part. I just have to sit there and look like I understand what you're talking about."

As usual, Molly is being humble. After her husband died, she started Molly Mack Chocolate in her kitchen. She managed to hold down a part-time job, raise two boys, and build the business into a multimillion-dollar corporation in a manner of years.

"We both know that you understand exactly what I'm talking about. But if it makes you feel better, you can just sit there and look pretty today."

"I'll try my best." She wiped an invisible speck of lint off her skirt.

"Is J.P. coming?" I asked. As head of marketing, my ex-brother-in-law doesn't always attend financial meetings, but I'd requested his presence at this one. Besides his calming presence, he'd also bring a plethora of marketing and industry knowledge in case I need backup.

"Yes, he's driving with us," she said. The fact that she averted her gaze before uttering the next sentence should have warned me I wouldn't like it. "And Stewart is meeting us there."

My ex-husband's attendance at the meeting shouldn't surprise me, but I had hoped something he deemed more important would keep him away. Even though I know the facts backward and forward, Stewart has a way of making me feel and look inadequate.

Squaring my shoulders, I resolved to ignore him during my presentation. And the rest of the time, for that matter.

"Do you know who we're meeting with?"

"Just the usual crew." She looked at the pile in front of me, then turned her attention to my right hand as it obsessively tucked a stray strand of hair behind my ear. "Don't be nervous, Barb. I've been dealing with First Allegiant Bank for almost thirty years."

"I know, but lending is still tight. The expansion is a great idea, but it's not a sure thing—nothing is. My job is to convince them we're worth the risk. I don't want to mess that up."

"You won't." She smiled. "I know you won't."

Tears filled my eyes, but before I could say or do something too sappy, J.P. stuck his head in the door.

"You want to grab some lunch before the big presentation?"

Even though food is the last thing on my mind, I echoed Molly's enthusiastic, "Yes."

Cal

I leaned back in the chair and looked around my office, trying to figure out what the fuck I'm doing here. I've made the thirty-minute commute to this soul-sucking place for the past six weeks and still can't believe this is my life now.

The corner office with its plush carpeting, mahogany desk, and floor to ceiling windows may be someone's idea of paradise, but it's definitely not mine. Grass, dirt, and smelly locker rooms are more my speed.

Sure, my degree is in finance, but I never thought I'd ever actually have to use it. College was only a stepping stone to where I really wanted to end up—the major leagues. Once I was drafted junior year, I figured I'd never have to get a real job. Yet here I am.

Not that I have to work. I was lucky enough to make a great living playing the best game in the world, so I could sit on my ass and do nothing for the rest of my life and never have to worry about money. But since I was forced to retire in what I consider to be my prime, I have to do something.

At thirty-three, I still had some good years ahead of me, but I was old enough to not act like a stupid rookie. I figured if I stayed in shape and kept myself healthy, I'd have at least another seven years in the hot corner. But after chasing a foul ball into the stands, I messed up my neck, and that was all shot to hell.

At least I'd made the catch.

I honestly never planned on having a career past baseball. My goal was to play as long as possible then retire and spend time with my wife and kids. Unfortunately, my marriage didn't work out and I never had kids. I'm blessed with family and friends, but they have their own lives.

The days are awful long when you don't have a purpose. It took me less than a year to realize I needed to work. I sat in the Waves' booth a couple times last season doing color commentary, but realized it's not for me. Not as a regular gig anyway.

My computer dinged and I sat forward and spotted the Outlook notification that filled the middle of the screen. I groaned and rubbed the back of my neck. Another conference call. Thankfully it's only for a half hour, because then I have that big meeting Mr. Robinson has been hopped up about all week right after.

Welcome to corporate America.